THE
WEDDING
PARTY

OTHER TRANSLATED TITLES BY LIU XINWU

THE WEDDING PARTY

LIU XINWU

TRANSLATED BY JEREMY TIANG

AMAZON CROSSING

Text copyright © 2016 by Liu Xinwu
Translation copyright © 2021 by Jeremy Tiang

Previously published as 钟鼓楼 (*Zhonggulou*) by Dangdai Bimonthly in 1984, by People's Literature House in 1985, and by Yilin Press in People's Republic of China in 2016. Translated from Mandarin by Jeremy Tiang. First published in English by Amazon Crossing in 2021.

Published by Amazon Crossing, Seattle

www.apub.com

Amazon, the Amazon logo, and Amazon Crossing are trademarks of Amazon.com, Inc., or its affiliates.

ISBN-13: 9781542031202 (hardcover)
ISBN-10: 1542031206 (hardcover)

ISBN-13: 9781542044790 (paperback)
ISBN-10: 1542044790 (paperback)

Cover design by Faceout Studio, Tim Green

Cover and interior illustrations by Xinmei Liu

Printed in the United States of America

First edition

SIHEYUAN RESIDENTS

1. Old Lady Hai

2. Zhang Qilin, a bureaucrat
    Yu Yongzhi, a doctor
    Zhang Xiuzao, their daughter

3. Hai Xibin, Old Lady Hai's grandson

4. Xue Yongquan
    Auntie Xue
    Xue Jiyue, their son
    Pan Xiuya, his bride

5. Zhan Liying

6. Mu Ying, a doctor
7. Hao Yulan, factory worker
    Liang Fumin, factory worker

8. Han Yitan, an editor
    Ge Ping, his wife

9. Tantai Zhizhu, an opera singer
    Li Kai, her husband
    Their children
    Li Kai's parents

10. Xun Xingwang, a cobbler
    Auntie Xun
    Xun Lei, their son

SIHEYUAN COURTYARD

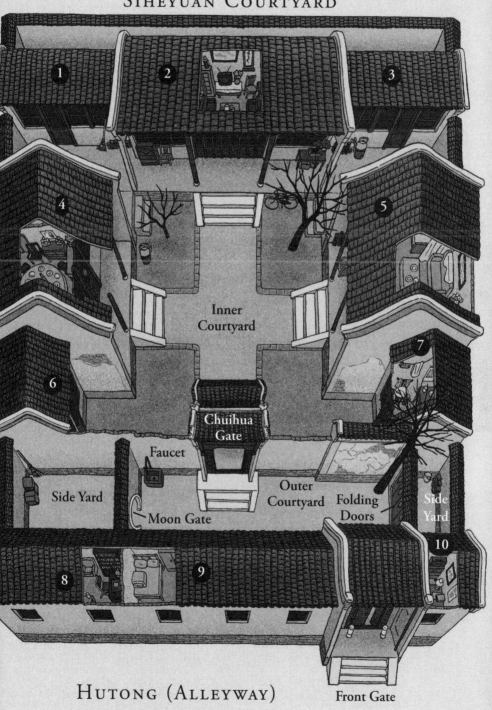

Inner Courtyard

Chuihua Gate

Faucet

Side Yard

Moon Gate

Outer Courtyard

Folding Doors

Side Yard

HUTONG (ALLEYWAY)

Front Gate

A NOTE ON THE TEXT

The original Chinese title of this novel translates to *The Drum Tower and the Bell Tower*, referring to the iconic Beijing landmarks. In the thirty years since the book's publication in China, many critics have likened it to *Along the River During the Qingming Festival*, the seventeen-foot-long scroll painting by Song dynasty artist Zhang Zeduan. It is a high honor in China to be compared to this work of art, which vividly captures twelfth-century city life in exquisite detail. Liu Xinwu has likened the structure of *The Drum Tower and the Bell Tower* to an orange: the various families and characters are self-contained, like segments of an orange, but it is only when they come together that you have a complete fruit. This approach was innovative in Chinese literature.

A NOTE ON THE TEXT

NOT THE BEGINNING

More than one hundred years before December 12, 1982

PROLOGUE

You can skip this section if you like, but why not
give it a read?

A dark night soon after the Guangxu emperor ascended the throne.

In a noble Manchu household not far from the Bell and Drum Towers, there was a bloodcurdling scream.

This mansion was the residence of a mere low-ranking princeling, but still magnificent. The night servants and watchmen heard the sudden cry and, in a panic, scrambled for lights. By the flickering red tongues of candles and the glow of sheep's-horn lanterns, they scoured the premises. Naturally paying most attention to the lush, twisting paths of the rear garden.

There wasn't a single star in the sky, and a gentle breeze ruffled the air. Discordant tinkling came from the wind chimes hanging from the great hall's eaves.

The housekeeper and majordomo gathered the servants in the official hall and asked them to report what they'd found. Not a single person had seen anything out of the ordinary, and there were no signs of intruders anywhere in the mansion.

It seemed the awful cry had come from a passing cat. This was, of course, a bad omen, and required precautions. The housekeeper gave instructions to send for Buddhist and Taoist monks from Longfu Temple and White Cloud Monastery at daybreak so they could carry out a sacrifice and avert catastrophe.

Everything seemed to go back to normal. The additional lights were extinguished, the off-duty staff dismissed. Soon there were just the usual night servants and watchmen patrolling the garden walls.

The thick cover of clouds cracked open, and a sliver of pale moonlight spilled to earth.

The mansion's silhouette gradually revealed itself, then all the buildings in the north of the city became visible. Right at the northernmost point of the city, the majestic Bell and Drum Towers rose high above them all.

From the Drum Tower—also known as the watchtower—came a flurry of drumbeats to signal the changing of the watch, shattering the night's stillness. A swarm of fireflies flew past its walls.

This seemed like an ordinary night, exactly like the one before and the one after.

Daylight slowly arrived.

As the sky turned from crystalline yellow to silvery blue, the slumbering city awoke. The street in front of the Drum Tower was crammed with shops. Banners in distinctive styles and eye-catching colors fluttered in the breeze. Mule carts passed by in both directions, metal-plated wheels scraping jarringly on the flagstones. Vendors of millet paste, tofu pudding, and roasted sweet potatoes were out in force, and artisans were striding down the street bellowing, "Hooped buckets here!" and "Scrap metal collector! Bring out your scrap metal!" Flower girls wandered the alleys, the hutongs, calling out alluringly, "Peonies for sale! Choose your own!" The street performers with powdered white noses clashed cymbals and begged for coins. Strangest of all these were the two mouse men, one behind the other, each holding a white paper flag with a picture of a rodent nibbling at stolen food. The man in front called out hoarsely, "Mousetrap—trap a mouse!" And the one behind in a gravelly voice, "Rat poison! One dose kills a whole nest—what a bargain!"

Not far to the southwest of the Bell and Drum Towers were the famous Shicha Seas. These "seas" were in fact shallow lakes, half-covered in lotus flowers, half-planted with rice. Apparently there used to be many temples on these shores, hence the name Shicha—"ten temples." Between the Front and Back Seas was a little stone crossing named after its shape: Silver Ingot Bridge. At one end of this bridge lived a family who sold bean juice out of their home.

Bean juice is a little like soy milk. You make it by soaking mung beans in water, then mashing and fermenting them. The resulting starch is removed to make glass noodles, and the bean paste and black powder filtered off. The sourish liquid left behind is bean juice. If you hadn't acquired a taste for it, particularly if you'd recently moved north to Beijing, you'd want to throw up after your first mouthful, whereas old Beijingers were hooked on this cheap and delicious hot beverage. Today, a hundred years later, many still adore this drink. Beijingers who've spent years abroad and sampled delicacies from all over the planet still immediately request "a piping hot bowl of bean juice—right now!" whenever they're back in town.

The little shop at one end of Silver Ingot Bridge had quite a reputation for its bean juice. It was owned by an honest couple in their fifties. Not only was their bean juice perfectly brewed, clear, and rich, they ran a shipshape business and treated their customers well. There was an old lady from a noble Manchu family who'd fallen on hard times. To save a few copper coins, she never bought warm bean juice, but got it cold in an earthenware bowl and heated it up herself at home. The couple never looked down on her but greeted her with a smile as warm and service as brisk as for their other customers.

Beijingers enjoy bean juice with certain accompaniments: pickled vegetables, dough fritters, flatbread. This shop offered generous servings of fragrant pickles, just the right color and texture, spicy or plain, sliced broad or thin, topped with diced kohlrabi and sprinkled with chili oil, cooled with ice in the summer—a peasant dish made with finesse. Their dough fritters were perfectly fried, golden and crisp. Biting into one of these sandwiched in a flaky, sesame-studded flatbread, followed by a mouthful of warm bean juice was, according to aficionados, an experience that could steal your very soul away.

A few days before our story begins, this couple suffered a great misfortune.

Their only child was a sixteen-year-old daughter, whom they doted on, and whom they refused to let serve at the shop or help with the cooking. They held her like a pearl in the palm of their hands and satisfied her every wish. This girl was extremely beautiful—by the aesthetic standards of the time, naturally: oval goose-egg face, long delicate eyebrows, flat nose with a pale tip, mouth like a cherry, Cupid's bow upper lip, perfectly sized mole to the right of her chin.

It was early summer, and the clove trees were in bloom. On their way home from a visit to Granny in Fengtai, mother and daughter passed the Shicha Seas just as the sun was setting. The lotus pads covering the lake stirred in the evening breeze, and the willow branches on the shore draped over the maiden's body, tangling with the sash at her waist and its betel-scented pouch. She stood at the water's edge with her mother, catching her breath, a couple of bends in the road from Silver Ingot Bridge.

It was at this moment of respite that the situation took a nasty turn.

To the south was the lotus-covered lake, and to the north, across a cart track, the famous Huixian Restaurant. From its eaves hung a black sign with gold lettering, and below that a red banner waved splendidly. Its two stories had twelve private dining rooms each, with walls of perfectly smooth brick, and on the upper floor was a wide balcony painted glossy green. Guests could lounge elegantly there and lean over the railings, gazing at the landscape as they sipped their wine.

Unfortunately, on this day, a certain wastrel carousing there spied the daughter of the bean juice vendors through the curtain of willow leaves.

This wastrel was the owner of the mansion at the start of this story—the princeling himself. He liked wearing outfits of dark crepe and was always armed with a large iron fan painted with a heraldic black butterfly over a bed of flowers like drops of blood. He wore at least five rings, two of which were fitted with spiked metal hooks. That should give you an idea of the sort of man he was.

As the bean juice vendors' daughter rested happily on the shore of the lake, she couldn't have imagined the tragedy about to befall her. Her thin pink blouse fluttered in the evening breeze, and standing among the rippling lotus pads, she herself looked like a lotus blossom rising pristine from the mud. Strands of hair escaped her bun and waved enticingly on the breeze, adding to her allure. As the princeling glanced in her direction, he felt his body weaken with desire.

The girl arrived home with her mother, but before she could even exchange a few words with her father, the princeling barged in with his entourage. He arrogantly announced his identity, declaring he wanted to take the young woman as his concubine—that is, to live in his mansion as a high-ranking maid and to serve him at night. The couple, he thought, would have no choice but to agree.

Stricken with terror, the young woman and her mother retreated into a back room. Unmoved, her father said sternly, "We are not worthy. My wife and I only have this one daughter. All we hope is to find her a husband, humble though his station may be, who can take over our bean juice shop. That would be enough for us."

Furious, the princeling and his men departed.

Tragedy struck early the next morning. The poor girl! Like her father and mother, she hadn't slept a wink all night, but she thought she'd at least managed to evade the princeling's clutches. As dawn seeped through the windows, she sat before her mirror—the most expensive thing in their home—and carefully began her toilette. Without warning, a gang of the princeling's men broke in and carried her outside. The maiden screamed and wept, struggling fiercely all the while. Hearing the commotion, her parents ran from the kitchen, where they'd been preparing bean juice, and flung themselves at the assailants. One of the men hit the father on the head with a metal bar, and he crashed to the ground. The mother collapsed on the doorstep and called for help, but by then their daughter had already been bundled into a waiting carriage. The neighbors came running and tried to stop the thugs, but the head thug scared them into silence by standing arms akimbo and hollering, "We're here on the princeling's orders to capture his escaped concubine! If anyone has a problem with that, step right up and we'll see if your head grows back."

At noon that day, the Bell Tower blithely tolled the hour. All around Silver Ingot Bridge and the Shicha Seas, everyone went about their day as always. A hawker passed by, striking a little pair of brass cymbals to advertise his wares: sour plum juice and stewed hawthorn berries. Then another holding a brush and clippers—the head-shaving man—followed by someone selling crane lanterns. From a street not far away, perhaps Tobacco Pipe Alley or Crow Hutong, came the sound of drums, horns, suonas, gongs, haidis—probably a sedan chair had arrived to pick up a blushing bride.

Meanwhile, the bean juice vendors were plunged into misery. The father lay in bed, felled by his injuries. Concerned neighbors tended to him, but it seemed unlikely he'd recover soon, if at all. In his delirium, a stream of babble escaped his lips. His wife, half-crazed with grief, sat slumped on Silver Ingot Bridge, howling with all her might and screaming the foulest curses.

According to eyewitnesses, not long after the Bell Tower tolled at noon, a young man appeared on horseback. He was dressed in a resplendent long robe and a cap trimmed with jade, with a jade-handled horsewhip in his hand. Although he looked like a scholar, there was something of a warrior's valor about his eyes. He dismounted by the grieving mother and gently asked why she was sobbing. She was near insensible with sorrow, so the crowd around her took it upon themselves to explain.

The handsome stranger furrowed his brow and audibly gnashed his teeth at this tale. Onlookers heard him say, "Weep no more, dear lady. Just wait for the good news!" By the time everyone had recovered their senses, there was nothing left of him but distant hoofbeats and an odd, lingering fragrance. Some wondered if he had been no more than a hallucination.

A few days later came the incident that began this story: a brief bloodcurdling scream in the princeling's mansion one dark night.

The princeling's servants didn't see anything out of the ordinary that night. It wasn't until the following morning that they found the princeling awakening from a death-like sleep, moaning weakly, two gruesome, bloody holes where once his eyes had been. It was said that a note was found pinned to the canopy over his bed: "This time your eyes were taken. Next time the knife will flash, and your head will be gone."

That morning, news of what had happened to the princeling spread like wildfire around the Bell and Drum Towers and the Shicha Seas. The neighbors fell over themselves to tell the bean juice couple.

As for who did the deed, both the couple and their neighbors had an inkling.

Word from the princeling's mansion, though, was that until the servants heard the princeling's moans and went in to him, the doors and windows of his bedroom were sealed tight and showed no signs of forced entry. The same went for every possible entrance to the mansion itself.

Time passed. The Bell and Drum Towers continued to stand there majestically.

What happened to the couple who sold bean juice by Silver Ingot Bridge? Were they ever reunited with their daughter? And a hundred years later, do any traces remain of their little shop?

The princeling's mansion is now a high school where students and teachers laugh and chat. Nobody thinks about that inky night and the strange event that took place in its darkness, how a profligate princeling let out a terrifying howl as he lost both his eyes in a sealed room.

Naturally, this became a popular topic for after-dinner gossip. Though it was a hundred years ago, you still hear old Beijingers discussing it in the neighborhood around the towers and Shicha Seas. Of course, each person adds their own seasoning and creates a different ending, so there are many different versions of this story.

Even so, few people in the perpetually bustling crowds around the Bell and Drum Towers are as innocent or as evil as the characters in the story, and you rarely see scenes of murder or mayhem around here. The rest of this novel, therefore, will not continue in this fantastical vein, but rather will focus on the mundane aspects of life, under which there is much depth to be found. I trust you will not object to this, dear reader?

As you read on, you will find that the events of this book are much closer to your own life.

Distant things feel mysterious, and closer ones unremarkable. The point is whether we can learn from them. Near or far, high or low, big or small, up or down, as long as we discover something new, we gain something, which brings us closer to happiness. Let's give it a try!

Keep in mind that at the northernmost point of central Beijing stand the ancient Bell and Drum Towers.

The Drum Tower in front, red walls and gray tiles.

The Bell Tower behind, gray walls and green tiles.

The Drum Tower is squat, the Bell Tower slender.

They no longer chime and boom at dawn and dusk, but to those who know, they remain majestic markers of time's passage.

Time flows on, until December 12, 1982.

In a hutong near the towers is a siheyuan courtyard, and in that siheyuan is a woman named Auntie Xue. Let's take a closer look.

PART ONE

卯时

Mao Shi

Time of the Jade Rabbit: 5:00 a.m. to 7:00 a.m.

CHAPTER 1

Beneath the Bell and Drum Towers, a family prepares for a wedding. Who is most anxious?

After her morning ablutions, Auntie Xue reaches out a hand perfumed by fragrant soap and ceremoniously tears a sheet off the calendar. Boldly announced on the red page is a day she's been dreading and anticipating with both rapture and anxiety: Sunday, December 12, 1982. Year of the water dog. Twenty-eighth day of the tenth lunar month. And a helpful reminder: winter solstice will be December 22, the eighth day of the eleventh lunar month.

DECEMBER 1982

12

SUNDAY
YEAR OF THE WATER DOG
Tenth Month, Twenty-Eighth Day (Lunar Date)

Auntie Xue has come to grips with the concept of a twenty-four-hour day, where a new day starts at midnight—it's the way young people talk nowadays. Yet to her mind, the day only begins when daylight enters the siheyuan.

On this day, Auntie Xue's younger son, Xue Jiyue, is getting married.

Auntie Xue stands staring at the calendar in the dim light. Like many Beijingers her age, she isn't really superstitious—when you come right down to it, it's just a bunch of random nonsense. Stories of old ladies fussing about visits from gods or ghosts have her slapping her thigh and making some cutting remark.

Yet, also like many Beijingers her age, she has her own ideas about summoning good luck. There are no fortune-telling stalls these days, and no one arranges marriages by compatible birth dates. City folk sigh to hear about tragic young couples in farming villages torn apart by ill-matched horoscopes. Beijingers have firm ideas about wedding dates, though. Who came up with these rules? Who disseminated them? No one knows. It's not just older residents like Auntie Xue. Even youngsters of Jiyue's generation place a lot of weight on this system. Which is what, exactly? Basically, you choose a day and month that are even-numbered in both solar and lunar calendars. A most primeval superstition: odd numbers mean singledom, hence widowhood. That's how it is all over the world—it's easy to get rid of complicated rituals, but you'll never eliminate the deepest, most fundamental beliefs of people's hearts. Auntie Xue is recently retired after more than two decades of working at a grocery store. Her level of education is precisely enough to read a calendar page, and now she stands before the red sheet of paper, going over the numbers again. Her heart fills with calm. Only the supplementary information leaves her uneasy. First, the number eleven pierces her eyes, then there's the "winter solstice," which doesn't sound like a particularly auspicious holiday. Still, these niggles are quickly banished by the redness of the whole.

Walking away from the calendar, Auntie Xue notices her son Jiyue in bed, still sound asleep. She almost wakes him, but no sooner has she taken a step in his direction than she reconsiders. Let him sleep a bit longer—he's going to be absolutely exhausted by the end of his big day!

Auntie Xue goes outside. The siheyuan is very quiet, with not a soul in sight. In the old system of carving up the day and night into twelve units, this would be mao shi—the time of the jade rabbit. The Xue family occupies two rooms on the western side of this siheyuan. Although they have added a kitchen to their home, it isn't big enough to handle the demands of catering. Yesterday, they set up a tarpaulin tent for the hired chef.

Her husband ought to be in the tent, but there's no sign of him. He must have snuck off to Back Sea Park for a stroll or some Bagua boxing. *Couldn't he have given it a rest on this day of all days?* Auntie Xue can't help grumbling to herself. She inspects the various ingredients and half-prepared dishes laid out in the tent—cabbage, washed and cleaned; mustard greens and carrots; yellow croaker fish dredged in eggs and flour, already fried once; tree fungus, chrysanthemum blossoms, and dried bamboo shoots, left to soak overnight. The chef they've found was once the meat-and-vegetable cook at Tongheju Restaurant, and he's planning to make the traditional "four fours to the end"—that is, sixteen dishes. No one's going to find fault with this banquet!

Auntie Xue feels unsettled. It's understandable that the chef isn't here yet—it's only just dawn, and he might have a long commute. But where's her daughter-in-law Zhaoying? Half a year ago, her older son, Jihui, and his wife, Meng Zhaoying, were living with the Xues. This meant the older Xues and Jiyue had to squeeze into one of the rooms, while Jihui, Zhaoying, and their little daughter, Lotus, had the other. Jihui works as a BJ130 light-truck driver, and Zhaoying handles accounts at the same company. The day they got married, they applied for a place of their own and finally got one this spring—a technician moved into an apartment block in a new residential development, and his vacant quarters were allocated to them. Now that they've moved out, there's enough space for little brother Jiyue to think about starting a family of his own. That's how things are in Beijing, each radish in its own little hole. Jihui and Zhaoying didn't move far off, just over to Gongjian Hutong, two subway stops from here. They agreed to come help out first thing in the morning, and now look—the sky is visibly lightening, and still no sign of them. Auntie Xue blames Zhaoying entirely, which is a habit of hers. When they come visiting with her granddaughter, she doesn't mind in the least if her son forgets to say hello, but if her daughter-in-law doesn't give Mom and Dad a greeting, or if she hesitates too long, or if her voice is insufficiently docile and sweet, Auntie Xue is filled with resentment. She doesn't normally say anything out loud, but when she's alone with her daughter-in-law, she doesn't so much as crack a smile. Now she walks out of the tent to the siheyuan entrance, silently grousing: *Honestly, Zhaoying, your brother-in-law's getting married—doesn't that mean anything to you? Couldn't you have shown up early?*

Auntie Xue passes through the chuihua gate separating the outer and inner courtyards and sees Xun Lei coming toward her. Xun Lei's a handsome guy—just twenty-two, three years younger than Jiyue. He lives in the side courtyard on the right as you enter, and his father, Xun Xingwang, used to work at a big factory in the eastern suburbs. After his retirement, he got an individual business license and now has a cobbler's stall by Houmen Bridge. With his fine pale skin and slender elegance, Xun Lei looks nothing like his coarse, swarthy parents—a golden phoenix emerging from a chicken coop. Good looks don't count for much, but he's also been a model student since elementary school and

13

surpassed the expectations of the entire siheyuan by getting a position in the Foreign Affairs Bureau. They sent him overseas for training, and he only returned this summer. Now he works as an interpreter at some important government department, and it sounds like he might get to work abroad in the future!

Right now, Xun Lei is holding two exquisite double-happiness paper cuttings, red on yellow. Full of smiles, he comes over. "Auntie, have a look. If you like them, I'll hang them up!"

Auntie Xue is delighted. What with all her little worries, she'd forgotten he'd said he'd do this. Uncle Xue put up a pair of double-happiness characters at the siheyuan entrance last night, but no sooner had they gone up than Xun Lei, passing by on his way home from work, stopped and studied them with his head tilted to one side. "These look uneven, and the background isn't great. I'll make a new set tonight, and if you prefer mine, I'll help you put them up." Now he's actually gone and done it.

Auntie Xue takes a closer look at the decorations he's holding up. They're really well executed. Apart from the neat strokes and finely balanced color scheme, the intricate border design of magpies and plum blossoms is a work of art in itself. How on earth did he do this?

"My goodness, it's gorgeous! Really gorgeous! Perfect for a celebration," Auntie Xue enthuses, clapping her hands. "How talented you are, Lei!"

"I'll go get some glue!" He darts back into his house exuberantly.

Her bad mood smoothed away, Auntie Xue walks out of the siheyuan.

They live in a hutong in the northern part of the city. And now, from the siheyuan entrance, in the pale-green silken light, the silhouettes of the Bell and Drum Towers delicately reveal themselves. The mythic beast's head that decorated the western end of the Bell Tower's roof spine fell off in the earthquake of 1976, and now only the eastern one is left, metal beard tufting upward, glinting in the gathering daylight. One of the pillars of the Drum Tower's wooden frame is prominent now, making the rather exaggeratedly solid silhouette take on a lighter, livelier air.

Auntie Xue looks up at these two towers, which have become a part of her life and soul. The towers seem to silently cast their eyes over the ancient hutong in which she lives, the shabby siheyuan, and her. For about half a minute, history and destiny stare at each other wordlessly, implacably.

A moment later, Auntie Xue's gaze shifts to the far end of the hutong. Why isn't Zhaoying here yet?

CHAPTER 2

On Di'anmen Main Road, the hired chef comes to cook the wedding feast. Why didn't he want a teapot?

The crossroads at Di'anmen look excessively broad. That's because the stately city gate of Di'anmen used to stand here but was torn down in the early fifties and replaced with this intersection. In the intervening thirty years, for some reason, no one has put up a landscaped traffic island and turned this into a roundabout. Everyone was busy doing other things, same as now. It's not yet light, and already the place is bustling. Not bustling like a park or shopping mall, of course, but in a much more colorless, joyless way—with people hurrying to work. The buses and trams are absolutely packed. At each stop, people stand obediently in neat lines, while some inconsiderate bastards are practically waiting in the express lane, ready to leap onto the bus as soon as it arrives. Then there are the bicycles, the glue holding this whole scene together. Most cyclists passively follow the streams of traffic, but there are also a few young things with asses lifted off their seats, darting swift as snakes into every gap they see, zipping ahead at an astonishing pace.

At least things are a little calmer today. It's Sunday, so the Party cadres and students are absent from this scrum. Nonetheless, there are still quite a few people passing through—laborers, sales clerks, administrators. The lofty Drum Tower to the north and the imposing peak of Jingshan in the south both seem to stare at this spot in the gloom, perhaps pondering: *Why has life in this place gone through such startling changes while consisting mainly of monotonous repetition?*

Lu Xichun pedals calmly amid the traffic, turning matters over in his head as he moves steadily onward.

He's twenty-six years old, and perhaps a little plump for his age, though his face, arms, and chest are firm and supple—he's just somewhat puffier than his peers and lacks planes or angles. He works at a restaurant in Huashi, just past Chongwenmen. This is pretty much Beijing's most lowly and unattractive establishment, and some self-proclaimed elites might regard it as utterly beneath their notice—a disposable cell in the city's anatomy. Yet as the saying goes, "The sparrow may be tiny, but its organs are intact," and all of Beijing, storms and sunshine, joy and sorrow, finds a clear, resounding echo in this tiny eating house.

Lu Xichun is an orphan. This is his brief answer, whenever anyone asks about his mother or father. If the questioner tries to find out more, he immediately gets upset. You might think there was a mystery surrounding his late parents.

Actually, it's a perfectly unremarkable tale. Xichun's father was a trishaw delivery man, and his mother a housewife. They didn't earn much but promised their only son they would provide for him just as well as any wealthy family. As a result, in elementary school, his bespectacled teacher frequently held him up for the edification of his classmates. "The old society and the new society are day and night. If we were still in the old society, Lu Xichun would be dressed in rags, scavenging coal cinders from the garbage dump." This same teacher once visited their home and invited his father to come talk to the students about his "miserable past and untroubled present." He found Xichun's father snacking on a head of garlic and drinking—he downed two ounces of baigan liquor after work each day. Unexpectedly for both Xichun and the teacher, not only did his father refuse, he went purple in the face, glared at them with bloodshot eyes, and ranted, "Don't make fun of me! Don't you dare try that with me!" His mother rushed into the room to smooth things over, claiming it was just the booze talking. "Don't pay any attention to him!" The teacher left dispirited and from then on never held Xichun up as an example again. Xichun was deeply confused about the whole business. Not long after that, his dad had a stroke and died.

After his father's passing, Xichun's mother took up the burden of providing for them. She'd been doing embroidery to supplement their household income and now needed to take on twice as much work, often plodding away until after ten o'clock at night. Thanks to her industriousness, Xichun lived just as well as before. As far as he can remember, though, his mom was never the kind, maternal figure one reads about in works of literature. Almost fifty, she checked herself out in the mirror at least a dozen times a day and was always pinching her forehead and temples between two fingers to remove toxins, leaving a neat row of purplish-red lines. Though they rarely ate meat, she insisted on plucking a bristle off the broom after every meal to pick her teeth as she sat in their doorway. From time to time, she got into an argument with a neighbor; though these occasions were rare, and his mom usually had a point, her sheer fury and filthy curse words left Xichun secretly ashamed for days afterward. She was diagnosed with liver cancer in the winter of 1972 and was dead by the spring of '73.

Lu Xichun lived in one of his siheyuan's south-facing rooms. After the death of his parents, the neighbors expected the place to turn into a complete rathole, or maybe even a gathering spot for all the hutong's hoodlums. Instead, just two days after arranging his mother's funeral, sixteen-year-old Xichun had transformed his home. First, he got a certificate of ownership from the neighborhood committee. He then took a set of ceramic vases, a hat stand, and a hardwood kang table to the pawnshop and got what seemed to him like a substantial amount of cash. Next, he painted the walls, cleaned every item of furniture with a straw brush, and completely changed the décor. Then he waited in his bright, clean house to be allocated a new job by the authorities. He was down to his last five yuan when he got the notification deploying him to this little restaurant.

In certain people's eyes, Lu Xichun was one of Beijing's "hutong hooligans," a young man with no prospects and little hope of reform. Against expectations, despite his occasionally puzzling behavior, he not only didn't go off the rails, but actually managed to lead an extremely respectable existence. This was due to the influence of two people in his life. First, his high school teacher Ji Zhiman, and second, Chef He from the restaurant. Teacher Ji is not a particularly well-known educator, and likewise Chef He isn't prominent in the food and beverage industry. Yet something wholesome in their essences, and the way they seek to constantly better themselves, seeped into Xichun's soul.

At first in order to avoid being sent down to the countryside, and then because of difficulties with labor deployment, the young people working at the restaurant mostly got there through the back door. Probably a hilarious thought to those people who don't think its front door worthy of notice. In a way, you could say that even when Beijingers share the same space or time, we're all at different levels. Lu Xichun's position might not be the lowest rung on the ladder, but even if it were, he'd have all kinds of things in common with those higher up. If a guy is swanking around in front of his coworkers because he got his job at the restaurant through connections, isn't that the same as a cadre getting extra respect from colleagues at the ministry because he happens to be some big shot's nephew? Xichun has wanted to pick up a spatula and learn to cook since he came to the restaurant but hasn't been given the opportunity—the "red" position of cooking meat and vegetables is one step higher than the "white" one of preparing rice and noodles. In the restaurant world, his origins and background are insufficient to earn him this honor. Instead, it's gone to a young man whose lips seem permanently fixed in a pout, who has better origins. Unfortunately, this guy's only aim in life is to get himself hoisted into a more exalted profession, and he has no interest in taking this red position seriously. Even so, the boss would rather keep him in this role than allow Xichun to step in.

Xichun is tormented by his ill fortune and the reality of his life. Is his suffering worth any less than that of a college graduate unable to put his degree to good use? Or a talented writer who pours his blood and guts into a manuscript only to have it rejected? Or a high-ranking cadre whose progressive reforms are blocked by conservatives? Surely not. Especially when that other guy doesn't listen carefully to the chef's instructions and distractedly allows a dish to get burned so badly that customers complain. Xichun suffers greatly at those moments. Sometimes he can't resist grabbing a steamed bun as it slides down the chute, squeezing it so tightly that white goo oozes between his fingers, then flinging the wad of dough back into the machine.

A few days ago, Xichun went back to his old high school to unburden himself to Ji Zhiman, who had been his math teacher when the Gang of Four were in power. You didn't learn much during math lessons back then, but in their conversations after class, Xichun gained a fair amount of true knowledge. Teacher Ji liked telling him about history, especially the recent past. The stuff he talked about wasn't anything you'd hear in history class. Xichun remembers one thing he said so often it was virtually his catchphrase: "You need to take a historical perspective."

Teacher Ji has always lived in a small room in a corner of the school. For some reason, he has never married. Each time Xichun visits, he sees a different female guest amid the chaos of Teacher Ji's room. Some appear young and, though not necessarily beautiful, are certainly fashionably dressed. Others are middle-aged and wear plain clothes, but have retained their charms. The woman that day was neither old nor young. She had a round face, slightly bulging eyes, and a booming voice. The way she behaved, you'd have thought she was Teacher Ji's closest companion. While Xichun was talking to Teacher Ji, she lounged on his bed smoking, casually flicking through one of Teacher Ji's stamp albums. From time to time, she let out a bark of laughter as coarse as any man's.

Xichun allowed his sorrows to pour out of him. Teacher Ji's expression didn't change, and he kept running a round plastic brush through his thinning hair. When Xichun was done talking, Teacher Ji grabbed a book off the desk and handed it to him. "Read this," he said simply.

The book was a yellowing copy of *The Anthology of Literature and History*. Lu Xichun glanced at the table of contents: Pujia's "Memories of the Qing Palace," Pujie's "Recollecting Life in the Northern Mansion," "Memoirs of Qing Palace Eunuchs." How would reading these essays solve his problems?

"Read this," Mr. Ji said again. "You need to take a historical perspective. You can't make sweeping statements about anything in the world, and there's never been an ideal time when everything made sense—it's just a question of how you look at the advancing tide and deal with remnants of the old order. Do you really think everything changed overnight when we became a republic after the 1911 Xinhai Revolution? Inertia is a powerful force. Right up until 1924, when we finally chased Emperor Puyi out of the Forbidden City, the Bell Tower was still striking the hours! That's nothing. Guess what else? After the Bell and Drum Towers sounded at dusk, people with bells hanging from their belts would appear in the streets—the night watch. Butt ringers, we called them. And who told them to patrol the city? They were led by old guardsmen from the Ninth Gate provincial governor's office. The guy in front held a lantern, and they walked along the road, just like that. This was a whole five years after the May Fourth Movement, three years after the Communist Party was formed, after the Beijing–Hankou Railway workers' strike sent shock waves around the world. Yet you could still see such a sight on the streets of Beijing. This book will tell you more facts like these. Go read it."

Xichun brought the book home. He was shocked to learn that Pujia's so-called "Memories of the Qing Palace" described events after 1919, which meant these awful feudal scenes took place well into the Republican era. Prince Pujie's recollections told him that the strict hierarchical order within the Northern Mansion held sway for even longer. The various Qing palace eunuchs' memoirs made his jaw drop even further. One father, determined to get his son into the palace to improve his family's situation, "cleansed" his son's body by crushing his testicles with his own hands, after which he sold the boy to the imperial officials who provided eunuchs to the court. That alone was enough to make anyone boil with rage. But when did it happen? In Republican times!

When he'd got to the end of the anthology, Xichun sank into thought, and gradually his raging emotions stilled. Why let himself get so worked up over these dark events? With the times moving so fast, of course any debris from the old era they hadn't got around to clearing away was going to look even more egregious. It was all a matter of having a historical perspective, of dealing with these things calmly and rationally. From this point of view, what was so strange about his little restaurant having a boss whose supercilious eyes were tainted by the values of the old society?

His boss's elitism may have blocked Xichun from getting a red position, but Chef He took him under his wing anyway. He brought Xichun home with him and taught him to make the standard banquet dishes, plus a few additional showstoppers. Chef He had been the head cook at the famous Tongheju Restaurant until he retired two years early so his son could take over. He still needed a bit of income, which is how he ended up at this little restaurant near his house. Quite a few big restaurants almost as good as Tongheju had clamored for him to join them as an instructor, promising him a hefty stipend, but he refused them all. "People who go to small restaurants deserve good food too," he said. He brought his exquisite craft to making forty-eight-cent bowls of braised tofu, and within a few months, the little restaurant had gained quite a reputation. Unfortunately, that reputation began with high praise and ended with "but the quality isn't consistent." The main reason for this inconsistency? The pouty bastard. How Xichun would love to take his place and make the restaurant known for unwavering excellence. Sadly, so far, he hasn't had the chance.

Xichun often goes to Chef He's house. When Xichun points at a recipe he's brought with him and asks about some detail or other, Chef He keeps his lips clamped around his pipe, frowns and shakes his head, and mutters a word or two of advice. But if Xichun shows up with ingredients, ready to start cooking, Chef He puts his pipe aside and begins animatedly instructing him. When the chicken in egg sauce or fish in rice wine is emanating delicious odors from its white porcelain plate, Chef He will insist that Xichun carry it out to the siheyuan to share with his neighbors. "Let's find out if our little offering passes muster," he'll say. "We'll let them taste it, and ask what they think." The neighbors are invariably delighted and offer little gifts in return, perhaps a dish of fresh or candied fruit. Chef He doesn't let Xichun refuse. In fact, he accepts the treats on Xichun's behalf, then gets out the erguotou, the sorghum liquor. As they sit and drink, he points out all the ways that day's dish could be improved. The recipes Xichun has found are sometimes unclear or wrong in places, whereas Chef He's words come from his own experience and are worth far more than any printed page.

"Don't you resent anyone," Chef He often says reassuringly after he's taken a swig, wiping the back of his hand across his mouth. "You'll get your turn."

Chef He is genuinely fond of his protégé, but there are times when Xichun's behavior is a little odd. A few days ago, the restaurant got twenty porcelain teapots from somewhere or other. They decided to keep a few to hold vinegar, soy sauce, and so on in the kitchen, and distribute the rest to the staff as a perk. Everyone took one, but Xichun refused. Chef He said, "Why not just take it? Sure, it looks a bit old-fashioned, but it'll be better than that glass jar you store boiled water in." Xichun insisted he didn't want one, and when they asked why, he wouldn't say. Someone shoved one at him but he didn't take it, and it smashed on the floor. While everyone exclaimed what a shame that was, he turned on his heel and walked away without a word.

Apart from these occasional inexplicable moments, Xichun comes across as a good-hearted young man who's always trying to better himself. He longs for the day Chef He spoke of, hoping it will come as soon as possible so he can not only wield the wok but eventually run the whole restaurant. He has plans to improve it in all kinds of ways, and completely change its appearance, so every customer who walks in will remember it for the rest of their lives.

Because of this, he doesn't pass up a single opportunity to improve his skills. Today, for instance, he's heading to a hutong near the Bell and Drum Towers to prepare a wedding feast in place of Chef He. He's heard that this family has prepared a good array of ingredients, and he'll have more than enough assistance. This is his chance to show them what he's made of—the Xues and their friends are sure to beam with delight when they taste his cooking!

CHAPTER 3

A Beijing opera actress with problems of her own is asked to
join the bridal party.

Tantai Zhizhu sings to herself as she walks up to the siheyuan gate. After vocal warm-ups and sword exercises, her voice feels smooth and relaxed, and every joint in her body is limber. Now that her attention is no longer taken up by the practice, though, wisps of heavy sadness rise from the bottom of her heart, increasing with the noise of the bustling marketplace.

Will they actually get to perform *Zhuo Wenjun*? Another troupe is already staging Mr. Wu Zuguang's arrangement of *The Phoenix Seeks a Mate*, in the Zhang style. Strictly speaking, this *Zhuo Wenjun*, which references Mr. Xun Huisheng's version, combines elements of the Cheng tradition and Ouyang Yuqian's performance style, so they wouldn't be treading the same ground. Yet the deputy troupe leader, who is in charge of programming, remains ambivalent, her fellow performers are all over the place, and the musicians don't seem enthusiastic either. Some said, "Will this really bring in an audience?" And others, "Why bother with a new arrangement when there are already so many? As long as people keep buying tickets, we can keep putting on the same old shows and make as good a living." It's true, these days audiences want to see battles and pageantry on stage. A poetic piece like *Zhuo Wenjun* isn't going to attract much attention. Besides, Tantai Zhizhu wants them to incorporate the Kun opera techniques of Han Shichang and Bai Yunsheng, to create what she calls a more "literary" effect. Would a show like this do well at the box office? It's hard to say! Still, she wouldn't be content with yet another production of *The Bean Juice Tale*, or *The Story of Su San*, or *Wu Family Hill*. Even their recent well-received effort, *Mulan Joins the Army*, can be set aside for a while, she thinks. She longs to see constant innovation on the stage, to show their existing audience something they've never seen before, while attracting new, younger viewers. But it's difficult! All she wants to do is what any performer ought to, honoring both her craft and her audience, yet to certain people, she might as well hope to pluck the moon out of the sky and eat it like a moon cake. These "certain people" are not just in the troupe, but also in her own household: her husband, Li Kai, has tried to stop her! He means well, of course. How can Zhizhu get his good intentions out of her way? Is he still in bed? Is he still torturing himself over the fight they had last night?

Zhizhu is almost at the gate when her eyes light up—she's just caught sight of the paper cuttings on either side and remembers this is the younger Xue boy's big day. She recalls the decorations from last night, but these are different: they have a yellow background, with exquisite magpies and plum blossoms around the red border. It's clear the family is taking this wedding very seriously, the way they've tweaked even this little detail. If only her comrades in the opera troupe would bring this spirit of constant improvement to their craft!

She goes through the gate and toward her home, which is in the outer courtyard, to the left of the entrance and diagonally across from the chuihua gate leading to the inner courtyard. She gently opens the front door, walks in, hangs her wooden sword by the door, and stands in front of the large wall mirror as she removes the pale-yellow mohair scarf from around her head, hangs it over the back of a chair, and smooths down her thick black hair with both hands.

They have three south-facing rooms. The middle one is a combined dining room, living room, and rehearsal space for her. To the east is her and her husband's bedroom, and to the west is where her in-laws live with her son, Bamboo, and daughter, Plum.

A cough from the western room. She immediately stops fussing with her hair, pulls aside the floral curtain, and goes in. A few days ago, her mother-in-law took Plum, who has not yet started school, to visit her auntie; they're not back yet. The room currently contains only Bamboo and her father-in-law, who used to work as a carver at a jade factory. He's seventy, and of course retired some time ago. Unlike most old people, he goes to bed late and seldom wakes up early. He is set in his ways and loves nothing more than to put on his reading glasses and work his way through a serial novel, never mind if it's classical or contemporary—as long as each chapter begins with the traditional couplet summarizing its plot, he'll read it. Right now, he's immersed in Jin Jishui's *Siqi*. It's a thin book, but after ten days, he's not even halfway through. He may be a slow reader, but he retains everything. Her father-in-law is fully dressed, while Bamboo is still sound asleep under the covers.

"Do you have a cold?" she asks loudly.

Her father-in-law coughs a couple of times more but bats away her concern. "Nothing to worry about. We have some loquat syrup in the house—that'll take care of it."

Zhizhu taps Bamboo's shoulder to rouse him and says to her father-in-law, "I'll go heat up some congee for you both." She also plans to slice up a steamed bun, dip it in egg, and fry it—that should do for breakfast.

Her father-in-law hesitates as if he wants to say something, and Zhizhu doesn't feel she can leave until he's got it off his chest.

He coughs twice more, picks up the novel from where it sits by his pillow, and says, "Aren't you about to start rehearsing a new show? How about adapting *Siqi*?"

"Dad," she answers loudly, "you make it sound as if all we need is an idea, and we can start rehearsing right away. First, someone has to write the script. Next, someone has to set it to music. You think any of this is easy?" She could mention many more obstacles, but sighs and lets the matter drop. It's clear that what he's trying to say isn't actually about the new show.

Finally, he can't stand it any longer and asks in the most conciliatory possible tone, "Last night . . . did Li Kai . . . did you two have another argument?"

Zhizhu feels blood rushing to her face. Her father-in-law is a little deaf, but their three rooms are joined together, and her quarrel with Li Kai was never going to be a secret. She glances at Bamboo, who is sitting up in bed rubbing his eyes, and forces a smile. "Well, it's normal for a young couple to exchange a few words now and then, isn't it? Don't worry, we never let the sun go down on a fight."

Unmoved, her father-in-law declares solemnly, "I'm going to teach Li Kai a lesson! You two aren't young anymore, but you're always yelling at each other in there. What do you think you're doing? Never mind if it bothers us oldies, how do you think it's affecting the children? And what if the neighbors hear you? Can't you just live in peace? What's wrong with Li Kai?"

Although the last part of the scolding is directed at Li Kai, Zhizhu feels it like a needle through her heart. He's right—how did things get so bad between her and Li Kai?

"Don't worry about us, Dad." She lowers her eyelids to hold back the tears. "I'll go heat up the congee."

Normally her mother-in-law rules the kitchen. Now that she's away, Dad tried to take over, but Li Kai put a stop to that—his wife would do the cooking, he insisted. This is one of the things they fight about.

Zhizhu pauses by the middle room. Instead of heading out to the kitchen, she can't stop herself going into the room she shares with Li Kai. She stands at the door a few seconds before stepping in.

Li Kai is sound asleep, his hair all mussed. He must have an unusually heavy head, because it always sinks right down into the pillow, making the pillow plump up all around as if sighing at the weight. One thick arm sprawls on top of the covers. His skin is dark and taut, and sinewy muscles ripple beneath it. On his upper arm are two large cowpox scars, like a couple of radishes planted in his flesh. He reeks of tobacco.

Zhizhu walks over and covers his arm with her blanket, which she hadn't folded earlier.

Gazing at her sleeping husband and the mound of cigarette butts in the bedside ashtray, Zhizhu's heart fills with confusion. Forgetting all about the congee, she sinks back into a padded chair.

How did they end up fighting again? Why does all of this feel so inevitable?

After last night's show, she emerged from the stage door just ten minutes late. Li Kai was supposed to pick her up, but there was no sign of him.

The theater is down a hutong. Yesterday's show ran late, and because it's winter, the audience dispersed very quickly. Her comrades in the troupe also went their separate ways without lingering. All by herself, she went to the usual spot, but for the first time, Li Kai wasn't there. She called his name, stomped her feet, almost burst into tears—still no sign. She began jogging along the alleyway, pulling up her sleeve to glance at her watch. She'd missed the last bus. Now what? Was she supposed to walk all the way home?

Who'd have thought it? Less than twenty minutes earlier, she'd been on stage in a comic role, tittering and capering around. Look at her now, miserable, scurrying alone down the street.

The cold wind found its way past her scarf, down her collar, and into her sleeves. Soon, she was shivering all over. In that moment, she felt as if all the things she normally thought were important—career, fame, reputation, eternal artistic values, and so forth—were completely meaningless. She was so unfortunate, what possible joy or attraction could life hold for her?

All of a sudden, a figure stepped out into the alley. Was she about to get mugged, or was he planning to have his way with her? She almost called for help, then managed to make her eyes focus despite her terror. It was Li Kai.

"Why . . . why didn't you wait for me?" How she wanted to go over there and give him a couple of slaps.

He glared at her with hatred. "Why didn't you come out after you changed?"

"I had to talk to the others about rehearsals for *Zhuo Wenjun*—"

"I know you've got your eye on that little gigolo!" he interrupted viciously, the words spewing out of him. "What the hell! I've seen the way he looks at you. Have you two already got it on? Why not just go home with him?"

This hurt Zhizhu more than a slap would have. Tears came to her eyes, and she felt fiery rage rise in her throat. "You're insane!" she yelled. "You're making this all up out of thin air! He's a whole generation older than us—he's about to become a grandfather! If he hadn't been cast as Sima Xiangru, I wouldn't be paying him any attention at all. He has BO—did you know that? How could you be so silly?"

She decided to ignore him and walk home on her own. He followed on his bicycle and finally persuaded her to hop onto the back. As he pedaled them home, she had no choice but to wrap her arms around his broad back, which now felt unfamiliar and icy cold. What should she do? What?

Back home, they felt the ceiling pressing down on them. Everything in their room felt unbearable, especially the twelve-inch color wedding photo above their bed: the two of them leaning toward each other, heads touching.

"We can't go on like this. Let's sit down, sit down, sit down . . . Let's calm down and just talk," said Zhizhu, lowering herself into the armchair without even taking off her coat.

Li Kai waited until the third "sit down" before doing so, on the edge of the bed. Right away, he started chain-smoking.

Back when Zhizhu graduated from the opera academy, could she have predicted this to be how her life would end up?

She was sent to a pretty good troupe and put all her energy into learning from the older performers. On stage, she poured her heart and soul into every role until a critic wrote, "She has great presence and emotive power, but lacks refinement. She does not seem aware that artistry lies in holding back. Her exaggerated acting feels excessive and indulgent." Just as she was working hard on increasing her refinement and learning restraint, the Cultural Revolution began. She was labeled a "feudal, capitalist, and revisionist black seedling," and when she said the wrong thing at the wrong time, she was denounced as an "active counterrevolutionary" and locked away. She felt as if everything was meaningless and lost all hope.

One day, when the guard dozed off, she grabbed the small bottle of insecticide under his chair and drank it. She didn't die. Instead, she went through unconsciousness, sluggishness, numbness, depression, pain, and despair, which gradually turned to calm, acceptance, endurance, tolerance, and optimism. In the spring of 1977, she began training again. Everyone was surprised when her raggedy voice recovered to be even more resonant than it had been a decade before, and her stiff body grew supple enough to once again fling herself around the stage. In the last year or two, her star has risen higher than in the old days, beyond anything she expected. Whenever she's on stage, even at the least convenient times or the most remote locations, the house will be at least seven-tenths full. This isn't bad at all, at a time when Beijing opera audiences are shrinking. Pictures of her in and out of costume frequently appear in the papers, the radio stations invite her for recorded and live interviews, the TV stations want her to appear, music companies want to press her records, fans show up backstage clamoring for her autograph and photos with her . . . and that same critic from before revised his opinion: "She doesn't have a great deal of presence, and her emotive power isn't the strongest, but she has such refinement that each smile or frown, each note that passes her lips, delicately plucks at the heartstrings and reveals the depths of each role. These beautiful portrayals seamlessly unite form and spirit."

If that were her whole story, extreme sorrow turning to joy, that would be very bland indeed. In 1973, five years after her suicide attempt, she got married. When she graduated from the academy, she had quietly told herself: *You're already married to the stage—don't be a bigamist!* This wasn't a line from a play but a promise that nothing would be more important to her than her craft. In 1972, her ruined body was deployed, as part of "implementing policy," to work on the packaging line of a button factory. She said to herself: *The stage has abandoned you—you can never go back to it. Might as well find a husband and get married!* Someone introduced her to Li Kai, a strapping salt-of-the-earth lathe operator. The first time they met, she ended up telling him everything about herself. Li Kai was visibly moved. While looking into his moist eyes, Zhizhu felt the first green shoots of love. She needed someone to love her and treat her like a wife, and she needed to love an actual person she could call "husband."

At the end of 1976, after another bout of "implementing policy," she returned to the opera troupe. During the Spring Festival of 1979, she took to the stage again. A hundred emotions warred in her as she stepped onto the red carpet! She still remembers Li Kai's excitement and delight, just as great as hers, and her in-laws glowing with pride for her. She was often cast in the big finale numbers, which meant finishing late. Li Kai always waited for her at the stage door to give her a ride home on his bike. He never came backstage. At first, this was because he was shy, but later . . . When did this start? Zhizhu hates herself for not noticing sooner that he had begun staying outside because of some complex mixture of inadequacy and arrogance.

Did it start when the radio producer came to interview her at their home?

The producer had asked in a carrying voice, "And what does your husband do? Does he play male leads, or is he more of a character actor?"

"He's not a performer," said Zhizhu.

Just as loudly: "Then what? Is he a stagehand? A drummer? A fiddle player?"

"He's not in my line of work," said Zhizhu.

The producer's voice grew even louder. "So what kind of artist is he, then?"

"He's not," said Zhizhu frankly. "He works in a factory."

Whether out of curiosity or a love of guessing games, the producer wouldn't let it go. Her voice rang out again: "Oh, in a factory? Which factory? Is he an engineer? A technician?"

That's when Li Kai walked out of the bedroom and said to the interviewer, deadpan, "I'm a lathe operator. A grade-two manual laborer."

If it were just a question of his self-esteem, she could have handled that. But Li Kai gradually began to detest the sight of Zhizhu and young male performers exchanging meaningful looks on stage, joking around, and getting married a few scenes later. Worse, Zhizhu recently shared the stage with two different leading men, and now she's planning to appear in *Zhuo Wenjun*. Li Kai knows very well what it is about the character Sima Xiangru that makes Zhuo Wenjun fall so hard for him.

Last night's fight was far from their first, but it was the most vicious one so far. All their arguments have a three-act structure. First, both of them unleash their anger and hurl hateful things at each other, culminating in "We might as well get a divorce." Next, none too calmly, they accuse each other of all kinds of sins. Whenever one of them talks their way out of something, the other finds a crack in the explanation and launches a new attack. Act three comes when they're both winded by this grim, hopeless struggle, and one of them—usually Li Kai, so forceful and unyielding to start with—cracks and tries to reconcile. Last night was no different. Zhizhu's brain had slowed down to the point that she could only repeat stubbornly, "Why do you hate me? Why?" Li Kai abruptly flung himself at her and held her tight, raining burning kisses down on her cheeks, her eyelids, her forehead, her nose, her mouth. Panting like a bear, he babbled, "I love you love you love you love you love you . . . If you don't love me, I'll kill you, then I'll kill myself!" Zhizhu struggled to get out of his arms, and yelled, "I don't love you, I don't! Kill me, then!" Li Kai sank to his knees with a thud and wrapped his arms around her legs, burying his face in her coat, sobbing and mumbling, "Zhizhu, forgive me, forgive me, I'll do anything, just don't leave me, don't . . ."

That brought Zhizhu fully to her senses. She lifted Li Kai to his feet and urgently hugged his sturdy body. "Don't be so silly!" she soothed him. "I love you, isn't that obvious? How could I ever leave you? Why would you think that? It's impossible, impossible."

With that, they went to bed. Like a prisoner in shackles, every movement Li Kai made exuded pain and regret. Zhizhu took a sleeping pill and thought that the next morning, not only would she have to work on her voice as usual, she'd also have to repair Li Kai's self-esteem. She'd cook for the entire family to prove she's still an ordinary wife after all.

And now, early in the morning, Tantai Zhizhu has returned from doing her exercises, spoken to her father-in-law, and is sitting next to her sleeping husband. With a twinge of pain, she reflects that they have once again reconciled, but her wounded feelings will never recover. And the circumstances that aroused this mood in Li Kai are still unavoidably there.

As she sits there deep in thought, Zhizhu hears a voice calling her name. She stands and listens: it's Auntie Xue, out in the courtyard.

In the few seconds it takes her to hurry out, she manages to put on a cheerful and lively face.

"Come in, Auntie Xue," she says as soon as she steps out. "I was just thinking I should stop by to congratulate you."

"No need for that." Auntie Xue takes her hand and studies her for a moment, then says in a voice overflowing with trust and admiration, "Zhizhu, I have a big favor to ask."

"What is it? Just say the word, and anything I can do . . ."

First, Auntie Xue has to complain. "A big day like this, and look! First thing in the morning, and already things are going wrong. There's still no sign of Zhaoying! I had to pull all kinds of strings to get that famous chef from Tongheju to cook the banquet, but now he says he's sick, and he's sending some young idiot instead. Jiyue's only just got out of bed, and already he's spilled water on his suit trousers while washing his face. About to get married and still so clumsy. I'm so stressed, I feel like my heart is about to jump from my throat. Meanwhile, my old man is shuffling around muttering, 'Don't worry, when we reach the mountain a road will appear.' You see?"

Zhizhu has to respond in some way, so she smiles and asks, "What did you want my help with?"

Auntie Xue gently strokes the back of Zhizhu's right hand, which she's been holding all this time. "You're a lucky woman, Zhizhu. Three generations under one roof. You get along with your husband, and you have a matched set: a son and daughter. You came through the other side of some tough times, and you're getting more and more famous. Our Zhaoying is going to pick up the bride today, and I'm hoping I can trouble you to go with her."

Before Auntie Xue has finished speaking, Zhizhu quickly agrees. "Of course! Just send Zhaoying over when she gets here. I'll get this place shipshape and put on a festive outfit. We'll give your new daughter-in-law a proper reception!"

As Auntie Xue walks away happily, Zhizhu remembers with a start that as they left rehearsal yesterday, she invited a few of her musician colleagues to come by for lunch. She'd completely forgotten, what with all the fuss last night. Now what? Will she have to wake up Li Kai to tell him and plead with him not to say anything about their quarrel in front of their guests? There's no meat in the house

30

and hardly any vegetables—what is she going to cook? Normally she'd dash to the market at Di'anmen and still be back in time, but she's just agreed to go pick up the bride and might have to set off at any moment. What should she do? Even if she sends Bamboo to the market, Li Kai and his dad will hardly be able to put together a meal fit for guests. Damn it. Why is life so full of frustrations? Why do other people's lives keep intruding on hers, messing it up?

Tantai Zhizhu stands in front of the mirror, at her wits' end.

CHAPTER 4

A bureau chief lives in a south-facing house but doesn't have
his own bathroom.

Several families have piled their unwanted furniture on either side of the dimly lit entryway, and on the roof hang a couple of old rattan chairs someone couldn't bear to throw out, even in their dilapidated state. The debris is like a single man guarding the choke point of a mountain pass, preventing ten thousand others from getting through.

Carrying a bamboo basket of fried pastries and bean-paste buns, Zhang Xiuzao bumps into Xun Lei by the entryway. For some reason, Xun Lei is holding a little brush and bowl of glue in one hand and a couple of sheets of paper in the other. What is he going to put up?

In an instant, Xiuzao feels a rasp in her throat, and her heart beats unevenly. For several months now, she's been sternly reminding herself that if she happens to run into Xun Lei she's only allowed to raise her chin a little, nod very slightly, and pass by without a single word. She lives in the farthest corner on the north side of the main courtyard, while Xun Lei is in a side yard to the right of this entryway—and moreover, she spends her weeks at Tsinghua University, where she studies hydroelectric engineering, and only comes home on Sundays (or sometimes not even then), so she hasn't had many chances to carry out these instructions to herself—just three, in fact. And now, one more. She tilts her chin up, but just as she is about to nod noncommittally at Xun Lei, he smiles warmly and says, "Could you give me a hand?"

It seems Xun Lei wants her help sticking up these pieces of paper. That's all it takes to shake the dignity and self-respect she's spent so much time building up. They look at each other in silence for two seconds. In his eyes she sees purity, sincerity, kindness, and the gleam of intelligence, a combination that drives her absolutely wild. She is intoxicated. No other young man possesses such adorable windows to the soul. Can she really stand before these open windows and speak the cold words of rejection she has prepared?

Xiuzao's lips quiver, and she is on the verge of blurting out, "All right," when Xun Lei suddenly grins apologetically. "I'm sorry! Look at me . . . You've just bought breakfast! Of course you'll want to get that to your family. I'll put these up myself."

Xiuzao's heart all but shatters. Why is she holding this stupid basket? Why did he notice it at this moment? Couldn't she have put it down on the stone bench by the entryway? This bench used to have a pair of lions on it, but in the summer of 1966, the hutong's Red Guards painstakingly removed them with chisels. Yes, she ought to have done just that, then gone with Xun Lei to help put up whatever it was. But he smiled apologetically and retracted his request, and now, like a gentleman, he's turned slightly aside to give her room to pass.

Keeping a tight hold on herself, Xiuzao raises her chin slightly, nods to him with an attitude of unmistakable frostiness, and angles her body to walk past him and through the entryway.

If there were a hundred strings in her heart, every one of them would now be jangling, and not in harmony either. All she wants right now is to find a corner to sit down in, rest her face in her hands, and quietly soothe those discordant strings until they're back in tune.

Unfortunately, she won't get her wish. As she walks through the ornate gate, the tarpaulin tent for the Xue wedding looms alarmingly. Yes, she saw it when she got home yesterday, and walked past it on her way to get breakfast this morning, but it was lifeless then. Now, Uncle Xue is bent over, lighting a charcoal stove—clearly they're going to need more than one flame today. From within the tent comes the frenzied sound of meat being chopped and a suffocating mix of odors.

Without Xiuzao's noticing, Auntie Xue has appeared in front of her, face wreathed in smiles. "Ah, Xiuzao, is your father leaving again this morning?"

Xiuzao isn't in the mood to smile back, but her parents have raised her well, and she can't brush off a conversation under any circumstances. She forces a cheerful look and says, "Yes, a car should be here after breakfast to take him to the airport. Oh, and congratulations, Auntie Xue! If there's anything I can do to help, just say."

Auntie Xue drops an assortment of candies into Xiuzao's bamboo basket and says with great sincerity, "I won't send Jiyue over, because your mom and dad both have official business—I don't want to disturb them. But here's a little something to pay our respects."

"Thank you," says Xiuzao quickly. "This candy looks so fancy. You've given us too much!"

Auntie Xue grins. "Well, in a few years when you return the favor, yours will have to be even fancier! And I'm telling you now—you'd better give us even more than this!"

Xiuzao can't even summon a smile. Auntie Xue has nothing but good intentions, but this is unbearable. How can she stand this? The figure of Xun Lei floats before her eyes. Why are they talking about her wedding? Who is she supposed to marry?

"I certainly will!" she manages to reply.

Auntie Xue doesn't seem to notice Xiuzao's distress—she just smiles and walks away. Xiuzao hurries home. She needs to get back to her bedroom to sit down and be alone.

Alas, that's not to be.

Xiuzao's family lives in three large south-facing rooms, and part of the wide corridor outside has been turned into a kitchen. Her father, Zhang Qilin, is fifty-five. He was part of an underground movement at college, before Liberation. In 1948, he went to the Liberation Zone from Beiping, as Beijing was known then, and the following year he entered the city with the People's Liberation Army. He was placed in the State Council, where he rose to be deputy section chief and then section chief. He'd just been promoted to deputy division chief when the Cultural Revolution erupted. During this time, he was denounced as a traitor, the "black teeth and claws" of his minister, and dispatched to a cadre school, where he raised pigs for six years. After the Gang of Four fell, he returned to his division as its chief. Not long ago, he was promoted again, and now runs a bureau. When the family returned to Beijing from the cadre school in 1977, they found their former quarters occupied. They stayed a long time at a guesthouse, and it wasn't until 1979 that they were allocated a space in this siheyuan. According to Old Fu in the Administrative Division, he had to deal with all kinds of red tape at the Housing Department to exchange four smaller houses for these three rooms. The family was delighted when they moved in. Xiuzao's older brother and sister were working elsewhere, so she and her parents had a luxurious six hundred square feet of patterned brick floors and pale-gray ceilings to themselves. Back at the cadre school, they were initially placed in separate dormitories, eighteen people to a room, sleeping on mats on the floor for the first few months. When they were finally allowed to live together as a family, it was in a tiny, plain hut. Day and night, compared to their current situation!

Now that they've lived here for a while, they've noticed a major flaw: they don't have their own bathroom. Instead, they use the communal one diagonally across the courtyard. The Administrative Division installed a phone line and running water quickly enough and had planned to put in a toilet too, but after studying their layout, the workers realized there was no easy way to run a waste pipe from anywhere in their home or the corridor outside to the sewer. And so it never happened. For the last year, Xiuzao's mother has been badgering Old Fu to move them to a unit in the new residential district. Old Fu's department has indeed been allocated some of these government-built apartments, and given Zhang Qilin's recent promotion, he feels confident that as soon as the next batch is given out, he'll be able to move them into a four-room unit—on a good floor with the best finishes, naturally.

Zhang Qilin isn't too bothered either way, but Xiuzao's mother, Yu Yongzhi, a doctor, is getting more and more worked up. Recently, she's been pestering her husband about the move. Last night, after Xiuzao got back, they had dinner and settled on the couch to watch the TV news. When an item about a new housing estate came up, Dr. Yu couldn't help mentioning it again. "I wonder if Old Fu will actually do what he promised."

Zhang Qilin smiled. "He's always kept his word to me. Though I think we'd be fine with a three-room place."

Dr. Yu disagreed. "A bureau chief should live in a four-room apartment. That's the rule."

Still smiling, Mr. Zhang said, "That's an old-fashioned rule."

"Nothing unreasonable about it. Look at your ministry—apart from you, how many bureau chiefs live anywhere smaller than a four-room?"

Mr. Zhang didn't want an argument; he was just stating his opinion when he said, "It's nice to live in a siheyuan, though. Rooms like ours are more comfortable than an apartment."

"But the bathroom!" Dr. Yu returned to a familiar theme. "We have to use the communal bathroom every day—it's so unhygienic!"

The smile never left Mr. Zhang's face. "The old folk in the siheyuan have always used that bathroom, and they look healthier than we do!"

"So you don't want to move? Is that it?" Dr. Yu was getting agitated. "I can't live here a moment longer. Never mind that there's no toilet, I can't even have a shower in my own home."

Zhang Qilin was leaning back on the couch, his whole body relaxed, eyes fixed on the screen. "The bathroom at the cadre school was horrible, and we made do just fine for six years, didn't we? As for showering—"

Dr. Yu leaned forward, all worked up. "How could you say that? We had no choice! I know what you're about to say—you think I can just go to the public bathhouse. But you know what? These bathhouses double as hotels these days—traveling tradesmen stay the night there. Some of them have fleas, and those fleas get left on the mats. You think anyone bothers to kill them? As soon as the sleepers are gone, they let in the bathers! The women's section is still okay, but I've heard the men's side is a complete hellhole!"

Zhang Qilin gently nodded the whole time she was speaking to show he didn't disagree. Then his smile abruptly broadened—he'd just remembered a moment last summer when he went for a pee at night and heard water gurgling as he approached the communal bathroom. Inside, he found the older Xue boy stark naked, having a shower by the faucet, which he'd fitted a rubber hose to. This sight jolted him into working harder to improve living conditions for all Beijingers, even though that was only tangentially related to his job. Now he couldn't help laughing as he recalled Xue Jihui's well-built body, his wet, smiling face. He said to his wife, "Sure, it's not the most pleasant thing to use communal toilets and bathrooms, but there is one advantage: they bring us closer to the people, to the whole of society. If we retreat into a government apartment, all our problems will be solved, which is very nice for us—but we'll be cut off from the masses."

Dr. Yu shook her head. "You think if we move into an apartment, the phone will ring less often? Fewer people will knock on your door? It may be easier for people to find you there! Look at this place. Never mind tea leaves, we don't even have hot water to offer people."

Zhang Qilin nodded in agreement, but explained, "When I say 'the people' or 'our society,' I don't just mean those from my workplace. I'm also talking about our neighbors here in this siheyuan and everyone who lives in this area. They may not have anything to do with our work, but it still makes a difference to interact with them. At the very least, they broaden our worldview and our thinking. We can't just look at a single point, or a line, or a surface—we need to consider every issue in three dimensions . . ."

Dr. Yu slumped back on the couch, and this time she was the one who nodded gently. Xiuzao, who'd been listening quietly, said, "So, Dad, if Uncle Fu phoned tomorrow to say we could move into a new apartment, what would we do?"

"We'd move," said Zhang Qilin, smiling.

"But you were just talking about being in touch with the masses and with society," Xiuzao couldn't stop herself saying. "How about them?"

"Where we live isn't the most important thing," said Zhang Qilin frankly. "What matters is how much we ask of ourselves. If we move away, we can still come back here to visit while getting to know our new neighbors and making new social connections!"

Now that it seemed they were more or less on the same page, the mood grew less tense. Even so, Dr. Yu couldn't resist one last gibe. "You say that, but you know how busy you'll be. You think you'll have time to come back here? You may not even have time to meet our new neighbors!"

In Xiuzao's family, the atmosphere is controlled by Zhang Qilin, who is always calm and rational but never inflexible or lacking in humanity. Even during the worst moments of the Cultural Revolution, he was never flustered or at a loss, at least on the surface. Xiuzao still remembers one day when she was just seven and had no idea what was happening in the world. She and her mother, brother, and sister were ordered to attend a struggle session in the square. First the ministers and deputy ministers were hauled up, then the bureau chiefs and deputy chiefs, and finally the "black teeth and claws." Her father was in this group. Xiuzao was terrified—every "black element" had their head shaved and a big black placard hung around their neck and was made to do the "airplane pose," bent over with their hands clasped behind their back. As a lesser offender, Mr. Zhang was allowed to return home that evening. Xiuzao's mother wept when he showed up but didn't dare say a word. Her older siblings were forced to "draw a boundary" and move into their school. That night, there was a big disturbance in their building—one of the other "black teeth and claws" had committed suicide during the night. Before her father left for work, the whole block knew about it. Her mother looked at him, shivering with fear. He said calmly, "I'm not going to." Just those four words. Xiuzao remembers them to this day, his face and voice as he spoke them. Then he asked Xiuzao, "How much candy do you have left?" She had a little candy jar, which she now opened and counted. "Twenty-six pieces." Her father knelt down and ruffled her hair. "Why don't you leave all those candies for your dad? One per day." Xiuzao held up the jar and said, "Why just one? Eat as many as you like, Dad. When they're gone, we'll buy some more!" Her mother dabbed at her eyes, and her father said with utter serenity, "We don't have any more money for candy. Leave these for me. Hide them away, and when I come home, you can feed them to me. One a day is too wasteful. I need you to do something for me. Unwrap them all and cut them in two. Then I'll have enough candy for a month and a half." And with that, he walked away. When he came home each evening, he bent down, and Xiuzao stood on tiptoe to pop a half piece of candy into his mouth. He didn't kill himself, didn't give in, didn't despair, and didn't compromise. When all of this had receded into the past and they'd moved into these three south-facing rooms, the day their twenty-inch color Hitachi television set arrived and the whole family was sitting in front of it—not just the three of them, her brother and his wife happened to be home for a visit—a picture of candy happened to appear on the screen, and Xiuzao tried to awaken her father's memories. "Dad, do you remember back when you had to attend a struggle session every day, and when you got back, I would feed you candy?" Her mother's eyes reddened with tears, and her brother and sister-in-law stared at Zhang Qilin, waiting for him to speak. He took a sip of tea, face blank, and said to Xiuzao, "What have you done with the evening paper?"

That's the sort of person Zhang Qilin is. To be honest, Xiuzao doesn't really understand him. What on earth is going on inside him? Likewise, he doesn't really understand his daughter, especially not today.

CHAPTER 5

A college student's infatuation—fair enough, the guy is
cute.

So, Zhang Xiuzao is on her way home with a bamboo basket full of breakfast
items when she bumps into Xun Lei at the entryway. Shaken, she plans to dump
the food on the table, claim to have eaten her share at the stall, then go to her
room and pull herself together. As soon as she steps inside, though, her mother
says, "We just got a phone call—the plane to Frankfurt's been delayed until four
p.m. Your dad won't be flying this morning."

Her father has changed out of his traveling outfit and is sitting at the dining
table in casual clothes. "You're not doing anything, are you, Xiuzao? You can
help me tidy the bookshelf after breakfast. It's been two years since we've done
that, now here's our chance."

Xiuzao would love to say she isn't feeling well or that she has an assignment
to complete, but her upbringing makes it impossible for her to lie. On the other
hand, she can't possibly confess that her feelings are in disarray because of Xun
Lei. So she sits in silence at the table, takes the hot congee her mother is passing
to her, and nods.

Tidying the bookcase! Why that, of all possible chores?

It was by her father's tall, sturdy bookshelf that she first saw Xun Lei.

One evening this past summer, she got home from college and heard her
father calling her as she came in the door. She went to her parents' room, and
there was a handsome young man by the shelf flipping through an English book.

"Xiuzao," said her father, "this is Xun Lei—he's a legendary figure in our
siheyuan."

Xun Lei's eyes rose from the book and shot their gaze directly at Xiuzao. She was startled. How could these eyes she'd never seen before look so familiar?

It's true, Xun Lei is a legendary figure, in not just their siheyuan, but also their neighborhood, and perhaps the whole of Beijing too.

He's two years older than Xiuzao, which means he was born in 1960, during the Great Leap Forward. The Second Five-Year Plan didn't just starve people to death in rural areas, it also caused great deprivation in the cities. Xun Lei's father bore the brunt of it: Xun Lei's grandmother was still alive and living with them; a wave of layoffs at the neighborhood factory his mother worked at sent her back to being a housewife; his two older sisters were still kids. His father, Xun Xingwang, single-handedly supported those five dependents. He was only in his thirties and in excellent health but never got enough food to satisfy his hefty appetite. At work, he frequently had to pause to tighten his belt another notch. The whole family doted on Xun Lei, though undernourishment left him unable to speak at a year and a half; his head looked abnormally large, and his fontanels never hardened.

For a while there was a popular chant that described Xun Lei's generation: "Starving when you're born, schools closed down, sent away to raise crops, came back to find no jobs." The difficult periods caused by the Party's missteps and U-turns happened to take place at key moments in their lives—that's indisputable. It was no easy task to battle this fate, overcome the objective difficulties placed in their paths, and flourish. Yet that is what Master Xun directed his children, particularly Xun Lei, to do. No matter what chaos reigned in the world, he required his offspring to be educated, understand human nature, and not cause trouble. In elementary school, Xun Lei was one of the few pupils listening attentively amid the general commotion. After class, he took his textbook and stood before the teacher, blinked his bright eyes, and politely asked a few clarifying questions. The teacher felt a bittersweet twinge and brought the boy back to his quarters, where he not only answered his questions but also earnestly added some additional information—all the material that had been brutally excised from the curriculum.

Between 1973 and 1976, when he was in middle school, cultural knowledge classes came and went, though at least he was taught some English. There were some problems in the teacher's past, for which he was severely denounced. From then on, he was under "their" control, and each time he stood at the lectern, it was as if he were skating on thin ice or standing before an abyss. How many of his pupils learned any English? Halfway through the term, the class was asked to write out the English alphabet, and most failed. By the end, he was practically teaching with his eyes shut, in a classroom noisy as a teahouse. Several of the boys, who couldn't even be bothered learning Chinese properly, played cards at the back of the room. In all the confusion, though, one voice steadily repeated after the teacher—Xun Lei, sitting in the front row. Despite finding himself in this impoverished intellectual soil, he was determined to greedily extract every drop of knowledge he could.

The way Auntie Xue and the other neighbors tell it, Xun Lei might as well have not existed. He'd come straight home from school and sit in his family's side yard studying. Now and then he'd bring a bucket to the communal faucet for water, his face pale and clean, and if he ran into anyone he'd smile shyly and greet them, so overly polite that he came across as a bit odd. Tantai Zhizhu remembers one time when she had to go talk to Mrs. Xun—this was back when Zhizhu was at the button factory, probably her stove had gone out and she needed to borrow a match—and there, in the yard, was Xun Lei on a bench, engrossed in something or other. She bent closer and saw that he was poring over a stack of desk calendars. When she asked where he'd got them, he flushed bright red and said, as if this confession might gain him a lesser sentence, "Grandpa Hu gave them to me, Auntie Zhizhu. He collects scrap paper from all over the hutong, and someone threw these out." She took a few from his hand and glanced at them. They were from the year before, and on every page was a line or two—a quote, a proverb, a historical or geographical fact, the brief bio of some notable person. The writing wasn't particularly elegant—in fact, the language was clumsy and suffered from the extreme leftist restrictions of the time. Nonetheless, at a time when books were hard to come by, these were like treasures for Xun Lei. Something stirred inside Zhizhu at that moment: a desire to start training her voice and body again. If this little seedling could strain so hard to burst through a crack in the stone, why should she, a young tree who had already blossomed, be content to wither under the assault of frost?

These days, people often ask Master Xun, "How did you educate Lei?" He never replies, because he feels there's nothing to say. Xun Lei also gets asked, "What did your dad teach you?" But he can't answer either—it all feels so formless, he doesn't know where to begin. Of course, there are a couple of moments he'll never forget, but are those worth mentioning? For instance, sometime in 1969 or so, his father brought him to the factory to use the showers. While they were in there, one of his dad's coworkers, an older mechanic whose whole body was thickly covered in hair, playfully pinched Xun Lei's bottom with his thick fingers. Instinctively, Xun Lei lashed out with his sharp little voice, "Motherfucker! Go smash your stupid dog head!" The mechanic smiled bashfully, but Master Xun snapped off Xun Lei's shower and roared, stone-faced, "What did you just say? Listen carefully: you're not allowed to talk like that under any circumstances! You shouldn't even know those stupid, wicked words. Now say you're sorry." Xun Lei hung his head and pressed his lips into a line but didn't say a word. The mechanic hastily turned his faucet off too and said, smiling, "Really, Master Xun, in this day and age, even young women are talking like that in the streets. Who hasn't said 'go smash your head' or 'go deep-fry yourself'? Forget it, just let it go!" Instead, Master Xun's face turned a shade of dark gray, his thick chest tensed like two cast-iron plates, and he thundered, "I don't care what day and age it is, my son is going to be a proper human being!" Xun Lei looked up at his naked father and saw the decorations he'd earned as a regular soldier during the liberation of Shijiazhuang: a scar across his collarbone and another across his waist. A jolt went through his tiny soul like an electric shock, and he blurted to the mechanic, "I'm sorry, sir! I shouldn't have said that!" Looking at this father and son, the other man had to quickly spin around and turn his shower on again so he could hide his scalding tears amid the hot water pouring over his face.

In 1976, when Xun Lei started high school, he asked his father for a pocket transistor radio, and Master Xun gave him the money without hesitation. *This child has never asked for so much as an ice cream,* he thought sadly. With this radio, Xun Lei was able to listen to English-language broadcasts every day, which his schoolmates found hysterical. "Xun Lei's set his sights too high! He thinks he can gobble down English, find a good foreign affairs job, and he's all set. With a mom and dad like his? Ha!" Eventually, those words were spoken to his face, and he just smiled in silence. Was he really angling for a diplomatic position? He hardly knew anything about foreign affairs, but given the circumstances, English programs were all he could bear to listen to. Besides, one of his father's sayings had stuck in his mind: "Extra knowledge doesn't weigh you down."

In 1978, just before Xun Lei was due to graduate, one of the foreign affairs bureaus was recruiting trainees from various Beijing high schools. Their main requirement was excellent foreign-language grades, so the English teacher encouraged Xun Lei to apply. This teacher's "problematic past" had since been resolved—he'd taught in Taiwan for half a year in 1948, but that didn't make him a bad person. Wherever he was, all he did was teach high school English, and whether you thought of that as his job or service to society, it was definitely no threat. He invited Xun Lei to come to his home each evening for extra coaching, and when Xun Lei walked into the exam hall, the teacher paced outside with his hands behind his back, looking so agitated that some people thought he'd gone insane.

Afterward, Xun Lei recounted every single question and his answers. With shaking hands, the teacher picked up a pen and calculated his score: 84. Even if this wasn't the highest mark, it would surely meet the entry requirement.

But then they started hearing all kinds of stories about how many people—not just the candidates themselves, but also their parents and other relatives—were using underhanded techniques, both primitive and advanced, to get into the department through the back door: hosting dinners, sending gifts, exchanging positions (you arrange one for me, I'll arrange one for you), calling the hotline with threatening messages, or soliciting recommendations from important people. Angry words were spoken within the bureau, but there seemed no way to shut the back door. One by one, candidates with mediocre results, or who hadn't even bothered taking the exam, received acceptances. Later, someone wrote a letter to the newspaper that was printed on their readers' page along with a very stern editor's note. You can imagine how Xun Lei and his teacher felt when they saw that.

It was said that in the end, about 74 percent of the people who got in did it through the back door. At least it wasn't 100 percent. And who got in without pulling any strings, without a helpful family background, with parents who were in fact ordinary working folk? Xun Lei alone, apparently. He came in first in the exam, with a score of 87—three more than his teacher had calculated. The second-place grade was 64, a whole 23 points less. Even one of the organizers was later said to have remarked, "If we don't take someone like Xun Lei, then there really is no justice in heaven and earth."

Everyone awarded a place in the program received a year of training in China before being sent to England for further studies. Through all this, Xun Lei maintained his first-place ranking, even increasing his lead. His jealous peers had to acknowledge he was a language genius, though some suggested it might be hereditary. Genius? Hereditary? Sitting on the bank of the Thames and listening to Big Ben chime, Xun Lei remembered the incident in the shower room when he was nine. Tears filled his eyes, but he choked them down. He felt his soul vibrate and thought he had never loved his fatherland so much as now. His solid, faithful fatherland. The dust flying through the hutongs, the ancient Bell and Drum Towers with withered weeds sprouting from their roofs, the dark hole of the siheyuan entryway, the old rattan chairs hanging above it, his father with shrapnel wounds on his collarbone and waist, his mother who loved making everyone egg and black bean noodles, his kind sisters who had dedicated themselves to service, the neighbors he adored, the huqin music and singing from Auntie Zhizhu's house, his English teacher with the perpetually startled expression . . . these were the origins of his genius. They were his heredity. He was going to be a proper person for the sake of his fatherland, and he would make a real contribution to his country.

After their studies in England were over, his classmates couldn't wait to get on a plane back to China, where there was another battle to be fought: securing a decent position in a desirable department. Xun Lei got the embassy's permission to return by train, which took half a month: cross the Channel, pass through the whole of Europe and the USSR, through Siberia, back to Beijing, back to his ancient siheyuan in the hutong near the Bell and Drum Towers. Nothing had changed. The rattan chairs still hung over the entryway, the cicadas still chirped in the tree of heaven, and water from the communal faucet still hit the bucket with the same crisp tinkle. He did notice one difference: a family named Zhang had moved into one of the south-facing rooms. He heard that the father was a bureau chief with quite a few shelves of English books, so while he was waiting to be allocated a workplace, he went over to see if he could borrow some.

Zhang Xiuzao saw Xun Lei for the first time standing at her father's bookcase. For reasons she didn't understand, she felt compelled the next day to keep asking her parents about him. Her mother said, "It really is a miracle. Born into a family like that, with everything going on at the time, he learned a foreign language all by himself—who'd believe such a thing? But maybe we shouldn't broadcast his story. It shows too much of our society's darker side, don't you think?" Her father had another way of looking at it: "Yes, there are a lot of darker elements—the Great Leap Forward into poverty, the Cultural Revolution closing down the schools, turning against intellectuals, all that back-door stuff, the children of cadres getting special privileges—but Xun Lei's achievement shows that our society also has a powerful enough light to shine through the darkness. Such strength might be scattered, lowly, formless—but still victorious in the end." Xiuzao wasn't particularly interested in her parents' earnest analysis. "How brilliant," she breathed. "To come back by train instead of flying. You can learn so much more looking out a train window than you ever could on a plane. Besides, they'd all already experienced flying on their way there. He said he kept a journal of his voyage back. I wish I could borrow it!" To which her parents chorused, "Go ask him for it, then!"

She did just that the following Sunday, and Xun Lei happily gave it to her. She read it that very night, brought it back to school with her, and reread a section every night. Even though they'd only just met and had had such different experiences, she was surprised to find his worldview mirrored hers in many ways. She kept the journal under her pillow and experienced insomnia for the first time in her life. Her young heart was undergoing the torments of adoration and yearning.

The next weekend, she went to Xun Lei's house to return the journal but found someone else there: a girl about her age, with a high forehead (what Beijingers call a "hatchet head"), deep-set eyes, inky-black pupils, and bright-red lips. Her petite body moved with grace. Her hair was combed into short plaits in a style that wasn't really fashionable anymore. One look at her blouse and you could tell from the cut and fabric that it was imported. Xiuzao's first impression was: *Ah, she must be overseas Chinese, I guess he meets people like that in foreign affairs.* Her next thoughts were: *It seems he's close to this woman. Even if he's found a job, he would hardly bring a regular coworker home like this.*

"Let me introduce you. My friend Feng Wanmei, my neighbor Zhang Xiuzao." Xun Lei's voice, right in her ear.

Xiuzao and Wanmei shook hands. When they let go, Xiuzao felt the floor drop away under her and the roof turn into a puff of smoke. There was no hope. She was a mere neighbor, while this other girl was a friend!

Which is why the seas of Xiuzao's heart are now choppy, not that her father notices. He wants her to help sort out the bookcase. On a morning like this, how will she be able to avoid recollecting her first sight of Xun Lei? The memory is so clear, she feels she could reach out and touch him: standing just there, flipping through the English book in his hand, sunlight pouring through the window and spreading itself over his shoulder.

"What's wrong, Xiuzao? Aren't you feeling well?" Her mother has noticed something is amiss but seems to think the cause is physical.

"No, it's nothing. I'm fine." Xiuzao steels herself and bravely walks over to the bookcase. In a steady voice, she says to her father, "Where should we begin?"

PART TWO

辰时

Chen Shi

Time of the Dragon: 7:00 a.m. to 9:00 a.m.

CHAPTER 6

An annoyingly enthusiastic person.

"My goodness, that doesn't smell right."

Lu Xichun is preparing the cold appetizers and Auntie Xue is frying the rice. At the sound of these words, her heart falls with a thud and she tenses. Without turning around, she continues tossing the rice in the wok and calls out to the speaker, whose voice she recognizes, "Ah, you're up, Nanny Zhan."

Zhan Liying is a woman of forty-eight who lives in two west-facing rooms that happen to be opposite the Xue residence. She's actually deserving of sympathy, having encountered many unjust blows on the road of life and punishments most people would find hard to bear—and yet, both now and in the past, very few people have felt any sympathy for her. Now why would that be?

Auntie Xue is a big believer in not saying inauspicious things. If you come over to someone's house as they're preparing for a wedding, the first thing you blurt out should definitely not be "My goodness, that doesn't smell right." That thought doesn't cross Zhan Liying's mind, though. She has nothing but good intentions and is happy to help in any way she can. That's just how she is. This Sunday morning, she lingered in bed a little longer than usual and has only now got up to wash her face and rinse her mouth. She was running a comb through her hair when, senses perhaps heightened by her unusually good mood, she detected the odor of burning rice across the way. Now she dashes across, still combing, and cries out, "Quick, sprinkle some vinegar on it! Hurry!"

Xichun glances at Nanny Zhan, thinking to himself that people who aren't professional cooks are inevitably the most eager to dispense advice. He doesn't know who Nanny Zhan is to the Xues, so he keeps his mouth shut for now.

Nanny Zhan's barked instructions panic Auntie Xue. As if this weren't enough, Nanny Zhan sticks her head over the wok to sniff, still combing away. It takes all of Auntie Xue's restraint not to give her a couple of raps with the ladle. Who knows how much dandruff she's dropping into the rice? How is this any of her business, anyway?

Zhan Liying has never been able to tell when others are upset with her. This failure means she never curbs her words or behavior in time, which is the source of all her problems in life. Now she sticks the comb into her hair, grabs the bottle of vinegar from the table, and pulls the lid off.

"Don't!" cries Xichun as he takes the bottle from her hand. "Vinegar won't get rid of the smell. I'm going to put that in a pot to steam. Some chopped chili and a bit of cooking wine will sort it out."

He expects her to be angry that he snatched the bottle away, but now that they're face-to-face, her eyes widen abruptly and she grins in delight. "Hey, aren't you one of Ji Zhiman's students?"

He freezes for a moment, then looks again. Oh right, he's seen her in Teacher Ji's quarters. So, she lives in this siheyuan. Teacher Ji is such a somber man, how could he be friends with such a loudmouth?

Seeing Nanny Zhan talking to this young hired cook, Auntie Xue gets even more frustrated. She bangs her ladle meaningfully on the side of the wok to let Nanny Zhan know she's in the way, but Nanny Zhan remains oblivious. In her blaring voice, she asks Xichun a few more questions, then suddenly seems to think of something and dashes back home.

"How do you know her?" Auntie Xue asks as soon as Nanny Zhan's front door closes.

"Oh, I've only met her once before. Your neighbor is weird!" Xichun doesn't want to be associated with this woman.

"She's, how can I put this? Not very well liked." Auntie Xue can't resist lowering her voice and adding, "She was a rightist!"

In Auntie Xue's eyes, even though the new regime has pretty much rehabilitated all the former rightists, it's still a stain to have ever been one. By contrast, as soon as Xichun hears this, he begins to have somewhat more respect for Nanny Zhan. In the last few years, all the novels, films, and TV shows he's seen have portrayed rightists as having lofty ideals and superior educations. To people of Xichun's generation, being a rightist is glorious. Nanny Zhan might come across as a loudmouth, but for all he knows she might be a heroine! No wonder Teacher Ji is friends with her.

Zhan Liying was indeed a rightist for a time. How did that happen? Did she long for Taiwan's Chiang Kai-shek to overthrow the mainland, like a character from a novel written between 1958 and 1966? Or was she a fellow traveler of the "capitalist roaders," who opposed the revolutionary rebels' assault on counterrevolutionary revisionism, like someone from a Cultural Revolution novel? Perhaps she lurked in a dark corner, a puppet master of henchmen for the revolutionary rebels (actually the Gang of Four) who went around usurping the authority of "capitalist roaders" (actually old revolutionary cadres), as depicted in certain novels written in 1977? Or maybe, as in a more recent novel, she'd suffered a heavy blow thanks to her defense of rationality but endured more than two decades of hardship with the support and care of the masses, until her patriotic, revolutionary heart was finally held up to be recognized and admired by everyone?

The answer is: none of the above.

By the time the anti-rightist movement began, she'd graduated from college and been deployed as a technician at a design institute. Her professional skills were above average, and no one could find any fault with her work. It was her personality no one liked.

Zhan Liying speaks raucously, hoarsely, and expressively. Let's be frank—she loves to exaggerate. Anything that passes through her mouth sounds ten times more exciting than it actually is. For instance, during a work break at the design institute, she announced loudly, "Hey, guess what? There's a new deputy director in the Party committee office who's married to a minister, tiny little thing—she's called the 'three-inch wonder,' or 'ground-creeper' in Beijing slang." Even if this were true, it would have been terribly rude to point out. What's worse, when her coworkers actually met this lady, she was only somewhat under average height, with a well-proportioned body, and married to a deputy bureau chief, not a minister. You can imagine how little her comrades believed Liying each time she passed on news of this kind. With this voice constantly clamoring in their ears, could they help getting sick of her?

Another problem is her inability to understand or care about other people. Although she's never set out to deliberately wound someone, her words often end up being hurtful. She once said to a coworker who was sensitive about her weight, "Hey, have you gotten fatter? What delicious food is your husband

51

feeding you to plump you up like that?" That wouldn't have been so bad, except this woman had just lost her husband and was still grieving. Liying forgot and invited her to go watch a foreign comedy film. When the woman refused, Liying giggled and kneaded her shoulders. "Why so prim and proper? Everyone likes to laugh, don't they? Come, or I'll have to drag you there!" Finally, the woman lost her temper. When Liying realized her blunder, she didn't apologize, just grimaced and pestered someone else to go with her. How many people has she offended through small incidents like this over the years? Even she herself isn't sure.

Worst of all, she doesn't know when to stop. When she gets riled up, she doesn't just rain thunder down on the person she's arguing with; anyone trying to intercede, even if they're clearly on her side, gets caught in the cross fire—sometimes becoming so enraged they end up quarreling with her too. One time, she got into an argument with a cafeteria server. She'd been in the right to start with—there was a little green caterpillar in her food, but when she complained and asked for a new helping, the server simply flicked the creature away and vigorously defended the cafeteria's honor. The deputy director she'd once labeled a "three-inch wonder" happened to be standing in line behind her and tried to stick up for her by saying to the server, "Miss Zhan's words might be a little harsh, but shouldn't you be—" That's as far as he got before Zhan Liying interrupted, "Me? Harsh? Are you saying I've done something wrong? You think I should stay calm and swallow the caterpillar? If they served us caterpillar stew, you people wouldn't care, would you? You blame me for being harsh? Let's see how harsh you sound when you get a bug in your food!" With some impatience, the deputy director said, "Please calm down, Comrade Zhan. I agree with your critique of our cafeteria—" Once again, Zhan Liying cut in with such a burst of fury that the director could only say, face red and breathing hard, "We'll talk about this after lunch. The comrades behind us are still waiting for their food!" Zhan Liying flung her enamel dish onto the floor and stormed out of the cafeteria, not even stopping to consider what onlookers might think of her.

During the anti-rightist movement, she inevitably said some things that weren't strictly correct according to the standards of the time. These sentiments were on a knife's edge between rightist and anti-rightist, and when weighed on the scale, her unimpeachable background and hardworking attitude ought to have shifted the balance toward anti-rightist, but because of the aforementioned character flaws, everyone was sick of her and inclined to add an extra weight to the scales, which shifted her to the side of the rightists. The design institute hauled her into a struggle session, and when her status was announced, she lost her loud voice and willfulness for the first time in her life, just stood there as if she were made of stone. After being labeled a rightist, she worked for a while making blueprints, then was sent down to a farming village to be reformed through labor. Before her departure, the deputy director called her into her office. "But how should I reform?" cried Zhan Liying. "What part of me needs reforming?" Seeing her eyes brim with tears, the deputy director was moved. There was no one else in the room, so she was able to say sincerely, "It's a question of cultivation. You're afraid now because you lack inner refinement. That's your fatal weakness." With that she opened her desk drawer and pulled out a copy of Comrade Liu Shaoqi's *How to Be a Good Communist*. Zhan Liying hastily accepted the gift, thinking, *I'm an anti-revolutionary now, and she's still willing to teach me how a Communist should cultivate herself. I should never have treated her so poorly.* With that, she burst into loud sobs. Startled, the deputy director swiftly flung the office door open so anyone walking past could hear what she was about to say. By the time Zhan Liying had finished purging her emotions, the deputy director's warm voice had turned frosty. Zhan Liying was confused. Why the sudden change of tone? And what was she being berated for?

After that, Zhan Liying went through more than twenty years of reform. She carried out the coarsest labor, endured the most cruel humiliations, accepted countless rebukes to her face, and was picked apart just as often behind her back. She wrote out reams of self-criticism, probably enough to encircle Beijing, deserved and undeserved, sincere and half-sincere. She gained a deeper and more accurate understanding of society and human existence, but her character didn't change much—a great shame. The work unit that eventually took her in asked only that she reform her thinking and didn't require her to adjust her personality. No one in all her life ever talked to her like that short deputy director had—to this day, the only person who's put a finger on exactly what Zhan Liying's problem is.

What's worse, even if her past experiences had caused her to curb her weaknesses, when the charge of rightism was overturned four years ago, that only brought her personality defects back to the surface. Just as few people pitied her when she was denounced as a rightist all those years ago, not many people expressed concern when she was allocated a job at the same design institute as part of "implementing policy." The deputy director, the only person who'd understood and wanted to help her, had unfortunately passed away during the Cultural Revolution. Zhan Liying may never meet another such coworker or boss during the course of her life.

The most difficult thing to change about a person is their personality. And the most difficult thing to describe about a person? Also their personality. No one has just one dimension, and no one presents just one side of themselves. The negative elements in Zhan Liying's psyche caused her great misfortune, but the more positive things—the directness that came with her thoughtlessness, the endurance with her coarseness, the inability to bear grudges with her reck-lessness, the helpfulness with her overbearing enthusiasm—have also failed to gain her any affection.

In 1962, after she was denounced, someone introduced her to a metallurgy technician who worked in Sichuan, and she married him. He, too, had been branded a rightist. They were only able to be together for about a month out of every year, which didn't give either of them the opportunity to detect the other's bad points—both put their best foot forward, so they were a sweet and con-tented couple. Now they've both been reinstated as engineers and have the best chance so far of living in the same place. Zhan Liying heard there's a shortage of foreign-language teachers in Beijing high schools, and college graduates with language skills can easily get transferred to the capital. That's why she mobilized herself to go see her college classmate Ji Zhiman, to ask if he could verify this.

Her visit was only meant to solve her own problem, but as they chatted, she learned that he'd never married, and a wave of enthusiasm came over her. Never mind what he wanted. She was determined to find Ji Zhiman a mate.

That's the sort of person Zhan Liying is—always passionately helping others in the way most likely to annoy them. She's doing it right now—dashing back to her house, grabbing a packet of fried-rice flour, and barging exuberantly into the tent. She snatches away Auntie Xue's rolling pin—Auntie Xue is in the middle of smashing the fried rice into powder—tears open the plastic packet, pours the grains onto the table, and booms out, smiling, "Don't waste your energy! Look what I have here—see how yellow and fragrant it is? My husband brought this when he visited in the fall. That should be enough for a big pot of steamed beef."

Her abruptness is as enraging as ever, but when Auntie Xue brings the stuff to her nose and sniffs, she has to acknowledge that Nanny Zhan's good intentions have paid off. This is authentic Sichuanese rice powder! Who'd have thought the Sichuanese were so ingenious, selling this crucial ingredient ready-made? If she'd known, she needn't have wasted all that time stir-frying raw rice.

Auntie Xue smiles and says, "Your husband brought this all the way for you, you ought to keep it for yourself." And Zhan Liying says, sincerely and passionately, "Don't be silly, I'll ask him to bring a hundred, a thousand packets next time. You think he'll dare say no? This is just my tiny contribution to Jiyue's big day—it's nothing at all. If there's anything else I can do, don't be shy, just ask!"

That's what Auntie Xue likes to hear. Her smile lines deepen and she shows the rice powder to Lu Xichun. "Shall we use hers?"

Xichun glances over and nods. "Let's. We can use the batch you made too. No need to grind it, just mix it all together. We'll have to steam it a little longer, that's all."

Just at this moment, Auntie Xue hears a voice calling, "Mom!" She looks outside the tent, and sees her daughter-in-law Meng Zhaoying and granddaughter Lotus arriving.

CHAPTER 7

Will this mother-in-law and daughter-in-law be at odds
forever? A chef deals with his feelings.

As soon as she sees Zhaoying, Auntie Xue's rage returns.

"Why are you only getting here now? If you don't care about us, then stay away—if you dare."

Zhaoying knew her mother-in-law would scold, but this is more vicious than she expected. She stifles her resentment as best she can and explains, "Lotus woke up feeling sick. I took her temperature—ninety-nine. I couldn't just ignore that, could I? I was so anxious, I took her straight to the clinic at Changqiaomen without even stopping for breakfast. We were the first ones there. The doctor saw her as soon as the doors opened. It was fine, nothing wrong with her insides, just the beginnings of a cold . . ."

As Zhaoying talks, Auntie Xue reaches out to feel Lotus's forehead. It's a little clammy but not noticeably warm. Lotus cries out, "Granny! I want to eat fish!" She has spotted the yellow croaker in its aluminum basin and it's making her mouth water. It's hard to get fish at this time of year, and they haven't had it at home for a while. Right away, Auntie Xue knows she can't be sick, because the first thing to go when you have a cold is your appetite for strong-tasting foods. As she ponders her granddaughter's condition, Auntie Xue realizes that her elder son isn't with them. "Where's Jihui?" she says loudly. "Why didn't he come with you?"

"He had to do an extra shift first thing this morning," says Zhaoying. "Just one trip, then he'll put his truck away and come straight here."

An extra shift first thing in the morning! Auntie Xue's heart throbs in pain for her son, which increases her antipathy for Zhaoying. "How very kind of you!" she snaps. "Letting him do an extra shift on a Sunday. Do you really need that little bit of money? Did you forget it's Jiyue's wedding day? I suppose it makes you happy that we can't have the whole family together. To think I was standing on my doorstep at dawn, waiting for you. I should have known you'd be busy setting traps!"

This is more than Zhaoying can bear. After all, she's a modern woman—financially independent and in charge of her own life. Why should she put up with this? She sets her jaw and raises her voice to defend herself. "He wanted to do it—why are you blaming me? I said to him, if you don't show up first thing, Mom is sure to grumble. And he said, so let her grumble. If I'm making any of this up, may my tongue rot in my mouth. He said it's not like the old days, when you just did as much or as little as you could. There are quotas to fill, and they're a man down because Old Zhao is ill. Jihui's the team leader—he has to set an example, doesn't he? So he's taking the morning shift, and Qi will do the afternoon. It was all arranged yesterday, and he couldn't change it. He insisted. Was I supposed to cling to him so he couldn't leave? Then Lotus woke up with a fever, and did he care? He just said bring her to the clinic and went off to work. I took the child straight to the doctor. Didn't even stop to brush my hair or eat breakfast. You think this is easy for me?"

Zhaoying is very articulate, and when she gets going like this, one unstoppable sentence after another, there's no way Auntie Xue can defend herself against the assault, however willful she finds her. Back in the house, Uncle Xue hears the raised voices of his wife and daughter-in-law and hurries over, wondering how to defuse the situation so both sides can step back with dignity intact. Before he can open his mouth, Zhan Liying has inserted herself into the conversation. In the tone of someone righting an injustice, she says to Auntie Xue, "Let it go, Auntie! This isn't worth getting upset about. How many young people nowadays can understand their elders?"

Auntie Xue is choking with rage, but Zhan Liying's words do indeed calm her down. She lets out a long sigh, but her breath goes down the wrong way, and she starts coughing.

Zhaoying has never liked Zhan Liying, the busybody. She says curtly, "Nanny Zhan, you really shouldn't speak without knowing the facts. How could you say I don't understand my elders? If you were in my shoes, would you really stay calm and talk nicely to her? With that temper of yours, you'd have started shouting long ago!"

Uncle Xue braces himself for Zhan Liying to respond. Instead, she throws her head back and roars with laughter. When she's done, she agrees heartily with Zhaoying. "You have a point! If it were me, I'd have steam coming out of my ears! Oh my god, that temper of mine." She takes the little girl by the hand. "Come on, Lotus. Auntie Zhan has some candy for you." And they go off to her house.

Seizing the moment, Uncle Xue scurries over and says nonchalantly, "Ah, you're here, Zhaoying. Would you like a cup of tea?"

Zhaoying smiles and greets him, then puts an end to the argument. "There's no time for tea—I got here so late. I'm just going to wash my hands, then I'll help with the cooking."

By the time Zhaoying washes her hands and comes back to the tent, Auntie Xue is back to normal too. She tells Zhaoying which tasks to assist Xichun with, then walks away. That's standard practice for Auntie Xue—once her daughter-in-law arrives, she doesn't do any more cooking. Zhaoying silently curses her but always knows to go straight to the kitchen. To maintain a sort of equilibrium, as she gets to work in the tent, she calls out to her mother-in-law in the house, "Mom, could you pop over to Nanny Zhan's place? There's some medicine in Lotus's pocket. Nanny Zhan should have her take it according to the directions. Make sure she gets the dose right!" As she watches Auntie Xue walking toward her neighbor's house, she can't help thinking: *Sure, I'm young, I ought to do a bit more work. But you can't just push everything onto me while you get to relax just because I'm your daughter-in-law! Everyone is supposed to be equal now, and we should all do our share of chores.*

Zhaoying chats with Xichun as she works—just small talk to start with, but she soon realizes this kid has some interesting ideas, and there's quite a few things they agree about.

She says, "Back when my husband and I got married, weddings were never such big events. And now look—never mind that they tried to hire your boss, they're insisting on this four-fours thing, sixteen dishes, no repetitions allowed. And there's still the car to come! At first they wanted my husband to borrow a car, then they said it wasn't appropriate for the older brother to be the driver and asked him to go by the back door and get a friend who owns a taxi to show up. My husband refused. You have no idea how progressive his thinking is. It's not that he couldn't make it happen. No matter how strict the regulations are, drivers will always be able to sneak in some trips for themselves. He just wouldn't do it. My mother-in-law got so worked up, she almost wept. She dotes on her elder son, and even when she thinks he's being a bad son, she doesn't yell at him like she does me. She just had to shed a tear and nag a little, and my husband's heart softened. He put away all his talk about a thrifty wedding, slapped his thigh, and said, 'Don't cry, Mom. We'll do as you say. Our Jiyue will have a car to fetch his bride—we'll rent one. I'll pay!' It's arriving any minute now to pick us up, then we'll go fetch the bride and come back here again. Back and forth, back and forth—think how much that's going to cost!"

"Right," says Xichun, "that must be expensive! I've heard that it's becoming fashionable to do away with the bridal car because they cost so much more to hire than regular cars."

"Exactly!" says Zhaoying. "It ended up costing two months' salary for both of us. It's such a rip-off, and even if you're okay with that, they aren't always available. This was a few months ago. At first my husband said he wasn't going to pull any strings, but he had to in the end—otherwise there was nothing available until the New Year. Luckily, he had a few words with someone and we managed to get a car for today."

Xichun says, "Then again, getting married is a really important moment in your life, so it's right to make a bit of a fuss. Other people get to ride in cars every day, but I'll probably only do it once in my life, and I'll pay with my own money—a ride in a car, a few tables at home for a decent spread, eat a little, drink a little, have a bit of fun, and that's that. It's fine as long as you stay within your means and don't get dragged into debt."

Zhaoying laughs. "That's what I think too. But you think I don't envy them? If I could marry my husband all over again, I'd insist on a bridal car, a photo session at China Photo Studio on Wangfujing, a sixteen-inch color portrait, and I'd throw a veil over my head, put on a white dress, pull on some white gloves, and hold a dazzling bouquet of flowers. That's what I call a wedding!"

Xichun nods. "Completely. When I pass by that photo studio, I always stop and look at the wedding pictures in the window. Even ugly people don't look too bad when they're all dressed up and posed properly. The grooms never wear their gloves, just hold on to them. Who came up with that? They look so cool."

"Have you had your picture taken like that?" Zhaoying asks bluntly.

Xichun blushes and tries to change the subject. "Why don't you have a rest, ma'am, and I'll take care of the rest. I just need to quickly fry the sliced meat and vegetable sides. The main cooking won't need to happen until the guests start arriving."

Auntie Xue calls from the house—it's almost time for the car to arrive. Zhaoying smiles at Xichun and exits the tent.

Xichun puts the beef with powdered rice on the stove to steam and, having nothing to do for a moment, settles into the chair they've thoughtfully provided for a quick rest. He notices they also left a cup of tea and a pack of Peony cigarettes for him. He sips the cooling tea, puts down the mug, and after a moment's thought, takes a cigarette and lights it. He doesn't usually smoke, but for some reason, this conversation with a woman he's never met has left him a little dazed. This might help steady his nerves.

Has he ever been photographed like that? Will he ever be? Why on earth would he tell a complete stranger that he likes looking at shop-window wedding photos? If he ever does get such a picture taken, who will be in it with him? Could it be her—the plain, round-faced woman? She lives near the restaurant and comes by almost every morning to pick up some scallion pancakes. Always four pancakes, never more nor less. Her hair is perpetually messy, as if she didn't have time to comb it before leaving the house, and she always has a dreamy expression on her face.

Xichun didn't notice her right away—they get a lot of people coming in for pancakes. One day, though, there were only three pancakes left when she arrived, and it was taking longer than usual to make more due to technical problems with their new fryer. She waited by the serving hatch, holding her enamel basin and staring into space. All of a sudden, a well-built man who didn't seem to have trimmed his hair or beard for some time came charging in, walked right up to her, and began yelling at her in a coarse voice. She tried to defend herself, but he barked something and dragged her out. The enamel basin fell to the floor with a clatter. Then a smacking sound—he'd hit her. She was sobbing and protesting but still went with him. Xichun tried to run after them, thinking he could reason with the man, but a customer stopped him. "They're a married couple," he said.

"The man's a bastard, and the woman's a punching bag. But that's their business, and no one ought to get involved. Let them sort it out on their own!"

Later, he heard that these two had both been sent down to the same village when they were young. One time, the educated youths went to the next village to see a film. The boy was with several friends, while the girl, for some reason, went alone. It was quite a long distance, over a hill that wasn't too high but could still be exhausting to climb—but they didn't care. In that time and place, they would have scaled two mountains if it meant getting to watch a movie. It got dark, and the boys' talk turned filthy. Out of nowhere, they started daring each other to score a girl. They weren't natural lotharios, but out of boredom and having nothing else to compete over, that's what they ended up betting on. One of them said, "I'll do it! See that chick over there? I'm going to nab her!" They settled the terms of the bet: a bottle of local baijiu liquor. The boy left his friends and went after the girl. He was chivalrous to start with, saying he wanted to keep her safe and watch the movie with her. But then he began working it and placed some candy in her hand—he'd been sent this treasure from home, and there was hardly any left. Finally, on their way home from the screening, he had his way with her in the wilderness. Not long after that, she found out she was pregnant. The boy held his hand up and took responsibility and said he was willing to marry her right away—so that's what they did. They had a son and later moved back to the city together, where they both found jobs. In this new existence, the woman recovered her self-respect and reason and asked for a divorce. She took it all the way to court, but the judge ruled that even if her husband was guilty of improperly pressuring her into sex, the statute of limitations had long passed. The man's workplace and the district office believed the most important thing was to keep the family—the basic unit of society—intact, and so they urged reconciliation. The woman was left deeply hurt and confused.

But how is her life as a whole? There's no way to know. Xichun sees her early every morning with her enamel dish, timidly buying pancakes. Whenever Xichun happens to serve her, he always flips through the pancakes with his bamboo tongs, trying to find her four of the best ones: puffy and well shaped, golden and shiny. As he places them in her enamel dish, her eyes focus on him as if returning from a dream, full of gratitude. He wishes he could tell her, "You'll escape from this misfortune and find happiness—I promise!" But he's never had the opportunity to speak these words.

He doesn't even know her name. All he's worked out is she's three or four years older than him.

Will he go with her to China Photo Studio on Wangfujing for a wedding portrait someday? Her in a white dress with a ring attached to the train so she can loop it onto her wrist, him in a suit, holding a pair of gloves and standing by her side. Is this a ridiculous idea? Or even a thought crime? He's never told anyone about this fantasy, not even Teacher Ji or Chef He, the two people he's closest to. He'll never tell anyone. Whenever this forbidden thought rises to the surface of his mind, he pushes it down again. "This is complete nonsense," he tells himself. "Just as harmful as smoking."

Yet here he is, cooking for someone else's wedding, a cigarette in his hand and this fantasy in his mind.

The smoke chokes him and he starts to cough.

CHAPTER 8

Not only can former lamas get married, married men
can be lamas.

The hired car is due to arrive at half past eight, and the wall clock shows 8:20 now. In order to make sure nothing goes wrong at any stage today, Auntie Xue deliberately set it ten minutes fast last night. Better early than late. She pricks up her ears and strains to catch every sound coming from the hutong. Uncle Xue has been dispatched to keep a lookout in case the driver misses their siheyuan, but she still feels uneasy. She believes she's the only person who'll hear the car horn right away and also that she's the best person to arrange every detail of this wedding.

Uncle Xue stands at the entryway. He could fetch a folding stool or sit on the stone bench—plenty of time to stand when he sees the car turning into the alleyway. But no, he stands with his legs slightly apart, hands behind his back, neck craned as he stares keenly toward the far end of the street. Most people walking past are residents of the hutong. Some wave hello and offer their congratulations, which he accepts with a broad smile and nod. Others who don't know him personally say nothing to him, just whisper to their companions, "See that? The old lama is marrying off his son." "Ha, really? I'd never have guessed the old lama was a rogue monk." Uncle Xue's ears don't burn, and the smile doesn't leave his face even though he hears these words clearly. Nor is there anger in his heart.

It's true, Uncle Xue used to be a lama. He doesn't understand why certain people, particularly the young, think being a lama is such a mysterious business. Xue Yongquan was the fifth child of a poor family in Hubeikou Hutong near

Hademen (now renamed Chongwenmen). His father hauled goods in a cart, and his mother cut cloth petals for the artificial flower trade. To a family like this, a job was whatever you could do to fill your belly. His eldest brother reared horses for the Peach Palace. His second brother was a "one-eyed dragon"—he lost his sight in one eye as a child, then later became a beggar, and at the instructions of his guild leader, wandered the streets knocking two cow hip bones together, chanting, "I beg here and everywhere, when big shots eat, then I'll be there—hey, you big shots, don't be rash, give me cash and off I'll dash!" One big sister married a man who made his living performing feats of strength at temple fairs, the other, a man who roamed the countryside collecting pig bristles for tooth-brushes. None of his older siblings' lives were seen as better or worse than their peers'. Even his second brother's begging was regarded as a proper profession, given that he was under the command of a guild leader. When the silk-flower factory where Yongquan was apprenticed went bust, his eldest sister's husband used his connections to get him taken in by Lama Ao Jinba, the head of Longfu Temple. Not only did his whole family celebrate the news, their neighbors also joined in with admiration and envy. What a fantastic opportunity, being a lama at a big temple like Longfu. Hard to believe that a few decades later, the descendants of those same families find themselves completely unable to understand the values of their elders. Jiyue has always forbidden his father to talk about his past as a lama, and has lately been reminding him not to breathe a word to his bride-to-be. But this woman isn't just an occasional guest, she's going to be living here, and even if Uncle Xue and his wife keep their mouths shut, Jihui or Zhaoying might mention it—they don't see it as a taboo. Many of the neighbors also know the whole story—Zhan Liying, who speaks without thinking, might blurt it out. It looks like Uncle Xue's time as a lama is going to cause ripples in this family sooner or later.

Uncle Xue doesn't find his lama past demeaning, only sad. No one in society looked down at the Longfu Temple lamas back then, though the junior ones like him didn't have it easy. After Liberation, he went from being a lama to a street peddler, then a sales clerk at a shop that was part private, part national enterprise. One time, his shop manager sought him out with some questions. This man knew nothing at all about the lives of lamas, and everything he asked seemed to come out of some startlingly simplistic assumptions. Yongquan answered as honestly as he could, which only further aroused the man's curiosity. The manager asked him:

"Did the old lama Ao Jinba treat you young ones badly? How hard did he beat you?"

"Ao Jinba didn't beat us. He taught us to chant scripture and took us out to chant in public."

"Did he just sit around while you chanted? I bet you young ones did all the chanting."

"He chanted alongside us. Back then, rich people's funerals usually had two or three pavilions of chanters. The wealthier ones had four: one for Buddhist monks, one for lamas, one for Taoist monks, and one for nuns. The very richest had five: an extra pavilion of Buddhist monks. We chanted sitting down, starting at eight-something in the morning, when the bell rang, for more than an hour. Another three rounds in the morning, then two more in the afternoon."

"When the hosts gave you money, did any of it go to you young lamas? I suppose Ao Jinba put it all into his own pockets."

"We got some. Ao Jinba led our chanting, so he got an extra half share. For instance, if we got three yuan each, he got four fifty."

"That's corruption, don't you think? Why should he get more money?"

"I don't think he did anything wrong. He was the one who taught us scripture, after all. The sutra of return, the white Tara, the green Tara, the heart sutra. Even the master sutra—that's a really long one, and he made sure we learned it. He also taught me to play the zangs dung. That's a type of Tibetan horn, more than six feet long, that only plays two notes: one high and one low. It took a lot of effort just to produce a sound, I can tell you!"

"So it sounds like you guys had a pretty good life back then."

"No one beat or scolded us. Later, banknotes became worthless—even the price of corn flour rose several times in one day. Ao Jinba wasn't that well off. That's why his eldest son left the city and ran off to join the People's Liberation Army."

"Is that true? Ao Jinba did say something about that to us. But why didn't the son ever come back to see him? He didn't even write a letter."

"Of course it's true. Someone was passing through Tianjin, and he saw young master Ao in a soldier's uniform. Apparently he'd been promoted to platoon leader!"

"Tell the truth—were things better before Liberation, or now?"

"Do you even need to ask? After Liberation, of course! At the very least, you don't need to worry what you'll find every time you go to the grain store with your sack. Don't you agree?"

These observations of Xue Yongquan's might sound shallow, but they are heartfelt. After he became a sales clerk, he kept his head down, worked hard, and was content. No extravagant desires here. In order to allow Jiyue to take over his position, he retired two years early. To make up for his lost income, he's taken a job as a warehouse guard. At his security post, he maintains the same calm and hardworking spirit and feels satisfied with his existence. Hence even when sunk deep in thought, it is rarely the patchy images of his time as a lama that flow through his mind. Instead, he imagines the richly colored life he will lead after he truly retires: a huge tank of tropical angelfish, striped like zebras; a hwamei thrush chirping in a cage hanging from a brass hook; a pair of dark-brown walnuts being turned over in the palm of his hand.

As he waits for the bridal car to arrive, a tide of emotion surges in Uncle Xue. It was his wife who insisted on getting the car, and he understands how she feels. Even now, people still ask him, "Hey, lamas are different from monks, right? You guys can get married?" He invariably nods politely but feels the questioner is making a big deal out of nothing. Not only can former lamas get married, married men can be lamas. Hasn't he done the same himself? At seventeen, before entering Longfu Temple, while still an apprentice in the artificial flower trade, he got married in a match arranged by his dad. His father-in-law hauled carts alongside his dad until he got a better job and went off to push a train for Zhongnanhai officials. No one nowadays would believe this, but in the early days of the Republican era, Zhongnanhai had a railway track left from the late Qing dynasty, with carriages but no locomotive. So how did they move? Brute force. Uncle Xue's father-in-law spent a few years pushing that train, and many impoverished city people would have said he had a cushy job.

Marrying the daughter of a "train driver" was a big event and had to be done properly. Of course there was no way they could set up a wedding pavilion fit to hold five generations of both families, and they didn't feel up to hiring a go-between to organize a banquet at a "cold restaurant" (that is, one dedicated to weddings and funerals). In the end, they decided a dinner at home for three tables would do—a token celebration. Even with this simple ceremony, the bride had to be received with sufficient pomp, so the Xues pooled their resources and hired a sedan. These days, when movies show weddings in old Beijing, they only ever have a single sedan chair—but in real life, one would never be enough! Naturally, the bride would have a red one with four or eight bearers, and you'd also need a green one with two or four bearers for the receiving matrons (the groom's aunts, sisters-in-law, and so on) and the sending matrons (the bride's aunts, sisters-in-law, and so on). Walking alongside would be two umbrella-holders and two fan-bearers, four flag-wavers, various musicians with cymbals, drums, suona, and horns, every one of them costing money. This wedding hollowed out the Xues' finances. Yongquan's mother had already been ill and needed to brew a pot of medicinal herbs each day. In an attempt at paying off their debts, she stopped taking her medicine, and not long after Yongquan entered Longfu Temple, she passed away from her sickness.

As for the bride, every time she saw sedan chairs and attendants passing by, she'd insist on pointing out the inadequacies of her own wedding. For instance, the phoenix-tail fans ought to have been real peacock feathers embellished with tiny shards of mirrored glass, but hers were just wild pheasant feathers with glass baubles clouded like cataracts. How humiliating! You couldn't have said her complaints were unreasonable. She was just a human being alive on earth, like everyone else, so why should she settle for less? You'd have thought that with the passing of time, as circumstances changed, Auntie Xue's resentment would have faded away. When her elder son, Jihui, married Zhaoying during the Cultural Revolution, they had a simple ceremony in keeping with the times—didn't even consider getting a car, just handed out some wedding candy and called it a day. Auntie Xue was perfectly fine with that and didn't breathe a word of complaint. When Jiyue's turn came, all her buried emotions bubbled thickly to the surface. It's not difficult to suppress someone's thoughts, but the mysterious process of changing them is much harder.

Auntie Xue is counting the arrival of the car as the first big event of the day. In the house, she is urging Zhaoying to finish combing her hair and getting dressed while she dusts Zhaoying's padded jacket with a new palm-leaf brush, though both her cotton jacket and plum-colored pongee blouse are already spotless. She listens for the sound of a car horn in the hutong, but nothing happens for a long time. Then out of nowhere, she screams, "They're here!" Has she really heard an engine or the gate opening? She drops the broom and hustles Zhaoying out the door, turning to shout at Jiyue, "Tidy up in here, they'll be coming any minute!" Either out of boredom or anxiety, Jiyue is slumped in a chrome folding chair, bent over a newly bought cassette tape, scrutinizing the list of tracks on the insert. He is already dressed: a glaringly new navy-blue suit, a scarlet tie with a gold dragon motif, a gleaming pair of black leather cap-toe shoes. He doesn't react to his mother's order. What's left to tidy up? He just wants the whole thing to be over and done with as quickly as possible, like fast-forwarding a cassette tape—what's the point of dragging it out?

The two women go out together. Auntie Xue sends Zhaoying ahead to the siheyuan entrance while she heads over to fetch Tantai Zhizhu.

Meanwhile, Uncle Xue is at the main gate greeting the rental car. He bends down to have a look and blinks in disbelief. How come the vehicle is full of people?

CHAPTER 9

The Beijing opera performer has to drop out of the
bridal party.

Three men jump out of the rental car, looking flustered, and make directly for
the siheyuan, not even glancing at Uncle Xue or Zhaoying, who is just stepping
through the gate. What to make of this? Uncle Xue is about to stick his head
in the window and ask the driver what's going on when the car starts moving,
clearly ready to turn around and leave. Confused, Uncle Xue stands frozen by
the gate, as if he's suddenly turned to stone. Zhaoying, a little quicker on the
uptake, says to her father-in-law, "This isn't our car, Dad."

These three are Tantai Zhizhu's colleagues. Their leader is a horse-faced man
with very pale skin and inky-black hair (anyone who knows these things can
tell right away it's dyed), long sideburns, and a pair of gold-rimmed glasses. His
padded satin jacket, ocher with a pattern of ancient coins, is open at the collar,
revealing a blue silk scarf decorated with white calligraphy. This is Zhizhu's costar
in *Zhuo Wenjun*, Puyang Sun, who plays young male leads. As for the other two,
the short, fat one plays the erhu, and the tall, scrawny one plays the ruan. They
are rushing to Zhizhu's house, but on the way they run into Zhizhu herself, all
dressed up and on her way to the siheyuan gate with Auntie Xue.

Zhizhu knows right away that something's wrong. She invited the five principals of their orchestra to lunch, so why are only two of them here? The two
main musicians—Old Zhao, the jinghu player, and Old Tong, the percussionist—haven't shown up, and young Qin the pipa player is absent too. Puyang Sun
wasn't invited, yet here he is. This is a mess.

As soon as Puyang Sun catches sight of Tantai Zhizhu, he raises his eyebrows and yelps, "Hey, Zhizhu, what the hell are you playing at?"

Zhizhu wants to ask what's going on, but Auntie Xue is right here, and she can't bring herself to wriggle out of her promise. Instead, she simpers at the three visitors. "So sorry, gents, I have to pop out for a moment. Why don't the three of you wait inside? I'll be back in a sec."

"Where are you off to?" Puyang Sun persists, full of emotion. "What have you got to do that's more urgent than this?"

Zhizhu glances at Auntie Xue. "I'm helping a neighbor out—fetching a bride."

Puyang Sun doesn't look at Auntie Xue. He claps his hands and points a circling finger at Zhizhu. "Like the old poem says, the singing girl doesn't know the pain of nations falling."

Zhizhu is even more confused. "Could you just tell me what you're talking about? Enough ominous hints, just tell me!"

From behind Puyang Sun, the erhu player says, "Old Zhao and Old Tong are climbing to a higher branch."

The ruan player, by his side, says, "We have to find a way to stop them quick, or we might as well close up shop."

There is a sickening crash in Zhizhu's heart, as if something has fallen and broken apart. This is the worst scenario she could imagine—and to have it happen today!

Auntie Xue was already uneasy at the appearance of these three strangers. Hearing their words and seeing Zhizhu frown and gasp, she can't help feeling even more anxious than Zhizhu herself. The rental car is already at the gate. Now what? She wishes Zhizhu could just set this business aside and go fetch the bride with Zhaoying—but it doesn't look like this is something she can walk away from. All she can do is force a smile and say, "Zhizhu, why don't you take your visitors inside? We'll wait by the main gate—come meet us there when you've got them settled." Then to the men, "Sorry to inconvenience you—we need to borrow Zhizhu a little while—she'll be back in no time at all."

Zhizhu ushers the three visitors into her home while Auntie Xue hurries to the siheyuan gate, where she is startled to find no car waiting, only Uncle Xue and Zhaoying staring at the far end of the hutong. Everything goes dark before her eyes. Has she offended some god? Isn't a single thing going to go right today?

Meanwhile, as soon as Zhizhu's guests are seated, she doesn't even offer them tea before urging them to tell her everything. It seems Old Zhao, the jinghu player, and Old Tong, the percussionist, paid a visit first thing this morning to the home of an actress at least one rung above Zhizhu in terms of experience, earnings, and fame. The details are murky, but it's obvious that this woman, whom Zhizhu is obliged to call "Elder Sister," is setting out to poach from her, and equally clear that Old Zhao and Old Tong are willing to cross over.

As they make their report, the erhu player and ruan player express their loyalty to Zhizhu and pour scorn on the turncoats, but also don't hide their feelings. "We might say we're working together for our careers, but after all, who wouldn't rather be drinking clear soup without specks of grease?"

It's true—Zhizhu understands how they feel. They all make the same living whichever orchestra they're in. But if they were working with Elder Sister instead of her, there'd be occasional dinners at fancy joints like Quanjude or Fengze Garden, and rehearsals at Zhizhu's place come with beer and soda, platters of cold cuts, cake, and fruit. Elder Sister's memory is excellent. If you have a son in kindergarten, she'll make sure to slide a bar of chocolate into your hand from time to time. If your old mother's teeth are in a dreadful state, she might show up at the holidays with a soft Western-style cake. Elder Sister has connections in Hong Kong and farther abroad, and when she gets invited to a performance or event overseas, naturally her musicians get to travel with her. Zhizhu thinks: *But what if they stick with me? I'm certainly nice to them, but how many perks can I offer when Li Kai and I are earning so little? I've never had the opportunity to perform abroad, so my musicians are stuck here too.*

Zhizhu's nose twitches as she comes close to tears, though she can't say if this is out of shame or anger. She recalls the promise Old Zhao and Old Tong made, and can barely contain herself. They said to her, "We're collaborating for the sake of art, to discover a new voice, and that's more delicious than roast duck." Their work together was about to come to fruition, yet they've had a change of heart! They happily allowed Elder Sister to pluck them like a couple of flowers. Which hole did they bury their consciences in?

Noticing how agitated Zhizhu is getting, Puyang Sun inches his chair closer to hers and says sincerely, "The horse may have bolted, my dear, but it's not too late to shut the stable door. Just say the word, and I'll go see Old Zhao and Old Tong tonight. We can all meet tomorrow evening at Cuihualou on

Bamiancao—you, me, Erhu, Pipa, and Ruan. We'll appeal to their emotions and make them see sense. They've worked with you for so many years, after all; I don't believe they're opportunistic or disloyal enough to just walk away."

Zhizhu has also been thinking along the lines of duking it out with Elder Sister. The other woman might have all the advantages, but Zhizhu has right on her side. Besides, she hasn't touched the hundred yuan she received for cutting that record a while back. She has to break herself of her miserly habits—getting money from her is like drawing blood from a stone, even at crucial moments. And it's not like Old Zhao and Old Tong have nothing to gain—after such a long collaboration, they're perfectly simpatico with Zhizhu, whereas there'd be a period of awkward adjustment if they crossed over to Elder Sister. Yet Zhizhu instinctively starts calculating: Cuihualou is a first-rate establishment. If she books a dinner in advance, that's seventy yuan for the seven of them, drinks extra. But if they just show up and order, they may not be able to get a table, her guests will feel she's being stingy, and she might not even save any money. Then she'll need to book taxis afterward to get them all home. Her hundred yuan might not be enough for this—she'll need to head to the bank with her passbook and withdraw another thirty or fifty. Oh dear, what will Li Kai say? He's had his eye on a Japanese Konica "idiot-proof" camera. Is he going to have to put off his purchase again?

As these thoughts run through Zhizhu's mind, strength drains from her and she begins to despair. Curling up in her armchair, she fiddles with the tassels of her yellow scarf and says feebly, "Forget it. Everyone has free will, just let them do what they like! The troupe will find me some other musicians—they're not going to keep me off that stage!"

Erhu and Ruan shake their heads vigorously. "We can't let Old Zhao and Old Tong leave," they protest. "We have to find a way to make them stay!"

Puyang Sun raises both his voice and his eyebrows. "Don't lose your resolve, Zhizhu! Frankly, if we can get them to Cuihualou, I can handle this. I've got a secret weapon up my sleeve, you know. Once they learn the truth about this woman, Old Zhao and Old Tong will come scurrying back to you. Wait and see!" He reaches into the sleeve of his satin padded jacket and pulls out a snow-white handkerchief, as if this were the secret weapon, and daintily dabs at his face. "Old Zhao and Old Tong have to sit at the same table as us tomorrow night," he says with emphasis. "That's crucial."

As they speak, Li Kai is nearing home. He was extra sweet all morning, having regretted how brutishly he treated Zhizhu last night. When she filled him in about her lunch party and needing to join the Xues' bridal party, he offered without prompting to go grocery shopping. He's now on his way back, having gone to Di'anmen Market for some good lean pork and garlic shoots, which aren't easy to get hold of these days, and then stopped off at the independent market by Houmen Bridge for a chicken and a couple of carp. While he was there, he spotted someone selling red pears and, recalling that Zhizhu prefers these to white or snow pears, quickly bought her a couple of pounds. There were a few other things too. Now the straw basket in his right hand and the string bag in his left are both stuffed full to bursting.

He sees Zhaoying and the Xues at the siheyuan gate and calls out a greeting. Auntie Xue says, "Our car is almost here, tell Zhizhu to come out quickly." And he answers, "Of course!"

When he steps into the house, though, the scene that greets him is not one he expected.

It's not just that a couple of the musicians are here early—what's that awful Puyang Sun doing here? He wasn't invited, was he? When Li Kai heard that Puyang Sun was about to start rehearsals for *Zhuo Wenjun* with Zhizhu, he said to her, "Make sure you don't bring that pansy into our home!" Zhizhu immediately replied, "Of course not, do you think I'm insane? He's sour on stage and off. I'm really sick of him. But it's hard to find young male leads, and he's trained with Mr. Yu Zhenfei, so there's a certain pedigree to his singing and acting. He's not actually a bad person. You shouldn't go around calling him a pansy—it wouldn't sound good if that got out." And indeed, Puyang Sun has never darkened their door—until today of all days. Not only is he here, look where he's sitting—and with such insouciance!

Zhizhu is in an armchair, across the coffee table from Erhu, also in an armchair, and Ruan, who is at the dining table. Puyang Sun has placed himself neither here nor there, between the dining and coffee tables, and he's pulled his folding chair as close to Zhizhu as it will get. When Li Kai comes in, the two musicians instinctively turn to look at him, but Puyang Sun's eyes remain fixed on Zhizhu, face expressive, hands gesturing, voice droning on. How could Li Kai not be filled with rage?

He takes a few steps into the room and drops his groceries onto the dining table with a thud. Only then does Puyang Sun notice him. He turns and meets Li Kai's eyes but doesn't realize this is Zhizhu's husband. A brother or some other relative, he thinks, and doesn't bother nodding a greeting before he turns back to Zhizhu to resume his speech. "This rival of yours is a silver-plated prop knife—impressive-looking, but won't cut anything. You have nothing to worry about."

The moment Li Kai stepped inside, Zhizhu saw storm clouds forming around his head. How is she going to explain this? Will he even listen?

Erhu and Ruan have met Li Kai before, so they smile and greet him as he comes over. He doesn't even glance at them, so intently is he glaring at the other two. Zhizhu can see the electric gleam in his eyes that means a thunderbolt is about to be unleashed, and quickly gets to her feet, cutting Puyang Sun off to say awkwardly, "Sun, this is Li Kai—my husband."

Puyang Sun's eyes bug open and he jumps to his feet, clasping his hands in greeting. "Ah! I'd never have guessed you were Zhizhu's guy. What an honor!"

It takes Li Kai several seconds to suppress an urge to smash him in the mouth. "Who are you?" he growls. "And what are you doing here?"

Realizing he's offended his host, Puyang Sun's eloquence of a moment ago deserts him. His face turns bright purple and he stares, uncertain how to defuse the situation.

Li Kai knows who Puyang Sun is, of course, but Puyang Sun hasn't encountered Li Kai before. Puyang Sun is actually a kind, timid man in his fifties. He was born into a family of bureaucrats and, under their influence, grew up loving Beijing opera. On the eve of Liberation, he was studying chemistry at Fu Jen Catholic University, but it was amateur dramatics that truly enraptured him. He's never been interested in politics—as long as he can get on stage, that's enough for him. At the age of twenty-one, he paid a troupe of artists to accompany him in a performance. That was a high point of his life, and his spirits still soar to think of it today. He started out playing "dan" roles—female parts, which are often played by men—in the mold of Xiao Cuihua, then later moved on to the more mature black-dress characters, with his most successful performance in *Three Ministers in Court*. After Liberation, he decided to turn professional. The opera troupe he joined was short of young male leads, so he switched to playing those instead. Even though that meant playing second fiddle to a string of second-rate actresses, he remained content. When young male leads and dan parts were prohibited during the Cultural Revolution, he took small roles in Madame Mao's model operas instead—Villager A, Bandit B, that sort of thing. After the Gang of Four fell, he returned to young male leads. There is still a shortage of performers who could take these on, so his position in the troupe has steadily risen. Recently, a couple of big name dan singers invited him to play opposite them. Forgetting his age and the frustrations he's suffered, he now happily throws himself into a life of rehearsing and performing. He feels as though he's regained his artistic youth.

Half a year ago, he made a trip to Shanghai at his own expense to pay a visit to Yu Zhenfei. This show of devotion moved the elderly artist, and he granted Puyang Sun the great honor of a thirty-minute audience. Back in Beijing, Puyang Sun took to referring to the old man as "Maestro Yu." When Zhizhu wanted to take the lead in *Zhuo Wenjun*, he insisted on playing opposite her so he could "recapture Maestro Yu's essence from way back when." He has a high opinion of Zhizhu and regards her as the most promising dan actress in their company. "She combines the best attributes of the Big Four dans, and there's no technique she hasn't mastered. She's going to hit the big time any day now—just wait and see!" All he cares about right now is bringing the story of Sima Xiangru and Zhuo Wenjun to the public as soon as possible, and he truly has no designs on Zhizhu herself. That's why, in all the time he's known her, he's never asked about her husband. Even earlier today, as he hurried to her home, it didn't cross his mind that he might run into her spouse. Now that Li Kai has shown up and made his enmity plain, Puyang Sun is completely taken aback and doesn't know what to do next.

Zhizhu's heart explodes in rage to see Li Kai speaking so bluntly, not yielding an inch, and in front of Erhu and Ruan too! This is sure to become a news item to be circulated around the troupe. She spends a few moments trying to tamp down her anger, and when it refuses to go away, gleefully lets it rip. Her face hardens as she snarls at Li Kai, "What the hell is wrong with you? Don't you know when to stop? Mr. Puyang rushed here to give me important news. What good does it do you if my career is torpedoed? You think that helps us?"

Now that Zhizhu has stepped in, Puyang Sun hastens to be conciliatory. "Comrade Li Kai, you've misunderstood. We mean you nothing but good. When we heard that someone was digging the ground out from under Zhizhu's feet, what else could we do but come and tell her at once?"

Erhu and Ruan rise to their feet too, and talk over each other as they try to explain the situation. When Li Kai finally understands, he feels a flash of regret—they didn't mean any harm after all—but when they get to Puyang Sun's plan for a dinner at Cuihualou tomorrow evening, he gets angry again. *They're helping themselves to our money, and it's clear they don't think I need to be at this meal—but I'm her husband, damn it!* Emotions swirl inside him and his face remains as dark as steel. "Don't tell me all that," he snaps. "This is my house, not your rehearsal room. Stop causing trouble here."

Now Erhu and Ruan are offended too, and Zhizhu is so agitated she's actually shaking. Her father-in-law hears the commotion from the other room and comes stomping in to lecture Li Kai. "Why are you talking like that? You're in your forties and still can't control yourself! These people came to do you a favor, but even if they were complete strangers who got the wrong house, they wouldn't deserve to be spoken to like that!" He turns to the visitors with a smile. "Please, have a seat. Take your time, say what you have to say." Then to Zhizhu, "Make your guests some tea! Li Kai and I will get some snacks from the kitchen." For the sake of the old man, the three visitors sit down again. Zhizhu goes over to the sideboard to fetch cups and the tea canister, and busies herself brewing the tea while trying to calm down. Li Kai remains by the dining table, still fuming. His eyes fixate on a couple of red pears that have tumbled out of the string bag. His feelings are jumbled and painful.

At this moment, Auntie Xue barges in and cries out, "Zhizhu, quick, the car's finally here! You and Zhaoying need to leave now!"

Startled, Zhizhu drops a glass, and it shatters on the floor. Everyone jumps. Auntie Xue freezes for a second, then tries to laugh it off. "Never mind, call it a lucky break! I'll get the bride to buy you a new one." She is surprised when Zhizhu turns around to reveal a furrowed brow and moist eyes. Has something happened?

Sure enough, Zhizhu says, "I'm really sorry, Auntie Xue, I can't go with Zhaoying—something urgent has come up."

Auntie Xue's heart sinks with a clunk of despair. Another problem! There really must be some kind of hex on today. Too agitated to ask questions, she mutters, "I won't trouble you, then," and hurtles out of Zhizhu's home back to the main gate.

A little crowd has gathered next to the car. Apart from Uncle Xue and Zhaoying, there's Zhan Liying holding Lotus by the hand; Xun Lei; Zhizhu's son, Bamboo (who was playing diabolo in the alleyway earlier); and other neighbors. A red satin banner hangs sloppily over the front of the car, and in its center is a fabric ball with a plastic double-happiness character—for some reason in magenta, which doesn't go with the scarlet banner at all. The driver sticks his head out the window and urges them to get in quickly.

Seeing that Auntie Xue has returned alone, Uncle Xue and Zhaoying clamor to ask, "What happened? Can't she get away?"

Flustered, Auntie Xue gabbles, "Something came up, she's not coming—oh lord, why did I have to be an only child? Jiyue doesn't have a single aunt to his name, that's why I had to grab her at the last minute!"

Zhaoying doesn't see what the big deal is. "I'll just go alone," she says, opening the car door. "One person can fetch a bride just as well."

In a rush of enthusiasm, Zhan Liying comes over, Lotus in tow. "Hey, what's wrong with you?" she says to Auntie Xue. "I'm basically your little sister, aren't I? I watched Jiyue and Jihui grow up, and all along they've called me Auntie. So what does that make me? If Zhizhu can't go, then I will!" And with that, she makes to burrow into the back seat along with Zhaoying.

Auntie Xue didn't expect Zhan Liying to mount a stealth attack, as if she's General Cheng Yaojin or something. Quite apart from her unstable temperament, Zhan Liying is bad luck—just last year, her father died of liver cancer in their hometown, and besides, she and her husband live in two different cities. Auntie Xue didn't forget to ask Zhan Liying; she was avoiding her. Yet here she is, with her usual lack of self-awareness, insisting on getting in the car! Auntie Xue feels a great weight on her chest. No longer bothering to be polite, she grabs the other woman by the arm and says, "I don't want to trouble you, Nanny Zhan! Please don't put yourself out."

Zhan Liying completely misunderstands the situation. She assumes Auntie Xue initially invited Tantai Zhizhu because of her fame and glamour and now feels embarrassed not to have asked Nanny Zhan in the first place. It doesn't occur to her that Zhizhu is a "complete person" (her grandparents, parents, husband, son, and daughter are all still alive), whereas Zhan Liying is very much incomplete. And so, laughing merrily, she wrestles free of Auntie Xue's grasp and hustles into the car. With the passengers on board, the driver starts the engine, and soon the vehicle has disappeared into the distance, leaving Auntie Xue to wait uneasily by the siheyuan gate amid the crowd.

Life flows exuberantly through this little siheyuan near the Bell and Drum Towers. A flock of pigeons belonging to someone in the hutong now rises up into the clear winter sky. The flapping of their wings can be heard back on earth.

CHAPTER 10

Here's a cobbler. What kind of daughter-in-law does he want?

If you draw a line from north to south right down the middle of Beijing, you'll pass, in order: the Bell Tower, the Drum Tower, Houmen Bridge, Di'anmen (meaning "Di'an Gate," though the gate itself has been torn down), Jingshan Park, the Forbidden City, Tiananmen Square, Zhengyangmen, Qianmen Street, Zhushikou, Tianqiao, Yongdingmen (here, too, the actual gate no longer exists). Of all these landmarks, the one outsiders are least familiar with is probably Houmen Bridge. It lies on the middle stretch of road between the Drum Tower and Di'anmen; in ancient times it was called Wanning Bridge, then Chengqing Lock. Water used to flow from the Shicha Seas under this bridge, make a sharp turn southeast, past East Buliang Bridge into the southeast quadrant of the imperial city, then into Tonghui River, a tributary of the Yongding. These days, the white marble balustrades are still there, but water no longer flows beneath— it's a dry bridge. Water from the Front Sea passes instead through a covered drain into the North Lake, Central Lake, South Lake, then the Jinshui River in front of Tiananmen, along another covered drain to Paozi River by Dongbianmen, and thence into the Tonghui.

Back in the day, according to local records, the area around Houmen Bridge was full of rustic charm. In the Yuan dynasty, the poet Zhang Zhu wrote, "Step onto the golden bridge, amid fragrance of lotus blooms. Paving stones after autumn rain, sunset on jade waters. Deep within the trees, crows are dappled with water. Smile away your cares, as a joyous breeze blows." Nowadays, though, Houmen Bridge is a busy commercial street. At the west end of the bridge is a Heyizhai Snack Bar, which also operates a shop selling traditional Beijing treats such as starch sausages and fried liver, and on the east side is a grocery store and a beef noodle restaurant. Recently, a group of young people pooled their resources and opened Yenching Bookshop there too. In other words, whether you're looking for spiritual or material sustenance, you're sure to find it at either end of Houmen Bridge.

Xun Lei's father, Master Xun Xingwang, sets out his cobbler stall on the sidewalk at the southwestern corner of the bridge. The whole thing consists of a couple of paint tins and several wooden boards, a couple of yards long, that fold up small enough to fit onto the back of his bicycle. He lays out his tools: nails in various sizes, metal plates, real and artificial leather patches, ready-made soles and heels, molded plastic. Once he's all set up, he ties a white banner to the front of his stall that reads "Leather Shoes Repaired" above his license number. When he's not working, he sits back with his hat pulled low (tufted wool in winter, cloth cap in spring and autumn, straw with a short brim in summer), lays a thick piece of fabric across his lap, and rests his "one-horned dragon" (an essential tool consisting of a baseplate, held in place by his feet, and an iron last on a rod on which the shoe can be placed) idly between his legs, smoking a pipe he made himself out of a piece of cypress wood. When a customer arrives, he puts his pipe aside and nimbly sets to work.

This morning, he's been here since a little after eight, and the jobs started pouring in as soon as he set up: resoling, fitting new heels, stitching front uppers, gluing insoles. All his customers seem in a big hurry to get the repairs done and the shoes back on their feet. Master Xun receives each pair and says cheerily, "Come back in an hour. I'll do my best to make them as good as new." As the customer walks away, he puts on his glasses and fixes his gaze on the one-horned dragon, and then his callused hands get busy.

When Master Xun is absorbed in his work, he doesn't see or hear anything around him. That's why he doesn't notice Meng Zhaoying and Zhan Liying's car crossing Houmen Bridge and passing right in front of him.

Someone else spots the car, though, and its inhabitants see her too. They even exchange a quick greeting. This is Feng Wanmei, heading north on her bicycle.

Feng Wanmei and Xun Lei are coworkers. She recently graduated with a degree in Spanish from Beijing Foreign Studies University. Though she and Xun Lei speak different languages, their work sometimes overlaps. It was love at first sight, and in the first heat of passion, they were so wrapped up in each other that despite all the words they exchanged, neither asked about the other's family. Their relationship wasn't public knowledge, so they didn't hang out in cinemas, theaters, or parks. Instead, they sought out places where you didn't need to buy a ticket and it was easy to get in and out—little scenic spots most people overlooked, where they could linger. Their frequent haunts included Tongzi River near the Forbidden City, tree-lined Zhengyi Road diagonally across from Wangfujing, Silver Ingot Bridge at the Shicha Seas, and the field on the east side of the National Art Museum. In these shady corners of the city, they embraced tightly, and with their eyes shut, sought out each other's fiery lips. Their hearts were full of poetry. At a certain point, after their blazing emotions cooled down a little, Xun Lei began learning Spanish from Feng Wanmei, and she English from him. They teased each other mercilessly as they studied. Xun Lei would ask, "How do the Spanish say 'moon' and 'stars'?" Wanmei told him, and after he'd memorized the words, she said, "And what do the British call maple trees and red leaves?" He told her, and she painstakingly repeated after him. Then they started making sentences. Xun Lei said, "Amo la luna y las estrellas, no te amo." Quick as a flash, Wanmei replied in English, "I love red leaves on maple trees, I hate you." Naturally their sentences were full of mistakes, and they corrected each other. He said something quick in English, and she demanded to know what it meant; then she pouted and spoke a Spanish sentence, and he asked what she was complaining about. Through this back-and-forth, they picked up a fair bit of vocabulary and syntax. Then he stretched his limbs, she shook her hair back, and they chorused, "I'm exhausted!" Leaning close, they murmured in a mix of both languages, "Te adoro . . . love you to death."

Of course, neither of them actually died. Indeed, they continued living with gusto. The day finally came when they had regained enough rational thought to understand that the end point of their love was a family consisting of them both, and this family would have to be connected to each of their individual families—that's when they began telling each other about these families and asking questions. Aren't they just a little too romantic? Haven't they been somewhat divorced from reality? Perhaps the reason they've conducted their relationship in this way is they've read too many Western books, and absorbed the ideology of humanism.

Xun Lei said to Feng Wanmei, "My dad is a cobbler."

"Don't brag." She giggled. "What right do you have to compare yourself to Hans Christian Andersen?" For indeed, the Danish storyteller was also a cobbler's son. Feng Wanmei has absolutely no prejudice against cobblers, whether Danish or Chinese. Cobblers are absolutely equal to her and everyone else. Yet she wasn't prepared for this. Xun Lei comes across like an English gentleman, and she'd assumed his father must at the very least be a high school teacher.

"My dad is a cobbler," he said again.

Wanmei glanced at him and knew right away he wasn't joking. She wiped the teasing smile off her face, settled her head more comfortably against his shoulder, and shut her eyes. "Do you love him? Tell me more."

Xun Lei stroked her hair and said slowly, "My father's name is Xun Xingwang. Our ancestral home is Boye County in Hebei. My grandpa died young, and my grandma suffered a lot raising my father and two aunts all by herself. Then my dad joined the Eighth Route Army. He was only fourteen, and his rifle was half a head taller than him. Later, he became the most ordinary kind of soldier in the People's Liberation Army and took part in the battle to liberate Shijiazhuang. You know that film by August First Film Studio, *The Liberation of Shijiazhuang*? No, of course you don't, you never watch movies like that. I don't either. They're far too lowbrow, right? But when it came on our TV, my dad couldn't tear his eyes away from the screen. He sat on our couch, which he made with his own hands, holding his cypress pipe, craning his neck forward, completely absorbed. Now and then he'd call out, 'Yes! That's how it was!' . . . 'No, they're making that up! It was never like that!' It's been broadcast more than once, and every single time he watches it with the same attention. Strange thing is, quite a few of his comrades were killed, but he wasn't seriously injured—and he took part in a bayonet charge. You don't believe that? I do. My dad's not very articulate. He struggles even telling us things that actually happened—making something up would be beyond him. One time, he told us about using a bayonet, and just a couple of sentences in, my heart was beating so fast. Only someone who'd done it for real could talk like that. He said enemy bellies were all he could see, and though these bellies tried to get away, he made sure to stab the bayonet right in so their intestines came pouring out. That pleased him. On the front line, it was life and death. My grandma and two aunts would stand at their village entrance all day long, and whenever anyone was carried by on a stretcher, they'd rush over to pull aside the blanket and see his face, but it was never my father. They would burst into tears, and when anyone asked why, my aunts would say, 'We're just happy. Our brother is slaughtering the enemy, but there's not a scratch on him.' Then my grandma would say, 'Oh no, what if he's lying dead somewhere, and they can't find him to bring him back?' After the war, when my dad came home, they got him to take off his shirt and were overjoyed to see his limbs were all intact. He'd been hit by shrapnel on his left shoulder and right hip and had a chunk of flesh scooped out of his left calf, but none of that mattered. If he'd stayed with the army and gone south, he might have ended up as a cadre down there. Who knows what kind of wife he'd have married then and what kind of children they'd have had, but anyway I wouldn't have been one of them. The family didn't have any farm laborers after the land reforms, so he got his discharge and started working on the land. After a few years of this, both my aunts were married, and a job opening came up in the city. A little while later, my grandma followed him here. First he learned carpentry, and then machine work. My dad is good with his hands and could have done anything he wanted to. He rose all the way to grade seven. The scale goes up to eight, but they had no grade eights in his factory, so he was the highest-ranked technician.

"You must be wondering if my dad's a Party member, given his talent and experience? Well, he's not. Apparently, when he first started out, the secretary of his factory committee was very taken with him and said to the branch secretary, 'If you don't promote someone like Xun Xingwang, who are you going to promote?' But that put the branch secretary in a tough spot. My dad was known for his devotion to his mom. My grandma loved eating red bean rolls, and though they weren't sold anywhere nearby, he'd ride his bicycle all over the city on his day off and wouldn't give up until he'd tracked some down for her. Of course, that wasn't a problem. The thing was, Beijing was promoting cremations at the time, and Party members were supposed to set an example. But when my grandma died, no matter how much people tried to persuade him, my dad couldn't bear to burn her body, so he bought a coffin and sent her back to be buried in their hometown. This kind of backward behavior was hard to explain away, and so there's no way the branch secretary could have recommended my dad for Party membership. Besides, my dad used to be illiterate. They had compulsory reading classes at the factory, and he made a heroic effort to pick up some words. He went for culture classes too, but never got beyond elementary school level. He's never enjoyed reading but loves working with his hands. He can do anything—make furniture, install plumbing, mend fishing nets, repair bicycles, fix shoes, carve pipes—everyone's always astounded by his handiwork. Ask him to read a book, though, and he gets a headache. He's only read two in his whole life: *Nobody's Boy*, not the French novel by Malot, but some sob story published right after Liberation, and *Lu Ban Learns His Craft*—apparently that came to him all torn up, and he read it by piecing the pages together one by one. There are two people he admires a huge amount. The first is from ancient times, Lu Ban, and the second is more recent: Peng Dehuai, the former defense minister. Because my dad remained uneducated, the branch decided he wasn't studying hard enough, so he was never inducted into the Party. My dad gets on well with everyone, but no one thinks he'll ever be a Party member, let alone an official. During the Cultural Revolution, he didn't join any faction, and no faction tried to recruit him. The Maoist propaganda teams didn't need him, and he never took part in the farming support squads either. He just went to the factory and worked. He kept going even after the factory stopped production, even when he was the only one left. He just waited there, wiping the place down and sweeping the floor. He might look like a blockhead, but he's actually very strong willed. His favorite opera is *The White-Haired Girl*. When he was in the army, taking part in the land reform movement, the artistic troupe performed *The White-Haired Girl* every night, and he was there for every performance. Every time they got to the part where Yang Bailao is murdered, his eyes would fill with tears. One time, someone in the audience tried to stir up trouble by shouting anti-revolutionary slogans. My dad launched himself like an eagle swooping, ran two hundred yards, and caught up with the guy. If the other people hadn't talked him out of it, my dad would have shot him dead on the spot. During the Cultural Revolution, someone told him Madame Mao had denounced *The White-Haired Girl* as a poison weed, but he wasn't shocked or angry about that, because he simply didn't believe it. Even after he learned this was true, he didn't get worked up. It was just a temporary way of thinking, and he still believed this opera was good. Later, *The White-Haired Girl* was turned into a ballet, and as he watched Xi'er getting kidnapped, he was just as moved as before. He said to everyone, '*The White-Haired Girl* is good after all, isn't it? I knew they wouldn't be able to ban it forever.' Everyone tried to explain to him that this *White-Haired Girl* wasn't the same as that other one, this one was revolutionary but the old one was anti-revolutionary. For example, Yang Bailao is brave and unyielding in this revised version, rather than weak and helpless. He didn't take any of that in. The others spent a lot of time explaining the whole thing, but in the end he just sulked. 'I don't see any big difference, and I wish they wouldn't keep dancing on their toes, it's not very nice to look at.' There was no budging him! Then the Gang of Four was brought down, and the opera could be staged again. He saw it on TV, and once again his tears flowed. I said to him, 'They can't perform the ballet version anymore.' He objected to that. 'Why can't they perform it? I thought that was good too, if they'd only stop walking around on tiptoe.' So you see, nothing sways how he looks at the world. I love my dad because he's a solid, sturdy, earnest person. His strength of character inspires me. It makes my soul kinder and purer.

"I guess you'll want to ask me next, 'If he was a grade-seven technician, how come he's a cobbler now?' The year before last, he retired, even though he was only fifty-four, so my second sister could take his place. Now I need to tell you about the rest of my family. Let's start with my mom. She's from Shunyi district in the Beijing suburbs and was introduced to my dad by his mentor. They fell in love right away and got married soon after. Then my mom started working at the factory too. At first, we stayed in the factory housing, in a room of maybe one hundred and thirty square feet. Those little houses you see rows and rows of, one family per house. At our biggest, before I was born, there were six people in our family: my grandma, my parents, my two sisters, and my elder brother—who died when he was seven. At the New Year, we'd buy a decoration to stick on the wall, and over the course of that year we'd learn every detail of that image. That was the extent of cultural life in my family. Then my grandma died, my sisters grew up, and during the three years of famine, I was born. Sometime after that, there was a fire. One of the families must have got careless with their stove and set their house on fire. Soon, the flames had spread to all of them, and the fire truck couldn't get there in time. All the workers' accommodations were burned to nothing. That turned out lucky for us—along with another family, we were given a room in the side courtyard where we still live now. A year ago, the factory built new quarters. Both families were suffering from lack of space, so my dad gave his slot in the new quarters to the other family, and we took over their room. Now at least we have two rooms to live in. My mom has gradually transformed from a village woman to a typical Beijinger. She's getting to look much more youthful than my dad (actually she's only three years younger).

When she gets home every day, the first thing she does is clean herself thoroughly, then she runs a brush through her permed hair and rubs silver-fungus pearl cream into her skin. She has two Western-style dresses, one of them specially tailored at Blue Sky on Wangfujing. On her rest days, she's always neatly dressed and sometimes even puts on a ring with an artificial pink gemstone. Before she has tea, she washes the cup until it's spotless. Despite all this, one look at her and you'll see she's a country bumpkin at heart. I love my mom too. She's suffered so much over the years, raising the three of us, and now she has breathing space to appreciate the finer things in life, she can express herself a bit more, and that's a wonderful thing. She might seem to have a vulgar side, but just overlook that. When it comes to housework, she's just as hardworking and capable as ever. If you saw her work, you'd think it was in her nature and that she longs to bring about her ideal vision of the world through labor. She keeps the house in perfect order, with not a speck of dirt to be seen. Before the bed sheets, blankets, curtains, and couch coverings have a chance to start looking grubby, she'll soak them in a basin, then roll up her sleeves to reveal arms sturdier than mine, and happily scrub away. She seems to take pleasure from those suds. My elder sister tells me that back when she was a kid, the house was always a mess, and our mom didn't have the energy to tidy up. Now that she has two rooms and the time to keep them shipshape, no wonder she's so contented. Of course her aesthetic sensibility was formed by the environment and culture of her upbringing. You'd understand if you had a look at my house. Every single item was painstakingly picked out by her. We could buy everything we need at the department store near our house, but if she needs curtain fabric, she'd rather run off to Xidan and Dashilan, carefully comparing all the options before making a selection, then come back covered in sweat. The drapes hanging in our outer windows are her handiwork: a pale-blue base with a design of dark-blue pine trees and brown cranes, and a knitted lace bottom border that she sewed on herself. And our couch covering? A rust-brown fabric with a print of two scarlet fairies scattering flowers. Then there's the plastic cloth over the liquor cabinet and dining table, which might strike you as gaudy to start with, but I trust you'll come to respect my mom's point of view as much as I do, and over time, you'll understand that the simplicity of these strong colors and clashing hues has a sort of rustic charm. The interior room belongs to me. My mom doesn't appreciate the things I brought home from England, just as I don't share her taste in curtain fabric, but likewise, she respects me. I hung an abstract painting over my bed, and every time my mom comes in to tidy up, she laughs. 'My god, what kind of picture is that?' But instead of taking it down, she gently cleans it with a feather duster. That's the sort of person my mom is. She's due to retire soon. After that, she says, she wants to plant flowers. I imagine when the time comes, our little courtyard will turn into a beautiful garden.

"As for my sisters, I can tell you about them in a few sentences. My elder sister came back from the countryside after the Cultural Revolution. She and her husband are both sales clerks. My second sister was unemployed for a while after getting discharged from the army and started doing temp work. Then she took over my dad's position, and now she's an elevator operator in a fourteen-story dormitory block. She got married last year, to an electrician at the factory."

Xun Lei paused. "Well? Did you get all that? Have you heard enough?"

Feng Wanmei lifted her head from Xun Lei's shoulder, smoothed her hair back with both hands, and sighed. "I was enraptured. You've given me a complete world. One I didn't understand before. A mysterious universe I'm about to step into."

Not long after that, she did indeed step into that world.

On that day, she set off half an hour early on her bicycle. Crossing Houmen Bridge, she saw Master Xun at his cobbler stall. This first sight of her future father-in-law filled her with loving respect.

Most people would look at the way Feng Wanmei dresses and behaves and peg her as a "modern" young person—that is, they'd assume she has a preference for foreign things. For instance, her favorite movie star must surely be Alain Delon or Mifune Toshiro. But in fact, ever since she was a little girl, Wanmei has only had room in her heart for two idols of the silver screen: Li Xiangyang (played by Guo Zhenqing) in *Guerrilla in the Plain*, and Company Commander Zhang (played by Gao Baocheng) in *Battle on Shangganling Mountain*. Apart from anything else, she finds both men absolutely gorgeous. Now that she's grown and works as a translator, her opinion hasn't changed, though her devotion has gained an intellectual layer: both these characters, she tells herself, embody a physical ideal of masculine beauty refined by generations of laborers, with folkloric and ancient historical connections, grounded in the vast land of China. One time, she was talking to a Latin American acquaintance, and found to her surprise that she happened to have seen *Guerrilla in the Plain*. The woman said frankly, "Li Xiangyang is adorable! I love men like that! If you ever meet the actor who played Li Xiangyang, be sure to let him know I worship him! I want to kiss him passionately!" Wanmei didn't find anything laughable about these sentiments at all. Beauty is there to be admired.

As she pedaled toward the cobbler, she thought how Master Xun was imbued with the spirit of Li Xiangyang and Company Commander Zhang. After all these years of working outdoors, his skin was tanned the color of soy sauce, but the lines of his face were full of vigor, his eyebrows bushy and black, his forehead broad, his eyes spirited, his nose perfectly shaped, his philtrum clearly outlined, his lips full, and there was a slight dimple in his chin. The street was full of handsome men in fashionable clothes, and no one noticed that this roadside cobbler was far more magnetic than any of them. Wanmei could see in him the elements that attracted her instantly to Xun Lei. Xun Lei might have the fine, pale skin of a gentleman, but his sturdy bone structure, the self-respect imprinted on his brow, and the manly thrust of his jaw were clearly the genetic legacy of his father!

Without realizing it, she came to a halt by the stall. Master Xun had just finished repairing a middle-aged woman's shoes. Wanmei heard the woman ask, "How much?"

Master Xun dipped a brush into black polish and rubbed it over the newly mended shoes. He could definitely skip this step, but did it for his own satisfaction. All his work must be executed as fully as possible. When the shoes were pristine, he handed them over and said, "Twenty cents."

"So expensive!" The woman took the shoes and cast a disparaging eye over them. "Twenty cents for this little bit of material? When did your prices go up so much! Twenty cents for a new heel!"

Master Xun began stuffing his pipe with tobacco. "Just go, then. Take them and go."

Startled, the woman hesitated a moment, then handed over a coin. "Of course I'll pay. Here's ten cents."

Master Xun didn't take the money. He lit his pipe and sucked on it. "Just go. The material isn't even worth five cents."

The woman thought about it, then produced a smaller coin that she tossed onto the stall. "Take five cents, then."

Master Xun picked up the coin and deposited it in her shopping basket. "Take it," he said calmly. "I won't accept a single cent from you."

The woman was clearly upset, but in the end she walked away without paying.

Witnessing this scene made Wanmei even fonder of her future father-in-law. She understood how he felt: he just wanted his labor to be valued. He didn't need charity. The money he collected was not for his materials, but his craftsmanship.

Master Xun looked up and saw her. "What's wrong with your shoes, young lady?"

Wanmei smiled at him. She wished there were some problem with the wedges on her feet, but they were regrettably new. Then again, why pretend to be a customer? Couldn't she just tell the truth?

She leaned her bicycle against the stall, sat on a folding stool, and said, "Are you Master Xun? My name is Feng Wanmei. I'm Xun Lei's girlfriend."

Master Xun was thrown into confusion. Li Xiangyang definitely wouldn't have gotten so flustered in this situation. His face flushed red. He put down his pipe, picked it up again, put on his glasses, then removed them again. It took him a long time to get any words out. "Xun Lei's girlfriend is you, I see. What's your name again?"

Wanmei told him again and explained how to write the characters, but he clearly only retained her surname.

"It was only last night that our Lei said he was bringing a girl home. So that's you." Having got over his initial surprise and recovered his dignity, Master Xun was now studying Wanmei intently. Kindly, he said, "You haven't been to the house yet, have you? Why don't you head there now and visit a little longer? Lei's mom is making dumplings. I'll close my stall early and head home. You're a southerner, aren't you? Do you like dumplings? Fennel filling okay?"

Wanmei nodded, though she actually can't stand fennel—her family has never eaten fennel, cilantro, or celery. She noticed a row of cans on Master Xun's stall, each containing a magnet covered in nails, like a curled-up hedgehog. "That's cute!" She picked up a "hedgehog" for a closer look, laughing merrily.

Master Xun had assumed from the way she was dressed that she looked down on cobblers, so this was reassuring. Was she going to become his daughter-in-law? Would they get along?

That was more than six months ago. Since then, Wanmei has been a frequent visitor to the Xun household. Each time she crosses Houmen Bridge, if Master Xun has his stall out, she stops for a chat. Her affection for him keeps growing as she discovers more glittering facets of his personality, which reflect well on Xun Lei. Nonetheless, Master Xun is only putting up with her—she does not fit his image of the ideal daughter-in-law. This is something she's come to realize.

On this day, the mellow sun pours over Houmen Bridge, making the winter day unusually warm. After Wanmei passes the bridal car, she pushes her bicycle over to Master Xun's stall. He nods to offer her a seat, hands never pausing in their work. "Have you had breakfast?" he asks cordially.

Wanmei takes a folding stool and smiles. "At this hour? Of course I have! Look, the Xues' car is setting off to fetch the bride."

Master Xun's eyes remain fixed on his monkey guide—his shoe-mending needle—and he says nonchalantly, "We're going to have quite a spread tonight."

"Is it crabs?" Wanmei guesses. "Frozen sea crabs? They were selling them in my neighborhood, at Ganjiakou Market."

"No, not that." The monkey guide somehow pricks Master Xun in the hand, which hardly ever happens. He shudders, then starts sewing again. "Our hometown dishes. You'll see," he proclaims, a little uncertainly. "Today . . . we have a visitor."

"Who?" Wanmei tries to guess again. "Is Eldest Aunt coming from Boye? Or Second Aunt from Tangshan?" She hasn't quite worked up the courage yet to address Master Xun and his wife as Mom and Dad, but is happy to refer to Xun Lei's aunts as if they were her own.

"No. It isn't anyone you've heard of. Someone from our hometown."

"Really?" Wanmei replies distractedly. "Then we'll have to give them a good reception."

A couple of customers arrive, and Wanmei surrenders her stool. "I'll head off now," she says to Master Xun. "Any messages?"

Master Xun thinks about it and says no. He waves as she cycles off.

For a while after this, Master Xun isn't going to be quite as adept at mending shoes as usual. Something is weighing on his heart. His visitor today is the daughter of his old comrade-in-arms, Guo Dunzi, a Jizhong man who joined the army around the same time as Master Xun. They ran through hails of bullets together and miraculously survived. Afterward, they came to work in the city. In 1960, both their wives got pregnant. Times were hard then. The factory was shrinking its workforce, and Guo Dunzi decided to move his family back to the countryside. He reckoned that with his severance payment, he'd be able to take over his ancestral home and start afresh. Perhaps life would be better there than in the city. Before he left, Master Xun threw him a farewell dinner. This one meal used up the entire family's meat ration. After clinking a couple of glasses of erguotou, the two men began reminiscing about their brotherhood on the battlefield. One time, Master Xun was knocked out cold by a blast; Guo Dunzi carried him to safety and woke him up by pissing on him. Only people who've lived through these experiences can understand how invaluable they are. They didn't know how to express their friendship, so when they got onto the subject of their pregnant wives, they had the same idea simultaneously: "If one of us has a boy and the other a girl, let's marry them off when they're grown!" That was more than twenty years ago. They've exchanged a few brief letters since then but haven't been able to meet. This chaotic world extinguished the promise they made at the dinner table, though it hasn't weakened their mutual affection. And they did indeed have a boy and a girl, who in the blink of an eye are now in their twenties.

Two days ago, Master Xun got a letter out of the blue, from Guo Dunzi's daughter, who is apparently no more educated that Master Xun. She called him Uncle and, in a few brief lines, informed him of the following: firstly that her father had unfortunately died more than a decade ago; secondly that her mother's health was declining; and thirdly that her mother wanted her to go into the city to visit her uncle. She told him her travel dates: she's due to arrive today. Last night, Master Xun took the letter from his breast pocket and pored over it for ages, line by line. Why didn't she say more? How did her father die? Why did she wait so long to tell him? What's wrong with her mother's health? Has she not named the illness to keep him from worrying? What are her intentions in coming here? Does she plan to ask her uncle for financial assistance, or is there a deeper motive? Late that night, Master Xun confessed all these worries to his old lady, but his old lady—she's not actually that old—only complained that he shouldn't be smoking his pipe in bed—the smoke chokes her! As for this country girl, she had only sympathy and kindness for her. "We should ask her to stay," she said, "and treat her like our own daughter. We're doing well now, and whatever is ours can be hers too. We'll all work. I'll find her a temporary job, or maybe she can be a nanny for a nice family and go back to her village when she's saved some money. Maybe we can find her a nice boy. Now, who are the bachelors in our factory, let me think . . ." Master Xun said, "We don't know if she has brothers or sisters. If she stays here, would there be anyone left to take care of her mom? What if her mom remembers our vow from all those years ago, and she's sending her daughter here to claim her husband?" His old lady didn't share his anxiety, but lightly said, "Oh that, well, that's no big deal. Even country folk understand about freedom of marriage these days. When she sees that our Lei is spoken for, she'll give up on that plan. As long as we treat her well, her mom will be happy when she goes back." Master Xun puffed on his pipe for a while more, murmuring to himself, "She's a country girl, and sure, Lei will treat her well, but will Miss Feng? Miss Feng will look at her like she's nothing and make her feel bad! And am I letting down Guo Dunzi? Besides . . ." He didn't carry the thought to its logical conclusion, but deep in his subconscious, he believes he ought to fulfill his promise and marry this country girl to Xun Lei. When he imagines this girl's appearance, and how she carries herself, she is clearly superior to Feng Wanmei in every regard.

Houmen Bridge gets busier. The sunlight slants down onto the broad bulk of the Drum Tower, which looks down imposingly upon all living things. What might it be pondering?

PART THREE

巳时

Si Shi

Time of the Snake: 9:00 a.m. to 11:00 a.m.

CHAPTER 11

The groom doesn't necessarily feel happy.

"It was fine a minute ago, how did you jam it already?" Auntie Xue scolds Jiyue. "Pay attention to what you're doing, don't ruin the stereo."

"I won't, Mom!" Jiyue can't be bothered to explain any further. He is sitting on a new chrome folding chair, frowning with concentration as he fiddles with the tape player.

The player is brand new, as is the cassette tape: a collection of Zhu Fengbo's solos, accompanied by a small orchestra and electronic keyboard. Jiyue can't explain to himself why he doesn't have the patience right now to sit through every track. Quite a few times now, he's pressed stop and fast-forwarded, only to hit the next song halfway through and have to rewind back to the beginning, and then he rewinds too far . . . All this back-and-forth is getting him hot under the collar. Tormented by him, Zhu Fengbo's voice suddenly erupts into a shriek and vanishes. Auntie Xue had planned to be tolerant of Jiyue today, but no wonder she can't help complaining.

Finally, Jiyue settles on a tune filled with breathy vocals and trills. Auntie Xue looks at him with pity, sighs, and gets back to her many chores.

Jiyue sits staring into space, his mind in a jumble. Beyond logic or reason, his head is stuffed with a tangle of colliding, jumbled thoughts. He knows a situation he can't avoid is about to take place, and though he's been waiting a long time for this moment, he's also dreading it.

How ridiculous that this tape deck can't automatically skip tracks. It's a quad-speaker, but the brand is lousy. It's not difficult to get hold of good brands these days—there are plenty in the electronics department of the store where he works—but they're so expensive! "What do you need a quad for?" Master Xu from the electronics department said. "A two-speaker Sanyo sounds just as good as the one you've got your eye on—the same quality for much less money." He felt himself being swayed, but Pan Xiuya was unyielding. "I don't care, I want a quad-speaker!" she insisted.

Jiyue looks around the room. Xiuya's quad-speaker energy is present everywhere.

Still, it has to be said that Pan Xiuya—his bride, who is due to arrive in the car any minute now—isn't one of those insatiably greedy people who doesn't know when enough is enough, as if she doesn't know how high the sky is, or how low the ground is. She battled her way out of her family, which gave her a very keen sense of just how low the ground is. Her parents had six children, three boys and three girls. She's number five, with only one younger sibling, an unemployed brother. Her dad works at a laundry and dye shop, and her mom sells ice pops from a wooden cart three months of the year. Her family is significantly poorer than the Xues and wish they could split every cent in half to make it last longer. Take cucumbers—they only buy sprouted ones, which go for ten cents a heap. How many short, bendy, plump-bellied, big-seeded cucumbers have they gotten through? Chopped for salads, stewed, shredded to fill dumplings. Money doesn't run through her hands like water as it does with some people. Now, thanks to her job at the photo studio, she also understands how high the sky is. They sometimes get booked for group photos, and she tags along as a photographer's assistant—so she's seen big government offices and grand events. Sometimes she gets there early and, if the organizers are nice, finds herself being invited to join in a tea party or banquet. She's met many celebrities and tycoons, and now the most luxurious scenes no longer faze her. She also understands there's no use hankering after this lifestyle—it's something she'll never attain, and yearning for it will only hurt her. That's who she is, a woman who knows not only the distance between sky and earth, but also how to conduct her life on this scale.

Just look at their room. Apart from gifts, the whole place has been outfitted according to her calculations. She put in two hundred yuan of her own money, her parents gave three hundred, and her siblings contributed the bed linen, bowls, and basins. Jiyue has no money of his own—he hands his wages over to his mom and asks her for cash when he needs it. His parents set up a savings account for him, which has accumulated seven hundred and eighty-odd yuan. Three hundred was set aside for the dinner, wedding candy, and so on, which left under five hundred for the household. Xiuya took charge of their money, about a thousand yuan total, like blowing up a balloon—stretching it as far as it would go, but not so far it would pop. Everything she buys has to sound good when they brag about it, as well as actually be useful. A double bed with a spring mattress, the sort with support on both sides—not a genuine Simmons, but still better than the bare boards her brothers and sisters sleep on. A three-door wardrobe. A couch completely contained within its hemp slipcover (real leather is beyond their means, but artificial leather is unthinkable). A writing desk with drawers on either side. Only a dresser topped with a mirror will do. The collapsible table must be the sort that can be changed from round to square (no need for chrome plating, it's going to be covered with a plastic cloth anyway—who's going to see? Varnish will do). The folding chairs, though, absolutely do have to be chrome plated. The liquor cabinet must be higher on one side than the other, and its sliding doors must have grooves, not handles. Even the stand for their washbasin requires a tall towel rack and two soap dishes. No wonder when she went shopping for a tape deck with Jiyue she was willing to compromise on the brand, as long as it was a quad-speaker.

Jiyue tried to talk her out of it. "Rather a two-speaker from a brand I've heard of, than a garbage quad."

She pursed her lips at him. "I'd rather have the head of a little goat than the tail of a big ox."

Fine! And now look—their room is stuffed full of little goat heads. The way she talks about it, you'd think they were drowning in high-end goods, but actually, they went to virtually every furniture shop in the city in search of a double bed—Jiyue thinks his legs lost half their mass from running around—before finding this one at a clearance shop near Yongdingmen. The quilting was slightly soiled, so it was ten yuan cheaper than anywhere else. "You won't even see that once we've put a bedspread on," she exclaimed to Jiyue, as if she'd won the lottery. The couch and wardrobe they got from a guy with a mouth full of yellow teeth, at the farmers' market by the Temple of Heaven. For everything else, they pulled strings to get hold of rejected yet undamaged goods, or spent hours choosing, comparing, and hesitating, all to save a yuan or less, for which they had to trek miles and persuade Jihui to help them bring it home in his truck.

Uncle and Auntie Xue have noticed Xiuya's thrift, which fills their hearts with joy. They've praised her more than once, both to her face and in front of Jihui and Zhaoying. One time, Auntie Xue kept going on until it started to feel like a comparison, and Zhaoying's round face lengthened into a rectangle. Did they stop at words? No, they were happy to spend two hundred yuan on a gold-plated Swiss Rado wristwatch for her. Even now, they're keeping that gift a secret from Jihui and Zhaoying.

Of course, no one knows better than Jiyue how this gift came about. Looking at Xiuya, you'd be hard pressed to say she was angling for wedding gifts like a village girl. Like so many other couples, after the initial meeting, they began their courtship with a walk in the park, then another walk, and gradually they started spending more time sitting than walking, not just talking but also getting physical. At the earliest stages, each took the other's hand to look at their watch, obviously not to tell the time, but to ask: "What brand is this? How much did it cost? Who bought it for you? Is it accurate?" Xiuya swiftly grasped the implications of Jiyue's timepiece: a quartz digital watch from Hong Kong. Two years ago, this was so in demand it must have cost at least a hundred yuan. Now it was still fashionable but worth forty-five at most. The day before Jiyue started work, Uncle Xue took him to the department store and solemnly bought it for him. From which you can tell, even now that he's grown, his parents still dote on him. It's hard to blame them. They have only two sons, and not only is he the younger one, he's spent more time living at home with them. What about the one on Xiuya's wrist? Jiyue stared at it for a long time without working it out. "It's a Swiss Rado watch," she teased him. He couldn't make out the English letters on its face, knowing neither Hanyu Pinyin nor any foreign languages, so he believed her. He hummed the Rado jingle from the TV ads and said, "Wow, a Rado watch, that's quite something." Xiuya snatched her hand back and felt a sour jolt in her heart. "A Rado? As if!" she snapped. "It's some garbage brand from overseas. My second aunt got it for me through the back door—she said it's a new product they were testing out internally for sales. Sixty yuan. I thought it looked good when she first got it. Gave her a thousand thanks and six crisp ten-yuan bills. Three months later, it became erratic. Now it gains up to half an hour a day, or loses ten minutes. I tried to get it fixed but they said there's no point, the spare parts for a garbage brand like this wouldn't work either. That made me so mad! But there's more. I heard that when they were testing the market for

98

this model, the sales price was fifty yuan. So my aunt skimmed ten yuan from me! I got into a big fight with her, and now she doesn't dare come visit if I'm at home. You see how hard my life is? My mom and dad wouldn't dream of buying me a watch. If I want one, I have to go out and hustle for it. If I really—you know—with you, will you buy me a nice watch?" Jiyue thrust his chest out and said, "Yes! I'll get you a Rado!" Xiuya flung herself into his arms, startling him. An instant later, she'd pulled back and was saying calmly, "How much money do you have?" He blushed and said, "Enough for that." Their next date was a trip to the Rado store on Wangfujing. When it came time to get married, Jiyue told her, "My mom and dad want to buy you a gold Rado watch, but you're not to wear it until our wedding day. It's for good luck. That's what the old people want, so let's just go along with it. Don't say anything to them about it, though. It will make you seem ungracious, and if Zhaoying gets wind of this, there'll be hell to pay." Since that day, the little gold watch has been glittering nonstop in Xiuya's imagination and dreams.

The elder Xues would never have come up with the idea of buying their soon-to-be daughter-in-law a gold watch if Jiyue hadn't urged them time and again. When they finally agreed, they decided to go for a Chinese brand that cost more than a hundred yuan, but Jiyue hinted this might damage their relationship with Xiuya. "Not that she's materialistic, but it would be a slap in the face." The old couple talked about it and decided that taking the long view, buying a gold Rado watch for their son's wife would be worth it. Apart from what they'd stashed in the current account in Jiyue's name, they had no cash on hand, just a five-year fixed-deposit they put ten yuan into every month—which, by good fortune, happened to have matured the day before. Auntie Xue was very calm as they went to the bank for the money but began getting agitated on the way home. She felt a tightness in her chest and her body grew heavy, and Uncle Xue had to hold her so she could hobble home. There was nothing physically wrong with her; she had just lost her psychological balance. All of a sudden, her wrists felt bare. On her own wedding day, the only jewelry she had on in the sedan was a pair of silver bracelets. And really, that "silver" was probably at least one-third tin. One time when Jiyue got sick, Auntie Xue tried to pawn those bracelets and couldn't even raise enough money for the medicine! It was only many years after Liberation, when Jihui was in high school, that Uncle Xue got hold of a Shanghai brand all-steel watch, and handed his Soviet half-steel one down to her.

For the first time in her life, her wrist had a watch on it. It started going slower, and then not going at all. It wasn't worth getting it repaired, but she felt it would be a shame to throw it away, so in the end she stowed it in a drawer along with some copper hairpins that had lost their baubles, a tarnished silver ear cleaner, and other odds and ends. That's how her life went. Brides today weren't the same at all—imagine demanding a two-hundred-yuan gold watch the moment you crossed the threshold! With that on her wrist, would Xiuya be respectful to her in-laws? Would she treat Jiyue well? Telling the time isn't difficult; if only you could read people's hearts the same way! She was still unhappy when she got home but didn't let it show on her face or in her voice. She counted out the ten-yuan notes, placed them in Jiyue's hand, and told him to go get the watch quickly. He hopped on his bicycle and headed straight to Wangfujing, where he purchased a slim gold lady's watch from the Rado store.

Right at this moment, Auntie Xue isn't thinking about that gold watch. She's bustling around the tent, getting the meal cooked and urging Uncle Xue to hurry off to Makai Restaurant to pick up the beer they've ordered.

Still unsettled, Jiyue abruptly walks away from the tape deck and goes to the mirror-topped dresser, where he almost instinctively pulls open the second drawer on the right. There are two things in it: a clothbound photo album—a wedding gift from their neighbor Xun Lei—and the Rado watch with its gold-plated braided strap. Xiuya chose the design herself. He remembers the day they visited the store on Wangfujing and bent over the reinforced-glass display case to peer at the glittering specimens. Xiuya spent a very long time deliberating, and the final speck of Jiyue's patience had been exhausted when she declared, "That's the one!"

That very watch is in the drawer. Xun Lei's gift came in a cardboard sleeve, but Jiyue removed it so the fabric cover, printed with an image of silvery pavilions, red peonies, green bananas, and purple hills against a bright-blue background, could perfectly set off the splendid gold watch.

As Jiyue gazes at the watch, his eye lands on a little booklet stuffed into the back of the drawer—the first in China Youth Publishing's series of handbooks for young people: *What Kind of Love Is the Best?* Yang Jiguang, secretary of the store's Party committee, gave this to him. He and Xiuya don't own any bookshelves, for the simple reason that they don't own any books, so this slim publication lives in this drawer. That wasn't a conscious decision, just a careless gesture on Jiyue's part. He thinks about finding somewhere else for it but can't be bothered. As he shuts the drawer, the glistening gold watch and red words on the book cover merge together, leaving him more unsettled than ever.

Jiyue looks up and finds his reflection gazing back at him. He is startled by his own face. Is this person really today's groom? Behind the groom is an expanse of double bed, shrouded in pink. Can this mystical moment truly be approaching, minute by minute, second by second?

He's flicked through *What Kind of Love Is the Best?* hoping to find a passage that answered the doubts in his heart, but there was nothing. He's gone through many other books, but they didn't have any answers for him either. He's even tried asking the sort of people who might be able to enlighten him, but either they let him down, or he wasn't able to bring himself to speak the words.

Jiyue is of the cohort that has a middle school certificate, but in practical terms hasn't really finished elementary school. They'd just started third grade when the Cultural Revolution kicked off, so they rattled around until 1970, spent a short time in middle school, then got packed off to the countryside. He was originally supposed to work on the land, but Uncle Xue moved heaven and earth to get him transferred to the Inner Mongolia Production and Construction Corps. There'd be more discipline there, he reasoned, and Jiyue was less likely to be led astray.

The company Jiyue ended up in was indeed extremely strict. He was assigned to the cafeteria, and when he thinks back to that time, those years feel like a single long, monotonous day. In the last couple of years, a guy from a different company in his regiment has become quite a famous poet. Jiyue happened to see some of his verses in a magazine and marveled that his old comrade could find such lyricism in that period of their lives. The last poem in that sequence was called "I Want to Return," and spoke ardently of his yearning for the land on which their regiment once stood, expressing a desire to go back "so my spirit might become your music, and melt into the heroic melody of our new era!" Of course, this might be a sincere distillation of his soul's longing, but no poet who ever wrote such lines actually applied to transfer his household registration back to Inner Mongolia. Jiyue ran into the poet at the mall once. He'd gotten a hefty fee for his writing and was planning to buy a baby grand.

Jiyue doesn't envy his former comrade. They were never the same sort of person, he thinks, and so shouldn't be compared to each other. Their regiment had all kinds of other talented individuals: one went on to do a PhD, another is now a well-known actor, and a third wrote an entire book—but Jiyue knows their parents were pretty much all intellectuals, and some were in the Party (and even held leadership positions). When they stopped classes in schools, these folk could go on home-schooling. Ordinary city folk like Jiyue showed up with wooden chests filled with clothes and toiletries by their ordinary city-folk parents, whereas these other comrades arrived with bundles and crates of books. When the regiment needed propaganda materials, written reports, or scripts for the cultural troupe to perform, these people stepped up; in recent years, the newspapers and magazines have published various unsparing accounts of these years, filled with deep reflection, also by these people; they're also behind this latest wave of nostalgia for those bygone times. They have a knack for coming out on top, and their years in the regiment will be treated as a precious experience, a sort of spiritual capital they will be able to draw from forever. Yet they are a tiny minority. For most young people, like Jiyue, these years of army life were a psychological wasteland, and they've emerged with their already impoverished souls even more shriveled.

Two incidents from this barren, dull time left a deep impression on Jiyue.

The first: A pond near their camp had a sort of fish that looked like a slimmer version of the bighead carp, which grew to be about a foot long. The local folk refused to eat it, apparently out of superstition. The regiment had run completely out of meat, so they decided to risk breaking the taboo and cast their nets. Jiyue was working in the kitchen when the spoils were delivered and was given the task of cleaning them. He cut open the first fish, and a wave of nausea came over him—a starkly white tapeworm stretched from its mouth all the way down its intestine. He'd thought that was just bad luck, but when he sliced open a second and third one, they too had worms. He stopped work and said they shouldn't feed these to the regiment, but his commander said, "Why so scared? Just toss out their guts, the flesh should be fine to eat."

Even now that he's back in Beijing, Jiyue doesn't dare eat fish. It reminds him too much of those parasitic worms. Sometimes he has nightmares of them wriggling, and wakes up screaming.

The second incident was the wedding of two members of the regiment, with their commander officiating. They stuffed themselves at the banquet and got through a dozen bottles of baijiu. The next morning, the bride went to the commander to denounce her new husband. For what crime? "Sir!" she said furiously. "He . . . last night, he wanted to . . . be indecent with me!" The commander stared at her for a moment, then threw his head back and laughed. Within half an hour, everyone in the regiment knew what had happened. Jiyue chuckled along with the others, but his heart was thumping all the while. To be frank, he was probably as ignorant as that bride about what goes on between a man and a woman.

For many years, the education of young people has been influenced by a kind of puritanism. This trend reached its height during the Cultural Revolution, with sociology, ethics, psychology, and other social sciences being abolished, until kids were denied even basic physiological knowledge. This led to three outcomes: Some young people grew depraved due to uninhibited sexual activity. A small portion became frigid out of ignorance, such as the military bride who construed her husband's loving touch as "indecency." The vast majority relied on instinct, speculation, and hints from their elders and more experienced peers to grope their way from confusion to understanding. Many mastered the subject without a teacher, but a few ended up completely lost, an insurmountable psychological barrier plunging them into doubt and misery.

Right now, Jiyue is a member of that last group.

One snowy night after the Gang of Four had fallen, the regiment had been disbanded, and Jiyue had put in the paperwork for his return to the city, he ended up in an intimate scenario, entirely at the initiative of the woman—and failed to rise to the occasion. This tragic defeat left a deep wound in his heart that has yet to heal.

That snowy night was a deeply private moment. To this day, he doesn't blame her, and he trusts that she doesn't blame him. He hopes never to set eyes on her again, of course, and presumably she feels the same way. He will never speak of her, and vice versa.

Even so, this has left Jiyue riven with unceasing self-doubt and self-loathing, which have in turn resulted in forced displays of bravado and machismo.

With the fall of the Gang of Four, love resumed its rightful place in society and in people's minds. *What Kind of Love Is the Best?* came out in this new atmosphere, was very warmly received, and resolved many young people's questions. Even so, many young people in Jiyue's situation urgently require some form of counseling, but this has not been widely recognized and wouldn't happen anyway due to lingering attitudes from previous generations. It is said that when young emperors in the Qing dynasty were due to get married, they would go to the lama temple to view sutras of "joint pleasure" in order to gain this rudimentary knowledge. If only society provided people like Jiyue with similarly reliable and accessible information!

Xue Jiyue, the groom, stands by the dresser in his nuptial chamber. Feelings are surging through him that oughtn't be present on a day like this.

He looks up at the sixteen-inch color wedding portrait hanging above the dresser. They got this done at the studio where Xiuya works, using their best people and equipment, with a great deal of posing and fussing. Xiuya is in a cloud of tulle, clutching a bouquet of flowers to her bosom, radiant with happiness. Jiyue is in a suit and leather shoes, hair oiled and face powdered—but looking at it now, he can see that his pride and contentment are clearly fake.

He's only twenty-five. Why the rush? Xiuya's the same age, but her twenty-five is very different from his. She's anxious; she's got her hands on something good and isn't about to let it slip through her fingers. Never mind what the brand is, as long as it's a quad-speaker. For the most part, he's gotten to this point in a most peculiar state of mind: he wants to prove to everyone, including himself, that Xue Jiyue is beyond a shadow of a doubt an absolutely real man.

"Hey, man, stop daydreaming!" comes a coarse voice from the doorway. Jiyue spins around and sees a short, tubby body with a vulgar face atop it.

Luo Baosang has arrived.

CHAPTER 12

A country girl shows up with a valuable gift.

Guo Xinger wears a watch but hasn't yet got into the habit of looking at it. Besides, both her hands are full, and it would take some effort to glance at her wrist. Instead, as usual, she works out the time by the quality of the light. Gazing at the imposing Drum Tower, she wonders: *Will anyone be home at this time? Should I be barging in like this?*

The gentle winter sun kisses Xinger's sweaty, ruddy face.

She arrived at Beijing Railway Station first thing this morning. Even walking down the ceramic-tiled underpass leading from the station, she felt this place was strange and mysterious. At the far end of the tunnel was an ad for Seiko watches, with a row of blockish black words across the top: "Welcome to Beijing!" Apparently this illuminated case was a "gift" from some Japanese businessmen—basically, free advertising for them and a way to hurt the patriotic feelings of Chinese travelers. No wonder so many people have written to the relevant authorities and published op-eds in the newspapers urging them to get rid of the poster. Sometime later, it would indeed be exchanged for something else. When Guo Xinger walked past this ad, though, she didn't feel any rage, just the vague thought that this lit-up case exuded a sort of metropolitan atmosphere (or, as she would put it, "big-city smell") she'd never encountered before, and this was exactly what she'd come in search of.

This is Guo Xinger's first-ever trip to Beijing, and also to any city—unless you're counting the county town, which consists of little more than a crossroads. It's not unusual for a village girl her age not to have seen a city, but the thing is her father, Guo Dunzi, left Beijing for the countryside in 1960, and strictly speaking, since her mother was pregnant when they left, Xinger is a city girl who happened to be born in the countryside. From early childhood, she heard her father's tales of the city—and not just any city, but the capital, Beijing! He frequently opened with "If this were to make it to Beijing . . ." or "They really need to shift this to Beijing . . ." or "Anyone comparing our cadres to the ones in Beijing . . ." or "You just try making that argument in Beijing . . ." Which has left her with the impression that no one and nothing in Beijing is ordinary, and even their ideas are sacred, more noble.

Guo Xinger has had a hard life. Her mother was racked with illness when she was born and, after her brother's birth the following year, was confined to bed for a whole twelve months. Her father looked desperately for a job, and though the production brigade tried to take care of them, the village never managed to raise its production quotas. Even the families who weren't afflicted by sickness or catastrophe had to tighten their belts, so you can imagine what deprivations the Guos suffered. No sooner had her mom finally recovered than her dad's strapping body suddenly collapsed. He was swollen all over, his face so puffy he couldn't open his eyes. When Xinger was nine and her brother seven, those eyes closed for good. The Cultural Revolution was at its height then, and their village was riven with the "seizing power" and "anti-seizing power" movements, during which the production brigade's cadres were denounced and had placards strung around their necks. Loudspeakers blaring propaganda slogans all day long were fitted to the telephone pole outside their home. When Xinger and Zaoer were grown, their mother told them, "That loudspeaker aggravated your dad so badly that he died." She sighed. "Your dad knew his own mind. He refused to become a cadre, whether by appointment or election. If he'd accepted, they might have denounced him too, even with him being so ill."

People dropped by to advise their mother to remarry. She always gave her visitors tea and even invited them to stay for dinner, but no matter how much they tried to talk her into it, she would only say, "I'll bring up Xinger and Zaoer by myself." Xinger grew up quickly. By the age of twelve, she'd dropped out of school and found a job. She was now a second parent to Zaoer. Time and again, she showed herself to be stronger than her mother.

Xinger has always wanted to be on top. When she was paid a lower "child wage" by the brigade, she complained to the commander: "Hey, I'm doing just as much work as the big sisters and aunties, how come I get less than them?"

At the age of fourteen, when she finally graduated to the "woman's wage," she marched up to the commander again. "Do you think my work is less good than the guys? Why can't I get the same as them?" When Chairman Mao started the campaign against Lin Biao and Confucius, the commune held Xinger up as a role model of "fighting for equal wages for women." The cadres found her immensely troublesome, though, and kept giving her the hardest, dirtiest jobs, usually ones unsuitable for a woman. Of course, they couldn't send her alone, so some of the other women workers got dragged down with her, which turned them against her too. "Let Xinger go be a role model on her own, we don't want equal wages!" At one point, Xinger gave up too. She went to the commune secretary and said, "I wanted equal wages, but you can't give me equal work!" Startled, he asked, "Why not?" Wide-eyed, she said, "Because I'm just a woman!" So much for being a role model.

Xinger fought for higher wages because she wanted her family to be better off—not for herself, but for Zaoer, and therefore for her mother. She knew her mom loved her, but the way she loved Zaoer was different. Xinger would eventually be married off, but Zaoer would be by his mom's side forever. Between them, mother and daughter put Zaoer through elementary school, then high school. One yuan at a time, they built up a nest egg for him.

Some village girls cast their lines into the ocean of matrimony, angling for a city husband. They didn't always seal the deal, but even if all they'd managed was a visit to town, they'd still swank around when they returned as if they were Empress Cixi herself. One time, when they were taking a break in the fields, a girl named Peach who'd recently returned from Shijiazhuang showed everyone a photo. The city! A tall building in the background—they counted a whole six floors. Sure, they'd all seen skyscrapers in movies, but Peach herself was standing in front of this one. What's more, for the few days she'd been in Shijiazhuang, she actually lived in that building. This was something else. According to her, the people in that building didn't sleep on heated kang platforms, but in beds. Hers was so soft, she couldn't get to sleep. So they brought out a metal thing like a waist-high bamboo steamer and said, "Sleep on this." She was confused, but they opened it up and said it was a "folding bed." This was stiffer, but she still felt like she was falling, and it took her three nights to get used to it. Then she spent a long time describing trolley buses. Someone asked, "But why are they called that?" Peach blinked. "Because they're on wheels, silly, just like a trolley." Xinger, who was already annoyed at the way Peach was blabbing on, snapped, "What do you know? They get their power from a trolley pole." But then someone asked, "So what's a trolley pole?" Now it was Xinger's turn to blink and stutter. She knew the answer but couldn't put it into words. Her face flushed bright red. Peach pointed at her and giggled, and then everyone was laughing. Xinger got worked up and hollered, "Hey! My pa's been to Beijing, you know. Have you forgotten? I have a photo of him at home." Tucked into the mirror frame above their dresser, right in the middle, were two pictures of her father in Tiananmen Square. One alone with Tiananmen Gate in the background, and one with Master Xun, both men sternly standing at attention for no reason. Anyone who'd ever been to her house had seen those photographs, but that wasn't the same as Xinger herself having been to Beijing, so the others continued siding with Peach, who poured fuel on the flames by jeering, "Don't pretend to be so sophisticated, Xinger. You haven't even been to our county town, have you? We don't need you to explain what a trolley is."

From that day, Xinger grew determined to visit a city. After the wheat harvest in 1977, she heard about a farmers' market in the county town, so she headed there with a basket of eggs. Her mom said she should just sell them at the nearby commune, but she insisted on trekking the more than five miles to town. Step by step, she trudged along the road. It didn't take long to sell all her eggs at the market, but that wasn't her real reason for coming here. She set about exploring the town—which disappointed her. Apart from the Big Crossroads, nothing about this place was any better than the commune. The Big Crossroads were three-story buildings at the four corners of a crossroads, a commercial district stretching a few dozen yards in all directions. Beyond that, though, were just regular countryside houses. Xinger went into the northeastern "mall," and found it full of trinkets that made her eyes gleam and her hands itch, especially the translucent silk scarves in red or green, shot through with gold and silver threads. Peach was always ostentatiously wearing one she'd bought in Shijiazhuang. Xinger wanted one too. Peach's was pale pink, so she'd get a jade-green one. Let their scarves duke it out to be prettier, more eye catching. She'd gotten more than twenty yuan for her eggs and could definitely afford a scarf. But then she thought about Zaoer's school fees and textbooks, the little fuzzy mustache on his upper lip, the nest egg that still wasn't enough to buy him a house. She swallowed painfully, walked away from the alluring scarf counter, and wandered up the stairs. Out of nowhere, someone screamed, "What are you doing here? Get out!" The third floor, she realized, was offices, and the staircase leading up from the second floor was marked with a wooden sign: "Staff Only." Ears burning, she hurried back down as the voice shouted behind her, "What an ignoramus! Barging in here like that."

Xinger's first trip to town brought her nothing but humiliation and an unsettled mind. As she walked home, she reevaluated her sense of self-worth. If her father had left her a legacy, it was knowing her worth, which meant a cheerful willingness to help anyone weaker than herself. The person who'd shouted at her so vulgarly was the true ignoramus, she decided. Her dad once told her—she remembered this very clearly—there's a street in Beijing called Wangfujing that has a big department store full of goods, from the first floor up to the third. Surely it was this image that had led her up to the third floor. What a shame this mall was so lacking, and didn't that reveal how little the people in this town knew about the world? In the department store on Beijing's Wangfujing, everyone was free to walk up to the third story!

As she walked past the farmers' market again, she saw a crowd and instinctively squeezed in to have a look. A woman even older than her mom was crying and sobbing—she'd managed to sell two live chickens for four yuan and was going to buy medicine for her husband, but someone picked her pocket before she could leave the market. Xinger didn't go through any rational process of thought; she was just moved by the woman's hands, wrinkled and curled like chicken claws, and the murky, red eyes those hands were dabbing at. She pushed to the front, reached for the satin handkerchief her money was tied up in, and pulled two yuan from the roll. "I'll give you half of what you lost, Auntie," she said simply. "I can't offer any more. My mom is waiting for me at home; I need to bring the rest to her." The crowd began to murmur. As she made her way back through the crowd, Xinger yelled, "You shameless thief! Have dogs eaten your conscience? You see this? I have more money on me. Try to take it—and see what happens to you!"

She strode off. Everyone watched her go, thinking she must know martial arts or something. The old woman was more thrown by this generosity than by the theft, and forgot to thank her.

Then Xinger got lost. The more she walked in circles, the more flustered she got. This was the farthest she'd ever been from home. As the sun slipped behind the distant hills and color leached from the fields, anxious tears seeped from her eyes.

Finally, after walking in a big circle, she managed to find the road back. The sky was almost completely black, and her heart plunged like a bucket into a well. All of a sudden, she understood how tiny this village was that she'd lived in for seventeen years, how far from the city. She'd never felt so lonely and hollow. She tripped on something and fell, sprawling. The basket rolled far away. She clambered to her feet, sat on a mound of earth, and sobbed.

Just then, someone called out, "Xinger! Sister!"

The familiar voice filled her with strength and tenderness. She leaped to her feet and ran toward it.

Zaoer's face was etched with anger and panic. When they got home, her mom slapped her across the face without saying a word. This was the first time in many years her mom had hit her in anger, but still this blow felt like the sweetest gesture, carrying such deep concern and so much indescribable love. She flung herself into her embrace and howled, "Mom!"

By the next day, her mom had forgiven her everything, including the impulsive generosity of the two-yuan donation.

After the wheat harvest in 1980, the village instituted a system of accountability for getting the crop packaged and delivered to purchasers. Twenty-year-old Xinger quickly became well known as a pillar of this process. Zaoer graduated high school and sat for the college entrance exam but failed to get in. He hadn't actually thought he stood a chance, but Xinger insisted he give it a try. In the end, not a single person from their district got through, so everyone was fine with that. Neither of them wanted their mom to keep working, and Xinger took over her duties in the fields. She told Zaoer to rear quails at home. Zaoer, an educated person, got a book about quail-rearing and did what it said, adapting the instructions to their local conditions. He became quite the expert, and five or six other households joined him. They signed a contract to provide a food company in the county town with quail eggs and birds, both layers and broilers. At home, all their mom had to do was cook and feed their pig and ten-odd chickens. The pig would be slaughtered and eaten at the New Year, and the chickens provided eggs for the household. Xinger's family gradually became prosperous, and before Xinger went to Beijing, not only were they able to refurbish their house, Zaoer built three extra rooms with verandas and tiled roofs. He was now the most eligible man in the village, and several girls were fighting over him. His mother and Xinger were poised to throw him a magnificent wedding as soon as he made up his mind and picked a girl.

One crisp autumn day after the harvest, the family was having dinner under the willow tree in the courtyard. Xinger asked her brother, "Who the hell do you plan to marry? If it's Jade, I'll probably fight with her." Jade was Peach's little sister and had followed Peach to Shijiazhuang for a time, where she worked as a nanny for a cadre's family. Xinger found both sisters annoyingly full of themselves. They'd both set their hearts on marrying a city man, though in the end Peach settled for Carpenter Zhang, who had the fattest wallet in their village. As for Jade, she seemed to visit Zaoer in his quail barn at least three times a day.

Zaoer blushed and tried to laugh it off. "Don't worry, Sis, the passion is all on her side." He looked at Xinger, face reddening, and allowed the words he'd bitten back for a very long time to finally rise to the surface. "Sis, if you don't get married first, I don't think I'll be able to."

Their mother looked at Xinger too, and sighed.

Xinger's heart burned. Her mom had said this to her before and suggested that they send her off in style before receiving a new daughter-in-law into the family just as gloriously. Xinger had retorted, "Well, I haven't fallen in love, have I? Anyway I can't leave this family until I know I've done everything I can for Zaoer, including marrying him off. Once I'm married, I'll belong to another family. I won't be able to come back and do stuff for you. How do you expect me to just walk away?" At the time, her mom nodded. In these moments, she always brought up Master Xun and his son, Lei, who was the same age as Xinger. Master Xun had been close friends with Xinger's father, so naturally the sworn brothers had betrothed their unborn children to each other. Back when they were poverty-stricken, her mom hadn't had the heart to think about this. At most, she'd bring it up as a joke to lighten their monotonous existence. Now that they were prospering, she felt the vast gulf between them and the Xuns had shrunk, bringing this previously unattainable match within reach. More recently, her mom had begun saying things like "I wonder if dear Master Xun still lives near the Bell and Drum Towers." Or "What kind of job has Xun Lei got, do you think?" Or "Mm, I'd love to know if Mrs. Xun has a daughter-in-law yet . . ."

Now that she was growing into the role of head of the household, Xinger no longer felt the need to hold back in front of her mother and brother. Since

Zaoer had brought up the question of her marriage, she told them her plans. "I'll make the arrangements for Zaoer, but to be honest, my own wedding can't be put off too much longer. I'll be twenty-three next birthday—how many girls in our village are still unmarried at my age? You could count them on the fingers of two hands. Still, you know I like to get my own way. I'll have to find someone who'll go along with me. I have one wish in life, and that's to visit Beijing. I plan to go there later in the fall. Firstly, to visit Master Xun and his wife. Secondly, to get some nicer household things for Zaoer than we can find here. And thirdly, well, I'd like to try my luck."

Her mother and brother nodded at each of these statements. And now, here she is, in Beijing, with a large traveling bag containing ten boxes of quail eggs. She'd planned to go straight from the train station to the Bell and Drum Towers, but at the bus stop, the list of destinations set her soul ablaze: Wangfujing, Tiananmen, Zhongshan Park. Unable to help herself, she made her way to Tiananmen Square, stood in line, and got a couple of photos taken: one with the gate in the background, and one with the Great Hall of the People. As the shutter clicked a second time, she thought, *This one ought to have two people in it.* Still lugging her huge bag, she made a round of Zhongshan Park and went into the Forbidden City, then wandered out the east gate onto Donghuamen. Just as she was taking herself to task for gallivanting, she overheard some people talking and realized Wangfujing was not far away. She happily walked over there and, with her heart in her mouth, entered the department store and went straight up to the third floor, stamping her feet on the mirror-smooth terrazzo floor. An enormous sense of contentment settled over her. She browsed the goods as she made her way back downstairs, and remembered her mom telling her, "Master Xun is fond of a drink, and Mrs. Xun loves sweet things." On the ground floor, she bought four bottles of the most expensive baijiu, crammed them into the side pocket of her bag as best she could. Then she picked up three frosted cakes in fancy boxes. Even though she now looked fairly comical with a stuffed-to-bursting bag in one hand and three cake boxes hanging off the other arm, she felt amazing as she walked out of the department store. She could walk into Master Xun's house like this, she thought, and have nothing to be ashamed of.

Several friendly people showed her the way, and she found the stop for the number 8 bus, which has brought her all the way here to the foot of the Drum Tower. All that's left now is to find the right hutong and siheyuan.

The Drum Tower! It's even bigger than she'd imagined. That makes her happy. Behind it is a large metal bell, probably from the other tower. She feels sorry for it, sitting there without a roof over its head. Then she spots the Bell Tower. How elegant it is. For some reason, she thinks they're like a married couple: Mr. Drum Tower, Mrs. Bell Tower. Standing side by side for eternity, never to be parted. She walks past a bar—First Fragrance Tobacco & Liquor— and asks quite a few people for directions, turning several corners until she sees Master Xun's hutong.

Making her way down this hutong is a startling experience. So Beijing isn't all imposing and grand? Who'd have thought it also had cramped, dingy places like this! She reaches the siheyuan gate and finds a little crowd gathered there. One of the kids holds a bamboo pole with dangling firecrackers that look like they might go off at any moment. An instant later, she spots the red double-happiness decorations on either side of the gate. Why does that make her heart clench? She didn't find her burdens heavy on the way here, but just like that, her arms begin to ache. What are the odds? Why did it have to be this day that Xun Lei—

"Are you here for the wedding?" asks the firecracker boy. "Quick, go in, the bride will be here any minute now."

Jiyue's aunt got here early and is now in the crowd waiting for the bridal car. She can tell this girl isn't from the city, and the Xues don't know anyone like that. She says, "Who are you looking for, girlie?"

Xinger recovers her senses. "The Xun family. Xun Xingwang is my father's—"

"Oh, you're Master Xun's niece? You're in the right place. Just turn right after the gate, and your uncle's house is in the side yard."

Xinger enters the courtyard, still tangled in her misunderstanding, but having regained her self-respect. *Act natural,* she tells herself. *Be generous and sincere when you congratulate Xun Lei.* She'll have to get him a really good present.

Two rattan chairs hang over the ancient entryway, decrepit and useless, but not yet thrown away. Earlier this morning, the graceful Zhang Xiuzao stood here a brief moment, going through an intense emotional struggle. Now another young woman passes through: the strapping country lass Guo Xinger, with a bulging bag in her right hand, three cake boxes tied together in her left, her footsteps heavy, and a storm raging in her heart.

Pyak pyak pyak, go the firecrackers outside the gate. The bridal car has arrived.

CHAPTER 13

An unusual guest at the banquet. Did you know about the
beggars' guilds in Beijing back in the day?

In 1982, most people get married like Xue Jiyue and Pan Xiuya. Only the children of cadres and intellectuals go in for destination weddings, and although the newspapers are always promoting mass weddings, only a tiny minority actually take part in them. Naturally, just as willow trees aren't the same as poplars, mulberry trees, or elms, each willow is different from all its fellows. Weddings like Jiyue and Xiuya's generally follow these steps: First, the bridal car arrives at the groom's house, to fireworks and confetti, with red double-happiness decorations at the gate. Second, the wedding ceremony is held at the man's house. All the friends and family at the reception are from the groom's side, and the more important ones stay for a meal. If the woman lives far away, only the people giving her away (usually her aunts or sisters-in-law) show up. Her parents and other friends and relations generally aren't present. Third, that day or the next, the groom accompanies the bride back home, usually on bicycles or the bus—now it's the bride's family's turn to throw a reception for friends and relatives, with the more important ones staying for dinner, generally a less-costly one than the groom's family threw. Fourth, about a week later, the bride and groom and their immediate families meet for another meal—usually at the groom's home, though occasionally the bride's side gets to host. And that's the grand finale to the whole wedding.

There are, of course, variations. Some aren't satisfied with a single bridal car and insist on a convoy—not of regular rental cars, but larger vehicles, typically a couple of cars plus two or three vans or mini-jeeps. Some choose to have the banquet at a restaurant instead of the groom's family home, which allows families and friends on both sides to be present. The bride still returns home, but there's no separate celebration, just a simple reception with tea and candy. The restaurant bill is split between both families, though naturally the man's side is expected to pay more.

On Jiyue's wedding day, the first guest to show up—not counting his sister-in-law Zhaoying—is Luo Baosang. This is surely a bad omen.

Jiyue doesn't feel just annoyed, but actually repulsed. Even so, he has no choice but to force a smile and walk over from the dresser. "Oh, it's you! Come in! Sit! Have some candy?"

Luo Baosang is sloppily dressed and hasn't bothered to shave—he could not make his contempt for his host any clearer. He plops himself onto the new couch and surveys the dishes of candy on the coffee table. "Nobody wants your crappy candy," he bellows. "How about a cigarette?"

Jiyue tosses him a packet of filter-tipped Firework cigarettes. Baosang catches them, purses his lips, and drops them on the table. "Is that all you have to offer? Come on, go get your Triple Fives. I know you've fucking got some. Who are you saving them for, if not me?"

Jiyue does indeed have some British 555 cigarettes, obtained with foreign-currency coupons from Xiuya's family, but he really doesn't want to share them with Baosang. "No swearing, okay? This is all I've got, take it or leave it."

Baosang glares at him for a moment, then chuckles and helps himself from the packet of Fireworks, producing a lighter from his pocket that shoots a tall flame. Lounging back comfortably, he smokes like an infant latching onto a nipple. Jiyue notices the lighter he is turning over in his other hand: a slimline imported model, plated with some smooth, shiny alloy. The contrast between this fancy lighter and his shabby clothes doesn't seem paradoxical to Jiyue. This juxtaposition contains the very Luo Baosang-ness of Luo Baosang.

Luo Baosang sprawls ostentatiously on the sofa. His appetite is in optimal condition, and his digestion is excellent. He's planning to eat a huge amount at this banquet—and according to him, he has an absolute right to.

Baosang's father, Luo Shengqi, has a younger sister who married Xue Jiyue's father's sister's husband's brother, which means Baosang also calls Jiyue's aunt "Aunt." By the same token, he calls Jiyue's parents "Uncle" and "Auntie," and as he's around the same age as Jihui and Jiyue, they've grown up like brothers. What could be more natural than showing up at his own brother's wedding?

That's not their only connection. Baosang works in the same place as Jihui and Zhaoying, so they're all coworkers. Also, when Jiyue and Xiuya were getting their furniture, Baosang went to a lot of trouble to get this huge wardrobe brought in, and he was the one shouting instructions, directing the movers where to put what. Isn't that what a brother should do?

Baosang is twenty-nine years old and still unmarried. The influence of his family—or maybe we should say his clan—over him is very clear.

So far, no sociologist has done any research into Beijingers, not in the broad sense of people who live in Beijing, but what you might call the "indigenous" folk—that is, those whose families have been here at least three generations, the ordinary working folk of the city, the "lower rungs of society." Of course, the term "lower rungs" is considered wrong these days. In the new society, every resident of Beijing is equal, and the categories of exploited and exploiters, oppressed and oppressors, no longer exist. Instead, to be more accurate, let's list the characteristics of this group: First, they're not cadres. Second, their wages are low. Third, they haven't had much schooling. Fourth, they have some sort of service job, or something else requiring less technical facility and more physical labor. Fifth, they mostly live in the hutongs and siheyuans of inner Beijing that haven't been modernized. Sixth, they've clung to many of their traditions. Seventh, their lives are much more stable than those of other inhabitants of Beijing—unlike ministers, who are subject to dramatic reversals of fortune; or artists, whose reputations might soar or crumble at any moment; or politicians, who are in constant danger of being denounced or landing on the wrong side of some faction or movement. You don't read many novels about these people. Some dismiss them as "little city folk" or, even worse, "the masses."

Yet their existence has a huge impact on the ecosystem of Beijing, and there is no way to raise the material and spiritual conditions of Beijing as a whole without observing this community so as to guide them upward. Any "big city people" who think this has nothing to do with them should ask themselves: Are you really able to keep your existence separate from the little folk? You encounter them in shops, on trams, on sidewalks, in parks and movie theaters, in restaurants and diners—in other words, it's impossible to avoid them. You're only able to maintain your sense of elitism precisely because of the myriad little folk serving you and your peers, filling in the cracks that would otherwise cause you discomfort. These cracks aren't always small ones either.

People are always complaining: Why do some service workers have such bad attitudes? Why are young factory workers so vulgar, so careless, so unruly? Many issues can be resolved through education, praise and criticism, rewards and punishment. At the same time, it is necessary to study social attributes and culture, intelligence, psychology, and education in order to come up with pedagogical tactics more suited to effectively addressing these problems.

Of course, within this group, everyone's circumstances are different.

So what is Luo Baosang's situation?

Both his parents come from generations of poverty in Beijing.

During the late Qing dynasty, those on the lowest rung of society were housed in two districts. The first was the inner city around the Bell and Drum Towers, where beggar gangs frequently gathered before dispersing east, west, and south, returning to their headquarters (doorways, street corners, lobbies, shacks) after a hard day's panhandling. The second was farther off in Tianqiao, and though there were also beggars there, they mostly performed tricks for money, rather than roaming around, and tended to live in run-down houses in siheyuans south of Longxugou and Chuziying.

Luo Baosang still remembers his grandpa, who took ill and died in 1957. The thing that sticks most vividly in his memory is that Grandpa always slept with his shoes on. Only when Baosang was grown did he learn this was because back in the day, vagrants survived winter nights by huddling together in "fire huts"—dilapidated government outbuildings, perhaps where imperial officers patrolling the streets used to meet. In these empty rooms, they would dig a pit, gather branches to build a fire, and fall asleep huddled together around it, men and women, young and old. The beggars who owned shoes were afraid they would get stolen, so they never took them off to sleep. The credo of the beggars' guilds was: If you snatched or stole something another beggar was holding or wearing, you'd be sentenced to death. But if they put down or took off that object, it was fair game.

For a time, Luo Baosang's grandpa was a guild leader. In the Beijing opera *The Bean Juice Tale*, which still gets performed frequently, Jin Yunu's father, Jin Song, is also a guild leader, and gets portrayed as a good person. Thanks to *The Bean Juice Tale*, Luo Baosang is fond of Beijing operas and also of the Xues' neighbor Tantai Zhizhu. This has added a layer of tenderness to his otherwise coarse soul, but we won't go into that now.

Beggars of Luo Baosang's grandpa's generation regarded begging as a profession, and just as the pawnshops around the Bell and Drum Towers were known for their cruelty, the beggars in this neighborhood had a reputation for giving people a hard time. When wealthy folk had a wedding or significant birthday, the beggars would show up to help them celebrate. If the doorman or family accountant wasn't sufficiently receptive, or even dared to chase them away, then a short while later, under the direction of the guild leader, teams of beggars would show up in shifts to hassle the guests, giving them such a tough time that eventually the host would order the guards or accountant to give them money to go away, at which point the beggars would beat a graceful retreat.

There used to be different types of beggars, just as Beijing opera performers are divided into young leads, character actors, clowns, and so forth, with further subdivisions: ingenue, coquette, comic sidekick, martial arts lead, sword-and-horse lead, and so on. Similarly, each category of beggar had a different style of work. "Soft beggars" were generally older, frailer, or female. They operated through weeping and wheedling and approached each target with a litany of woe: "Madam, please give me a couple of yuan, may you live ten thousand years, madam," or "Be generous to me, sir, and you'll surely be blessed with sons and grandsons!" This group was further divided into "sitting" and "calling." The latter roamed the streets and interspersed weeping with displays of rage: "Give me your money—or hold on to it and pay for your coffin!" Odd as these statements might be, they still fell within the scope of softness—unlike "hard beggars," who were generally young men, less glib and more reliant on action to get results. Many did what was known in the trade as "street work": hitting their bare chests repeatedly with swords or bricks until they'd drawn blood, or wearing around their necks a barbed metal chain attached to a heavy iron ball that clunked along the pavement as they walked. "Trick beggars" utilized fairly basic acrobatics, such as the "falling lotus" (dancing to the rattling of coins in a hollow bamboo stem), "stealing the limelight" (balancing a bowl on the tip of a needle between your eyebrows and encouraging people to drop coins into it), and so on.

Master Xun Xingwang begged alongside his mother as a little boy, but in a rural village during the years of famine—unlike the professional beggars in

Beijing. Not only were their motivations very different, the way they presented was also miles apart.

Luo Baosang's father, Luo Shengqi, took on the role of a "hard beggar" when he reached adulthood. He was thirty-six and still unmarried at the time of Beijing's Liberation, and only in 1950 did he start pedaling a trishaw cart with the help of government relief funds, thus gaining a stable job and making a positive contribution to society for the first time in his life. In 1952, pushing forty, he married Luo Baosang's mother, who was thirty-five. Having married later in life, this couple only produced one child: Luo Baosang.

Trishaw carts used to play a central role in the business of transporting goods around Beijing, and even now are still in use. For a long time, they've been operated by workers' cooperatives and collectives that owned the means of production, but when you look closely, although the bulk of the haulers are impoverished city folk with proper backgrounds, there are also two groups who could fairly be called the detritus of the old society: One, like Luo Shengqi, is poor through and through, with no history of work—mostly former beggars, gangsters, or wastrel offspring of declining families. The second group is military men, police officers, and hangers-on whose offenses pre-Liberation weren't too grave, so that after a spell of interrogation and education, they were placed under surveillance or spared punishment, but in any case, being as bereft of skills as the first group, some of them would also be allocated jobs hauling goods in trishaw carts. These two groups have several characteristics in common: first, lack of a strong work ethic, preferring instead to smoke and drink, and second, absence of self-respect, with a weakness for the opposite sex. They're grasping yet loyal spendthrifts who can put up with suffering where necessary. Naturally, not everyone was like that, and after the People's Republic of China digested and reformed them, many went through a laudable transformation, sloughing off the chaff and cultivating the finer parts of themselves.

Even so, it's no easy task to completely break down and remake a person. Think about it—with Emperor Puyi or war criminals, you're dealing with educated individuals, so you can make a rational appeal and shift their political stances, rendering them worthy of love and respect. It's trickier with the dregs of society—they're ignorant and full of garbage. Even if they were ideologically impeccable, they would still emanate a revolting stench.

One time, Luo Shengqi, Xue Yongquan, and Xun Xingwang happened to run into each other at Xinyuan Bathhouse on Tobacco Pipe Alley. After soaking awhile in the hottest pool, they went out and flopped onto the mats for a rest. If anyone had been observing them, it would have been apparent at a glance that they were not cadres or intellectuals, but working men. Yet there were clear differences in the physical appearance and bearing of the trio.

Master Xun Xingwang had dark, coarse skin, but his muscles were firm and supple, and on the whole he gave the impression of unfettered virility—not just because he was several years younger than the other two, but because he was also a productive member of society and a warrior who'd taken part in regular physical activity from a young age: first on the land, then in the People's Liberation Army, and finally as an industrial worker.

Uncle Xue Yongquan had pale, yellowish skin. His body ran to fat, and his suffering had left marks everywhere. The way he draped and folded two snow-white towels over himself before settling onto the mat, even if you didn't know he'd been a lama, you'd still find yourself thinking of a reclining temple Buddha—not exactly a beautiful sight, but also not unpleasing to the eye.

Luo Shengqi's skin was a hard-to-describe muddy-brown color. There was an oddly shaped growth on his forehead—he'd driven nails in there when he was a "hard beggar." This is also when he acquired some peculiar scars on the right side of his chest, from shoving metal hooks through his flesh. Like many of his fellow trishaw cart drivers who didn't get regular jobs until their thirties or forties, he started too late to develop a good physique, but his musculature was stretched and enlarged through constant activity, which left him rather oddly shaped: a shrunken chest and taut belly, sinewy upper arms and enormous forearms, greenish veins protruding from the surface of his legs. Something about his body put you in mind of a praying mantis or spider.

Their behavior differed even more. Xun Xingwang was happy to settle for the tea provided by the bathhouse, and when the attendant came with hot water, he chatted casually with him, clearly seeing him as an equal. This man was serving Master Xun now, and Master Xun might serve him on another occasion. Xue Yongquan ordered tea too, but he only opened the packet a little and poured half its contents into the pot, folding the top over and stowing the rest to take home. As the attendant poured hot water, Uncle Xue nodded and thanked him politely and urbanely. By contrast, Luo Shengqi had brought his own tea leaves but waited for the other two to brew theirs before offering around his stubby metal canister. "Here, use mine, it's good stuff—one yuan twenty a tael." Naturally, they declined. He grabbed one of their teapots, lifted the lid, glanced inside, and sniffed the brew. "No, no, that's not right," he said crisply. "I bet that's fifty cents a tael. The color's all wrong, and it smells murky. That's going to scrape your throat raw." He pulled the lid off his canister. "Get a whiff of this!" He summoned the attendant in a resonant voice and asked for a teapot. When it arrived, he examined it and criticized everything from the lid to the spout. When the hot water arrived, he leaned back and half closed his eyes as it was being poured, enjoying the sensation of being served.

That's how you know Luo Baosang's father, Luo Shengqi, is not in the same league as Xue Yongquan and Xun Xingwang.

Luo Shengqi is sixty-nine years old, and retired a while back. He has a hwamei thrush and a grosbeak, for whom he has bought costly, exquisite cages, food bowls, cloth covers, and so on. The former he rears for its song, the latter for its trick of holding a little ball in its mouth. Unmarried and still living with his parents, Luo Baosang has covered an entire wall of his room with fish tanks he welded together himself, which he's filled with tropical fish: angelfish, kissing fish, gouramis, tiger barbs, zebra fish, rainbow fish, and all varieties of seagrasses: jade hairpin, crowns, lotus, banana, ox tongue, chrysanthemum. Baosang's spiritual and material circumstances might be very different from his forebears', but you can still somehow tell that his grandfather was the head of a beggars' guild and his father was a "hard beggar."

When considering what went into the making of Luo Baosang, we must also consider the maternal influence.

His mother, the former Miss Huang, hails from Tianqiao—the southern counterpart to the poor neighborhood around the Bell and Drum Towers. Between Occupation and Liberation, Tianqiao was known for its "eight eccentrics": Big Gold Tooth, who ran a peep show and had disciples called "little gold teeth." Soaring Through the Clouds, who was a street performer in a papier-mâché mask. Grease Gone, who peddled a sort of grease remover, singing the whole time. Piper would insert a little bamboo flute up a nostril and produce all sorts of tunes. Half-Immortal Wang performed with his daughter—strips of white paper would dance between their hands, rising and falling. Third Treasure was a flag dancer and tumbler. Sun Hongliang, a hawker who chanted as he sold insecticide, later bought a shop front and oppressed the masses. He was overthrown as a bully after Liberation. Soldier Boy Huang had been a low-ranking officer in a warlord militia. He became a vendor of healing ointment, and each day, he'd set up a circle of benches in Tianqiao, but instead of the usual acrobatics or martial arts, he sat there cursing the state of the country, corrupt officials, and their rancid history. Everything he said made sense, and he cursed with such fluency and pleasure, people came each day to listen. His strapping body was clothed in old gray military fatigues. With no regard for his place in the pecking order, he ranted away in his Shandong accent and made his name that way. Word on the street is that Luo Baosang's mother is Soldier Boy Huang's daughter, but that's just speculation; no one dares ask her to her face. Even the household registration officer at the police station, who could do so with impunity, never seems to develop an interest in this question. Whether or not it's true, Luo Baosang has certainly inherited a plain-spoken streak from her—he's always up for righting an injustice, usually in the fruitiest language.

So it's Xue Jiyue's big day, and Luo Baosang's the first guest to arrive. No sooner has he stepped inside than he starts making an annoyance of himself. His main reason for being here is to eat and drink his fill, and he makes no pretense of this fact. The first words out of his mouth, rather than the usual congratulatory speeches, are a demand for a 555 cigarette. When he's rebuffed, he grudgingly accepts a Firework instead, sprawls on the sofa for a moment, then paces around the room. He ends up in front of the dresser, standing on tiptoe to examine the wedding photo. Abruptly, he snorts and sniggers creepily. When he's done laughing, he leans over to Jiyue and murmurs into his ear, "How about it? Did you sample the merchandise? I bet she gave you a run for your money."

Jiyue flushes bright red and shoves Baosang away. "Fuck you! That's rubbish."

Baosang narrows his eyes at Jiyue. He strides out of the nuptial chamber, cigarette drooping from his mouth, and ducks into the temporary kitchen tent.

Auntie Xue feels obliged to be polite. "Hello, Baosang! Didn't your parents come with you?"

"Congratulations, Auntie Xue!" Baosang smiles mischievously. "My mom and dad would have loved to be here—but you didn't invite them, did you?"

"Gracious, why so formal?" Auntie Xue raises her voice to defend herself. "Since when does family need inviting? They know about the wedding, of course they should be here. No cash gift needed, we don't care about that. You helped

Jiyue move in, that's better than any gift!" The "cash gift" is a customary small present of money for the newlyweds, anything from two to twenty yuan. Now that she's brought this up, Baosang feels a little embarrassed and hastily fakes a sudden desire to see the rest of the kitchen. He catches Lu Xichun's eye over the cold appetizers.

Xichun smiles, having already recognized his voice. "Here to fill your belly again?"

"My man!" Delighted that Xichun is the hired chef, Baosang pats him heartily on the back. "Listen, these folks are practically my parents, and the groom's like my little brother. Make sure you do a good job, for my sake, yeah?"

"How do you two know each other?" Auntie Xue has to ask.

Baosang quickly answers, "His dad used to work on the trishaw carts with my dad. I've met his mom too. They've both kicked the bucket now. And he's a bachelor like me."

This little speech makes Auntie Xue uneasy. Over the last three hours, she's come to trust Xichun and admires his craft and dedication. But now Baosang says he's an unmarried orphan, which is terribly inauspicious! What if his bad luck seeps into the food and infects the family?

Lu Xichun shakes his head gently, sighing inwardly. He understands Luo Baosang only too well. They were at elementary school together. Baosang started out two grades ahead but got held back twice, so they ended up in the same class. Xichun can't stand Baosang's lack of respect for anyone, including himself. In fourth grade, the Cultural Revolution kicked off and they denounced their teachers and principal like they'd seen rebel factions in the high schools and colleges doing. Baosang was a year older than even the sixth graders and practically at his full adult height. To bolster his imposing physique, he wore a red armband, proclaiming himself to be among the "five red categories"—and at the time, it certainly seemed he had the right. Rumor had it that after Liberation, his father, Luo Shengqi, overthrew the evil tyrants in their neighborhood, then helped the People's Liberation Army's death squads drag them to the execution grounds. A most courageous, revolutionary act. As the principal was denounced and the teachers forced into struggle sessions, Baosang took on the role of making them "do the airplane." Not satisfied with twisting their arms and pressing their heads down, he came up with even more vicious ways to humiliate them: stomping on the soles of their feet, parading them around by their ears, pouring ink down their collars—all the while making faces at the "revolutionary student body" watching him on stage. Later, he turned his sadistic mind on his fellow students, forcing those whose families were from the "five black categories" to lean against a wall with foreheads pressed against protruding nails, scratching confessions onto their chests with safety pins. Not long after that, Luo Shengqi was hauled out of his workplace. Lu Xichun saw the poster denouncing him but didn't understand it at the time. Much later, he learned that on the eve of Liberation college students organized an "Against Hunger, Against Civil War" march protesting the Nationalists' anti-revolutionary tactics, so the Nationalist Army hired hoodlums to attack them, promising one steamed bun for every student they drove away. Luo Shengqi was one of those thugs, and he earned eighteen steamed buns that day! Now that his father had been exposed, Luo Baosang went instantly from red to black. The strange thing was, he didn't seem sad about this, only resigned. During those ridiculous struggle sessions at their school, Baosang never waited to be tortured but assumed the position himself, rump high in the air, arms raised behind his back. One time, he even stood on stage and slapped himself across the face—but just as Xichun was quietly feeling sorry for Baosang from where he sat in the audience, Baosang abruptly turned and stuck out his tongue at him.

Now that they're grown, Xichun often uses Baosang as a mirror to examine his own soul. He can forgive Baosang's past ignorance and tolerate the bad habits he still hasn't managed to shed, but he, Xichun, must take heed and always have respect for the dignity of other people and himself.

Xichun is not thrilled that Baosang has shown up at this banquet—his carefully prepared dishes are sure to be tainted now. Take this exquisite appetizer of two adjoined mashed-potato hearts with bright-red hawthorn strips forming words across them, surrounded by a colorful and finely balanced array of ham, shrimp, shredded egg, pig-head meat, cucumber cups, tomato flowers, century egg slices, and so on. When this dish is served, it demands that you first take it in with your eyes and fully appreciate it before tucking in. What do you want to bet that Baosang will dive straight in, reducing the whole thing to mush with his chopsticks?

Baosang has no idea what Xichun is thinking, and automatically puts on an air of superiority—today, Xichun is a server, and Baosang just so happens to be one of the people he's serving. He proclaims in ringing tones, "Don't you dare slack off, you bastard! Show us what you're made of."

Jiyue's eldest aunt arrives with her family at this moment. Hearing Auntie Xue greet them, Baosang goes out too, only to realize he knows them. Xue Yongquan's late second brother was in a beggars' guild. This aunt's husband used to work the crowds at Longfu Temple, which means he had dealings with Baosang's mother's family. Seeing this complicated web of relationships he is part of, Baosang is more convinced than ever that he has a perfect right to partake of this delicious feast.

Uncle Xue abruptly shows up now, sweaty and bearing a bulging straw bag. Everyone starts calling out greetings even more vociferously. With some urgency, Uncle Xue says to his wife, "Now look what's happened—Makai Restaurant says the beer delivery truck never showed up today. They didn't have much left as it was, and there's two tables of overseas Chinese booked in for later, so they can't spare us any. They canceled our order!"

"I knew it! You can't do a single thing right." Auntie Xue's first instinct is to start nagging. "Didn't I say we should buy the beer ahead of time? But no, you refused, you said the beer will spoil indoors and the bottles might break if we leave them out, better to let them sit in the restaurant fridge until we're ready for them. What are we supposed to do now? How can they just cancel our order?"

"I walked all the way from Makai to Di'anmen, but no one had any beer for sale. In the end, I stopped off at Di'anmen Market and got ten bottles of malt syrup."

"What the hell is that?" Baosang interjects. "You can't have a wedding without beer! How are Jiyue and his wife supposed to have a happy marriage?"

Auntie Xue's heart is a churning pit of mud. Another bad omen! Beijing weddings require three types of alcohol: baijiu to represent wealth (Dragon-Phoenix brand at the very least, if you can't afford one of the eight big labels), wine to symbolize prosperity ("Beijing red," at least 3.5 percent alcohol), and beer for contentment and harmony. Now there's a real danger they'll be missing one of the three!

Just as Auntie Xue is at her wits' end, Luo Baosang proclaims, "I don't believe Makai is really out of beer. I'm sure they saw your kind face, Uncle, and decided to take advantage. Just wait and see. I'll head over there, and I bet I come back with a crate. Give me some money and something to put the beer in. I'll go now."

Auntie Xue stamps her feet in agitation. "Xiuya is arriving any minute now. Is anyone waiting at the gate? Those kids are supposed to set off firecrackers and throw paper flowers—I hope they haven't run off."

The eldest aunt quickly leads Jiyue's cousins to the gate to await the bride.

Uncle Xue hands twenty yuan and two large net bags to Baosang, who rushes off on his mission.

The Xues retreat to their room for a moment. Auntie Xue grabs a brush and carefully dusts off her outfit, then does the same for her husband.

A short while later, the bright, explosive sound of firecrackers comes from the gate. Auntie Xue straightens her outfit and solemnly walks out of the room toward the nuptial chamber. Uncle Xue follows her.

CHAPTER 14

The bride finally arrives. Why do some sales clerks ignore
their customers?

The driver is not happy. This isn't his first rodeo, and he's met his share of difficult customers, but today has really taken the cake.

Pan Xiuya's family lives in a hutong with a "No Through Road" sign. Since
the street is so narrow, the car naturally stops by the entrance, dropping off
Zhaoying and Nanny Zhan to go fetch the bride. The Pan house is full of people,
and though there isn't time to ask who they all are, it's obvious at a glance that
the backbone of this tribe is the dried-out old lady Xiuya calls Seventh Aunt.

Seventh Aunt came over specially from Guang'anmen to be in the bridal
party, just like she did when Xiuya's two older sisters got married. Now it's Xiuya's
turn, and not only is Seventh Aunt shouldering her responsibility, she's doing it
with the gusto of a famous opera singer in the season's final performance. Apart
from the bride, she's easily the best-dressed person here. She's in her sixties and
there's no concealing the wrinkles on her face, but she has dyed her hair—which
is thinning, but not enough to reveal her scalp—and has slathered it with an
untold amount of hair oil, combing the gentlest possible wave through it, which
has the magical effect of, from a slight distance, making her look no more than
fifty. When Zhaoying and Nanny Zhan arrive, she is fussing with the bride's outfit. Xiuya is in a Western-style suit in a pale apple-green fabric with a faint stripe,
which she had made at Leiming Dress Shop on Wangfujing. The asymmetrical
jacket opening reveals a cerise nylon blouse with a large pointed collar. On her
lapel is a vermilion satin flower, from which dangles a ribbon stamped with the

word "bride." Seventh Aunt has decided this artificial flower has not blossomed sufficiently and is painstakingly rearranging its petals.

The two women's entrance precipitates a noisy round of greetings. Nanny Zhan sighs theatrically and says, "Isn't the bride just gorgeous? If I were a young buck, I'd want to marry you too."

Seventh Aunt glares at her and wonders why the Xues would send someone like this to fetch the bride—look at the way she's running her mouth! Deadpan, she says, "Is the car at the door?"

"You live in a dead end!" Nanny Zhan says, oblivious. "The driver couldn't get in, so he's waiting at the hutong entrance. We'll just walk out there. Come on, girlie, we're kidnapping you!" And with that, she reaches for Xiuya's arm.

Seventh Aunt smacks away her hand. It's clear she will have to work harder than usual to fulfill her responsibilities today. How could this Nanny Zhan be so rude? Dead end! Kidnapping! You don't say such inauspicious things on someone's wedding day! Whoever heard of a bridal car not coming right up to the door? "Tell the driver to drive in. The hutong's wide enough," she says sternly.

Everyone starts gabbing. Zhaoying says, "Sure, he can get in, but there's no room to turn around."

"Just get him in here! If he can drive in, he can drive out!" Seventh Aunt is unwavering. "Listen here, tear down the neighbors' houses if you have to, but he's driving up to the door." She turns to her niece. "Xiuya, sit and rest, I'll deal with this. Believe me, I'll get him in here." She strides determinedly out the door. Zhaoying, Nanny Zhan, and some of the Pans hurry after her.

The driver refuses to bring the car any closer, but Seventh Aunt's mouth is a crucible in which reason, bribery, and emotion are alloyed to ensure compliance. "Come on, Driver, don't be so stubborn. You think I don't know the rules? You have to drive to the address you're given, or I'll have to tell your bosses. What's it to you anyway, driving a few extra yards? You'll get a little more money, won't you? Tell you what, I'll write a letter saying what a good job you did. That's your monthly bonus guaranteed, isn't it? Young man, are you not married yourself? It's once in a lifetime, you know. If this were your wedding day, would you be happy with half measures? Help us out this time, and when it's your turn, your bad luck will turn good, and gray skies turn blue." As Seventh Aunt delivers this speech, the other Pans take the opportunity to give the driver a full pack of high-quality cigarettes. He doesn't accept them, but when they toss them into the little compartment by the driver's seat, he doesn't reject them either.

In the end, not only does the driver enter the hutong, he takes Seventh Aunt's suggestion and reverses in so he can drive straight out. It only takes everyone a moment to understand why Seventh Aunt went to all this trouble, and when they do, their respect for her only grows. Everyone, that is, except Zhan Liying, who still thinks this was all fun and games and hasn't fully grasped Seventh Aunt's state of mind.

The Pans and their neighbors hoot and cheer as the car emerges from the hutong. Nanny Zhan sits in front next to the driver, and in the back seat, the bride is flanked by Seventh Aunt and Zhaoying.

Xiuya's not at all worked up—she's in a state of calm contentment. Zhaoying is holding her hand and smiling, but her mind is on her daughter, Lotus—how is she doing now? Meanwhile, Seventh Aunt is pondering how she will show off the bride's family to its best advantage—playing these psychological games is the only way she can feel the joy of existence.

Nanny Zhan twists around to look at the bride, and as usual gives her unfiltered opinion. "I say, the cut of that suit is really not bad at all, it's a shame about the color—it just doesn't go with your blouse! Why would you match that shade of red with green? You need a third color between them to even it out." Being the sort of person who does something as soon as it pops into her mind, at a certain point in the journey, she calls out, "Stop over there, Driver! I have something urgent to take care of." The driver assumes she has to relieve herself and pulls over on the side of the road. This throws Seventh Aunt into a panic. "What on earth are you doing? Don't stop! You can't stop!"

Naturally, this annoys the driver. Why can't they make up their minds? Who is he supposed to listen to? Seeing as he's already at the curb, and parking happens to be permitted here, he decides to ignore Seventh Aunt's protests and hits the brakes. Right away, Nanny Zhan leaps nimbly out and cries, "Three minutes! I promise!" With a merry giggle, she disappears into the crowd.

"Who's ever heard of such a thing?" Seventh Aunt grumbles loudly. "The bridal car isn't supposed to stop along the way. This isn't proper, not proper at all!" She turns to Zhaoying. "What's going on with your mother-in-law? How could she send a flibbertigibbet like that to fetch the bride? Wasn't there a more suitable 'complete person' in your siheyuan?"

"It was actually Tantai Zhizhu who was supposed to come," Zhaoying explains. "You've heard of her? She's quite a well-known opera performer. Not at all like this scatterbrain . . . Shall we just go? We don't need to wait for her. God knows what nonsense she'll come up with next."

Seventh Aunt grits her teeth. Abandoning Zhan Liying isn't the answer either—losing part of the bridal party on the way to the wedding would be an even worse omen.

Three minutes pass, with no sign of Nanny Zhan. Five minutes, nothing. Not only is the driver grumbling, Seventh Aunt is simmering with rage, Zhaoying is frantic, and even Xiuya is on the verge of losing her temper. At the eighth minute, Liying appears, pulls open the door, and gets in, breathing hard. Before Seventh Aunt can let rip, Liying smiles and places something in her hands. "I pass by this department store on my way to and from work every day," she explains, "and I remembered the brooches there are rather special. I knew exactly what would complete the bride's outfit. You've got a good eye, Seventh Aunt. Have a gander at the cut and craftsmanship. Go ahead, put it on her. I know you'll find the right spot."

As the driver moves on, Seventh Aunt opens the pretty brocade jewelry box to reveal a gleaming brooch: silver strands gathered to form a twisted leaf, studded with fake gemstones in violet and amber. This is such an exquisite item, her anger melts away. "Is this what you ran off to buy?" she coos. "It's really not bad at all."

Seventh Aunt pins the brooch on the bride, and Zhaoying exclaims, "Nanny Zhan is right. Xiuya's blouse and jacket go together much better now—the brooch brings them together. It's not much to look at on its own, but with that on your lapel, you could be a movie star!"

Xiuya says sincerely, "But, Nanny Zhan, this must have cost quite a few yuan! You've already given a cash gift, and now this—it's too much!"

"This is nothing!" says Zhan Liying breezily. "Don't mention it! I watched Jiyue grow up, and now he's marrying you—no expense should be spared. If only I'd thought of this sooner, I could have taken my time and chosen an even nicer one."

In just a moment, the atmosphere in the car has reached a high point of happy harmoniousness.

Unfortunately, though Nanny Zhan can win everyone's affection with a single gesture, she can also make people hate her with just a few words.

As the car speeds toward the Bell and Drum Towers, she recalls her spontaneous purchase. "I was lucky to get in and out so quickly—that hardly ever happens. Usually the sales clerks are too busy chatting to pay any attention to customers—they ignore you even if you shout at them, or they just stand there counting banknotes and receipts, refusing to look up. It makes me so mad!"

Xiuya lowers her head, not out of shyness, but annoyance. What is wrong with Nanny Zhan? Has she forgotten that Xiuya herself works behind a counter?

Pan Xiuya is on the sales team at the photo studio. She can't operate a camera and doesn't know her way around a darkroom; her job is to greet customers from behind the counter, write out receipts when someone comes in for a photo, accept negatives for developing and orders for reprints, and hand over the finished pictures when they're ready for collection. She's also responsible for selling equipment, film, and photo albums, and hiring out cameras. Compared to most shops, they don't get too many customers, so the work isn't stressful, but Xiuya and her coworkers, who are all around the same age, happen to have the two bad habits Nanny Zhan just complained about. Quite often, when a customer comes up to the counter and starts speaking, Xiuya turns to a coworker and casually picks up a conversation from earlier, perhaps grousing about the movie tickets that were just handed out. "It's so rude, those guys in the darkroom took all the good seats again, and we're stuck at the far end of the back row. Look at my seat! Right by the toilet. It's going to stink! I tried to swap with Big Wang, and you know what he did? He just meowed at me. Imagine being so ridiculous, and at his age too . . ." At this point, the customer might impatiently clear their throat or raise their voice, or start lecturing, "Hey, what kind of service is this? Why are you ignoring me?" Only then does Xiuya turn around and drawl, "How can I help you?" Counting up cash and receipts is fairly important, particularly somewhere like a department store, where each business team has to hand their takings to the bank at a fixed time every day. Xiuya knows this and is aware she can use it as an excuse to delay. She likes to stand right by the counter, as close to the customer as she can get. The customer naturally hopes she'll stop and serve them, but Xiuya just counts with more concentration, not even glancing up. Some customers start criticizing her work attitude, which allows first her and then her coworkers, when they back her up, to self-righteously proclaim,

"This is our duty, understand? You think we don't need to check these things? When we're busy doing this, we don't have to serve you!" Some customers might protest, "Why not do that in the back room?" To which she and her coworkers retort, "We'll do our work where we like!" and "What's it to you?"

In Beijing at least, these two habits are a persistent sickness among counter staff, with frequent outbreaks and no apparent cure. Has anyone carried out a study of this behavior to understand the psychology displayed by Xiuya and her young peers?

If anyone were to look Xiuya in the eye and ask, "Why are you doing this?" she'd only be able to answer, "I don't know." And to "Where did you learn to be this way?" she'd reply, "No one taught me, I got it by watching others. Before I took this job, when I was a customer myself, that's how they treated me." If you persisted, "You didn't enjoy that, did you? Why turn around and do that to other people as soon as you're on the other side of the counter?" she'd have no answer, none at all, because she's not in the habit of thinking deeply about anything. Young people like her aren't equipped for deep inquiry. Faced with the world and the sweep of human existence, Xiuya only has shallow ideas—a little more than instinct, but far short of philosophical thought.

All of this can be traced back to her birth and upbringing, her life experiences thus far, and the social environment that has influenced her, consciously or not.

Like Xue Jiyue, Xiuya was born into a petit bourgeois family, albeit a more economically straitened one. Her father used to run a stall at a temple fair, hawking the sort of items you no longer see around, such as the "poo-poo-thud," a cheap glass tube shaped like a trumpet or bottle gourd. You put the end shaped like a bottle mouth between your lips and blew; the other end was thin enough that your breath went *poo-poo* against it. These gimcrack toys broke easily, slicing children's hands open, and all that blowing wasn't good for their lungs. They aren't manufactured anymore. He also made and sold sweet-smelling herbs roasted, pulverized, and poured into pouches sewn from satin scraps. You were meant to carry these about your person to get rid of the smell of sweat and other odors. He would brag that his mix included musk, but actually only the sample pouches did; the ones he sold were purely botanicals. These have gone out of fashion too. He sold these and other trinkets until temple fairs were abolished after Liberation. He then worked at a dye shop until his retirement last year. Xiuya's mother could be said to have married down. She, too, had a temple fair stall, but a far superior one: Xiuya's grandfather was a wigmaker. Every winter, during the off-season, he'd pack a bag and head northeast to the Tumen River, where he bought hair. Back then, the tresses of the Korean women in this region were much sought after because they had the custom of letting their hair grow undisturbed until marriage. He'd return home in the spring, and they'd turn his haul into braids and chignons for sale at the fair. A yellowish sheen was most desirable—plain black hair was considered brittle, and harder to sell. Naturally, this was a far more lucrative trade than peddling poo-poo-thuds or scent pouches, so for a long time after they got married, Xiuya's mother carried with her a sense of superiority. Then Xiuya's grandpa passed away, and her mother was a mere unemployed housewife who occasionally made ice pops to sell in the summer. Now that Xiuya's dad was responsible for supporting them, her mom's superciliousness faded.

A family like this, without much education or economic clout, naturally doesn't bandy about philosophical concepts in conversation. Although the petit bourgeois lived uncertain, difficult lives before Liberation, they don't have any great hatred toward the old society. Of course, they're grateful to the Communist Party and to Socialism for their stable, well-fed existences in the new society, but in the absence of material and spiritual riches, they don't have strong political feelings. Even at the height of the Cultural Revolution, their main concern was how high food prices were going to rise, and if the shops would run out or if they could still get their one-tael ration of sesame oil. As long as these basic needs were met, they weren't really bothered by newspaper announcements about who was getting denounced or rehabilitated. Hence "shallow ideas" are a basic condition of their lives, for good reason.

As for the children of the petit bourgeois, the vast majority shared their parents' fate, either drifting downward into Beijing's large service sector or taking on one of the more labor-intensive industrial jobs. Of course, a very few take advantage of the possibilities offered by society, making the most of their potential to become a cadre or intellectual. Some sons and daughters of cadres and intellectuals were forced into industry, farming, or the army during the Cultural Revolution, and some even ended up in service jobs, but with the reforms in 1977, they swarmed once again into colleges, government departments, research institutes, and cultural organizations. Hardly any stayed on in service jobs, and even if they did, it was usually in administration or related scientific research. Take Xiuya's photo studio. One guy here is the son of two intellectuals. He's appeared in a newspaper article (praising his parents for supporting him in his service job), and he takes care of the technical alterations at the studio (such as eye opening—if someone happens to have their eyes shut in a group photo, where it would be too much trouble to assemble everyone for another shoot, a little "eye-opening surgery" is carried out on the negatives), rather than waiting on people at the counter like Xiuya does.

Now that we know a bit more about her background, it's easy to understand why a salesgirl like Xiuya might neglect customers to chat a little with a coworker or even have a full-blown gabfest, and why she feels justified taking her time to check the stock and tally receipts.

This psychological state is a kind of resistance. Viewed through the lens of their "shallow ideas," we can understand that they achieve a sort of balance by ignoring their customers, or by serving them desultorily without bothering to pause their conversation. It's a way for them to assert their independence, to make it clear the customers need them more than they need the customers. They weren't born to serve, so a certain human cost is required from the clientele in order to receive service. Similarly, the reason they wait for a customer to show up before they begin checking the stock or receipts is to demonstrate the serious nature of their work, and to emphasize that their job comes with an easily over-looked technical aspect. (Who says they're just here to fetch and carry?)

In a Socialist service industry, there are indeed certain advanced individuals who wholeheartedly focus on the customers' needs. What makes them advanced is that they have carried out a deep humanist study of themselves and their community, allowing them to see their work at the counter as a form of noble sacrifice, part of a glorious whole. These people would never behave like Xiuya, but Xiuya and her ilk could never reach this deeper way of thinking, essentially because of their lack of education. For instance, Xiuya has no concept of three-dimensional space and isn't clear on recent events in Chinese history (or, for that matter, less recent events). She saw *The Hunchback of Notre Dame* and thought it was an interesting movie, but if you asked her which country or era it took place in, she wouldn't be able to tell you. She works at a photo studio, but has only the vaguest idea of what happens to light-sensitive materials to turn them into images. If you want a young petit bourgeois such as Xiuya to have a Socialist awakening and embrace the ideals of Communism, you must begin by inculcating in them the fundamentals of astronomy, the development of biological organisms, and basic Chinese history—because when you get right down to it, Socialism-Communism is basically a branch of science, which is to say, a form of culture, and a highly sophisticated culture at that.

Today is December 12, 1982, and civilization on our planet continues to move forward. In countries where technology and manufacturing are more advanced, computer usage is becoming widespread. In our fatherland, many modernizing projects are proceeding full steam ahead. In Beijing, progress is constant, without a moment's pause. The raised intersections of the second beltway have already been constructed, and new buildings are rising one after another from the ground like bamboo shoots. Yet Pan Xiuya, a most ordinary member of Beijing society, is unable to grasp the spirit of philosophical thought and enter the next stage of her existence.

After the mental prison of 1966 to 1976, it was only in 1978 that people began speaking publicly about love having a place in society. In 1979, Zhang Jie gave it even more prominence by proclaiming, "Love must not be forgotten." By 1980, love was all the rage in newspapers and on the silver screen. People no longer worried there was no room for love in society—instead, they grumbled it was taking up too much space. Since 1981, there've been ever more colorful and inventive ways of expressing love. Some brave souls have even begun discussing extramarital affairs and the "rational, changeable nature" of love. In this climate of increasing fervor, many fashionable young things choose the theories that accord with their own understanding and boldly put them into practice.

None of this has much impact on Pan Xiuya's life. Ignorant of the careful constructions of authors and the praise or criticism of reviewers, she reads nothing but magazines—in fact, only movie magazines, and even then only for the pictures. The photo studio does have a newspaper subscription, but she only ever looks at the cinema listings and cartoons.

Ever since she turned twenty-two, the shallow idea that she ought to get married has reared its head in her. Her thoughts on this matter are very simple: you need to find the best partner you can within your limitations. She lacks imagination and has no sense of romance whatsoever. She isn't the sort of girl who'd watch that British film *The Slipper and the Rose* and imagine herself as Cinderella before falling asleep each night. She's supremely pragmatic. Between the ages of twenty-two and twenty-three, she decided she ought to mount an assault on the intellectual world. Back then, the rallying cry for intellectuals was "implementing policy," but a girl like Pan Xiuya had long ago decided what policy she would like to implement with them, and what's more, yearned to join their circles. She once tried her hand with the "eye-opening" boy at the photo studio, and was so bold as to show up at his house with a bag of fruit while he was ill in bed. It became clear to her, not only from the boy himself but also from the way his parents looked at her, that this scheme would never come to fruition. At least she knew when to beat a retreat. Now she understood how both her older sisters had ended up marrying laborers. At the age of twenty-four, she went on an inordinate number of dates, set up by matchmakers, with guys from national enterprises. She'd meet them once, twice, thrice, sometimes even five or six times. There weren't many she liked who didn't like her back. Instead, they were generally happy to carry on, and she was the one to slam on the brakes—there was always something wrong with these boys. Either they were too short, or had too many family responsibilities, or annoyed her by pawing at her as soon as they stepped into a park. Only when she was pushing twenty-five did she finally lower her sights to people at her level. Her eldest brother's wife drove a motorized three-wheeler for a department store and frequently had to drop off makeup and other small items. As a result, she got to know the salespeople in the toiletries department, Xue Jiyue being one of them. He always helped her unload her cargo, and seemed like the reliable, down-to-earth sort. Xiuya's sister-in-law asked around and learned that this boy's parents were honest folk with good pensions, his elder brother was already married, and there were no other people in his family who might be a burden. They had a room he could move into when he got married. Not a bad setup, in other words. He was seven months older than Xiuya, five-foot-nine with a charming face, an even temper, and the endearing habit of blushing a little when talking to strangers. She decided to set her sister-in-law up with him. Xiuya went to the park three times with Jiyue and visited the Xue household twice. That's all it took—she declared she was willing.

Love! The word has never entered Xiuya's mind. She only has the idea of finding a "partner." The simple words "I love you" have never passed between her and Jiyue. All they've ever said to each other is "I'm willing."

She's going to get married. To be part of a new family. To live a new life. She wanted a husband who was "presentable," but not so presentable that he'd go around raising hell and embarrassing her in front of the family. That's exactly the partner she found. Just like that tape deck they got—the brand isn't great, but what matters is that it's a quad-speaker.

This is her wedding day. "Turning over a new page in her life," "the blossoms of love producing fruit," "someone to take an oar alongside you in the boat of life"—she's never heard any of these poetic sentiments.

Even so, sitting in the little car, she feels happy. Zhan Liying's thoughtless comment annoyed her, but the mild displeasure is easily blown away by the gusting wind of joy. And look, they've reached the hutong. *Pik-pik-pak* go the firecrackers. "Just one string?" Seventh Aunt grumbles. "They ought to have two, one on either side of the gate." Xiuya is grateful that Seventh Aunt is so protective of her, but also satisfied with her in-laws' arrangements. She's happy that there were firecrackers at all. The brand may not be so good, but after all, it's a quad-speaker.

PART FOUR

午时

Wu Shi

Time of the Horse: 11:00 a.m. to 1:00 p.m.

CHAPTER 15

This is how Beijingers get married.

The bride has arrived, and pretty much all the guests are here. Now it's time for the folding table to be carried into the center of the nuptial chamber, with extra leaves turning the square into a larger circle, ready for the first time to bear such a glorious load.

Of course, one room with a single table wouldn't be enough; Uncle and Auntie Xue's quarters are pressed into service too, and their old eight-immortals table is brought into the middle.

Don't imagine that the Xues' wedding banquet consists of a mere two tables. This is just the first round—their best friends and closest relatives. Later, from around two to seven, many more visitors will show up, and though some won't partake, that's another couple of tables' worth. Counting up the total number of visitors and the plates of food they'll get through, it's roughly equivalent to an eight-table banquet.

The first round of guests arrived before the bride. Among them are the bride's "accompanying matron," Seventh Aunt; Xue Jikui, the son of Jiyue's late uncle (that is, Jiyue and Jihui's cousin); Jiyue's eldest aunt, her second daughter and the daughter's husband (Jiyue's cousin and cousin-in-law), and their two children; Jiyue's second aunt's eldest son (another cousin, the only member of Second Aunt's family left in Beijing); Master Tong, Jiyue's manager (a scrawny man in his forties—Xue Yongquan included him in the first round because of his part in bringing the couple together); their matchmaker, Wu Shuying (Xiuya's sister-in-law, who does not have the day off—her motorized three-wheeler is parked by the gate, and after the meal she's going back to work delivering goods);

Manager Wang from Auntie Xue's workplace (a plump guy in his fifties—Auntie Xue has no living relatives, so she invited her boss to represent her side of the family); Xue Yongquan's sworn brother, Mr. Yin (five years older than Yongquan, still in good health), and his ten-year-old grandson; and of course the very first person to show up, our old friend Luo Baosang.

Auntie Xue is starting to feel she doesn't have enough eyes, ears, mouths, or legs. No sooner has she ushered someone to their seat than the next person is there to be greeted. Even as her heart churns with worry because her elder son, Jihui, hasn't turned up yet, she loudly exhorts her neighbor Nanny Zhan to come join the celebration, pastes a big smile on her face as she speaks to Manager Wang, then loses it when she catches a glimpse of Luo Baosang. She's trying to count how many people are here but somehow can't keep the numbers straight. Her heart is sweet yet bitter, joyful yet anxious. When she runs into Zhaoying in the crowd, she lashes out, "Look at you, having a good time while I do all the work. Nice of you to stand and watch the fun!" Zhaoying knows at least a third of this anger is aimed at her absent husband and only two-thirds at her personally, though the whole is unjust. Isn't her father-in-law over there earnestly greeting the guests too? Hasn't she been rushed off her feet herself? But this isn't the moment to pick a fight, so she smiles blandly and continues her hostessing duties.

Seventh Aunt's sharp eyes evaluate the scene before her. Among the guests are a prosperous-looking cadre (Manager Wang), a refined intellectual (Jiyue's cousin-in-law), and a kindly, honest man (Xue Jikui). That's all very satisfactory, but what's going on with that vulgarian (Luo Baosang)? And how does that random old man (Mr. Yin) fit into all this? She can't help feeling resentful on behalf of her niece—why are people like these in the first round of guests? While they were setting up the space, she insisted that the table and chairs be "whole"—nothing touching the bed, and certainly not using the edge of the bed as an additional seat. As a result, Zhaoying had to run out and borrow a neighbor's bench. She hadn't had an opinion about the tablecloth, but as soon as Auntie Xue said, "Let's remove the tablecloth, the plastic might get scorched," Seventh Aunt immediately simpered, "Oh no, we can't do that! Look, there are red flowers in the design—so auspicious! Leave it." Turns out she's here today as the bride's fusspot, an indispensable role in Beijing weddings. Xiuya is the last single woman in the family, and there'll be no more daughters to marry off after this. As a result, Seventh Aunt is throwing herself utterly into the role. Like a famous actor delivering a farewell performance, every move she makes feels completely familiar but is also imbued with melancholy as she fades away. "Oh no!" Having discovered yet another sign of carelessness from the groom's family, she points it out to Xue Yongquan right away. "These two bowls are quite handsome, but how could you arrange the fruit like that?" Xue Yongquan understands right away what she means. The two bowls on top of the dresser each hold a mixture of apples and pears—an inadvertent bad omen because they're splitting up the "pairs." He rearranges the fruit, and all is fine again. Like Auntie Xue, Seventh Aunt, too, is quietly trying to work out how many people are here, but everyone keeps moving, and she can't get an accurate count.

Lu Xichun, the hired chef, watching coolly from the sidelines, is the only one who manages to keep a tally: six hosts (it ought to be seven, but Jihui still isn't here) and fourteen guests. Twenty total in this first round, sixteen adults and four children.

Jiyue feels dazed amid this chaos, as if his brain is swelling, as if he's fallen into a pond and can't swim. His heart races; his senses go into overdrive. Through the cacophony, he clutches at the song coming from the tape deck like a lifeline, the one speck of comfort. For some reason, the only words that stick in his mind are "Happiness is not the drizzling rain." He can't stop thinking about it. If happiness is not the drizzling rain, what is it? A thunderstorm? He wishes it could be a light rain. Oh, if he could only run to the Shicha Seas right this moment, all by himself, and lean quietly against the railing by the water, how wonderful that would be!

For her part, Xiuya feels contented and smug. Seventh Aunt is going to make sure she doesn't get taken advantage of. She feels like someone who's paid her insurance premiums and no longer fears her house burning down. Watching the crisscrossing guests and hearing the sounds of celebration, she's like a butterfly fluttering over a flowerbed, enjoying the spectacle without having to use her brain. When she imagines the gold-plated Swiss Rado watch on her wrist, she feels a tenderness she's never felt before toward her husband, as well as her parents-in-law. For that she's happy to overlook her husband's awkwardness, her father-in-law's carelessness, and her mother-in-law's agitation.

The guests are experiencing a variety of emotions. Some truly wish the couple well and plan to stay for the entire day (Eldest Aunt); others aren't particularly enthusiastic but couldn't turn down such a warm invitation, so why not enjoy a good meal? (Manager Wang); or they're sincere in their good wishes but have gastric ulcers and regard the banquet with trepidation (Master Tong); or they've come in the role of senior relatives, though they aren't close to Jiyue at all (Mr. Yin); or they've been frustrated since they arrived, wishing they could leave after congratulating the couple and handing over their gift, but that would be far too rude, so they have to sit and eat (the bespectacled cousin-in-law, the only intellectual in the family—he graduated college before the Cultural Revolution, and now works as an assistant engineer at a design institute); and naturally, there's also Luo Baosang, who's just here to stuff himself silly.

The cold appetizers arrive. In the nuptial chamber, they get a big platter with a red double-happiness character, as well as four medium and four small dishes. In the other room, they only get four medium ones. Seventh Aunt inspects the display and deems the large platter auspicious and beautifully laid out, with plenty of food to go around. The four medium dishes are sausages (ready-made, flavored with garlic, tea, and egg white, neatly sliced and tastefully arranged), rice noodles (with shredded cucumber and ham), fried peanuts (large kernels probably intended for planting, cooked at exactly the right temperature), and Dezhou boneless chicken (ready-made; the chicken's head is a good size and color). As for the small dishes, there's fried beltfish, fried imitation shrimp, preserved eggs, and cucumber with tomatoes. Seventh Aunt is satisfied with this spread. She could do with a little more of that last dish, but she remembers cucumbers and tomatoes cost more than meat at this time of year and decides not to give them a hard time.

After a bout of confusion—chairs being offered, everyone deferring to everyone else, shuffling around, and rearranging themselves—everyone in both rooms is finally seated. In the nuptial chamber, the couple face south, with Xue Yongquan by the groom and Seventh Aunt by the bride, then Manager Wang, Master Tong, Wu Shuying, the cousin-in-law, Mr. Yin, Xue Jikui, Auntie Xue—her seat is empty as she's hard at work in the cooking tent—and Luo Baosang, who shouldn't even be there in the first place. Eldest Aunt is at the head of the table in the other room. Zhaoying's chair is also empty as she hurries between the tent and the two rooms.

One by one, the bottles of alcohol are opened. Some people alternate between baijiu, wine, and beer, some stick to just two, and some are happy with beer. Others claim they don't drink, but in the end everyone has at least two glasses of different liquids in front of them. Baosang got the beer from Ji's Roast Meats by Silver Ingot Bridge, and though there are only five bottles, it's impressive he was able to do this at such short notice. As he pours everyone a glass, he praises himself for these spoils of war and is filled with a sense of pride that surely justifies the amount of food he's about to gobble.

Before Liberation, Beijing wedding rituals were complicated, to say the least. As soon as the bride got out of the sedan chair, she had to pay her respects to the "symbols of heaven and earth" (that is, statues of the gods), though later this was changed to a red double-happiness character. The couple would then pay their respects to the bride's parents, the groom's parents, and each other (paying their respects, strictly speaking, meant kneeling and kowtowing). Next would be entering the nuptial chamber, lifting the bride's veil, sitting on the bed, changing outfits, eating dumplings (the emcee would feed the couple a dumpling and ask, "Raw?" and they'd have to answer "Yes," because "raw" sounds the same as "having a child") and longevity noodles (a small bowl containing a single very long noodle). After all these rituals, the couple would be exhausted, but a true banquet would only just be getting started—and they'd need to perk up to entertain their friends and relatives. After Liberation, the city cadres, who'd only just taken charge, got involved in wedding ceremonies. Sedan chairs, veils, and idols swiftly vanished from the scene, though the wedding itself remained a complicated ritual of many parts: First, the couple would bow three times each to statues of local leaders, their parents, the officiator, the guests, and each other, then the emcee would gleefully say, "And now three times to me!" A total of eighteen bows, if you were keeping track. Next, the officiator (usually one of their bosses from work) would offer a congratulatory message and the parents would make speeches, followed by more congratulations from the guests. Finally, the bride and groom would "honestly" tell everyone the story of their courtship, which was sometimes embarrassing, but compared to the rituals of the past, this was the segment that felt most revolutionary, unique, and humanistic. Then it was time for the ritual hazing: the couple had to chew on the same piece of candy or grab an apple in their mouths (dangling from a string held by a young man standing on a chair, so they had to leap for it) to break the ice between them. This went on until the Cultural Revolution. Afterward, people went in for quiet ceremonies in which only immediate family—parents and siblings—were invited to a meal behind closed doors, and only then would they distribute the usual wedding candy, inevitably surprising everyone: "Oh, have they already tied the knot?" "You've gone and done it? Why didn't you say anything beforehand?" There were also more formal weddings, of course, which required the following rituals: First, the couple waved Mao's Little Red Book at the local leader and said, "May you have ten thousand limitless lives!" Before 1971, they'd also have to chant, "Wishing you eternal health!" three times. Second, the chief of the Revolutionary Committee (or the Workers' Propaganda Team, or the Army Propaganda Team) would say a few words (usually exhorting the newlyweds to "continue the Revolution of our proletariat dictatorship"). Third, the Revolutionary Committee (or the Workers' Propaganda Team, or the Army Propaganda Team) would present a gift (usually a copy of the Little Red Book with a red silk ribbon around it, probably the fourth or fifth copy the couple would own). Fourth, the couple exchanged vows (generally following the "Three Loyalties" or "Four Boundlessnesses," taking the form of "And we must never forget . . ." or "Let's apply these lessons in our own lives . . ."). Fifth, the entertainment, usually a recitation of Mao's "Three Constant Texts" or one of Madame Mao's model operas. No banquet, just a reception with tea and maybe snacks, to show how thorough the family had been at "destroying the Four Olds and building the Four News." Since the Cultural Revolution ended, there's been a profusion of ways to get married in Beijing. People go in for destination weddings, mass weddings, restaurant weddings, home banquets. Some register the wedding and don't celebrate in any way, others take part in a mass wedding, have a banquet at home, then go off traveling. One trend across the board is worth noting: most ceremonies have cut down or done away with elaborate rituals. Many mass weddings barely bother with the bowing. Today, even Seventh Aunt hasn't made the couple bow to her. The only thing they have to remember is to make the rounds at the start of the meal, toasting their guests in strict order of hierarchy, and everyone's happy.

Jiyue is just standing to pour Seventh Aunt a drink as his father told him to, when Zhan Liying comes rushing in. When Auntie Xue repeatedly asked her to join the banquet, she smiled and declined, so why is she abruptly turning up in the middle of proceedings? She carries a plate of Sichuanese pickles, which she merrily plonks in the middle of the table and proclaims, "You're eating such greasy food today, I brought you a palate cleanser! I made them myself. They're better than the ones at that Sichuanese restaurant in Yarn Hutong. Try them if you don't believe me!"

Seventh Aunt can't believe her eyes. This flibbertigibbet created so much chaos on the way here, and now she's doing it again! Whoever heard of serving pickles at a wedding banquet? Besides, there are exactly nine cold dishes on the table, and nine is an auspicious number. Sticking another one in there spoils the harmony, surely she can see that?

Uncle and Auntie Xue ask Zhan Liying to join them, and Auntie Xue jumps to her feet, offering up her own seat. Liying doesn't accept, just stands there smiling so broadly that her eyes almost disappear. "Come on, quick," she commands Jiyue and Xiuya, "toast your Nanny Zhan. I'm going to be a big help to you from now on."

Jiyue hasn't given Seventh Aunt her drink yet, and now he stands with the bottle tilted in midair, in a quandary. Auntie Xue swiftly pushes her own glass toward Jiyue, and Xiuya nimbly grabs it and holds it up to the bottle. Jiyue understands and starts pouring, but doesn't stop in time and it overflows. Nanny Zhan chortles. "Right up to the brim—excellent!" Xiuya passes the glass over, and Nanny Zhan tosses back her drink, sets the glass down, dabs her lips, and says, "I hope you grow old together! I won't stay, I have guests of my own." She leaves the way she arrived, in a whirlwind.

Seventh Aunt is severely displeased. It seems to her the Xues need a lesson in manners, but she can't very well criticize Nanny Zhan directly. Looking around the room, an obvious topic occurs to her. She clears her throat and affects a shocked expression. "Oh my! Xiuya toasted the next-door neighbor but hasn't offered a glass to her brother-in-law yet! That won't do!" Jiyue's parents blush at these words. Jihui has really let them down. It's his own brother's wedding—how can he not be here yet?

Xiuya misunderstands her aunt, and stands to pour cousin Jikui a drink and light his cigarette, which he hastily declines. Seventh Aunt snorts in derision. Zhaoying happens to come in with the first set of hot dishes just then, so she grabs her arm and says, "Look at you, rushed off your feet. Where's your husband got to? He should be helping you out." Zhaoying smiles grimly. "Him? Help me? The Bell Tower will strike again before that happens."

Now that the four hot dishes are on the table, everyone's attention is drawn by the food, and Seventh Aunt's foray fails to have the effect she'd hoped for.

The first hot course Lu Xichun has prepared consists of moo shu pork, pork chops in tomato sauce, stir-fried lamb with scallions, and cauliflower shrimp. By this point, Luo Baosang has had two bottles of beer and two glasses of baijiu, and the cold appetizers haven't been doing it for him. As soon as the dishes are on the table, his chopsticks shoot out and grab a pork chop with such enthusiasm that tomato gravy sprays across the table, and one drop happens to land on the cousin-in-law's cuff. The cousin-in-law was already having a terrible time. His plate is full of tidbits placed there by the hosts, but he's only nibbled at them and not touched a drop of drink. All he's thinking about is how soon he can decently leave the table, ask his wife to excuse him, and head home. He also happens to be very fussy about his clothes, and today is wearing a jacket of melton twill that he's only just brought back from the tailor, and though his hosts urged him several times to take it off, he didn't want to risk dirtying his pure-white high-quality coarse-knit all-wool sweater, so he claimed he wasn't hot and kept it on. All through the meal, he's delivered each morsel of food to his mouth with the utmost care, partly in order to maintain a certain elegance, but also to keep his outfit pristine. One violent jerk of Baosang's chopsticks, and greasy sauce has spattered his sleeve. "Oh no!" he yelps, and everyone turns to look at him. "How could this have happened!" Seventh Aunt loudly commiserates. "Such good woolen material too. What a shame!" The cousin-in-law almost loses his temper but doesn't want to cause a scene, so he simmers down and sits staring morosely at his sullied garment. Quick as lightning, Baosang pulls out his filthy, wrinkled handkerchief and swabs vigorously at the stain, smiling impudently. "So sorry! A classy guy like you has to keep up appearances. Don't sink to my level!" Seventh Aunt shrieks, "Stop that! The grease will be harder to wash out if you rub it into the fabric." The cousin-in-law's face is turning purple, and he's glaring at Baosang, but it really wouldn't do to let rip in front of all these people, so he gets himself under control and says to his hosts, "Forget it, it's fine." Jiyue can no longer hold his tongue. "What's wrong with you, Baosang?" he says. "There's plenty of food—no need to snatch at it like that." Xue Yongquan chimes in, "Yes, don't get full too quickly, Baosang. There's more deliciousness to come!" Baosang's lips are slick with grease, and the rest of his face is shiny too—he's sweating from the amount he's eaten. Unconcerned, he helps himself to another piece of pork and says with his mouth full, "No matter how much you bring out, I'll eat it all. Can't blame me, I was born with a bottomless stomach!" Then he turns to Manager Wang and pesters him to play a game. Manager Wang thinks this young man is acting like a circus clown, but both hosts and guests have made several rounds of toasts, and it doesn't seem like there's anything more to be said. No point just drinking in silence, is there? Next thing anyone knows, the two men are chanting, "Three for long life, four for courses, six for good luck, eight for horses," as they launch into a thumb battle. Provoked beyond endurance, the cousin-in-law says he has to check on his children, and leaves the table. Seventh Aunt lobs a new bit of gossip toward Xue Yongquan, and Zhaoying brings in the next round of hot dishes: kung pao pork, lion's head meatballs, imitation crab, and mushrooms with rapini (usually it's mushrooms with mustard greens, but there weren't enough of those, so another vegetable had to be pressed into service). These dishes have been selected to present a complementary array of colors: rich red, powdery white, mild yellow, and jade green. Determined to find fault, Seventh Aunt inspects and tastes them, but all she can find to say is, "Where did you find this chef?" Auntie Xue quickly answers, "He's just a young fellow, but he trained under the red chef at Tongheju. He's doing a decent job. The chicken, duck, and fish will come out in a while, see what you think of those." Xue Yongquan says, a little apologetically, "We wanted to have more seafood, but good mussels are expensive right now, and there's no point buying the second-rate ones. Better to make sure the other meats are as good as possible." Seventh Aunt sympathizes. "The likes of us can't afford delicacies. You're doing well if you've got good chicken, duck, fish, and pork."

Seizing a moment when no one is looking their way, Xiuya leans over to Jiyue and whispers in his ear, "Where's the watch?"

Jiyue glances over at the dresser. The small room is even more crowded than usual with the brazier and dining table crammed in. Baosang's chair is right against the dresser. Rather than trying to squeeze past him, Jiyue whispers back, "Why so anxious? As if it could go missing." Zhaoying happens to be walking past just then, and Jiyue nods in her direction. Xiuya takes the hint and bends over her food.

After hours of hard work, Auntie Xue is finally able to sit down to the meal. She spies the two lovebirds whispering to each other, and a flower of happiness blossoms in her heart. This one moment has made up for much of the suffering and toil in her life.

CHAPTER 16

The Technical Report Unit chief who doesn't
acknowledge people.

In late 1982, it's not yet seen as rude to drop in on people unannounced. Visitors don't find it improper, and visitees don't think it strange. Of course, this is a function of societal norms, which, if you look at them closely, have to do with how educated people are. In rural villages, country folk are always going into each other's houses, not even bothering to knock, just stepping in without a word and taking a seat uninvited, or even climbing onto the heated kang platform. Among city laborers, it's fine to pop by a neighbor's place without knocking, but you do at least have to say hello, and anyone from farther off is expected to knock—a hearty thump is fine, though, no need for a refined rat-a-tat-tat. Among cadres, and particularly intellectuals, knocking is definitely expected, and too urgent or heavy a fist is frowned upon. If your gentle tap goes unanswered, slight escalation is permitted—a little louder and longer. (In 1983, doorbells would come into use, and the following year, electronic ones would become fashionable—though people would feel the same about bell-ringing as knocking.) If you hear someone knock at your door or ring your bell, you're expected to call, "Who's there? Who is it?" (Before 1982, not many people had peepholes—the sort you can see through without being seen—as these come from overseas, so you'd have to grab one while traveling or get your friends to bring you one from abroad; at the start of 1983, imported ones from Japan would appear on the market for just ten yuan each, and soon there was no need to ask this question.) Then you open the door a crack to verify the person's identity before letting them in. If the person for whom the visitor is looking happens not to be home, you say they've gone out and you don't know when they'll be home, then shut the door—or occasionally you might politely say, "Would you like to come in and wait?" But the visitor should see the look in your eyes and tactfully reply, "No need, no need."

As the siheyuan homes of Beijing fade away and are replaced by apartment buildings, people live in closer proximity, but the connections between them have atrophied, and neighbors are often cut off from each other. When visitors arrive, those tightly shut apartment doors feel heartless and stark, unlike the casual welcome that siheyuans offer.

Just as the wedding banquet is at its most raucous, a middle-aged man arrives at the siheyuan gate. He seems about to step in, then steps back again. Next, he paces in front of the gate. When someone comes along on a bicycle, he pretends to be passing by, quickly carrying on to the other end of the hutong, then doubling back.

He is short, with unremarkable features, though his clothes are neat and he wears a blue nylon baseball cap. It's clear at a glance what he is: an intellectual.

This is Pang Qibin, the new chief of the Technical Report Unit at the bureau that Zhang Qilin runs and the cause of a very heated debate between Bureau Chief Zhang and the rest of the Party committee, as they tried to verify that Pang Qibin was suitable for this position.

Mr. Pang is forty-two. Right after he graduated from the University of Science and Technology of China in 1963, he was sent to this organization to write technical reports. He is skilled at foreign languages and seems serious and responsible about his work. He's in the prime of life, and there shouldn't be anything controversial about promoting him to unit chief, except for one complaint shared by all his colleagues: he never acknowledges anyone. When someone walks toward him in a narrow corridor, he drops his eyes when he's still some distance off, and when he draws closer, even if the other person calls out a greeting, he brushes past with his head down. Or if he gets to a meeting early, he refuses to make small talk with anyone else present. When they try to strike up a conversation, he'll answer if he absolutely has to, but otherwise just sits there frostily. As a result, he's extremely unpopular at work. Even the doorman hates him—he picks up his mail in complete silence and hardly ever smiles. Why doesn't he acknowledge anyone? Some think it's arrogance, others that he's aloof and unworldly, but in any case it's definitely a sign of incorrect thinking. He submitted his application to join his local Party branch in 1963, but of course they never considered it seriously. Then in 1982, the first decision made by the newly reshuffled leadership group was to promote Pang Qibin to unit chief. There are eleven people in the Technical Report Unit, three of them Party members: sickly Miss Qin, who attended college in the early days of Liberation and only knows Russian, and two men in their twenties, one who joined the Party as a "Worker-Peasant-Soldier" student and the other when he enlisted in the army. Neither is much good at languages; frankly, they struggle with the actual task of writing technical reports, and you could hardly promote someone like that to unit chief just because he's a Party member. There've never been many Party members in Technical Reports, so they generally combine with members from another administrative division to form a grassroots branch. When the bureau was considering who to elevate to unit chief, debate raged in the branch committee, and someone posed the question, "If Pang Qibin gets the promotion, doesn't that mean we'll have to bring him into the Party soon? Is he qualified?" Miss Qin stood up for him. "Mr. Pang has requested to join the Party for years now. In the past, we didn't help him enough, but after this we can adjust our work. Even if he's not qualified, he'll be suitable once he's unit chief. I'm in my fifties, in poor health, and I only speak Russian—that's too many strikes against me. Not only does Pang Qibin speak good English, he can handle French and German too. Thanks to all the original-language texts he's read over the years, we've had a bird's-eye view of our sector, which has helped the speed and direction of our development. I reckon we should go ahead and promote him." But the bureau committee also heard several sharply dissenting opinions, and Zhang Qilin was at a loss. He sought out Miss Qin for a longer conversation, and they forensically discussed the question of Pang Qibin. What was going on with him? Miss Qin murmured, "People come and go in our team—turnover's really high. The only people who've stayed put from the beginning are me and Mr. Pang. After many years of observation, I can say that Pang Qibin's personality definitely bears the marks of his intellectual upbringing—the idea that if you earn your living through knowledge, you don't need to bend at the waist for anyone and can keep yourself proudly aloof. Of course, his experiences on the road of life will have shaped him too. For instance, I happened to hear that when he was in college, he was unlucky in love and got so depressed he almost killed himself. Maybe it's things like that which made him so introverted and cold.

There's one thing I ought to tell you: when Pang Qibin gets to know you a bit better, he'll suddenly become very lively and chatty, and you'll realize he's much more direct and warmhearted than you'd imagined. If I may draw an analogy, he's like a sugar cube. Put him in a glass of water and he won't dissolve right away, but after a very long time, the water closest to him will taste a little of his sweetness. Okay, so that's not a great analogy, but it does lead us to the problem: he might be able to dissolve more fully, but the process is always going to be slow and gradual. That's my rational analysis, but I also have some intuition into his character: I believe the reason he ignores people, particularly those who've just transferred into our unit, or those from other departments, or people he doesn't know, is extreme shyness. From a psychological standpoint, aren't there people of this sort? It isn't necessarily some deep moral flaw, it could be an unshakable bashfulness that prevents him getting along with people around him." Zhang Qilin repeated Miss Qin's words to his comrades on the Party committee, but the only reactions were shaking heads, sneers, and indifference, which left Mr. Zhang doubtful too. Can you really analyze a cadre the way Miss Qin did?

Sometimes, as the family watches TV, his daughter Xiuzao abruptly says something like, "Dad, in your Party committee, are you a reformist or conservative?" There's nothing odd about her asking this—TV dramas are meant to reflect contemporary society and hence depict only three types of cadres (the third is "fence-sitter"—the sort who just muddles through). Zhang Qilin only smiles at these questions and answers, "It's not that simple." It's true, life is not as simple as it seems on TV. He doesn't want to criticize any particular TV serial, not that he ever watches any of them all the way through. He'd like to, but there isn't time. When he gets home, even if he manages not to slump in front of the TV, it's still hard to avoid visitors or the telephone dragging him back into the busyness of work.

As for the question of whether Pang Qibin is suitable for promotion, it just so happens that the new Party committee members are of a reformist mind-set and are determined to pay more attention to the work of the Technical Report Unit—hence the heated debate over who should be the new unit chief. This dragged on until October, when they finally announced Pang Qibin's appointment.

What happened next was interesting: Reactions within the unit itself, whether they agreed with this decision or not, were rather muted. Those in other departments, particularly Party-member comrades, uniformly felt the bureau's new leadership had made the wrong choice. They'd even discuss it over lunch—"Just wait and see, the Tech Report Unit is going to fall apart." After more than a month, not only has the unit not fallen apart, it's flourishing. At the last all-bureau meeting, the unit shared its report on technical trends in other countries, with Pang Qibin "threading the needle" as lead presenter: making introductory remarks, bringing in each speaker and transitioning to the next, then wrapping the whole thing up so all this profound, brand-new information managed to smoothly and clearly penetrate every person's mind. Afterward, some people who hadn't had a good impression of Mr. Pang exclaimed, "So he doesn't always look so stern, after all!"

When Pang Qibin runs into colleagues in the corridor, though, he continues to ignore them. Just a few days ago, Zhang Qilin spotted him at a distance, but before he could wave, Mr. Pang abruptly ducked into the restroom. Evidently he's unable to break his habit of not saying hello and has begun to fear others doing it to him.

Now here he is at Zhang Qilin's siheyuan gate. He, too, finds his own behavior odd. Why can't he, a grown man, get rid of this detestable shyness? Determination to do battle with his bashfulness drove him, earlier this morning, to ride his bike all the way to the office, where he planned to force a smile and a pleasant word, as he picked up his mail, to chip away at Doorman Qi's implacable dislike. But Doorman Qi has endured enough of Mr. Pang's cold shoulder— how was he supposed to know he'd had a change of heart today? He didn't even look up, leaving Mr. Pang to slink in and out silently. Next, he headed upstairs to the report unit to retrieve a foreign-language booklet, and who should he meet coming down the stairs but Old Mr. Fu, the head of the Administrative Division. Old Fu called out a greeting, and Mr. Pang instinctively looked away, then immediately despised himself for falling back into bad habits, and exerted himself to turn his gaze back on Old Fu, by which time Old Fu was already brushing past him, forming the thought, *This Pang Qibin is really an utter . . .* , and Mr. Pang blurted out, "Mr. Fu!" Then, looking him right in the eye, "You, uh, you're here on a, um, Sunday . . ." Momentarily startled by this unexpected phenomenon, Old Fu gathered himself and replied, "I have work to do! Bureau Chief Zhang's going overseas today, and I'm driving him to the airport. He was supposed to leave first thing this morning, but now he's got me picking him up at two. I'm off to find a car and driver. How about you?" Mr. Pang relaxed a little and said, blushing bright red, "I'm, I'm just here to pick up a book." If Old Fu hadn't known about his peculiar temperament, this awkward display would have made him think Mr. Pang was here for some nefarious purpose. Further wrestling with his shyness, Mr. Pang made a supreme effort to chat a little more and learned that Zhang Qilin would be away for about a month in West Germany, France, and the United States before returning to Beijing via Hong Kong.

Pang Qibin fetched the booklet from his office. As he walked back down the stairs, an idea popped into his head: he ought to go see Bureau Chief Zhang before he left for the airport. He couldn't have said whether this felt so urgent because he had a request to make, or simply because it would be a further assault against his weak spot, this cursed shyness.

After making his way to the neighborhood, Pang Qibin parked his bicycle by a department store on West Drum Tower Street and went inside to give himself a moment to stiffen his resolve. He caught sight of himself in a mirror—he looked even more full of guilt and self-loathing than usual. He thought: *If I were a woman, or a slender, effete man, maybe people would understand my shyness, and I wouldn't be suffering like this. Instead, I've been saddled with this stubby body, protruding gut, and a face—how shall I put this? Objectively, it's bulging with unsightly chunks of flesh—yes, that's fair, you could slice off the two gobbets under my eyes and show them to writers to define the word "bulbous," or maybe put them in a literary museum. Who'd understand or believe this foolish, clumsy body could contain such a delicate soul!* He shivered and walked away from his reflection. Waves of cold passed over his body. A couple of days ago, he saw Bureau Chief Zhang in the corridor and instinctively took refuge in the toilet, only to run into someone else coming out, but before that comrade could nod in greeting, Mr. Pang had lowered his head in panic and hurried right past.

"This is a sickness," he decided. "I'm not well." The hospital affiliated with their bureau doesn't have a department that could treat such an illness. He's found enough information in foreign books to gauge his own symptoms, but other than increasing his anxiety, this hasn't done any good. It's incredibly difficult to treat a mental condition on your own, and he knows he needs the help of a qualified psychiatrist to patiently guide him through this. The strange thing is, his symptoms vanish when he's at home—he smiles and chats with his wife and kids, and with good friends when they visit, and he even displays a sense of humor. As soon as he steps out of his front door, and especially when he's among people he doesn't know well, the problem reasserts itself.

When Miss Qin hinted at what was about to happen, and when Zhang Qilin formally told him he was going to be promoted to unit chief, what went through Pang Qibin's mind? No one could ever guess. Was he shocked? Overwhelmed? Indifferent? Apprehensive? None of these things! His first thought was, "It's perfectly true, I'm the most suitable person for this job. I know how to guide us through the next stage of our work. I ought to be given this opportunity. I'll make sure our Technical Report Unit gathers the newest and most important information from all over the world at the greatest possible speed, then get it organized and analyzed quickly, so the higher-ups can use it in developing strategy. I can do this." He certainly can. When he's at work delegating duties, guiding younger comrades, inspecting everyone's work, going through data, and proofreading draft reports, he's not shy at all. Outside his actual work, though, when he has to participate in regular human interaction, he seizes up helplessly. People haven't shown him much sympathy, which has affected his ability to lead his comrades in the unit and made it difficult to coordinate with the bureau's other departments. He can feel this, which is why he's so determined to correct this deficiency in his character—but it isn't easy.

He walked out of the department store and stood for a while by the bicycle rack, staring into space, before deciding to leave his bike here and walk to Zhang Qilin's home. He knows the address because, after becoming station chief, he sent him a letter detailing the issues involved in increasing the unit's head-count, which startled Zhang Qilin—not because of its contents, but because the Technical Report Unit is in the same building as the bureau chief's office, and Mr. Pang could easily have sought him out for a conversation or phoned his office or home, but no, he wrote a letter. That's the sort of person Pang Qibin is: he'd rather write a letter than talk, even on the phone. Perhaps the unfortunate end of his college romance was brought about by this inexplicable behavior?

Today, though, Pang Qibin is doing battle with his damaged psyche. He sees the difficulty, and is charging ahead regardless. Having finally made it to Zhang Qilin's siheyuan, he is brought up short by the sight of a motorized three-wheeler by the gate. What's wrong with him? This vehicle, an inanimate object, is enough to make him shrink into himself. There will be complete strangers in there. Can he go in without acting bizarrely? Besides, he's just noticed the rich fragrance of cooking in the air. He glances instinctively at his watch, and oh no, it's past eleven. How can he barge into the Zhang household so close to lunchtime without an appointment? Wouldn't that seem abrupt and rude?

He almost steps in, but retreats. He paces in front of the gate and along the hutong. A strapping young man comes through the gate, looking furious for some reason, stomping quickly past him. This is Tantai Zhizhu's husband, Li Kai. Pang Qibin has no idea who he is, but his passing by is calming. Clearly, people live everywhere with their own joys and sorrows, rages and fears. He's not the only unbalanced one, so there's no need to be so hard on himself. With this realization, he summons his courage and walks toward the siheyuan. Only now does he notice the red double-happiness characters on either side of the gate and the confetti littering the ground. As he steps in, he feels his heart grow unspeakably heavy and has to tell himself: *I'm here to see Bureau Chief Zhang on a very important matter, yes, this really is important, truly important.*

CHAPTER 17

The bureau chief receives an uninvited guest and a
whistleblower's letter.

"Dr. Yu! Someone's here looking for your husband."

Dr. Yu feels a prickle of unease at this sudden cry.

It's Zhan Liying shouting. Pang Qibin quickly realized Zhang Qilin didn't
live in the outer courtyard, so he made his way inside, and deduced from the
commotion that one of the households was having a wedding. For a moment,
he couldn't work out who lived here and if Zhang Qilin was among them, or if
there was a third section to the siheyuan. Nanny Zhan happened to be passing
by and called out to Dr. Yu as she pointed him in the right direction.

Dr. Yu can't wait to move into an apartment building, precisely because
siheyuan living is full of these disruptions. She's given her husband strict instructions to get an electric doorbell and peephole while he's abroad. The first thing
she'll do in their new place is install these two essential items, and that's the last
they'll have to hear of people like Zhan Liying randomly screaming.

Although she can see Pang Qibin approaching through the glass panel in the
front door, Dr. Yu makes no move to let him in. Not until he's actually standing
there rapping does she pull the door open, look him up and down, and say,
"Who are you looking for?"

Pang Qibin flushes red, but he's got his back to the light, so Dr. Yu doesn't
notice. She also doesn't detect the tremor in his voice when he says, "I'm looking
for Comrade Zhang Qilin . . . I mean Mr. Zhang . . . Bureau Chief Zhang . . ."

Dr. Yu makes her voice as gentle as she can. "What a pity, he's just about to
head out. He's part of the delegation that's going overseas."

"I know, I know." Mr. Pang's tone turns brusque, which displeases Dr. Yu—why is he being so impatient? But actually, Pang Qibin is inwardly exhorting himself: *No matter what, just stay calm, make sure you get what you want.* He raises his voice a little. "I know he's flying off this afternoon, but I have something urgent to discuss with him. It's really important."

Dr. Yu laughs frostily. Everyone seeking out her husband thinks they have urgent business. She's seen far too many of them, and honestly, some have trivial issues to discuss, others just want advice about mistresses or divorces, all of which exhausts Qilin and does him no good at all. What might this individual be here for? Judging by his appearance, this "urgent" matter is probably something to do with his job title or salary or deployment. Keeping her face blank, she says, "Mr. Zhang is leaving shortly. If this is urgent, you'd do better to talk to one of the other bureau bosses."

She is about to shut the door when Mr. Zhang comes into the room. Looking over Dr. Yu's shoulder, he exclaims, "Oh, Qibin! I thought I heard your voice. Please, come in!"

Dr. Yu steps aside, leaving her husband to receive his guest, and goes into the kitchen. Her daughter Xiuzao looks up from the noodles she is cooking and asks, "Who was it?" Dr. Yu sighs. "Just imagine—news gets around so fast! Someone heard your dad's flight was delayed and came running to see him." Xiuzao says, "It's almost lunchtime. Should we ask him to eat with us?" Dr. Yu sighs even more heavily. "The two of us should go ahead and eat first, we'll see how it looks."

How it looks is extremely clear: more likely than not, they'll have to ask him to stay.

Zhang Qilin would love to know why this man has suddenly shown up at his door, when he normally doesn't acknowledge people, would rather write a letter than speak on the phone or in person, and ducked into the bathroom just a few days ago rather than say hello. When he has visitors from the bureau, Mr. Zhang will generally cut to the chase and ask, "What is it? Has something come up?" But now he suppresses the urge to be so direct. Instead, he makes tea and casually remarks, "Did you see? Our siheyuan is quite bustling today—there's a wedding going on. The bride and groom are both dressed Western-style, looking pretty good."

Pang Qibin was prepared to be asked "What is it?" as soon as he sat down, and is thrown by the way Mr. Zhang doesn't seem to find anything odd about this sudden visit. What's with this small talk, as if he's a regular visitor? This is the scenario he's least equipped to deal with. He sits bolt upright in the armchair, fists clenched and pressed rigidly between his thighs, staring at Mr. Zhang with no idea what to say.

Zhang Qilin carries on breezily, trying to dispel the awkwardness. "It's not too cold, is it? Looks like we're in for another mild winter. Our house is fitted with something called a 'radiator.' My wife and daughter put it in, seems to work quite well. If you're warm, feel free to take off your jacket."

"I'm okay, not too warm . . ." Pang Qibin feels as if he contains two selves, and one is mocking the other: *What are you so scared of? You look like a thief who's just run into a police officer.* The other self huddles in a corner, hugging his shoulders as if his clothes are too thin to keep out the chill, feebly defending himself: *But I really am innocent, I don't know why I'm like this.*

Zhang Qilin looks at him and sighs inwardly. How hard it is to understand another person! What kind of key does he need to unlock the door of Pang Qibin's character? Largely because of the headache posed by Mr. Pang, he borrowed a couple of books from the bureau library, one on psychiatry and the other introducing the foreign topic of "behavioral studies." Unfortunately, so far he's only glanced at their forewords and tables of contents. There just isn't time! Now he reminds himself, *When you're dealing with someone like Pang Qibin, it's best to engage him in professional conversation. That's when his mind is clearest, and his thoughts flow most smoothly.* And so he changes the subject. "In the latest issue of *Information and Documentation,* you had a piece on international trends in SP development that I found most interesting. I'm leaving for Frankfurt this afternoon with a delegation—we'll be in West Germany for a little while, and then we're heading to America via Paris. While I'm in the States, I'll make sure to take the opportunity to check out this new sequence you mention in your materials."

Sure enough, Pang Qibin's eyes light up. "Actually, according to Alvin Toffler in *The Third Wave,* the SP sequence we mention in that report is still in the second wave of historical change, even if it is the highest benchmark reached by SP so far. But this so-called third wave is going to transform the scale and standardization of series production, leading to short-term production lines that can be partly or wholly customized."

"I noticed that," says Zhang Qilin happily. "You came at exactly the right time—I was going to ask for your informed opinion. I recently read a couple of abstracts put out by the ministry—one was of *The Limits to Growth*, that book by American scholars, including the Meadowses, commissioned by the Club of Rome, and the other was of Toffler's *The Third Wave*. My instinct is we can't bury our heads in the sand and ignore the warning bell that the Meadowses and others are ringing, but their pessimism is unwarranted. Toffler's thesis is more persuasive and worth studying, though some of his conclusions are a bit arbitrary, especially where he talks about development in the third world. Miss Qin tells me you've read both these books in the original language. Could you tell me what Toffler says about the explosion of small businesses in the West? The abstract oversimplifies that section."

Pang Qibin frees his hands from between his thighs and leans back in his chair as he grows expansive. "It's hard to speak objectively about his point of view because I happen to think what he says about this so-called explosion of small businesses in the West couldn't be more biased. First of all, his premise doesn't have a leg to stand on. I've seen the data on American enterprises, and yes, there were ninety-three thousand new businesses in the States in 1950, compared to six hundred thousand in 1980, but while small businesses might be springing up willy-nilly, they're also folding in large numbers. On average, thirty percent of them go bankrupt within a year, fifty percent within two, and eighty percent within five years. So I believe the state of small businesses in the West is a much more complex economic issue, and it's hard to make such a glib assessment. But I'm not answering your question, am I? All right, let me begin by summing up Toffler's main points . . ."

And just like that, they're deep in conversation, getting on like a house on fire. By the time Xiuzao brings out the noodles and Dr. Yu urges them to come eat, they're laughing and chatting, both completely at ease.

As soon as he stops talking shop and faces the prospect of joining the family for a meal, though, Pang Qibin immediately grows flustered again. He jumps up from the armchair and clumsily refuses. "No need, thank you, I'm not hungry, not hungry at all."

Zhang Qilin tries to persuade him, and even takes him by the arm, but he won't budge. Then Pang Qibin has a realization: he hasn't actually mentioned the most important matter, the one he came here to talk about. Now's the moment! Quickly, before the momentum of their conversation can disappear altogether, he says loudly, "Mr. Zhang, there's actually something else I was hoping you could help me with. I saw an ad in a foreign magazine for a book being published in America this year that's even more groundbreaking than *The Third Wave*. I asked several libraries, but they aren't bringing it in. As you're going to the States, I wondered if you could get a copy? It's *Megatrends: Ten New Directions Transforming Our Lives* by the American futurist John Naisbitt." He produces a fountain pen and notebook and bends over the dining table to write the author's name and book title in English. He rips out the page and hands it over, then takes his leave. Seeing that nothing will persuade him to stay, Bureau Chief Zhang walks him out. As they pass through the courtyard, he says, "Really, would it hurt to stay and eat some noodles? Comrades from the bureau often stop by, and they always take potluck." Mr. Pang keeps walking. At the gate, Zhang Qilin shakes his hand and says, "I'll definitely find a way to get the Naisbitt book for you. And you must visit again—see you when I get back!" Pang Qibin walks away, not looking back. His heart is suddenly lighter, and he feels somehow more substantial.

As Zhang Qilin heads back, Xun Lei pops up from the side courtyard and smiles to see him. "Oh hello, Uncle Zhang! What a coincidence—I was on my way to your place."

"Come on in," says Mr. Zhang. "Xiuzao's at home today, you young people can talk."

"I saw you had a visitor, otherwise I'd have brought this over sooner." He hands Mr. Zhang a letter.

Zhang Qilin usually gets his mail at the office, just as Dr. Yu gets hers at the hospital, and Xiuzao at her school. The mail carrier rarely brings anything—in fact, the siheyuan doesn't have a mailbox. The carrier just shouts into the entrance, "Mail!" (or sometimes, "Newspaper!"), and one of the Xuns or someone from Zhizhu's family picks up the item and delivers it to whichever household it needs to go to.

Puzzled, he accepts the envelope. Who could this be from? Apart from that one letter from his recent visitor, Pang Qibin, he can't recall anyone who's written to him at home in years.

Inside, he tears open the envelope and reads the message as he tucks into his ground pork noodles.

Dear Bureau Chief Zhang,

We know you're very busy, but this needs to be brought to your attention. Mr. Fu Shandu, the head of your Administrative Division, has been using an ingenious tactic of "emptying out the reserves" to help himself to your bureau's allocation of govern-ment-built housing for midcareer intellectuals, in order to provide apartments to the so-called famous artist Luo Jishan, who is not an employee of your bureau. It's unclear if you're quietly complicit, or just in the dark. One thing we do know is that in your living room hangs a "masterpiece" that Luo Jishan "humbly" presented to you—although the landscape and figures are very beautiful, this artist has painted a similar style of picture at least ten times, and used his "masterpieces" as bribes to gain housing three times to our knowledge. We sincerely hope you still hold the Party dear in your heart, and will therefore curb your practice of collecting art. First wash your own hands clean, then investigate Fu Shandu's behavior. We have written to the ministry's disciplinary committee revealing this information, and also wanted to let you know, so you can exercise self-discipline for the sake of the Party!

For reasons you will understand, we provided actual evidence and used real names in our letter to the ministry. They have no knowledge of our letter to you. Please trust in our good inten-tions, and be magnanimous enough to forgive any offense we have caused.

With respect from,
Two members of another work unit
December 11, 1982

When he gets to the end, Zhang Qilin reads it again. He has lost his appe-tite. Involuntarily, his eyes drift to the painting on the wall—a traditional Chinese painting in a fancy frame, illustrating a poem by the late Tang poet Yu Fen, "Sunrise Musings in a Mountain Village." The artist scrawled the verse on the picture:

Outside the door lie fields of millet, and the neighbor stays
    at the flood.
Choppy waves on southern streams this morning, rain on the
    west river last night.
The shepherd boy in a short straw coat, flute at his waist,
    waits for the mist to rise.

Below that is a more intimate message: "Humbly presented in late spring 1982 to Brother Qilin, who banished weariness and stirred unworthy Jishan's brush." Beneath this dedication and the fine balance of black and white in the bottom-right corner are two stamps, one negative and square, one positive and the shape of a gourd. This picture has been hanging there more than six months, and Zhang Qilin sometimes gazes idly at it, which has indeed "banished weariness." True, Old Fu brought him the painting, and he accepted it after a quick glance, without much thought. He met Luo Jishan at a hotel, and they naturally struck up an acquaintance—Mr. Zhang was there for a foreign affairs conference, and Mr. Luo had been invited to create an artwork for the hotel—as their rooms happened to be next to each other, and they often ended up sharing a table at mealtimes. Zhang Qilin never asked him for a painting, not because he was worried about how it would look, but simply because the thought never occurred to him. It was completely the same to him whether or not he had a picture hanging in his living room. When Old Fu brought this to him, he thought he might as well take it, put it on his wall, and glance at it from time to time. How could he have known it was actually an ambush?

"Hey, what's wrong? You're not eating your noodles. Why are you just staring into space?" Dr. Yu asks. "Did that Pang person disturb you? Where did this letter come from? Are the noodles too bland? I can add some soy sauce if you like."

"No need." Zhang Qilin gobbles his noodles, then folds the letter and puts it in his pocket. Much calmer now, he goes to the armchair, lights a cigarette, leans back, and half closes his eyes.

"Why not have a nap? Old Fu's coming to get you at two, isn't he? I'll wake you up at one thirty," says Dr. Yu as she clears the table. "You're all packed, so you'll just need to get changed."

"That's fine." Mr. Zhang's eyes open wide, and he suddenly seems full of energy. He turns to his wife and says cheerfully, "I'll have plenty of time to sleep on the plane. I'm going to read for a while." He stands and heads to the inner room, then turns back at the doorway. "While I'm gone, get Xiuzao to take that painting off the wall, will you? Just roll it up, and it can stay in the drawer for now."

Dr. Yu is surprised. "Why? It looks good there. Are you afraid it'll get damaged? Did you hear that Luo Jishan's work is going up in value? But we're not thinking of this piece as an investment, so what's the harm if it gets a bit worn out?"

Zhang Qilin laughs. "How could this picture be worth anything? People tell me he's done at least ten similar ones. Just take it down. I've got my reasons." With that, he strides into the room and starts reading.

He isn't actually calm, of course. The book of psychiatry is open in front of him, but he can't focus. Apart from his inner turmoil, the external circumstances aren't helping—the Xues' wedding is still going on in the courtyard, and a barrage of noise hits him, more ear-splitting than ever.

CHAPTER 18

Why aren't the city girl and the country girl getting along?

Guo Xinger arrives to find Mrs. Xun home alone. Everything she sees is surprising and confusing to her. She'd vaguely assumed city people would be better off than country folk in every possible way and is dismayed at the Xuns' tiny, cramped home. Not only is it smaller than Zaoer's new place, these two rooms and kitchen aren't even half the size of her old house. The layout is awful too. She doesn't understand why Master Xun doesn't move the front door and windows so they open out onto the hutong, turning this into a south-facing house. In this small dwelling of a great man, many things seem out of proportion. She begins to feel prouder of where she comes from. In a rush of enthusiasm, she invites Mrs. Xun and her husband to "come stay with us for a bit" before they've exchanged a dozen sentences. After sitting for a while and studying her surroundings more closely, she's humbled again. The house may be small, but every single item of furniture and décor is much more exquisite than anything she's ever set eyes on. Take the couch she's sitting on. The basic shape and structure are nothing new—these "folding sofa beds" are available now in their market town—but its legs rest on chrome-plated casters, each slightly bigger than a walnut, that allow it to be wheeled around easily. That's special. Also, the fabric is the color of a walnut kernel, with a faint sheen to it, and feels amazingly soft to the touch. It looks like it's had nails driven through it, creating dimples in its surface, giving it an arresting appearance. The corners are impeccably finished, with no visible seams. Zaoer's been clamoring for a couch now he's getting married—they should get him something like this! The other furniture—wardrobe, dresser, liquor cabinet, and so on—are also better constructed and more handsome than anything she's seen. Even the tea set Mrs. Xun brings in and the candy box she's lifting the lid off are delicate and well shaped, with intricate designs in elegant colors.

"Try one of these sweets!"

Xinger takes the candy, which looks like a goldfish. She removes the wrapper by its "tail," to reveal a nugget the color of soy sauce. Milk sweets are the best sweets, but they ought to be white, the whiter the better. This is dark brown, but Mrs. Xun offered it to her, so she cheerfully takes a bite—it's sweet and bitter and spicy all at once, and spurts a dribble of liquid onto her. Mrs. Xun laughs. "The outer shell is chocolate, with liquor inside. Don't worry, it won't stain your clothes."

The candy is disgusting. Xinger asks how much it cost, and Mrs. Xun says, "Four eighty a pound. That's a lot, isn't it? My husband and I think they're expensive and don't taste good, but Xun Lei insists on buying them. He chose the couch you're sitting on too—it cost quite a bit more than a regular one. He earns a little extra on top of his salary, doing 'translation.' That means taking words that foreigners have written and changing them into Chinese. Every now and then, he'll get thirty or fifty yuan for that—he calls those 'royalties.' He hands his salary to me every month, but I let him keep his royalties. He likes throwing money around, and not just on himself—he insisted on getting the best of everything for this room. Said he'd pay the extra himself, and he did. Would you like to see his lair?"

Xun Lei's room is dazzling. The outer room was more beautiful than her home, but here it's not even possible to make a comparison. Shock turns to unhappiness, and unfamiliarity leads to contempt. Two boxes are suspended from the corners of the ceiling. Apparently they're called "speakers." So what if they can speak? They shouldn't be hanging in the air—it's weird! Why are they black? That's so depressing. That tray thing on the wall threatens to drive her insane the more she looks at it—the drawing on it could be a person or a dog, or maybe a cloud or a tree, a line here and a squiggle there, what ridiculous nonsense! The bookshelf takes up an entire wall, and wow, he sure has a lot of books, both Chinese and foreign ones. Books are well and good; even if you can't read, you know they're worth more than gold and jewels. It's the way the bookshelf is decorated that confuses her. In her village, tree branches are chopped up and used as firewood, but Xun Lei has placed one on his gleaming bookcase, as if it's a holy figure to be worshipped. Then there are pebbles, like the ones that lie in heaps on riverbanks, laid out like precious treasures. Also a few porcelain figurines: an ox with a cube for a head and a weirdly shaped deer, which is fine, but there's an owl too—that's a bad omen!

"Guess what we're having for lunch?" Without realizing it, Xinger has followed Mrs. Xun back to the kitchen, which is unexpectedly large and has doors connecting it to both rooms. There's a gas tank, a gas cooker, and a full set of cooking equipment, as well as a floor drain, a sink, and a washing machine, and a round dining table covered with a white plastic tablecloth so you can eat right here when you're done cooking. Xinger's eyes dart around the entire room before landing on the counter by the stove, where Mrs. Xun's voice is directing her. "We're making this specially in your honor. It was your Uncle Xun's idea!"

Oh! On the counter is a hele noodle mold. Xinger walks over for a closer look, trying to quell the rising panic. Why is Master Xun making her eat hele noodles? Their lives have been getting better and better—polished rice and wheat flour aren't that expensive anymore. When they have too many meals of steamed cornbread or skillet corn cakes in a row, Zaoer complains and their mom quickly rustles up some egg and chive dumplings. Nobody eats hele noodles nowadays. Their mold is languishing in a storeroom somewhere, long forgotten and probably rusty by now. Yet the first meal she's going to have here, after coming all this way to Master Xun's home in Beijing, is hele noodles!

"That's how nostalgic your Uncle Xun is. Lei and I thought it was hilarious when he first suggested it, but then we thought about it and understood his meaning. He doesn't just want to eat hele noodles with you, he wants Lei to try them too. Look, he made this hele mold himself a few days ago. He might not have much going for him, but he's kindhearted and good with his hands." Mrs. Xun grabs a wad of brown dough and pushes it through the mold so noodles are extruded from the little holes. She chuckles. "This doesn't look right, does it? We couldn't find sweet potato or sorghum flour, so this is just buckwheat. Our local dry-goods store has started selling it, alongside the rice and wheat flour, so people can try something different. We won't just dress this with scallions, vinegar, and garlic, we'll mix in some grilled lamb too. Ha! How about that? We're having meaty hele noodles."

This little speech makes Xinger understand what Master Xun is driving at. At the end of the day, he's treating her like he would his own daughter—or daughter-in-law. The clouds of suspicion dispel, and her heart opens wide. She rolls up her sleeves and says, "Let me make them, Auntie. I'll do it better than you."

Mrs. Xun doesn't try to be polite. "I'm sure you will," she says cheerfully. "Wash your hands and go ahead, then. I'll get on with my other chores."

While Xinger is making the noodles, Master Xun comes home. He hadn't felt like setting out his stall anyway, and when he did, he couldn't concentrate. He would have come home early, but a customer had left a pair of leather shoes the day before and promised to get them that evening. Master Xun had waited until the sky was dark, but there was still no sign of him. Today being Sunday, Master Xun thought this customer was sure to turn up, and being the sort of person who'd rather be let down than let someone else down, he set out his stall at the usual time. Sure enough, the customer showed up around ten and was delighted with Master Xun's handiwork. He's a performer with the National Traditional Orchestra and leaving town for a performance tonight. These shoes are going with him, and he was thrilled to see them ready on time, as good as new! Master Xun would have packed up after that, but then a lady showed up with a snapped high heel. He could hardly leave her to hobble all the way to the north side to find another cobbler, so he painstakingly fixed the heel back in place.

Hearing the bicycle trundling into the courtyard, Xinger looks out the kitchen window and recognizes her long-awaited Uncle Xun right away. Although she's only ever seen him in photographs from more than twenty years ago, his every move is exactly like she's dreamed and imagined! Her hands stop, and she stands frozen. She ought to rush out and call to him as if he were her own father, but somehow her legs have filled with lead and she stays rooted where she is.

As soon as Master Xun steps inside, his wife loudly announces, "Xinger got here early! Look how generous she is. Her mom said you like to drink, so she got you four big bottles of the good stuff. She knows I like sweet things, and got me three cream cakes. Also ten cartons of quail eggs—her little brother Zaoer raises quails. Why didn't you close your stall sooner? Quick, go wash up! Xinger's in the kitchen making hele noodles. Xinger, your uncle's here!"

Xinger comes in and stands before Master Xun. Her heart is full of the most intense emotions, though all she can do to express them is keep her head down, blush, and timidly murmur, "Uncle!"

Master Xun, too, is bursting with feelings he would love to give voice to, but he only smiles and says gruffly, "Xinger, you're here—that's good." With that, he goes into the kitchen to wash his hands and face.

Mrs. Xun quickly sits Xinger back down on the couch, offers her tea and candy again, and follows her husband into the kitchen. She knows what he's about to ask, and sure enough, he says, "Where's Lei? Why didn't he stay home?"

In a low voice, Mrs. Xun says, "He went out with Miss Feng."

Master Xun knows what time Miss Feng got here but hadn't expected her to immediately lure his son away. He's a little upset by this. Not wanting to deceive Xinger, he'd planned to have Lei and Miss Feng both be here when she arrived. He absolutely doesn't want to treat Xinger dismissively by avoiding the issue.

Mrs. Xun can see what he's thinking and hastily explains, "It was my idea—I told the two of them to go for a stroll and pick up some roast lamb from Ji's Roast Meats to have with the hele. I thought it would be better if we told Xinger that he's seeing someone first, before she meets them. If she'd stepped in our front door and been confronted with Lei and Miss Feng right away, without any preparation, it might have been too much of a blow."

Master Xun says nothing, just wipes his face with a towel.

Back in the other room, he settles into a rattan chair, lights his pipe, and begins talking to Xinger. Neither of them is good with words, or indeed facial expressions, and an eavesdropping stranger would wonder why their conversation was so stilted, just bland questions and answers delivered slowly and stutteringly. Their hearts, though, are bursting open like sprouting beans, sending out shoots of pure devotion.

When he hears that Guo Dunzi passed away in the recent turbulence, Master Xun's eyes don't grow damp, but he sucks on his pipe a little longer than before and lets out a strange guttural sound, and the cloud of smoke he exhales is thicker than before. Xinger finds this more moving than any words or tears would have been. When he hears how Xinger's family is now prospering, a faint smile floats lightly across his wrinkled face. He asks how things are going with finding Zaoer a wife, takes a few puffs of his pipe, then steels himself to say, "Xinger, child, I've let your father down. I didn't take care of you like I ought to have. You've come too late. Lei has found a woman he loves. You'll meet her in a short while. I hope you don't mind. You're like our own daughter, and this is your home. There'll always be a place for you here, no matter what you decide to do." He can't go on, so he returns to puffing furiously on his pipe, unable even to look at Xinger. Instead, his eyes rest on the New Year's illustration on the wall, *Child Bearing a Peach*.

Xinger's heart sinks. She'd guessed this; she'd predicted this. When she arrived at the siheyuan today, she thought for a moment it was Xun Lei getting married. Then Mrs. Xun greeted her so warmly, and Xinger asked, "Isn't Xun Lei at home?" Mrs. Xun told her, "He's just gone out, he'll be back in a while," so merrily that she allowed the fantasy and hope to resurface. Now that the truth has finally been revealed, she is honestly finding it a little hard to accept. Even so, how can she bear to watch this dear family friend feel guilty because of her? Is she a petty person like Peach, who thinks of nothing but climbing onto the highest possible branch?

Swiftly regaining control of herself, Xinger summons all the dignity, warmth, and rationality that she can muster and forces herself to sound perky when she replies, "What are you talking about, Uncle? Our families lost touch with each other because we were poor, and everything was so chaotic. My mom sent me to Beijing to visit you all, and also to get Zaoer some decent furniture. I came straight here from the train station. If I didn't think of this place as my home, I'd have gone to a hotel. It's wonderful that Xun Lei has a fiancée. I'm not being funny, but if we had heard this news a few years ago, we wouldn't have been able to give him anything at all; now we can get him a fantastic present! I don't know what to choose, though. I don't know his taste. Have they set a date? I'll leave some money, so he and his wife can get themselves something nice."

This little performance of Xinger's catches Master Xun by surprise. He looks up and, sure enough, she's smiling. For some reason, he feels as if the sight of her is being projected right onto his heart, and feels a sharp pang of regret. This is how his daughter-in-law should be—this face, this temperament, this generosity of spirit!

This is the moment that Xun Lei and Feng Wanmei arrive home.

Wanmei changes the atmosphere in the house, simply by coming in. Without waiting to be introduced, she walks briskly over and extends her right hand. "You must be Xinger? I'm Feng Wanmei. So happy to see you here!"

Xinger hastily gets up off the sofa and tries her best to act normal, but she isn't in the habit of shaking hands. Wanmei has to grab her hand, hold it tight, and pump it up and down.

After calling out "Sir" and "Ma'am" in a loud, relaxed voice, Wanmei bounds into the kitchen, merrily takes the hele mold from Mrs. Xun's hands, and cheerfully gets to work. "We're having hele noodles!" she cries out gleefully.

Master Xun frowns and sucks on his pipe. Xinger sits back down, uncertain what to do. Wanmei's voice is grating on them both. Noise blares from Xun Lei's room—Western orchestral music, which Master Xun detests, and Xinger has never heard before. Borodin's Nocturne. Xun Lei's tape deck came back with him from Britain, so it has newfangled functions like a timer; Wanmei set this before they went out, and now it's clicked on. She cheers when the music starts blaring. "How about it? Didn't I tell you we'd be back in time?"

Wanmei darts abruptly into the living room and calls out, as if she were the hostess, "Come and eat, everyone! We've got some tasty treats for lunch!" Without waiting for Master Xun and Xinger to stand, she spots Xinger's gifts on the liquor cabinet and makes a beeline over to examine them. The quail eggs cause her to hoot with joy. "Ah! The king of eggs! The most nutritious! And aren't they pretty? Like little handicrafts!" But the three cream cakes make her draw a sharp breath. "Xinger, Xinger," she says reproachfully. "I know you mean well, but no one in Beijing would bring so many cakes! There's no fridge here. We won't be able to finish these today, and the leftovers will go bad."

She seems oblivious to how she's displeasing Master Xun and embarrassing Xinger.

Everyone sits around the dining table. Mrs. Xun has prepared some snacks to go with drinks, but Master Xun says, "Let's wait until evening before we start drinking. We'll just have the noodles for lunch." So they stay sober and have the buckwheat noodles fresh from the pot. Xun Lei tries to serve his father some of the lamb from Ji's Roast Meats, but Master Xun moves his plate aside and says, "No, thanks. I'm fine with just the noodles. Give Xinger a little more." He does so, and without looking at him, she says, "That's enough, thanks, I don't eat much." Mrs. Xun asks everyone, "Well? Is it like the real thing? Does it taste good?" Wanmei is the first to answer enthusiastically: "Yes! It's delicious! I never expected it would be this tasty!"

The Nocturne finally ends. Now that his head is no longer full of the din, Master Xun turns to Xinger, who is bent over her food, and says, "Do they still eat cottonseed knots where you are?" Xinger looks up and nods. Wanmei is intrigued. "What did you say? Can you really eat cottonseeds?" Xinger says,

"Why ever not? You mix them with corn flour and boil them. While the water's heating up, you pull the mixture into knots, so some parts cook dry and some stay watery. That's why we call them cottonseed knots. A few years ago, we ate them all the time, but now we have more food to choose from." Wanmei wants to know, "Do they taste good?" And Xinger replies, "Why wouldn't they? They're quite tasty." Wanmei persists: "If they're so tasty, why don't you eat them anymore?" Xinger is silent, and Wanmei asks again. Mrs. Xun can't stand it anymore, and tells Wanmei, "When country folk say something is tasty, that's because they were hungry. Anything you eat when you're starving is going to be tasty. I've had cottonseed knots myself, and they weren't bad at all. Only thing is, if that's all you eat, you can forget about ever shitting again." Xun Lei protests, "Mom, we're trying to eat!" Mrs. Xun smiles and says, "It was Miss Feng who insisted on asking!" Wanmei giggles.

Master Xun's mind remains on Xinger and her father. He asks, "Do people still eat tree leaves?" Again, Wanmei can't resist butting in. "Can you eat tree leaves?" Xinger informs everyone, "Yes, some people still do eat tree leaves, but it's not common. The best ones are willow leaves. You soak them in a trough for a while, changing the water a dozen or so times, to get rid of bitterness. Then you dry them in the sun so they keep longer. Mix them with corn flour and sweet potato flour, and you can shape them into biscuits or steamed buns. When we didn't have enough rice or wheat, tree leaves helped fill the gap. Now that we're doing okay for food, people only eat them out of habit—they can't stop being frugal, or they're so used to living a harsh life that refined foods feel extravagant. When my dad was still around, we had leaves all the time. If he were still with us, I bet he'd insist we eat them now and then."

Master Xun doesn't hear the rest of the conversation. His old battlefield comrade Guo Dunzi has appeared before his eyes. Guo Dunzi was great at fighting, but not so good at his studies. He got the lowest marks in literacy class and couldn't sing to save his life. When the land reforms first started, though, he wrote a "Song of Emancipation" that got 78 points, with the fewest mistakes of anything he did before or since. When he sang this song, though every single note was out of tune, you couldn't hear it without being moved:

> *The sky above the borderlands is oh so blue,*
> *And our productivity will increase, that's true.*

We have houses and we have land,
Food and clothes too, everything's grand—
Oh! Food and clothes too, everything's grand!
No one in this world was born to be poor,
We'll dig up poverty by its roots, to be sure,
And feudalism will vanish now!
Don't forget the Communist Party,
And our great savior, Chairman Mao!

Digging up poverty by its roots didn't make everyone rich right away—instead, they went through a period of struggle. Master Xun thinks back to 1950, when he and Guo Dunzi were reunited on the steps of the Working People's Cultural Palace to the east of Tiananmen. Both of them were in Beijing looking for work after lack of labor and famine caused a poor harvest. Back then, folk up from the countryside would gather in Tiananmen Square, waiting to be hired. He and Guo Dunzi were taken on as temporary staff for an exhibit at the Cultural Palace. They worked there by day and slept at Magala Temple, not far from the palace's eastern entrance. It used to be an imperial palace in the Qing dynasty, then later got repurposed as a Buddhist temple—its official name was Puqing Temple. At the start of Liberation, many itinerant workers ended up staying here, and everyone helped everyone else. Neither Xun Xingwang nor Guo Dunzi had brought bedding, but they didn't go cold that first night—people were willing to share what they had and let them huddle under their blankets. Later on, many of these country folk were hired by Beijing's factories and construction sites as bona fide workers, and though this was a great change in their lives, the transition to prosperity remained slow and fraught with difficulties. Their work units would expand, consolidate, and progress—but also retrench, stagnate, and recede. Master Xun can't help recalling what happened in 1960, when Guo Dunzi's work unit urged its employees to return to their villages. They met at his house to drink after he decided to leave, snacking on Iraqi honey dates and feasting on noodles in thick gravy—back then, this was as good as a banquet. It was on this night that they came up with the plan to marry Xun Lei and Xinger. Guo Dunzi was very serious about this—to his mind, it was the only way to seal their brotherhood. Who could have expected that after saying goodbye, they would never again share a drink, or that so many unimaginable changes would creep over their lives? Now both families, like so many thousands of others, have prospered. If only Guo Dunzi hadn't passed, but lived to see these prosperous times, to see what Xinger and Zaoer have made of themselves. If they could meet once more for a drink, the food on the table and the words in their hearts would surely be sweeter and stronger than ever!

Mrs. Xun notices her husband looking odd, and asks, "What's up with you?"

He comes back to himself and says, dully, "A slight pain in my chest. I'll lie down for a while, the rest of you enjoy your meal." He stands up, and turns to Xinger. "Remember, this is your home, no need to be polite. Spend time with Lei and Miss Feng. You young people ought to have a good chat."

"What's wrong, Uncle?" Xinger is anxious. "Are you not well?"

"It's all right, just an old injury," Mrs. Xun reassures her. "He got it more than ten years ago during a war preparation exercise. You know what a hard worker your uncle is. They were supposed to unload a train. There were a dozen or so people on the ground. He and another fellow were going up into the carriage and bringing down sacks of cement. This other man was working at a snail's pace. Your uncle got impatient and sped up, not stopping until the last sack was gone. They emptied an entire carriage in forty-five minutes. The cargo weighed forty-five tons, which works out to a ton a minute. He kept going like this for a few months, then his chest started hurting. At the hospital, they said he'd pulled a muscle. He keeps going for treatment, but to this day they haven't managed to fix it. From time to time it acts up and starts throbbing with pain, but it gets better when he's had a rest."

After the meal, they tidy up the kitchen. Mrs. Xun goes to their room to tend to Master Xun while Xun Lei invites Xinger to come sit in his room. She follows him and Wanmei in there, and he tells them to share the armchair while he takes a folding chair. He turns on the television, keeping the volume low so as not to disturb his father in the next room. The final match of the third Intercontinental Cup—the Toyota Cup—is being broadcast this afternoon via satellite: England's Aston Villa is playing Uruguay's Peñarol. The match is almost done when Xun Lei tunes in, and the atmosphere seems tense. When the camera pans to the stands from time to time, the spectators are roiling like a pot of bubbling congee.

TV sets are nothing new to Xinger. Zaoer bought a Shanghai Golden Star ten-inch black-and-white one some time back, and she goes to his place with their mom every night to watch. Another family in the village has a four-teen-inch color TV—in fact, it's the household Peach married into. Xun Lei's is different—an enormous twenty-inch full-color screen, far more vivid and clear than anything she's seen before. It's a shame the program isn't anything she's interested in. She can't understand why a girl like Wanmei would want to watch soccer like a boy. Look at her, eyes wide as she follows the skirmishes on the field, hands clasped to her chest, mouth wide open. She even lets out shrieks and groans from time to time. Does Lei like her because she can enjoy soccer like a guy?

The crappy program can't hide the excellence of the set. She asks, "Xun Lei, this TV set is great. Did you get it from the department store?"

"I brought it back with me from England," he replies. "I studied there for two years before starting this job."

Now Xinger understands. No wonder everything in this room reeks of the West. England! She valiantly combs through her knowledge of geography but can't recall where England is in relation to China, or even what shape it is. All she knows is it's very far away. Lei has been to the West—no wonder she's not good enough for him. Even if this fiancée weren't in the picture, Xinger still wouldn't stand a chance. Afraid these thoughts are showing on her face, Xinger steadies herself and says, "This British gadget is pretty good—that looks just like real, and the colors are so bright!"

"That's not a British set," Wanmei butts in. "It's a Sony—that's a Japanese brand." Before Xinger can respond, Wanmei continues, "Japan is such a powerful economic creature! Right now they make better compact cars than the Americans, better watches than the Swiss, better sound equipment than the Dutch, and better optical instruments than the West Germans! Lei got to England and went looking for a TV set that was a good value, and he ended up with an Asian one!" She pauses for a second, but before Xun Lei can say anything, she gestures at the screen and goes on, "See? In order to increase their influence, Toyota is willing to spend big bucks on this Toyota Cup. If you didn't know beforehand, you'd be hard pressed to say which country was actually holding this tournament—because all the advertising around the field is for Toyota cars, Hitachi appliances, Canon cameras, Fuji film . . . They've got you every which way!"

Xinger is still trying to digest this argument when Wanmei flicks off the television. "The match is over! It's just the prize-giving next—nothing worth seeing there. I'm not going to support Toyota." She stands and says to Xun Lei, "Let's have some music, but keep it low, we don't want to disturb your dad." And with that she goes back to the kitchen.

Xun Lei turns on the tape deck, which plays Debussy's *La mer* quietly. Now Xinger understands what the black boxes hanging from the ceiling are for. The music is still hideous, though. All of this, from the tape player to the speakers to the music, must have come back from England with Xun Lei. He feels further from her than ever, which is actually quite reassuring.

Wanmei returns with two steaming cups, which she hands to Xun Lei and Xinger. Xinger has no idea what this is, so she politely says, "You go ahead!" Wanmei nods toward the kitchen. "I made myself one too. Go on, have it!"

Xinger accepts the drink, though she still has no idea what it is. Xun Lei explains, "It's coffee—instant coffee. It comes ready-mixed with sugar. Drink, don't let it get cold."

Xinger takes a sip and frowns. Like the vast majority of Chinese people, she finds her first taste of coffee not just unpleasant, but actually nauseating. Why would anyone drink this bitter brew?

Wanmei comes back with her own coffee, as well as three slices of cream cake. She places one of the plates before Xinger and smiles. "It's the one you brought. This should go well with coffee."

Xinger picks up her slice and has a bite. It's delicious! Her first taste of cream cake—she had no idea it would be so sensational. She can't help laughing to herself at how ridiculous Westerners are: they make such scrumptious cakes, yet their version of tea, "coffee," is awful slop—but somehow they believe these two things go together!

Wanmei has no idea that Xun Lei and Xinger were betrothed to each other as fetuses, and Xun Lei doesn't plan to tell her until Xinger is on her way back home. As a result, Wanmei has blithely assumed that Xinger is a poor country relative of the Xuns'. As they drink their coffee, Wanmei says, "Xinger, hey, Xinger, tell us about the village you come from." She is curious about life in the more rural parts of the country.

It's not that Xinger doesn't want to tell her, but she doesn't know how. Where should she start? She puts her coffee on the table, blushes, and rests her coarse hands in her lap, looking like a student who hasn't done her homework getting called on by the teacher.

Xun Lei tries to help. "After they brought in the 'household responsibility' system, did things actually improve?"

Xinger doesn't know how to answer that either. She's bad at summarizing things.

Wanmei jumps in: "Country folk don't have to worry about their basic needs anymore, and some of them have even gotten rich. We've all seen that—Xinger's family is one example. We can talk about that later. But why don't you tell us what the issues are?"

Xinger thinks about it. "True, there are problems. When they first divided up the land we'd be responsible for, some people in my village fought over it. One guy got allocated a plot near the well, so he could water his crops all the time, and they grew really tall. Everyone hated him. Finally, someone got so jealous, he went over in the middle of the night and blocked the well."

Wanmei's eyebrows rise in shock, and she laughs. "Wow, did that really happen? Then what? If the well was blocked, no one could water their crops, right?"

"Yes, we all had to find other ways to get water. To this day, they haven't managed to unblock the well. Everyone has so much money now, plenty of people are playing for cash—"

"Playing for cash?" Wanmei doesn't understand.

"She means gambling," Xun Lei explains. "There's two things it's difficult to avoid in the countryside: superstition and gambling. The more money you put in the hands of rural folk, the more likely it is to happen. Unless you provide them with not just money, but also education."

"Oh right. Xinger, another question," says Wanmei earnestly. "I was reading the newspaper, and I saw two different items. The first was a dispatch that said farming villages are so wealthy now, everyone is clamoring more than ever for knowledge and education, and all the kids who were pulled out of school to work on the land are being sent back. The second thing was a letter from an elementary school teacher, who wrote in to say more parents are withdrawing their children from school and sending them out to earn money, and the situation's getting desperate. Xinger, which of these is true of your village? Let's have some firsthand intel!"

Xinger doesn't quite understand the question. "What does that mean, 'intel'?"

"'Intel' means knowledge or news or trends. Humanity is currently transforming into an information society . . ." Wanmei enthusiastically explains all this at length to Xinger, who is patently uninterested. She looks down, hands writhing together, and tries hard to pay attention.

Xun Lei gazes at these two young women, sighing. An hour ago, all he could see was their exterior differences: they both have thick brows and large eyes, but Xinger's expression as she gawks at everything in the house makes him think of those gaudy red paper-flower cut-outs country people decorate their windows with, while Wanmei's every frown and smile is as elegant as He Luting's *The Cowherd's Flute*. They both have darkish skin, but Xinger's has an undertone of yellowy-black, with large pores, inextricably linked with the sunlight and earth and toil of the countryside, whereas Wanmei's is more of a dusky-pink hue, its fine-grained, gentle glow indicating this sheen was acquired through boating on the river and hiking in the hills. Of course, their clothing presents an even starker contrast. Take their sweaters alone—Xinger's is made of thin crimson acrylic, with an embroidered design of leaves and yellow blossoms below the open collar, while Wanmei's is soft to the touch, violet marbled with indigo and heather gray, with an oversized high collar that flops appealingly around her neck. Half an hour ago, Xun Lei began to understand the differences in their psychology. Now he can detect an even deeper gulf between them. Will this gap become a sharper conflict or eventually erupt into open confrontation? Naturally, this isn't just her versus her, but them versus them—that is, the clash is fundamentally about two separate cultures. Isn't it?

Indeed. Feng Wanmei might be the closest a young city intellectual could be to an uneducated worker, but for all that she is trying to extend as much kindness as she can muster to Xinger, whom she still thinks is part of the Xun family, she is beginning to get frustrated at the amount of explaining she has to do. Faced with Xinger's headshaking, lip-biting, and blank stares, she is forced again and again to shrink and simplify the knowledge she is trying to transmit, to make it shallower. Even phrases like "information tool" or "electronic technology," or statements such as "For example, this TV set is an information-receiving device" or "The firewood you burn in your village is a natural resource" seem completely incomprehensible to Xinger. Wanmei has reached the point where she's starting to wonder whether this woman, who's about her age, actually deserves her respect—and indeed, whether there are any grounds for optimism about the future of the Chinese people.

What about Xinger? By the same token, for all that Xinger is one of the most confident and progressive young people in her village, and for all that her affection for the Xuns should extend to Wanmei too, this endless overexplaining and the frequent interjections—"Do you understand?" and "Got it?" and "Is that clear now?"—are beginning to raise in her an old, unyielding disdain, or perhaps even hatred, for the intellectual superiority of city people.

When Wanmei begins once again to explain breathlessly that a "computer" is a type of "electronic brain," Xinger can't stand it any longer. She rears back her head and snaps, "What are you talking about, electronic brain? Is that like a monkey brain? I've eaten monkey brains, and sheep brains too. What the hell would I do with an electronic brain?"

Wanmei is startled into silence, and Xun Lei is surprised that Xinger would suddenly display such vulgar countryside rudeness.

Fortunately, Mrs. Xun comes in and says, "Xinger, you must be tired. Come have a rest in the other room, I've got it ready for you."

Xinger follows Mrs. Xun and finds she's pulled a curtain across the other room, dividing it in two. On her side, the couch has been opened out into a bed, complete with sheets, pillows, and blankets. Mrs. Xun leads Xinger to it and says, "Have a little nap, dear. When you get up, we can wrap some dumplings for dinner. Your uncle's chest has stopped hurting, and he's resting up now. He wants dumplings tonight. A full day of meals from his hometown!"

Xinger lies down. The sofa bed is too soft for her to find it comfortable, and Mrs. Xun has sprinkled some sort of floral fragrance on the pillowcase that bothers her. For some reason that she doesn't understand, all her excitement at coming to Beijing has evaporated. She misses Zaoer and her mom like crazy. What's Mom doing right now? Have any of Zaoer's quails taken ill? Oh, Zaoer, don't forget to make Mom some honey water to drink, and please be careful not to get entangled with Jade again!

PART FIVE

未㊝

Wei Shi

Time of the Sheep: 1:00 p.m. to 3:00 p.m.

CHAPTER 19

A major character in this novel: the siheyuan.

How many intact siheyuans does Beijing still have? Which government office has the exact number? Nowadays, people are beginning to understand the importance of protecting wildlife. In 1980, a few white swans were seen in Yuyuantan Park, and when a passing laborer killed one with an air rifle, there was public outrage. China has far fewer siheyuans from the Ming and Qing dynasties than wild swans, yet their wanton destruction—indiscriminate alterations, damage, even demolition—has attracted virtually no public condemnation, except from a few experts in historical architecture. Siheyuans, particularly in Beijing, and most particularly the classic Ming and Qing ones, are relics of China's feudal society, and all the more valuable for being steeped in this culture. You could say there's no better way to understand urban society in the late feudal period: family structures, lifestyles, aesthetics, construction techniques, folklore, psychology, human interaction—all are reflected here. To modernize Beijing, a number of siheyuans will have to be removed; yet we must preserve some of the intact ones, and restore others. Perhaps certain neighborhoods could be designated heritage zones, conserving the Beijing of bygone eras. If we were to do this, our descendants would surely be grateful to this generation of Beijingers.

This siheyuan near the Bell and Drum Towers, where the Xue family is holding a wedding celebration on December 12, 1982, has undergone some deterioration and alteration, but remains a classic Beijing siheyuan.

The word "siheyuan" literally means "unified four-sided courtyard," and indeed they consist of four rows of houses, arranged in a square with a space in the middle. People who haven't been inside one might now be wondering: What's the big deal about these structures? Aren't they a bit, well, dull?

Not at all. These squares are full of variations, and their strict proportions contain untold multitudes.

Let's take this siheyuan, which we are beginning to get familiar with. It faces south, the most ideal and proper position for a siheyuan, and its layout and décor are also exemplary. If you look at the courtyard as a square, the main entrance will never be in the center of one side, but rather in the southeast corner (or the northwest one, if it's reversed). This positioning is an embodiment of how the standard family in feudal times (usually three generations under one roof) were meticulously managed and closed off to the outside world. This main gate will usually have a high "hanging mountain" roof and, at either end of the ridge, two unornamented protuberances known as "sparrow-hawk beaks." The gate is raised so there are three to five stone steps leading up to it from the street, with a sturdy foot-high sill before it. The two wooden doors fit together tightly, making it almost impossible to peep in through the crack. In days of old, these doors would be engraved or painted with a couplet: "Pass loyalty and virtue through the generations, study hard and learn from those who came before." There were also gate cymbals, named for the folk music instrument they resembled, attached to a rope that you pulled to summon someone to let you in.

Siheyuans built on the cusp between Ming and Qing tend not to have been residences of the elite. In *Dream of the Red Chamber*, the elite live in mansions far larger than the humble siheyuan; only when the aristocrat Jia Lian wants a place to stow his mistress does he temporarily rent her a place in a siheyuan on Flower Branch Hutong (which still exists today, not far from the Bell and Drum Towers). Generally, siheyuans were home to the middle class: palace staff, merchants, gentry, peasants who'd struck it rich, and aristocrats who'd suffered reversals.

Push open the doors and you're in an entryway, with a "screening wall" ahead that hides the rest of the courtyard from view while relieving the dark monotony of the entryway, as these walls are generally made of pale water-smoothed bricks, which gleam beguilingly when they catch the sunlight. The top of the screening wall is designed to mimic a gable roof, also rising at both ends into sparrow-hawk beaks. There'll be some sort of relief carved into the wall itself, perhaps pines and cranes for longevity, or blossoming flowers to represent prosperity. The corners and bottom border will be decorated with something to echo the main design, perhaps a design of leaves or lotus lamps. Sometimes there'll be a shrub or vine to the right of the wall, depending on the season—blooming wisteria in spring, thick green foliage in summer, bright-red leaves in fall, something to soothe the eye as you enter the courtyard.

Let's go farther into the siheyuan. At the moment, the entryway is cluttered with an assortment of objects, and above the entryway are a couple of tattered rattan chairs—we've mentioned these before, and you're going to meet their owner soon. The design in the middle of the screening wall has been destroyed, though the tree of heaven growing beside it is still there, now about three stories high with a trunk as thick as a water pail.

East of the entryway and screening wall is a set of folding doors that, when closed, present the appearance of four wooden boards. You can tell that back in the day these were painted pea green, with a red "calligraphy square" (actually, more of a rhombus) on each board. There used to be words in each of these squares, but it's impossible now to say what they were. Past these doors is a side yard, presently occupied by Master Xun's family. To the south are two smallish rooms, to the north the east wing, and to the east another siheyuan. In the old days, this would have been servants' quarters. These side yards are generally screened off with similar four-panel folding doors. I'm not sure why, but perhaps it's to emphasize that its inhabitants are of a lower status than the rest of the courtyard and are expected to come running when summoned.

Heading west from the screening wall, you arrive at the long, narrow front courtyard. To the south are a row of five rooms—the three easternmost ones form Tantai Zhizhu's family home, and the other two belong to another household (we'll get to them in a while). Let me draw your attention to a little wall, running north–south, that carves off the space in front of the last two rooms into another little yard, about the size of the Xuns'. This one has a different entrance—a moon gate (round like the full moon; some siheyuans have jar- or bottle-gourd-shaped ones instead). In olden times, these two rooms would have been set aside for visiting friends or relatives. The latrine would have been here too, usually in the northwestern corner. Past the northern wall of this little yard is the inner courtyard's west wing, and on the other side of the western wall is another siheyuan.

The three rooms that Zhizhu's family lives in would have been used as an external living space and study. During the Republican era, the easternmost room often had a door put in, opening out onto the entryway, and a window installed near the courtyard gate. A male servant would have lived here and served as a sort of sentry or doorman.

Naturally, there's yet another wall between the inner and outer courtyards, with a chuihua gate. In contrast to the stern austerity of the main gateway, this is jauntily decorated, with the unusual feature of a wooden screen below the "hanging mountain" roof, its two sides stretching out and delicately carved with lotus blossoms or passionflowers. These engravings and inset pieces are exquisitely crafted, decorated here and there with vivid oil paintings: detailed illustrations of various flora and fauna, or pavilions and pagodas, or incense burning, or classical allusions. The chuihua gate always displays the highest standard of craftsmanship and the most cultural riches of the entire siheyuan. This one has not been maintained, and its paint is peeling, but at least the main structure is intact, and it still manages to convey a great deal of its bygone charm.

The wall that the chuihua gate is set into was once smooth gray brick on its lower half and painted white above, with a ridge of glazed tiles on top. Now the glazed tiles have been ripped off by residents to use in their newly installed little kitchens, and the wall itself is about a foot shorter. In the 1970s, during the campaign to "dig deep holes" (build air-raid shelters), the residents' committee gave an order to make up the shortfall of bricks from these walls. The more sophisticated siheyuans have openings in these walls in the shape of fans or linked rhombuses, peaches, or pomegranates—but the siheyuan we're talking about was never that classy, not even back in the day.

Step through the chuihua gate, and you'd once have seen a "clasped-hands veranda," with sides stretching left and right past the east and west wings before coming together at the door of the northern quarters, like linked hands—anyone who's seen the two wings of the Hall of Happiness and Longevity in Beijing's Summer Palace will have no trouble visualizing it, though of course this is much less magnificent. The only relatively intact stretch of walkway left is along the northern wall. During the time of "digging deep holes," there wasn't enough wood to fire the bricks, so these verandas were hacked up and flung into the kilns.

In feudal times, these inner courtyards were where the noble families actually resided, with the head of the household in the three spacious south-facing rooms where Zhang Qilin's family now live. The middle one would have been a reception room where younger members of the family greeted him each morning, and where he met with important visitors or close friends. The family's meals would also be taken here. The rooms on either side were bedrooms. At either end of the row is one more room with a much lower ceiling, which gets less light because the east and west wings are blocking them. These smaller, dimmer spaces are called "ear rooms," and would have been used as studies or retiring rooms, where the head of the household could do anything from admiring his antique collection to smoking opium. These ear rooms are, of course, separate from the Zhang family's dwelling. Two relatives, one old and one young, live in them—and we're going to talk about their unusual existences later.

In feudal times, the east and west wings were side residences—for concubines, children, and grandchildren. As descendants proliferated, a single siheyuan might grow too small to accommodate them all, in which case one or more younger families would move out, or they'd make do with rooms on the northern side of the outer courtyard. The unity implied by the "he" in "siheyuan" actually meant that the younger generations on the south, east, and west sides of the inner courtyard would serve and obey their senior relatives on the north side. This layout displays in every line a rigid sense of order, with an atmosphere of restful ease and the calm stillness that comes with being completely cut off from the outside world.

We already know that the two northernmost rooms in the west wing house the Xue family, whose younger son is getting married today. What about the southernmost room? Its door is often locked, and its owner doesn't come back here every day. As for the east wing, the two northern rooms are inhabited by Zhan Liying and her unguarded tongue, while the remaining one is home to a young couple, both factory workers. They're on the early shift today, so their door is locked.

In order to make sure everyone has the most accurate possible image of this siheyuan, I must remind the reader that almost every household has installed a "little kitchen" or extension in front. These come in a variety of sizes, heights, and styles, and since the 1970s, they have surpassed the function of a kitchen. Certain families kept renovating and expanding them until they were larger than their actual homes, but they're still referred to as "little kitchens." According to building regulations, anyone renting a home in a multifamily courtyard from the Housing Department doesn't have the legal right to build additional rooms, but there was a period when the ministry was unable to keep up with the urgent housing shortage, so Beijingers took matters into their own hands. By the late seventies, every siheyuan was at full capacity, and the authorities had no choice but to close one eye and accept this state of affairs. With little kitchens appearing like bamboo shoots after rain in all sorts of residential courtyards ("multifamily courtyards" refers to converted former palaces and official ministerial residences, which are mostly more than one floor, as well as the more common siheyuans), the ecology of Beijing's older residences changed enormously.

In this siheyuan, Zhang Qilin's family has installed a water pipe for their own use, while the other households share a single spigot just to the west of the chuihua gate. To keep the pipes from freezing in winter, residents have to first lift the lid on the nearby dry well, which contains the water meter, and open the valve inside with a long-pronged spanner before turning on the faucet. If the weather's not too cold, they can leave it when they're done, for the convenience of the other families. But in the evening, or when it's particularly freezing, they have to clear the pipe by putting their mouths over the spout and blowing hard, pushing the leftover water back into the dry well. Then they close the valve and put the lid back on so no matter how cold it gets, the pipes won't freeze. This is what tens of thousands of Beijingers do each day, and while it may seem like a small, unnecessary detail, spare a thought for future generations of Beijingers. If we don't tell them the minutiae of our daily lives, how will they get this information decades from now? Any way of living, in all its detail, is a specific form of culture. This doesn't solely consist of literary or artistic creations, but also what people eat or wear, where and how they live.

Right now, in this siheyuan near the Bell and Drum Towers, we're in a particular cultural milieu of early-eighties Beijing. By observing the various people who live in this courtyard, their joys and sorrows, their conflicts and clashes, we keep a faithful record and leave a richer tapestry behind for tomorrow's Beijingers.

Life flows on without a pause in this little courtyard. It's now the afternoon of December 12, 1982. The people we have already met are still to reveal their full selves, but new characters are already coming into view. So much waiting for us to find out, and so much to comprehend, in this world, this life, this humanity!

CHAPTER 20

A middle-aged woman's romance. Why does she ask a
stamp collector for a sheet of stamps?

Zhan Liying leaves her home feeling smug. So many people have arrived for
the wedding that they no longer fit into the Xue residence and are crowding
around the doorway, from which riotous noises of celebration escape. Nanny
Zhan quickly reaches the main gate. The motorized three-wheeler outside is no
longer there; a multitude of bicycles have taken its place by the rack. She walks
to the end of the hutong, heading to Springtime Tea Shoppe on East Drum
Tower Street. She said she needed to buy some tea leaves, but actually that was
an excuse to leave Ji Zhiman and Mu Ying to chat alone.

Ever since freeing herself of the "rightist" label, Nanny Zhan has taken it
upon herself to serve as a self-appointed matchmaker. Sometimes she brings a
couple together; other times they fall apart and spin out of her control. In either
scenario, she gets a certain psychological satisfaction from the process. If she
didn't pour her abundant enthusiasm and energy into forging these connections,
she wouldn't be able to go on living. That's just the way she is.

She doesn't see introducing Zhiman to a woman as meddling in his life. She
was at college with Zhiman, and though they studied different subjects, they
danced together at parties and were good friends. After graduation, Zhiman
was given an unfortunate job: high school math teacher. Then they both went
through whatever fate had in store and almost forgot about each other. They
reconnected a couple of years ago when Liying looked him up, hoping he
could help her husband find out if Beijing high schools really were short of
foreign-language instructors. Zhiman was largely indifferent to Liying's sudden

reappearance, but she felt it was an enormous shame that he was still single. Regardless of whether he actually wanted help, she began introducing him to possible partners with the bubbling enthusiasm of a Dong Lai Shun special mutton hot pot. She quickly realized that Ms. Mu Ying, who'd recently moved into the single room in the west wing, would make an ideal companion for Zhiman. Although she's divorced, she isn't encumbered with elderly relatives or children, and she's a highly educated intellectual. Right now, she's a doctor at a government department's in-house clinic. She looks a little like Wang Danfeng, the old-time movie star, and always dresses with elegant refinement. When you get to know her better, you realize how kind and gentle she is. Since she's single, rather than waste time and energy cooking, she often eats at her work cafeteria and sleeps at the clinic while her room in the west wing is "guarded by an iron general"—that is, padlocked shut. Because she just moved here and is seldom around, no one in the siheyuan knows her particularly well—apart from Zhan Liying, who claims they got along right away and often shows up uninvited for a chat when Mu Ying gets home, or even drags her over for a meal. In Liying's subjective opinion, they had an immediate connection.

She went to see Ji Zhiman and gushed about Mu Ying for half an hour without pausing to draw breath. When she finally stopped—her mouth was dry and she needed a sip of tea—Zhiman asked a few questions while tending to his sparse hair with a brush. He spoke slowly and calmly, in contrast to Liying's frenzied answers.

"So her surname isn't 'Mu' as in Mu Guiying, but 'Mu' as in 'admiration'? Why would anyone have such a weird name? If it was 'Murong,' I would understand, that's a real surname, you can find it in the register of names."

"What's the big deal? Names are just symbols. Who decided that the horizontal axis would be X, and the vertical axis Y?"

"Why did she get divorced? What did her first husband do?"

"According to her, they just didn't get along. He had an awful temper, and he beat her. You hear me? He beat her! He dispenses medicine at a walk-in clinic. They parted quite amicably, and she let him have custody of their child."

"Ms. Mu Ying must have very high standards. I'm just a poor high school math teacher—I don't think I'd catch her eye."

"Why do you have to look down on yourself like that? You're a level-three teacher at a well-known high school, and you call yourself poor? Isn't the Finance

Institute trying to recruit you? If you take that offer, you'll be able to fill your classes and get an assistant professorship, easy as snapping your fingers."

"You know I'm not interested in that—I'm used to teaching high school and living in the staff dorm. At the end of the day, I've been alone for so long, I'm quite happy like this."

"But what happens when you get old? Are you going to retire in this room? You ought to have a partner, and Mu Ying is the perfect woman for you!"

"The way you describe her, beautiful as Wang Danfeng and so on . . . Listen, there's a mirror in this room, and I look at it often enough to know my looks aren't—"

"Hey! Don't you know me by now? I always exaggerate! Obviously she isn't in Wang Danfeng's league. She just knows how to dress and do her hair nicely, and she has big eyes and an expressive mouth—she's very charming! If I'm honest, she's a little on the short side. Anyway, you have no idea what women find attractive. Hardly any of us like those pretty boys with oil in their hair and powder on their faces. Someone like you, almost six feet tall with broad shoulders and a craggy face? That's what I call manly. So what if you're thinning on top? You're still not bad looking! I know for a fact that Mu Ying is looking for a mature man like you."

"You're exaggerating again, aren't you? If I were really that attractive, wouldn't you pursue me yourself? And then your husband would find out and come running from Sichuan to fight me."

"Ugh, I can't stand you! Enough nonsense. Will you meet her or not?"

"I think it's better if we don't meet."

That actually did make Liying angry. She flounced out the door.

That was her first attempt. Liying's not one to bear grudges, especially not against Ji Zhiman. She owes Zhiman—thanks to his intervention, it's looking more and more likely that her husband will be transferred to Beijing. Zhiman's high school has a surplus of math teachers and a shortage of English ones, so the Ministry of Education has agreed to move Zhiman to the Finance Institute and give his place to Liying's husband. With this debt of gratitude on top of her usual overenthusiasm, she tried again and again to persuade Zhiman, until he finally said yes—and here he is, this Sunday afternoon, meeting Mu Ying.

The reason Liying was so determined to lure Zhiman over is something she discovered by chance: Mu Ying is also a stamp aficionado. Stamp collecting has an important role in Zhiman's inner life. People who aren't into stamps may find this hard to understand.

As agreed, he shows up at Liying's home with two stamp albums under his arm—of course, this is just one-tenth of his collection. These are "mobile albums," specially designed for meeting other hobbyists. One holds the highlights of his collection, for display purposes, and the other the specimens he will swap.

A day before this meeting, Zhan Liying made a large bowl of ham salad and bought a tea-smoked duck from the Sichuanese restaurant on Yarn Hutong in Xidan. This lunch menu would have an East-meets-West theme. For a starter, she made tomato soup by mixing milk powder with tomato sauce from her fridge. Next came the ham salad, with vermouth to drink. Then the tea-smoked duck, heated up and served on a bed of rice, eaten with chopsticks and fork. Finally, homemade fruit ice pops. Because most of these items were pre-made or ready-made, she was able to spend a leisurely morning getting dressed, and even found time to insert herself into the bridal party. When Zhiman and Mu Ying arrived, she swiftly served this rather eclectic meal with pickles on the side—and with her usual misplaced energy and enthusiasm, ran next door with another plate of pickles to add to the Xues' wedding banquet.

Both Zhiman and Mu Ying sincerely applauded Liying for the effort she put into this meal. The tea-smoked duck got Mu Ying talking about the concept of food as medicine. She mentioned a Sichuanese restaurant near Chongwenmen that had added specially designed medicinal foods to their menu, with the idea that the food would make the medicine more effective, while the medicine would enhance the food's nutritiousness. With her insider knowledge, she spoke of the health benefits of pairing gingko with pork ribs, kidneys with *Eucommia* bark, goji berries with snowflake chicken, shredded beef with xiangsha. Zhiman mused that the Cantonese usually drank their soup at the start of the meal, just like Westerners, which led him to how Western lifestyles, and hence Western civilization, had been infiltrating China in recent years. This in turn grew into a discussion about the late Ming idea of Western scholarship spreading to the East, and the "rational opposition" and "gradual melting" this policy encountered, and how through a bold and active absorption of the finest that the West had to offer, we could build upon our strong foundation to expand and develop a brand-new Chinese civilization. Liying watched, listened, and served her guests, thinking to herself, *They were made for each other!* After the meal, they sat sipping coffee and admiring each other's stamp collections. Now that she was no longer needed, Liying claimed she was out of tea leaves and slipped out the door.

Liying's impression of how things are going, though, is completely mistaken. She's been unable her whole life to know herself, and can't accurately perceive others either.

Strictly speaking, her understanding of Mu Ying's personality is pretty much nonexistent.

So what kind of person is Mu Ying?

The people who know Mu Ying fall into two camps: one group thinks she's a paragon of our times and practically has a halo around her head; the other thinks she's dog shit, barely human, and the people in this camp froth with rage whenever her name is mentioned.

To start with, Mu Ying isn't her real name. She was born in a small, remote town in the south. In the spring of 1958, just as she was about to graduate from high school, she came across a feature that took up practically one whole page in the newspaper. It was about a hero of their time: a soldier who was left disabled after the War to Resist America and Aid Korea, who donated his entire compensation payment, returned home empty handed, and set up a neighborhood factory in a Beijing hutong. He now led a team of former housewives and disabled homeless people in manufacturing products that sold extremely well, and his business took off like a satellite into space. Mu Ying will never forget the moment she read this article. It was the afternoon break, and she was sitting under an old mulberry tree in the schoolyard. Now and then, overripe mulberries fell onto her newspaper, leaving bright purple stains. The report was brilliantly, lyrically written. The hero's photo was also printed, and Mu Ying spent a long time staring at it, developing a fierce love and admiration for him. She worked for the school radio station, and during their afternoon broadcast two periods later, she read this story out to the entire student body. Several times, her tears fell onto the page, mingling with the mulberry stains. Her voice was rich with emotion, and quite a few students and teachers felt their eyes moisten as her passion touched them.

This was an era of sincerity. When she thinks back now, Mu Ying can't recall a single speck of hypocrisy in herself. That very evening, she wrote a long letter to her hero in Beijing, copying out her rough draft in careful, neat handwriting.

Instead of her actual name, she wrote "Mu Ying"—"in admiration of a hero"—at the bottom. On her way to school the next morning, she solemnly put this letter into the green mailbox hanging by the doorway of the co-op. She remembers the moment with utter clarity—how it was awkward to stuff in because it was so thick. Now she realizes the letter was probably overweight and she hadn't put extra stamps on it—yet the post office didn't return it undelivered. This would be a dramatic turning point for her destiny.

Ten days later, she got a reply from the hero. A brief letter with a weighty message expressing the hero's warmhearted humility and support for high school students. She'd put her home address on the envelope, and this message addressed to "Mu Ying" found its way unerringly to her. Right away, she brought it to school—she remembers running there, so eager she stumbled and fell. The letter from the hero was put up on the noticeboard. This was the most earth-shaking event ever to take place in her high school.

From then on, she kept up a correspondence with the hero in Beijing. Not long after that, the newspaper published a second feature about him by the same reporter. The language was just as poetic as before, but even more detailed and moving—probably because his professional accomplishments had already been covered, more could be written about how he'd overcome his personal struggles. Although the article mentioned the care he received from the people around him, what left the deepest impression on Mu Ying was that he returned home each evening and mended his own clothes, even though he was blind in his left eye and partially sighted in his right, so it took him dozens of attempts, more than a hundred sometimes, to thread the needle. This one detail conjured up an image deserving of her worship and sympathy. Quite naturally, she spoke in her next letter about her willingness to fly to his side, take care of him for the rest of his life, and sacrifice everything she had.

She never expected the hero would quickly reply the way he did—inviting her to Beijing. She was shocked. Surely she was unworthy? Completely unworthy. Even so, she went. Her family and a representative from the school accompanied her to the train station, which was quite a distance from her home. She felt like she was riding on a cloud. She arrived at Qianmen Station in Beijing and found the newspaper editor and reporter waiting on the platform. Her first letter had been sent to the newspaper, and they'd passed it on to the hero. Now he'd given them the task of meeting her.

It was like swimming through an ocean of happiness. One splendid moment after another: checking into the guesthouse, gazing up at Tiananmen Gate, visiting the famous neighborhood factory, attending a poetry competition at the Beijing People's Commune. All brand-new experiences. Naturally, the high point was meeting the hero himself. For him, it was love at first sight. Even though she was only eighteen, a whole twelve years younger than him, and she wasn't registered to live in the city, when he formally proposed to her, she accepted without hesitation. After that, it was green lights all the way. The housing office transferred the hero to one of its best apartments, and her residency was easily changed to Beijing. The newspaper and factory worked together to throw them the most magnificent, awe-inspiring wedding, and eight days after the ceremony, the newspaper published a third profile by the same reporter, in prose even more lyrical and stirring than before. This time, the photograph accompanying the article showed her sitting by the hero's side, mending his shirt.

She gave herself entirely to the hero and felt content. At the beginning, when work units invited the hero to speak, she always went along and shared in his glory. When shrapnel in his body caused a chest inflammation, she stayed by his side, caring for him in the hospital, except when she had to stand in for him at speaking engagements at kindergartens and elementary schools. Now it felt like she was taking his glory for herself. The hero received the very best care and soon recovered enough to come home. Despite being blind in one eye and riddled with shrapnel, and having a slight limp, he was still in fairly good physical condition. Not long after that, they had a son. The country went through three difficult years, but they experienced no hardship at all—their special status protected them from the famine and natural disasters ravaging the land. Life felt like it would continue to be peaceful and joyous forever.

Bit by bit, she formed the idea of wanting to continue her studies. The hero fully supported her in this, so they left their child at the neighborhood nursery— he was too young to stay full-time, but an exception was made. They reserved a place at medical school for her. No one could have expected what an abrupt change would take place in her life after that. Another staggering turning point.

These recollections now fill her with emotion. Right from the start, she was the most honest, hardworking, and respected student in the school. As she hadn't had to take an entrance exam, she lacked some basic knowledge and found it hard to keep up. Soon, she was going almost nowhere but the classroom, lab, library, and dorm. She went home every Saturday afternoon and returned in time for Sunday-night self-study. Everything according to schedule, like clockwork.

Eventually, though, something changed in her. When did it begin? What started it? She can't say. Maybe it was the violet dress. Her roommate Jin Liming, an intelligent girl from Shanghai with an abundance of energy, sewed herself a violet dress in the Soviet bragi style popular at the moment, and asked Mu Ying to try it on so she could alter it—they were about the same height and build. Still holding her lecture notes, Mu Ying obediently slipped it over her head and went on studying. Liming got her to turn this way and that, now and then sticking a pin into the fabric. All of a sudden, she walked a few paces away, clasped her hands to her chest, and exclaimed, "Mu Ying, my god!" Startled, Mu Ying dropped her notes. Liming dragged her out of the room and stood her in front of the large mirror on the landing. Mu Ying will never forget this life-altering sight. This was her genesis; now she was cast out of paradise. For the first time in her life, she saw a side of herself that had been hidden. Could she really be this alluring, this radiant? Some of her classmates happened to be passing by, and they flocked around her, agog. Liming restyled her short hair and got another girl to let Mu Ying try on her low-heeled leather pumps. Everyone spontaneously gasped and cheered at this transformation.

For Liming and the others, this moment probably slipped to the backs of their minds. Mu Ying pretended to do the same as she returned to her short-sleeved blouses, trousers, and cloth shoes with button-loop fastenings, but it was as if a patch of spring grass had suddenly sprouted on her previously barren heart. Back at home, she would blush to find herself lingering in front of the wardrobe mirror.

It was a long time before she put on her own bragi dress. The hero didn't react—he neither complimented her nor so much as frowned. Liming had made some exquisite little alterations to the dress. Like a thief, Mu Ying kept sneaking out to the landing, looking around to make sure no one was coming, to stare furtively at herself in the mirror.

She continued studying hard, and her classmates continued regarding her as someone particularly worthy of respect.

One Saturday, Liming asked if she'd like to see an art exhibition. Mu Ying hesitated before saying yes. She lost track of Liming at the gallery, and looking around, flustered, she ran into Ge Zunzhi. She already knew who he was, of course—he was the general branch secretary of their department's Youth Party, who often spoke rousingly at branch meetings. He knew who she was too, naturally, and took the opportunity to express his admiration and concern. Noticing that she didn't seem to know much about visual art, he guided her from room to room for a closer look, giving her quick pointers on some of the key pieces, niftily leaving her with a good dose of artistic knowledge. When they left the gallery, he walked with her to the tram station and patiently waited until she got on her tram before he left.

Afterward, she didn't remember a single painting. The only thing that lingered in her mind was how he looked and talked.

To an outside observer, everything probably seemed to happen very fast, but she felt the changes took place extremely slowly, without her even being aware of them. One day at home, she realized with a start that, for the first time, she couldn't bear the hero's breath, which reeked from his lifelong habit of eating raw garlic at every meal. She encouraged him to brush his teeth before bed and not just in the morning. For some reason, she spoke unusually harshly, and they had their first quarrel. Then, one Saturday she didn't come home. Liming had urged her to stay at school for a weekend party. She'd asked before, and although this time was no different, Mu Ying said yes. She put on her bragi, telling herself she'd just sit there and watch for a while before leaving. In the end, she stayed a long time. It was astonishing that she'd never been to any of these events. When she saw Ge Zunzhi inviting another girl to dance with him, the perfect gentleman, and then the two of them gliding across the floor as if on a cloud, something rose up in her heart that she'd never felt before. Much later, she realized this was jealousy. Someone from another department came and asked her to dance, and she brusquely turned him down, feeling guilty as she did so.

At the end of that semester, her exam grades were middling. Liming gave her an American novel, *The Scarlet Letter*, and told her to "lighten up a little." Mu Ying devoured it in a state of high tension, then borrowed more novels from the library. She read Yang Mo's *The Song of Youth* and thought how much the dashing Lu Jiachuan resembled Ge Zunzhi.

Back home, she felt stifled. The hero wasn't interested in anything she had to say, and vice versa. The general public had long since forgotten the three newspaper features about him. New heroes kept coming to prominence. There was no longer a market for the goods produced by her husband's factory, so finally they gave in to the downsizing trend and merged with another neighborhood factory. Her husband was the deputy foreman in this joint venture and almost immediately began clashing with the foreman.

Mu Ying's field of vision rapidly expanded while the hero's radiance dimmed. Their neighbors began asking questions long before they did: Are they really suited for each other? Will they go the distance?

Their first truly hurtful argument began over the most insignificant thing.

She stayed away from home two Saturdays in a row. She'd begun to find her past behavior ridiculous—how could she have been so stupid, not to know the difference between adoration and love? Between a spirit of sacrifice and desire? Between class solidarity and marital bliss? Well and good, allowing a noble, high-minded spirit to possess her soul, but why on earth had she let this surly old man possess her body?

Screwing up her courage, she approached Ge Zunzhi in the cafeteria and invited him to see a new art exhibit, having decided she'd have no regrets even if she ended up humiliated. He didn't seem surprised, nor did he angrily reject her. Instead, he accepted with casual nonchalance.

She began spending more and more time with Ge Zunzhi. She truly loved him.

One evening, as she was leaving the library, Mu Ying caught sight of Ge Zunzhi walking very close to a female classmate, slowly heading down the path toward a little grove. Something twisted in her heart, and she instinctively ducked behind a tree, pretending to be absorbed in reciting an English-language poem to herself, keeping a sharp eye on Zunzhi and the girl. His hands were clasped behind his back, and she toyed with a sprig of leaves as they strolled along the edge of the grove. They seemed to be having a pleasant chat, which made flames shoot from Mu Ying's heart. As dusk began to fall, they finally turned around, and parted at a fork in the path. Afterward, Mu Ying didn't remember how she went up to Zunzhi, what she asked him, or how he tried to explain himself. All she was aware of was his shocked face, bright as a mirror in which she could clearly see her only option was to burn her bridges. She also has no memory of leading Zunzhi back toward the grove, deep among the trees, only of the moment they stood facing each other and he said, "What's wrong, Comrade Mu Ying?" She flung herself into his arms and screamed hysterically, "I want you to love me! I want you to, I want you to!" He stood still as a statue for a moment, then peeled her arms away and moved her a little way from him. In a trembling voice, he said, "We can't do that! We really can't do that!" But then their eyes met with a charge like electricity, and now he was the one throwing his arms around her, kissing her on the forehead, and murmuring, "We can, we can . . ."

When their relationship was exposed, Ge Zunzhi was expelled from the Party, which not only meant losing his branch secretary position, but also halted what ought to have been a glittering future. Jin Liming was implicated too—the Youth Party censured her in private. School and department officials counseled Mu Ying, pointing out that she'd been corrupted, urging her to recognize her mistake, awaken from her stupor, and rebuild her relationship with the hero "until it recovers to its previous historic height."

By this point, she was about to graduate. Then something happened that the school authorities had not foreseen: the hero asked permission to divorce Mu Ying. She'd previously asked the same thing, but the school had said they would not support her request. Still, a hero is a hero, and Mu Ying misses him a little to this day. She didn't love him but will always respect him. He gave her the opportunity to enlarge her world. They parted on good terms, and she gave him custody of their son. She didn't want a child. She didn't want anything.

Ge Zunzhi was given the very worst job: prescribing and dispensing medicine in a neighborhood clinic. Her own post was scarcely better: in the outpatient department of a similar clinic.

Amid a storm of public criticism, they got married. She changed the "Ying" in her name to mean "cherry blossom," not "hero." Their quarters were tiny and their finances strained, but as far as Mu Ying was concerned, all she'd lost was the burden that had been weighing her down, and clearly, she'd gained the contentment of loving and being loved. Not long after that, the Cultural Revolution began. Their tiny vessel of love was nowhere near the whirlpool, but they had to carefully steer clear and try to move ahead with as much stability as they could find. They had a daughter. The Tang poet Yuan Zhen wrote, "In poverty, husband and wife have a hundred sorrows," but life can't always be, to quote the Song poet Lu You, "a series of endless bright vistas." Ge Zunzhi set to work with his hands, building them a little kitchen and making all the furniture they needed. His knowledge of art melted away, drop by drop, as he became absorbed in the enterprise of constructing their small household. None of their neighbors could have guessed he'd once been the general branch secretary of his department, that he'd once sat before a microphone and, in a speech that flowed like a raging river, moved an entire cohort of first-year students to tears. They called him a househusband—he even did all the cooking. Mu Ying spent a great deal of time reading—mostly Western classics, which were forbidden at the time, that she'd borrowed from trusted patients. While Zunzhi was in the yard varnishing the liquor cabinet he'd just assembled, she'd be in a reclining chair absorbed in a copy of *Jane Eyre* with its cover torn off. Or he'd be in the kitchen cooking shredded pork in garlic sauce from a recipe while she lay back on the couch holding the novel she'd just finished, Zola's *Nana*, eyes shut as she pondered its contents. She was satisfied, in an enlightened way—and that included sexually. When she thought back to the nights she'd spent with the hero, her hair stood on end. Thank heavens she'd severed what needed to be severed and attached herself to the right thing.

One morning early in the winter of 1975, Mu Ying was desultorily examining patients at the clinic. She called out the next name on her list, Qi Zhuangsi, and the man who walked in caused her eyes to light up. She saw so many people, yet something about this one caught her attention right away.

He was in his sixties, with an imposing physique and a face that smoldered with virile energy. All very nice, but what made Mu Ying react as if to a jolt of electricity was the absolute noble dignity with which he carried himself. Neither the one-eyed hero, nor Ge Zunzhi, nor any man she'd ever met, had possessed this quality. She knew immediately he was someone special. Really, he shouldn't have been seeking treatment at a shabby little street clinic like this one.

Here's how Dr. Mu Ying usually worked: Without even looking up, she'd ask, "What's wrong?" and before the patient could answer, she'd impatiently say, "Unbutton your shirt." After pressing the stethoscope sloppily to their chest and listening for less than a minute, she'd snap, "Open your mouth," and before they could ask any questions, she'd grab the tongue depressor from its beaker of disinfectant, press down on their tongue as if to punish them, and shine a flashlight into their mouth for a quick look. She didn't listen to a word the patient said, whether they were trying to describe their symptoms, or ask what was happening to them, or request a particular treatment. She simply scrawled a prescription, signed with a squiggle that could have been anything, ripped the sheet off the pad, and handed it to the patient. Then she'd open the door and call out "Number fifty-four!" and the next name.

Without her realizing it, her bedside manner changed completely with Qi Zhuangsi. She asked detailed questions, examined him attentively, and got him to lie on the high table so she could tap his back and ascertain the condition of his liver and spleen. Then she wrote out a list of tests she wanted him to have.

Right at the end, she said, "It looks like you have a respiratory infection . . ."

He raised his thick brows. "Pneumonia?"

"No," she said firmly. "It's fine, you caught it in time. If you hadn't, well, it's hard to say."

He solemnly thanked her, and walked out.

At lunchtime, she found out that Qi Zhuangsi hadn't gone for any of the tests she'd ordered, just collected his medicine and left the clinic—and instead of submitting triplicate forms to cover his treatment, he'd paid cash.

She began vaguely hoping he would come again, but he never showed up. Finally, she made inquiries and found out he was a "capitalist roader" who'd been put through many a struggle session. He was still labeled, and lived nearby in his eldest daughter's home. He was no longer eligible for special medical treatment, but wasn't willing to show his face at the public clinic, so he put up with the pain when he got ill and used medicine from the drugstore if it got really bad. Only when he thought it might turn into something serious did he go to the neighborhood clinic, where he paid cash.

Still, he lived near her clinic, so she might meet him again. Sure enough, not quite intentionally and not quite by chance, she ran into him on a street corner one sunny winter's day. He was in a worn-out black woolen coat, with a long, thick grayish-blue woolen scarf around his neck, apparently out for a stroll. Mu Ying called his name. He froze for a second, then recognized her. She asked how he was doing, advised him to go for the tests she'd ordered, and made sure he was eating and drinking properly. Before saying goodbye, she asked where he lived and said she'd be happy to check up on him on her own time. He politely declined, and they parted without his revealing his address. They hadn't talked about anything serious, yet this encounter left an indelible impression on Mu Ying. When she thought about it afterward, it felt as if they'd said so very much.

The Tiananmen Incident of 1976 took place a few months later. Early on, she and Ge Zunzhi had gone to the square out of curiosity, to see the magnificent spectacle. During that first visit, they saw all the floral wreaths people had left and were stirred by the atmosphere. After that, Mu Ying went twice more on her own. Now poems were appearing, all rather well written, mourning the death of Premier Zhou Enlai. Seeing other people writing them down, Mu Ying pulled out her own pen and notebook to write down some of the more moving ones. Back home, she read these to Zunzhi, and he agreed they were excellent. Over the next few days, more and more verses showed up, less about Premier Zhou's death and more openly criticizing Jiang Qing and Zhang Chunqiao. Some were so full of fury they couldn't be called poems at all, but naked attacks. Orders came to stay away from the square. Ge Zunzhi obeyed—out of cowardice? Or indifference?—while Mu Ying continued going—out of bravery? Or anger? Two days before the collective mourning of Premier Zhou was suppressed, Mu Ying met Qi Zhuangsi amid the crowd. She nodded a greeting, which he returned. Walking a little apart from each other, they made a round of the square. When he began walking in the direction of Dongdan, she followed him. He turned into the park that runs down the middle of Zhengyi Road, and she quickly caught up with him. He smiled at her, eyes gleaming so sharply she thought they could see right into her heart.

She pressed her booklet of Tiananmen poems into his hand and said, "I know you're afraid they're watching you, so you have to be careful—that's why you didn't write these down. I got more or less all the good ones. Take these home and read them!"

He took her red leather notebook, sat on a nearby stone bench, put on his glasses, and began reading. She heard him mumble approvingly to himself, "The People! The People!"

He didn't finish reading before handing her book back. "Thank you," he said. "You keep this. My grandsons made copies too, and they've already shown me."

Returning his reading glasses to his shirt pocket, he seemed lost in thought.

Mu Ying said, "But they aren't thinking about the People at all! What can the People do, anyway?"

Still silent, he stood up. Later, she realized: there was a police station along Zhengyi Road.

He kept walking toward Dongdan, and she followed. Finally, he started talking. He spoke to her of philosophy and explained social history from a materialist standpoint. His words were brief but incisive, and though he didn't name names, everything he said was aimed at a target. He finished by saying, "No matter how many difficult twists and turns there are, when you get right down to it, it's human hearts that determine the course of history. Flowers will always bloom when spring is here."

She got home full of excitement. Zunzhi was cleaning his shoes, and the whole house reeked of polish. This was the pair he'd bought for their wedding—each made from three pieces of cow leather, requiring a careful polish every few weeks, whether he wore them or not. They were already gleaming, but still he kept rubbing them with a chamois he'd got from god knows where, going over every inch. His behavior never used to bother Mu Ying, but on this day the sight offended her. As soon as she stepped in the door, she began berating him: "What do you think you're doing? Don't you have anything better to do? Do you know how big the crowds in Tiananmen Square are right now? And they're bravely speaking up on behalf of this country and its People? While you just sit here, completely numb. How could you be so backward?" He continued patiently working away and said blandly, "Of course I know. But what good will that do? Haven't they already said we're not allowed to go? You shouldn't be going either—you'll get into trouble." In a rage, Mu Ying snatched the shoes and flung them into a corner of the room.

They didn't split up right away. When society is in upheaval, individual lives get lost in its roiling ups and downs.

The more Mu Ying thinks about this next stretch of her life, the more she feels she has nothing to be guilty about. Many people think she's hopelessly corrupt, whereas she believes she has finally reached emotional maturity.

She no longer believes in the straight line of cause and effect. A human being can't simply select a goal and move directly toward it. Wherever we end up, it's never where we initially planned. There are all kinds of complex circumstances that determine a person's fate. Order comes out of chaos, and enlightenment rises from the miasma of unknowing.

One scorching summer day after the downfall of the Gang of Four, she hurried down Wangfujing to Central Brand Dye Shop, where she had to pick up some clothes. Before she could exit, she spotted the hero through the glass door, moving through the crowd with their grown-up son and a sturdily built woman—it was easy to guess who she was, just by the way the trio were walking together. A chill went through Mu Ying's heart, and many events from the past surged into her mind. She'd once passionately loved the hero, blind eye, limp, and all. Now he wore a pair of dark glasses, looked a little shriveled and hunchbacked, and was walking with some difficulty. She recalled the newspaper report through which she'd first gotten to know him on that historical afternoon, the tree she leaned against, stains from the fallen mulberries. Had one of them tricked the other? Her eyes lingered on her son. Good god, he'd be graduating high school any day now. To think she had a son that age! Everyone had called her heartless, and even she had to admit that she was missing an essential part of a woman's nature: mother-love. Just because it was weak, though, didn't mean she possessed none at all. When she looked at her son now, at his face just like the hero's, her eyes brimmed with tears.

Another time, in late autumn, boom boxes had recently become fashionable, and young people strutted down the street blaring a mélange of Teresa Teng hits, Apollo's electronic beats, breathy voices, and a digital cacophony like croaking frogs. It was in this atmosphere that Mu Ying ran into Jin Liming, whom she hadn't seen for many years, by the entrance of New Great North Photo Studio on Outer Qianmen. Liming shrieked with delight, flung her arms around Mu Ying, and spun her in a circle right there on the sidewalk. Mu Ying felt a spasm of guilt—Liming had been punished because of her and been given an inferior job. Before she could apologize, Liming was clutching her arm and waxing nostalgic about bygone days while leading her up to the second floor of Old Zhengxing Restaurant, where she ordered a couple of Shanghainese specialties so they could eat as they chatted. It turned out Liming didn't regard what happened to her back then as a misfortune. Laughing merrily, she said, "As far as I was concerned, I was like a fish they'd flung back into the water!" After graduation, she was sent to be a doctor in the clinic of a government ministry, and although this put the brakes on her medical career, it also brought her ease and quiet. Now she was about to be transferred back to Shanghai, where she would be reunited with her husband and children, not to mention her father, a prominent Shanghai industrialist. This was "implementing policy"—her family would once again enjoy a bungalow with a garden, and she'd been awarded a generous severance. She was content. She invited Mu Ying and her family to come visit her in Shanghai—they could stay at her place, and she'd treat them to chicken in Portuguese tomato sauce and grilled shrimp at the famous Red

House Restaurant. They prattled animatedly about moments from their college days, the violet bragi dress, Liming dragging her out to the landing to look at her reflection . . . Oh, what a thing life is. If not for this random, insignificant moment, Mu Ying's personality, psychology, feelings, and ambitions might have developed in a completely different direction. But would they have? Who can say!

As a result of this chance meeting, Liming arranged for Mu Ying to take over her job at the clinic. Not long after Mu Ying began working there, Qi Zhuangsi was put in charge of the ministry.

The people pointing fingers at Mu Ying now describe her as a devious woman who wormed her way into the ministry with the goal of seducing Qi Zhuangsi. That wasn't the case, of course, but even if she had done that, Mu Ying thinks, why would it be wrong?

One evening after dinner, while her daughter was skipping rope in the hutong with her friends, Mu Ying decided to act, and said to her husband, "Sit down. We need to talk."

Zunzhi was clearing the table and said distractedly, "What about? Can it wait? I'm about to do the dishes."

"Leave it, I'll do them later." Something about her voice and expression alarmed him. "Sit. I have to say this to you directly."

Zunzhi sat across from her, still blithely unaware of what was about to happen.

Mu Ying felt her heart fill with the purest, noblest enlightenment. Calmly and somberly, she said to Zunzhi, "I don't love you anymore. I loved you once. I'm grateful that you accepted my perhaps overzealous love and made such an enormous sacrifice for me, one I will never forget. But I don't love you now, not even a little bit."

Zunzhi stared at her, dazed from this sudden blow.

"I know it must be agony to hear me say these words. But if I were to hide this from you, that would be unethical of me."

"What's wrong with you?" Zunzhi roared. "What did I ever do to you?"

Mu Ying's voice, so level and unwavering that it was an act of cruelty, continued: "We need to face this reality calmly. That's just how things are now: I don't love you. I love someone else. I love him passionately, ardently."

"How could this be?" Zunzhi looked as if she'd driven a knife into his chest. "How could you do this? You—"

"It's no longer a question of what I can or can't do. We need to face the truth. What now?"

"Slut!" he thundered. His face flushed bright red, then the color drained away. In an excess of emotion, he flung himself onto the table. "Who is he? Who?"

She placidly told him Qi Zhuangsi's name and briefly described their first few encounters, how her affection for him was first sparked, how the flames grew to a blazing pyre.

Zunzhi couldn't accept this reality. He was shivering all over, like a malaria patient. Over the last few years, he'd sensed her feelings for him waning, and a growing frigidity to his embrace, but he'd never have imagined this was because she'd fallen for a ministry-level cadre!

"Have you . . . slept with him?" Zunzhi asked, staring at her and breathing hard.

"Not yet," said Mu Ying unhurriedly. "In fact, I haven't told him how I feel. But I believe he'll love me. Don't get so worked up. Please understand, the love I have for him is essentially spiritual. This is more than mere lust, more than starting a family and living together happily—"

Without waiting for her to finish, Zunzhi slapped her across the face. Through gritted teeth, he growled, "You shameless hussy! You tramp!"

She smiled magnanimously and stood to pack her suitcase. Zunzhi slumped across the table and sobbed.

The neighbors had heard them quarreling and now came flocking to ask questions and dispense advice. Mu Ying thought these common creatures were barely worth her notice, and sat there smiling coldly. They helped Zunzhi to the couch, but he just ground his teeth, too ashamed to tell them what had happened. Their daughter skipped through the door and burst into tears at this unexpected sight. Mu Ying went to hug her, and her heart softened as she stroked her daughter's hair. Thanks to this moment of connection, she didn't walk out that night. Instead, she slept on a folding bed in the kitchen. The next day, she asked one of the aunties in the siheyuan to keep an eye on her daughter, and left with her suitcase to take up residence in the clinic.

Once again, she'd burned her bridges, this time more decisively, resolutely, and fearlessly. That very night, she knocked on Qi Zhuangsi's front door—he'd moved into this apartment not long ago. His wife had died a decade ago, and he lived with his eldest daughter's family. The maid opened the door and led Mu Ying straight to Qi Zhuangsi's room. No one else paid her any attention—people of all sorts turned up day and night looking for Qi Zhuangsi.

Qi Zhuangsi was a little startled by her sudden appearance, but she wasn't unwelcome. Not long after he joined the ministry, he'd realized she was working at the clinic there, and when he stopped by to pick up medicine, he would stick around chatting for ten or fifteen minutes because he liked to hear what she thought about the workplace, and she passed on other people's opinions. They also spoke about random things, such as why the crab-claw cactus on the windowsill wasn't flourishing, and speaking of which, what houseplants did Mu Ying have? One time, the ministry held a big conference in another city, and he asked Mu Ying to come along with her medical kit. She showed up at his hotel room almost every day to take his blood pressure—of course she did this for the other older comrades too, but with him she would linger, and he liked her lingering. Some of her ideas and suggestions were very sound. She joyfully caught hold of every glittering principle he mentioned. She was completely intoxicated with her love for him. What about him? He was in the midst of carrying out the work of reform, which was a great strain on him. He had neither time nor energy for romantic love and didn't detect her soaring affection.

Even so, Qi Zhuangsi was a man with healthy appetites, as well as a scholar-general—a cultured individual. That night, when Mu Ying showed up at his home, he was sitting at his desk admiring his stamp collection.

Mu Ying will never forget this sight: his bent head, his thick graying hair, his broad forehead, the angled rectangular magnifying glass, light reflecting off his tweezers, the open stamp album.

He invited her to sit and naturally asked if she would like to view his collection. That's how she learned that his interest in stamps had begun while he was still in the Liberation Zone, and had gone on more or less continuously until the first half of 1966. During the Cultural Revolution, his house was ransacked and his albums confiscated. By the time of the Gang of Four's downfall, he'd forgotten he ever had this hobby. A few days ago, he suddenly recalled the four thick albums which had since been returned to him, and on this night he'd decided for the first time to steal a moment to revisit his former dreams.

"It's your lucky day, Mu Ying. You're in for a treat!" he said warmly. "I've got such a collection here, aficionados from all over the planet would jump on a plane to get a look at it."

Mu Ying already thought that the world Qi Zhuangsi represented was broader, more profound, richer, and more alluring than anything she knew. Looking at this stamp album, she believed even more fervently that she had to find her way into this world, to revel in it.

She was intelligent anyway, and love had turned her into a sponge. After just over an hour of conversation, she'd absorbed a huge amount of information about stamps. Now she understood postmarks, souvenir sheets, booklet panes, stamp blocks, bisected stamps, miniature sheets, first-day covers, canceled stamps, and so on.

Qi Zhuangsi had once owned a number of the so-called Large Dragons—the very first stamps issued in China, during the fourth year of the Guangxu emperor's reign—but they'd disappeared from his albums. Probably the inspectors deemed them "anti-revolutionary" and had them destroyed. Mu Ying could understand why this made him sigh so heartily.

After going through them once, she appreciated that he'd arranged his stamps thematically. First was "A Time of Hardship," with stamps from various Liberation Zones, commemorating post-Liberation events and sacred grounds of Revolution, documenting the entire journey from the time of the Heavenly Kingdom to the establishment of the People's Republic. Then there was "Our Magnificent Landscape," "Artistic Treasures," "Athletic Wonders," "Bright Colors," and others.

She turned the pages, admiring every single stamp, and forgot why she'd come.

The phone rang. Qi Zhuangsi picked up, and after a few minutes, he was swept up once again into the maelstrom of reform. Then he hung up and turned back to Mu Ying. "Why did you come to see me, anyway?"

"I'm getting a divorce," she said.

He stared at her, uncomprehending. This was none of his business. Ministry employees didn't need his permission to get divorced.

All he said was, "Why?"

She looked directly at him and said, "Because I don't love my husband any-more. I love you. You can do anything you like to me, but I love you."

He was clearly startled, but only as you would be by an unexpected distur-bance. His habitual solidity and dignity remained. The way he carried himself was what Mu Ying loved about him. She wished she could press her lips to his arm—that thick, hairy arm now resting on the desk, fingers drumming. He looked calmly at her and said, "I see. You should go home. I don't have the time or energy to get sucked into this. Please get yourself under control, and don't bother me again."

After leaving Qi Zhuangsi's home, Mu Ying didn't get the bus, but walked all the way against the wind back to the ministry. She was grateful for his hon-esty and understood the situation he was in. She hadn't expected an immediate response. Now that she'd confessed her feelings to the man she loved as well as the one she didn't, she was basking in the virtuous glow of having fulfilled her moral duty.

Within a few days, news of her divorce had spread through the entire office. Whenever people came to the clinic to pick up their medicine, they acted awk-wardly around her. Some female comrades spoke viciously behind her back and glared frostily to her face, but she remained completely serene and provided even better service than before.

And so she went through a second divorce. She said she didn't want anything from Zunzhi. On his own initiative, he went to the housing office and exchanged their two rooms (one of which he'd gotten someone to build for them) for two single rooms in different locations. Mu Ying chose the one in this siheyuan and felt once again like she'd been liberated. She'd won her freedom back.

To address the things people were saying about her at work, she took the opportunity when one of their internal magazines solicited contributions to send in an essay expressing her point of view: It's completely rational to fall in love outside the bonds of marriage, and it's the nature of love to shift constantly. Once love has evaporated, it's hypocritical to struggle on with a marriage—in fact, that's the truly immoral act. Demanding lifelong love is akin to the out-dated feudal idea of "one spouse for life," which forbade women from remarry-ing even after their husbands died. The most rigorous, pure, and moral version of love is that in which one dares to love truly and, when love is gone, to say to the former object, "I don't love you," and gladly, resolutely rid oneself of the loveless relationship. Any relationship that doesn't spring from compulsion is rational, and therefore moral. The increase in the divorce and remarriage rate, and the fact that people are now able to openly cohabit, isn't a sign of moral degradation, but rather of a more enlightened civilization.

Half her essay was cut, and it was clearly only published as an incorrect opinion because there happened to be space. She received more than a hundred readers' letters in response, slightly less than half cursing her, the rest expressing agreement and support.

Her essay also said, "Complaining that love is changeable is like criticizing the world for its rich variety. Someone who always stays at home will naturally only have a very small space in which to find someone to love. If she steps outside and into the open countryside, she'll see more to adore. And if she goes from level ground to the top of a hill, surely the greater vista will show her an even higher level of beauty. When we see more, we have more options. Everyone is always trying to refine their love—that's the most natural impulse in the world. The problem isn't that love can change, but whether we have used force to win the object of our affection, and if we can dissolve our legal ties to the husbands or wives we no longer love while respecting their humanity."

Since Mu Ying's divorce, she has neither avoided nor pestered Qi Zhuangsi. He'll soon retire and move to a second-tier city. After her blind infatuation for the one-eyed hero, and her worldly romance with Ge Zunzhi, she has refined her emotions and arrived at a spiritual, unearthly love for Qi Zhuangsi. She'll wait for him. And she believes he's actually waiting for her too.

By throwing herself wholeheartedly into her work, maintaining a pleasant attitude at all times, and not holding grudges for the nasty comments flung at her, she has gradually won over some of the people who hated her. Like a phoenix, she has risen purified from the immolating flames of love.

She began collecting stamps, paying particular attention to the most recent designs and specimens from the Cultural Revolution. Anything older she treats with a sort of reverence. Someone once offered to swap an eighteen-stamp set of S44 Chrysanthemums for a W2 Long Live Chairman Mao, but she said no. This surprised the other collector, because W2 stamps aren't particularly rare, whereas a complete S44 set is hardly ever to be found. But Mu Ying has a very simple reason for not wanting any chrysanthemum stamps in her collection—she remembers that *he* has some.

Although she rarely returns to her room in the siheyuan's west wing and tries her best to avoid her neighbors, she still gets pestered by Zhan Liying—who hasn't read her essay, knows nothing about her past, and doesn't seem to fully understand her present situation. She has no intention of laying herself bare to Liying, and only reluctantly agreed to meet Ji Zhiman because Liying mentioned he collects stamps too. She can't afford to make things awkward with Nanny Zhan—after all, they live right across from each other.

While Liying is off buying tea leaves, Mu Ying scans Zhiman's stamps with an insider's eye. She is very complimentary about his S15 Scenic Spots of Beijing series, particularly as she can see he has a rare alternate Tiananmen Square that shows the morning sun seeping through the clouds. Mu Ying spends a long time staring at this through Ji Zhiman's magnifying glass. Smiling, she says, "Last year, this was worth two thousand five hundred American dollars on the international market." He is taken aback. "Really? I bought these for six dollars each—including Tiananmen Square. Do you get the international catalogs? Which ones?" She does—Liming's little brother moved to America to take over their uncle's business, so she asked Liming to get him to send some over. Still smiling, she says, "The French one compiled by Yvert et Tellier, the American Scott catalog, and the Hong Kong one by Yang Nai-Chiang for stamps from the People's Republic. I've got them all, and they've taught me a thing or two." Zhiman can't help being a little envious. He only has a Japanese catalog, and not a recent one either.

Mu Ying goes on elegantly examining his album, and murmurs, "People like us don't collect stamps to get rich, but it doesn't hurt to know what's going on in the stamp market—and it helps our understanding of economics . . ." She breaks off, having turned the page and seen a C94 Stage Art of Mei Lanfang that leaves her shaken. The set consists of a four-cent stamp with Mei Lanfang in street clothes, eight-cent ones of him in *Battle at Mount Jin* and *Peony Pavilion*, a ten-cent *Farewell My Concubine*, a twelve-cent *Mu Guiying Takes Command*, a twenty-two-cent *Heavenly Maiden Scatters Flowers*, a thirty-cent *Remorse at Death*, a fifty-cent *Peak of the Universe*, and a three-yuan miniature sheet of *The Drunken Concubine*. Mu Ying distinctly remembers that Qi Zhuangsi is missing this miniature sheet from his collection. He once lamented, "I don't know how I missed it when it was released. I'll have to find a way to get hold of one after I've retired, even if I have to swap a full set of fifteen Peonies." Mu

Ying has checked her foreign catalogs and knows this miniature sheet is worth five hundred American dollars on the international market, while a full set of Peonies doesn't fetch much more than a hundred. The high price is one thing; the real thrill is in tracking down such a rare specimen—and yet this Ji Zhiman happens to have one, perfectly preserved.

Mu Ying can't stop herself holding the magnifying glass over this sheet and gaping. Zhiman looks on, happy to have found someone who understands—Zhan Liying has also gone through this album but had no idea what she was looking at. He has begun to feel warmly about Mu Ying—she's clearly a cut above, having such a breadth of knowledge and an excellent eye, and what's more, she speaks with refinement and moves with elegance. Hoping to learn more about her, he says, "You have quite an unusual surname—is it an ancestral one?"

She comes back to herself and says vaguely, "Oh, no, that's the name I gave myself in college. A spur of the moment thing . . ."

"Would you show me the best items in your album? I'd like to admire them."

She smiles. "Just this small sample of yours leaves my entire collection in the dust. I took this up quite recently and mainly focus on new stamps. I don't have a single rare one. If I may be so bold, though, I have to ask—if someone wanted your *Drunken Concubine* sheet, what stamps would you ask for in return?"

"I'll never give that up," he answers full-throatedly.

Her eyebrows rise and she says jauntily, "And if I insist?"

He stares at her, dumbstruck. This is all unexpected—the request, the attitude, the expression, the tone of voice. Zhan Liying said Mu Ying's in her forties, but she looks easily a decade younger, and the way she is pouting and flirting right now makes her seem like a college student in her twenties! Zhiman is flummoxed. He came here chaste as Liu Xiahui, but is he going to leave a Romeo?

Mu Ying's eyes are fixed on him, glittering like stars. Half-innocent, half-teasing, she says again, "That's right, what if I insist?"

He grows even more confused. *A moment ago, she said, "If someone wanted" and now she's saying, "If I insist." Well, it's true, it's different if it's her doing the asking. But hang on, let's think about this. If she really wants to be with me, why do we need to swap stamps at all? Won't both our collections be combined? Is she asking for a token of love? Isn't this moving a bit too fast? Of course, it's possible she's just joking. A woman who loves to play a classy little joke! It's unlikely, though. The odds of meeting such a fun-loving lady are pretty low.* Zhiman once proclaimed himself to have a "historical perspective," but at this moment, his perspective is failing to see through what's in front of him!

"Well, if you like it that much, I'll just give it to you." He thrusts his chest out, ready to walk through flames for her. For the first time in their conversation, he uses the informal "you."

"Really? Wow, thank you!" Taking him at his word, Mu Ying lifts *The Drunken Concubine* with her tweezers, and says in trembling voice, "I can't just take it without giving you anything in return. Would you prefer a postmarked Cultural Revolution Quotations or a northeastern 1949 Commemorative C3A World Federation of Trade Unions Asian and Australian Trade Union Conference? Or you could take . . ."

Zhan Liying gets back with the tea leaves and pauses to peep through the window before going inside. What she sees speaks volumes. *Oh, how wonderful,* she thinks. *Love at first sight!*

CHAPTER 21

*No need to rehearse Forging the Bell, but there is something
else that needs doing . . .*

Drum Tower Street is unusually busy this afternoon.

Its official name is Outer Di'anmen Main Road, but Di'anmen Gate was demolished soon after Liberation, while the imposing bulk of the Drum Tower is still there just to the north and will probably be preserved as a valuable cultural artifact—maybe the street name should change? Don't be too sad that the gate is gone. People who don't know old Beijing often wrongly believe that Di'anmen was a majestic city gate like Tiananmen or Qianmen. But no, it was a single-story building with three arched doorways and a hipped roof—nothing special. Beijing's temples—the Temple of Heaven, Temple of Earth, Temple of the Sun, and Temple of the Moon—still have this style of gate. The one at Di'anmen was a little larger, that's all.

Shortly after one in the afternoon, Tantai Zhizhu stands at the northern end of this street—that is, at the foot of the Drum Tower. Anger, worry, panic, and confusion mingle in her eyes.

She was already exhausted from her fight with Li Kai last night, then first thing this morning she received news that Old Zhao, the jinghu player, and Old Tong, the percussionist, were preparing to jump ship. She'd been supposed to host Old Zhao, Old Tong, and the other musicians at her home for a unifying lunch, but that turned into a breakup meal.

Puyang Sun is an agent of chaos. He might not be a bad person, and perhaps he came today with the best of intentions, but no wonder Li Kai can't stand the sight of him.

After the kerfuffle, they patched up the misunderstanding. Around eleven, everyone was sitting around the table eating as they discussed how to defeat Zhizhu's "elder sister" by making Old Zhao and Old Tong come to their senses. Even Li Kai joined in—he grasped the urgency of securing victory at tomorrow's Cuihualou dinner. Unfortunately, Puyang Sun had had quite a few drinks by this point and proceeded to talk nonsense.

To start with, he was just a little too insistent on keeping his idea on the table, at least as a backup. "If we manage to get Tong and Zhao, we'll really have to up our game. Let's build on the success of *Mulan Joins the Army*. Of course *Zhuo Wenjun* will have to be a smash hit, that goes without saying, but we'll also need to keep pushing ourselves to put on new shows. When I walked past the Bell Tower today, I remembered something. For my sins, I got my degree at Fu Jen Catholic University. The campus isn't far from here—on Dingfu Street, to the west of Front Sea. I often used to drink at Huixian Restaurant, north of the lake, and there I heard the story of the lady who was cast in the bell. It's a sad tale. The Bell Tower was being rebuilt during the reign of Emperor Qianlong. The artisan, Deng Jinshou, had a daughter named Almond Blossom, a lissome thing of just sixteen years with a lively intelligence, the bones of a warrior wrapped in the spring breeze. Deng Jinshou cast several bells, but none of them were good enough, and the deadline was drawing close. He was at his wits' end. Afraid that her father would be punished for his tardiness, Almond Blossom hurled herself into the flames, and the next bell he forged had the clearest, most resonant ring. Her father had tried to stop her but only managed to grab one of her embroidered shoes. When the Qianlong emperor heard of this, he declared Almond Blossom the Saint of the Crucible. People set up shrines to her in front of bell factories. It's said that in the past, when the bells rang out each night, mothers all over the city would whisper to their children, 'Go to sleep, the Bell Tower is ringing, and the Lady of the Crucible wants her embroidered shoe back.' Zhizhu, what if we turn this story into an opera, *Forging the Bell*, and you play Almond Blossom. Wouldn't that be perfect?"

The erhu player and ruan player praised the idea copiously, and even Zhizhu's father-in-law chimed in, "Oh yes, I remember that legend. You know about Bell-Forge Hutong off West Drum Tower Street? And Bell-Storage Hutong behind the Drum Tower? Then there's that abandoned bell by the Drum Tower, which goes to show the bell was forged more than once. Oh yes, and on Drum Tower

Street, heading south on Houmen Bridge, between Tianhui Courtyard and Walking Stick Hutong on the east side of the street, there's a little dead-end alley called Almond Blossom Paradise Hutong. Surely that's because Almond Blossom went up to paradise, and what's left of her spirit remained here."

Zhizhu was open to considering this idea but wasn't particularly enthusiastic. "That's easy to say, but it won't be easy to turn it into a show," she said flatly. "Take the scene where Almond Blossom throws herself into the furnace. How do you plan to stage that?"

Puyang Sun wasn't deterred. Gesturing wildly, he said, "All you need to worry about is singing! Leave the staging to me. For the furnace scene, you'll dance and sing at the same time, your voice choked with sobs, your body stumbling and falling across the stage. It's a Qing dynasty story, so that means we can't use water sleeves—but oh, I've just thought of something. Why not copy the greatest, Xiao Cuihua, and enter with a kick step? Back in the day, I copied Master Xiao's moves in *Haihui Temple* and kick-stepped all over the place—the whole audience burst out cheering. Sure, I'm old now, but I can still revisit old glories. Zhizhu, I'll teach you how to kick-step. Just say you'll learn from me, and I'll give you every trick I have—holding nothing back. A month from now, you'll be a success!"

Li Kai was clearly furious—he tossed back a full cup of baijiu and was staring at Puyang Sun with bloodshot eyes, ready to explode at any moment. No one else noticed the danger—all eyes were on Puyang Sun—apart from Zhizhu, who'd caught sight of him in her peripheral vision. Alarmed, she said sternly to Puyang Sun, "Forget it, enough of your nonsense. I'm not going to be able to do that—you go ahead and play Almond Blossom yourself."

Rather than taking the hint, Puyang Sun prattled on. "If I were twenty years younger, I might actually consider taking the part myself, but it's time to give way to the younger generation and accept a supporting role. You ought to be Almond Blossom, and I'll play a poor scholar. The two of us would naturally be childhood sweethearts. We'll get betrothed at an early age and await our nuptials—until Almond Blossom decides to hurl herself into the flames, and the scholar can't persuade her not to. Hey! For the furnace scene, why don't we borrow a trick from *The Butterfly Lovers* and turn it into a pas de deux? That will melt every heart in the audience . . ."

Li Kai abruptly rose to his feet and stormed out of the house. Zhizhu almost called after him, but then hesitated—maybe he was just going to the bathroom? Besides, no one had noticed his departure—he hadn't said anything, and they were still fixated on Puyang Sun's ramblings.

Choking back Li Kai's name, she frostily interrupted Puyang Sun's speech to urge everyone to have a little more chicken soup.

Li Kai never came back, and even Puyang Sun began to sense a little tension in the atmosphere. The erhu and ruan players tactfully stood and thanked their hostess, and Puyang Sun seemed to understand that he'd made a drunken faux pas. As they said their hasty goodbyes and departed, Puyang Sun reminded Zhizhu, "Don't forget, we're all meeting at Cuihualou tomorrow—see you there!"

With her guests gone, Zhizhu collapsed onto the couch. She felt as if not just her body, but her soul itself, was falling apart.

Her father-in-law patiently tidied up and sent Bamboo into the hutong to find his dad, but he didn't disturb Zhizhu by sending her into her room for a nap or offering her a few consoling words. He knew that at moments like this it was best to leave her alone. She reclined on the couch with her eyes shut, and stayed there drowsing for quite a while.

When her father-in-law was done washing up, he tiptoed back to his own room and lay down for a nap himself. Only then did Zhizhu jump to her feet, quickly wrap the pale-yellow mohair scarf around her neck, and hurry out to the courtyard gate.

As she had lain on the sofa, her mind was like a screen on which several movies were being projected at once, a confusing overlap of scenes past and present. Or maybe it was more like being on the Rocket to the Moon ride at the amusement park, spinning faster and faster. She imagined various rescue scenarios but couldn't decide which was best.

No use just sitting there being depressed—time to take action!

She rushes out into the hutong, then realizes she doesn't know what to do.

Where's Li Kai? How heartless he can be! Does she really need to go searching for him now? She has her rival to deal with—she doesn't have time for this! She had thought of something urgent a moment ago, what was it? Oh yes, making a phone call! Right, no time to waste, let's do this.

Zhizhu hurries to the public phone, which is in a nearby grocery store, only to find a young guy already using it, with a youngish woman and a middle-aged man standing in line. No point waiting around—she goes straight back out and along the hutong, searching for another phone. Without meaning to, she arrives at the foot of the Drum Tower. Diagonally across from the tower, at the southern opening to West Drum Tower Street, is an enormous propaganda poster with a slogan below, each character the size of a basin: "For a happier today and a glorious tomorrow . . ." Zhizhu often passes by this street corner but has never paid much attention to this billboard. Now the words seem to lunge at her. A happier today and a glorious tomorrow? Are they making fun of her? She steadies herself and reads the end of the line, ". . . a husband and wife should have only one child," and smiles mirthlessly.

"Zhizhu, is that you? Where are you off to?" She turns and sees her neighbor Old Lady Hai, who lives in the western "ear room" in the inner courtyard; her adopted grandson, Hai Xibin, has the eastern one. Grandmother and grandson have no one in the world but each other. At this moment, Old Lady Hai is basking in the sun by the Drum Tower wall, sitting on a folding stool she's brought out with her. Many of the neighborhood's elderly residents, more men than women, bring their own seats and gather at this spot on sunny winter afternoons. Some have birdcages too, though there's nowhere to hang them, so they just hold them. When they get tired, they stand and swing the cages around, walking their birds without actually moving from the spot. Others have chess sets, which they lay out on the ground and bend over to do battle, both players and onlookers growing so rapt they forget there's a busy road behind them. Most just chat idly, though a few get overenthusiastic and jabber away nonstop or start bickering for the sake of it. You'll find old people gathering like this on many Beijing street corners, just like in the common rooms of senior centers and care homes in the West, forming relatively self-contained and stable social islands. As for the middle-aged and young, teenagers and children, they often sail past these islands in the boats of their own lives, not even noticing them. Looking but not seeing. Zhizhu, for example, has never once observed this lonely island in the sea of humanity at the foot of the Drum Tower.

The inhabitants of these islands tend not to call attention to themselves, even when it's their neighbors passing by. When they do call out a hello, they don't stir from their spot—after all, it's the youngsters who ought to come to them. When Old Lady Hai warmly calls out to Zhizhu, however, she makes the most unusual move of standing up from her camp stool.

Zhizhu has no choice but to steady her nerves and force a smile. "Granny Hai, nice to see you."

Old Lady Hai waves to a nearby man. "Old Hu, Tantai Zhizhu's here!"

The old man has already gotten to his feet. Now he scurries over and enthuses, "We live in the same hutong, but it's rare to catch a glimpse of you. What's your next role going to be? I heard you doing *Mulan Joins the Army* just yesterday on the radio. Such a delicate voice you have! You remind me a little of Shang Xiaoyun from the old days!"

Old Lady Hai turns to Zhizhu. "This old codger is Mr. Hu from Courtyard Seven on our hutong. The kids call him Grandpa Hu. We were just talking about you—it's not just Shang Xiaoyun, Old Hu also heard Lu Mudan and Furong Cao perform in person! Over there on Tobacco Pipe Alley, which used to be Beijing's entertainment zone. There was storytelling, drumming, cross-talk comedy—you name it! Cao Baolu, Wei Xikui, and Wang Peichen all sang there. Wang Peichen's vinegar drumming performance was sharp and sweet as pickled almonds. Later on, opera troupes started putting in an appearance too. Oh yes, Yu Lianquan—you know him by his stage name, Xiao Cuihua—performed there too. There were some second-string singers: Liang Xiaoluan, Huang Yuhua, and the like. But look at me, rambling on. Once I get going, I just talk and talk, like that opera *Eighteen Conversations*!" Old Lady Hai tends to meander— Zhizhu already knows to respond with "Mm" or "Oh" where necessary. The old lady isn't done yet, though. She turns to Grandpa Hu and says proudly, "Zhizhu is the kindest person in our siheyuan. She might be a big star, but she never puts on airs. If you want to see one of her shows, don't be shy, just let me know and I'll ask her—I'm sure she'd be happy to get you a ticket." Turning back, she says, "Isn't that right, Zhizhu?"

"Yes, don't be shy, just ask Granny Hai, and tell me what you think afterward!"

Grandpa Hu is moved to tears. "Oh, that's—what can I say? I'm lucky to have met such a good person!"

Old Lady Hai is about to say something else when Zhizhu hastily cuts in: "Let's talk another time, I have to rush off now. Enjoy the sun!"

The two elderly people nod. "All right, off you go! See you again!"

Zhizhu darts across the road and walks straight ahead, moving fast in case they're watching her leave.

This encounter has soothed away Zhizhu's anxiety. As she walks, she thinks: *I'll also be old one day, won't I? Look at Old Lady Hai, with her face like a walnut shell, the way her mouth shrivels when she talks—so unattractive. But she was sixteen once, and there must have been a time when she was good-looking. That's in the past, though. All she has now are memories. That's why she called me over, to bask in my reflected glory, to convince herself and others that she's worth something. Life is a process of deterioration. Who can stay at the peak forever? I'm already in my forties—how much longer do I have left? So why do I care so much about what's happening? To get old and withdraw from battle is a good thing. Haven't I seen Grandpa Hu in the hutong, going through trash cans and picking up scrap paper? I heard he supports himself selling what he scavenges. Nanny Zhan told me he has a son, but his son and daughter-in-law treat him badly. They've stuck him in a tiny room of just forty square feet. The son has a TV set but won't let him watch—he says he stinks. So the son bought him a little transistor radio that was obsolete years ago—he even has to buy his own batteries. No wonder he's only heard me sing—he's never been able to see me perform on TV. Zhan Liying certainly gets around. She moved here a few years later than me and already she knows so much about what's going on in the hutong! Still, Grandpa Hu sits among the other old people at the foot of the Drum Tower, completely equal to them. And wasn't that Director General Wu I glimpsed playing chess? He's not a director general anymore. He's retired and lives in the next siheyuan. When he was still running the local Bureau of Commerce, he came to see me, and invited me to sing at their award ceremony for Most Progressive Workers. In the end I brought the whole troupe and we performed* Love in the Closet. *He looked so dashing, standing in front of all those people! Now he's in the old people's club, along with the cabbage sellers, trishaw drivers, and handymen. Even Grandpa Hu, who makes his living going through people's trash, is basking in the sun, chatting and playing chess, right alongside them! That's the funny thing about life. As a kid, everyone's about the same—we all play together. Then as we get older, the differences between us become more obvious as everyone gets competitive. At the end of our lives, though, we go back to being more or less the same, and we all play together again.*

Her thoughts in a tangle, Zhizhu wanders past Makai Restaurant, Tobacco Pipe Alley, and the department store, all the way to Yiliu Hutong before she comes to her senses. *Wait! I was supposed to be looking for a public phone. How could I get distracted from something so urgent?*

Next to Yiliu Hutong is the Di'anmen post office's newspaper shop, which also sells complete sets of stamps for collectors. Zhizhu finds herself among a gaggle of stamp fans, mostly young people. She's heard that "stamp fever" has been on the rise for a couple of years now, and practically every new release is met with a stampede of interest. Honest folk stand in line before dawn, while tricksters find ways to cut in. People have been known to pay more than a hundred yuan, and even high school students are buying entire souvenir sheets at one go. People who know someone working behind the counter are able to get hold of "side stamps," ones with an unperforated edge, particularly the distinctive ones with color blocks, a signature, or a serial number. What do they want these things for? Could it really be to admire them? Or for artistic reasons? No, it seems quite a few people treat stamps as vouchers that will never lose their value, or savings accounts with the highest interest rate. Some even resell them right away for a profit. As soon as you step out of the post office, an eight-cent stamp is worth fifteen and a ten-cent stamp thirty because of all the stamp fans who can't be bothered to stand in line. It's ridiculous! According to Zhan Liying, Dr. Mu, their neighbor who's never around, is a stamp fan too. Does she really show up at these gatherings with her album, ready to swap? Surely not! Would a civilized female comrade, and a doctor too, get sucked into something like this?

A young guy with wavy permed hair comes up to her and says, blinking, "Got a Monkey? Want to swap?"

Flustered, Zhizhu steps away from him. "I'm not a collector—I'm just passing by."

Ugh! Can't she do one simple thing without getting interrupted? She crosses the road and sees the post office. Perfect. She goes in and—wonderful!—the glass phone booth is standing empty. Finally, it seems, someone up there is looking out for her.

Stepping into the cubicle, she gets out her little phone book and quickly looks up the troupe leader's number.

She ought to have called long ago. Even though the troupe leader has always shown favoritism to Elder Sister, he will still have to treat this as an official matter. If he condones this poaching of musicians, it won't take long for the entire troupe to fall into chaos!

Bracing herself for the busy signal—his line is busy nine times out of ten—she is relieved to get through on the first try. "Who is it?" says a voice.

As if she's actually standing before him, she tilts her head to one side and pouts. "It's me, silly! Can't you recognize my voice? I'm not so old yet that it's started changing."

Maybe there's a problem with the line, because he says, "Who is it? I'm sorry, I can't really hear . . ."

"My goodness," she purrs. "Can you really not tell? It's your humble servant Tantai Zhizhu!"

"Oh, I see," says the voice. "You're looking for the troupe leader, I suppose? He's not here, he went out—I'm just a family member. Why don't you try again this evening?"

He hangs up with a click, and Zhizhu stares in disbelief. Now that she thinks about it, that didn't really sound like the troupe leader. She ought to have made sure before she went into her coquette act! When she recalls the voice she used and imagines how cheap she must have sounded, she blushes bright red.

She has thought about this before, how all of them—not just her, but virtually all the girls who've been through drama school—are pouty in the presence of their troupe leader. They graduated at nineteen or twenty, and first began making a splash in their early twenties—young and in showbiz, it's understandable that they played the minx when talking to the higher-ups. The strange thing is, they're now in their thirties and forties, but quite a few of them have clung to old habits, fluttering their eyelashes and putting on baby-doll voices for the boss. She'd thought she was more self-aware than most, but this phone call has exposed how deep-rooted this behavior is. Ugh! She's really let herself down. How embarrassing! She is squirming.

Okay, so the troupe leader's not at home. Now what? Should she phone Elder Sister herself? There's a public phone just downstairs from Elder Sister's apartment, and Zhizhu has its number in her book. She could just interrogate her and see what she has to say for herself!

In for a penny, in for a pound. She dials the number and asks the person who answers to go fetch Elder Sister. Instead, this neighbor insists that she give him the number of her public phone—he'll pass it on to Elder Sister, and she'll give Zhizhu a call back. Zhizhu has no choice but to do as he says.

Zhizhu stands in the phone booth, waiting for the call. Time seems to pass very slowly. She longs for the phone to ring but is also terrified that it will—they're about to engage in close combat, and she still doesn't have a plan of attack!

A sudden sound makes her jerk her head to the side. There's a guy standing outside, and he's just rapped on the door—apparently he thinks she's hogging the booth for no reason.

As frustration rises in her, she has a sudden realization: Elder Sister is never going to call her back. Why would she be so foolish? If she'd refused to hang up and insisted that the person who answered the phone go fetch her right away, that might have worked. But now what?

She flips frantically through her phone book, then suddenly has a thought and immediately dials a number. This is something that occurred to her while lying on the sofa: to get in touch with a well-known critic who'd mentioned her in an essay about dan roles in Beijing opera. She's met him on a few occasions, at talks and tea parties, and he's always been very thoughtful and encouraging. He has a fair bit of authority. Maybe at this crucial moment, he'll give her some much-needed help.

She gets through right away, but the critic's daughter says he's just gone for his afternoon nap.

Recklessly, Zhizhu pleads, "If he's not asleep yet, could you please go get him? It's really, really important!"

The daughter goes. The critic is a kind man and comes to the phone.

Zhizhu agitatedly explains the whole situation to him, spilling all her troubles and doubts. "So what should I do? Chalk it up to bad luck and make do with whatever jinghu player and percussionist the troupe assigns me next? Or go into battle with my rival, fight tooth and nail to hang on to Old Zhao and Old Tong? Or just throw up my hands, blow out the candle, and give up? I'll be honest—I don't think this sort of situation happens by chance. But my thoughts are all jumbled, and I don't know how to make sense of it all. Anyway, I've told you everything now. I know you only care about what's on stage, and behind the scenes isn't any of your concern, but I'm fresh out of ideas. I don't know what to do next. If you could just show me a way out . . ."

The critic is frank. "My word, this is a brand-new problem. I've never heard anything like it. This wind of reform is blowing into every corner—you know what they say: every wind raises waves! How should we manage arts organizations? How can we encourage harmonious artistic pursuits and prevent artists from tearing each other down? How can we smash the egalitarian idea of the 'big pot of rice' that we all sup from while ensuring that emerging artists stay economically competitive? If this is a race, where's a rational place for the starting line? This really requires careful analysis! Even so, Comrade Tantai Zhizhu, I don't think you need to be so sad, or confused, and certainly not pessimistic. Isn't it good to shake things up a bit? I heard your troupe is losing money year after year—"

"You're absolutely right," Zhizhu confirms. "Every year, every month, we need government subsidies to stay afloat."

"Which is to say, you need systemic reform or you won't be able to go on," the critic tells her. "Stand a little taller, look a little farther, and think a little deeper. Of course, poaching is wrong, and I can see why you'd be enraged that someone would jump ship without so much as a goodbye. Yet it's these disturbances that tell us a structure is so weak it can't withstand wind and rain. I can't give you an answer right away, of course, but why don't we meet for a chat?"

Zhizhu is delighted and grateful. She asks if she can drop by right now, and he says he would welcome her. She floats out, almost forgetting to pay for her phone calls at the counter.

As she steps out of the post office and into the bustling street, her mood darkens again. She experienced a sense of enlightenment as she listened to the critic's words, but now Elder Sister's haughty face is a rock weighing down her heart. Getting rid of abuse in the troupe through reform and letting these disturbances lead them in a healthier direction? Easy for him to say!

The critic lives some distance from the Drum Tower—she'll have to take a bus there. Suddenly, she remembers Li Kai. Is he back home yet? If not, where is he? What's he doing? My god, what if he does something foolish? And where's Bamboo? Why didn't she stop to check if he was with his grandfather before rushing out? What if he's gone in search of his dad and gotten lost? Why do life and work have to weigh so heavily on us? How is she supposed to bear this?

The wind is rising. She wraps her scarf more tightly around her neck as she walks toward the bus stop.

CHAPTER 22

An editor meets a literary youth.

Page four of the *Beijing Daily*'s classified ads on December 12, 1982:

> MISSING PERSON. Su Deyou, male, 36, 5'3", from Anshan, Liaoning. Last seen wearing a dark-blue padded jacket, workman's trousers, and black vinyl boots. He carries a yellow canvas bag and doesn't look normal. On November 14, he left home for Beijing with a big stack of poems, and that's the last we saw of him. If anyone knows of his whereabouts, please contact Su Dehua at Mount Dagu Mine Ore-Sorting Plant, Anshan.

Probably not many *Beijing Daily* readers even notice this. How many feel a sense of dread after reading it? Only one, and he's in the siheyuan near the Bell and Drum Towers that we're getting to know quite well.

In our tour of the siheyuan a couple of chapters ago, we mentioned that to the west of the front courtyard is a little space carved out by a low wall with a moon gate. A middle-aged couple live here: Han Yitan, a poetry editor of thirty years' experience, and his wife, Ge Ping, who's been teaching elementary school for twenty-seven years. Their only daughter, Han Xianghong, is in her early thirties, married, with a son who's turning five soon.

Being cut off from their neighbors by that low wall, and not gregarious by nature, the Hans never really got to know the rest of the siheyuan, even though they've lived here almost as long as they've been married. In early 1982, Zhang Qilin from the northern side of the siheyuan was flipping through *Enlightenment*

Daily after dinner, when he came across a piece praising an excellent editor: "Han Yitan, who tirelessly pans for gold." It said Mr. Han read almost a thousand unsolicited submissions every day, most of which were flavorless as wax and had nothing new to say. Even so, he insisted on reading every single poem, and when he happened upon the rare shining exception, he was always thrilled to forward it to his editor in chief with his highest recommendation. One time, he'd just read an excellent verse of only twelve lines when he was called into a meeting. When he came out, the wind had blown the jumbled stacks of paper on his desk onto the floor, and a well-meaning colleague had picked them up—but though he went through these new piles, the poem he remembered liking was nowhere to be found. As he despaired, the others urged him to forget it—after all, the poet was a nobody, and according to their editorial guidelines, a mere twelve-line submission would not be returned nor responded to. Even so, he couldn't get it out of his mind, and spent the entire afternoon going through every scrap of paper from his desk and drawers, with no luck. The next day, he set to searching with even more determination, getting down on the floor and looking under the cabinets—and finally found that little poem in a cobwebbed corner. The poem was published, which was a shot in the arm for its author. Encouraged by this initial success, the poet's passion for his craft reached new heights. He produced many more poems and pamphlets in quick succession, eventually becoming one of the brightest literary stars in our province. When the reporter asked what Han Yitan had learned from this experience, he replied, "I learned that I need to buy a paperweight." Sure enough, a bronze weight now rests on his desk.

After reading this report, Zhang Qilin sighed wistfully. "Every profession needs people as good at spotting talent as this Han Yitan. If only my bureau had a few Han Yitans!" His daughter laughed at him. "Dad, did you know Han Yitan lives in our siheyuan?" Zhang Qilin was taken aback. "What? He's our neighbor?" Xiuzao giggled even harder. "Dad, you are such a bureaucrat! He's got that place on the west side of the front courtyard. Did you really not know?"

As a result of this article, an explosion of poetry manuscripts arrived at the Editorial Department, every one of them marked "For the attention of Comrade Han Yitan" or with a letter enclosed for Mr. Han. Actually, even before the profile was published, Mr. Han had already stopped reading unsolicited submissions—two "proletariat students" who'd just joined the department had been put in charge of plowing through them. Anything addressed to Mr. Han, though, they brought straight to his desk and placed beneath the paperweight. When he was truly overwhelmed and sent some back to the students, they simply sat on them. After all, the submitting instructions clearly said, "Please do not address correspondence to individual editors, as this may result in delays." In other words, "Any correspondence addressed to an individual will be mercilessly delayed." Of course, these thousands of innocent submitters would never have imagined this might be the case.

That wasn't the only outcome of this profile. One evening about half a month later, Han Yitan and Ge Ping were eating dinner when Tantai Zhizhu's father-in-law ushered a young man into their yard. "Editor Han, Teacher Ge, one of your relatives from the northeast is here to see you."

They turned to look at the young man, only to realize with a start he was a stranger. Later on, they cleared it up—the young man had never claimed to be a family member; he'd just asked to see "Uncle Han." Noticing his luggage and northeastern accent, Tantai Zhizhu's father-in-law had jumped to his own conclusions.

Mr. Han hastily put down his bowl and stood. "You wanted to see me?"

"Are you Uncle Han Yitan?" asked the stranger.

Mr. Han nodded. "Yes, I am."

The young man set down his luggage and wrapped both hands tightly around Mr. Han's right one, tears glinting in his eyes. "Finally I've found you, Uncle Han!"

Mr. Han was starting to understand. "Where did you come from? And what did you want to see me about?"

Even his actual family didn't behave so warmly. The young man bent down and unzipped his travel bag, from which he pulled out a plastic packet of large dried mushrooms. He set these on the table and said to Ge Ping with utmost respect, "And you must be Mrs. Han? Sorry to trouble you, Mrs. Han."

Han Yitan wasn't mentally prepared for this situation. All he could do was ask more questions. "Are you a literary youth? What are you doing here? How did you get my home address? Are you asking me to read your manuscript?"

It took them a short while to get the full story. He was a literary youth from a province in the northeast, and he loved poetry. Naturally, he'd been submitting his work for some time, to everywhere from *Poetry Journal* and the *People's Daily* arts supplement to regional newspapers and magazines in his part of the country. Not a single poem had been published—mostly he got no response. It was like dropping a stone into the ocean. The profile of Han Yitan had been hugely inspirational, and he wept hot tears while reading it. Apparently sincere, he said this was the one beam of light in his kingdom of darkness, so he felt he had to see Mr. Han in person. He got off the train and went straight to the Editorial Department, but the receptionist told him the entire department was out at a talk (this was true), so he asked for Mr. Han's home address and managed to get it after some pressing. Now here he was.

Ge Ping's maternal instincts took over. "Have you had dinner?"

"I couldn't eat anything before I found Uncle Han," said the young man frankly.

She invited him to stay for dinner. There wasn't enough food, so she went into the kitchen to fry some eggs.

In the meantime, Han Yitan asked him to take a seat on the couch and said, "Have you brought some of your writing?"

The young man dragged his heavy bag over, slid the zipper all the way open, and produced stack after stack of poetry, which he laid out on the coffee table with a running commentary. "This is *One Hundred Lyrical Poems*, this is a set titled *Love of the Soil*, this is an epic, *Ode to the Sky*, and here's part one of my narrative poem *Prometheus of the Grasslands*, my verse drama *Waves on the Aegean Sea . . .*"

By the time he was done, the stack of poems was more than three feet high.

Staring at this tower of poetry, Han Yitan felt as if he'd just been handed a severe prison sentence. He was too flustered to say a word.

"Uncle Han, you have to read these and publish my work! I need you to guide me, support me!" the young man entreated.

Ge Ping came out with the fried eggs and asked the young man to join them at the table. He didn't try to refuse, but sat with them and wolfed down his food—he'd clearly been very hungry.

Not having noticed the tower of poetry, Ge Ping said, "Don't eat too fast. If you're still hungry after this, I'll make you some instant noodles. Do you have family in Beijing, by the way?"

Still gobbling, the young man said, "No, apart from you and Uncle Han."

Mr. Han's heart sank, but Ge Ping still hadn't quite understood. "What are you here for? Is it work? Which guesthouse are you staying at?"

He looked startled by this question, and declared, "I'm here to see Uncle Han, of course. I was planning to stay with you for a month, and then . . ."

Only now did Ge Ping realize the severity of the situation. Panicking, she pressed on: "Do you have a job? Where do you work?"

"Of course I do," said the young man indifferently. "I'm part of the repair and construction team in my county's Agricultural Machinery Brigade. Our bosses are all old country bumpkins, you know what I mean? They don't support my literary work. In fact, they even attacked me—"

"Did you ask for leave before coming to Beijing?" Han Yitan couldn't help asking.

The young man sneered. "What for? I don't care what they think!"

"That won't do," said Ge Ping anxiously. "You can't just come to the city without a plan!"

The young man finished his last mouthful of food and wiped his mouth with the back of his hand. "I'm not going back until my poems are published!"

Han Yitan shivered. How was he going to get rid of this intruder?

"Does your family know you're here?" asked Ge Ping.

"Of course! I got into a big fight before setting out."

"How could you do that?" said Ge Ping reproachfully. "Think how worried your mom and dad must be!"

"My mom and dad?" He smiled. "My mom and dad died long ago."

"What family were you arguing with, then?"

The young man suddenly got worked up. "What family? My wife, that's who! That unbelievably vulgar petit bourgeois. She doesn't know the first thing about poetry! She's poetry illiterate! A classic ignoramus! We don't have a single thing in common! I asked her for a divorce long ago, but she refused! It's like being shackled! Think about it, Uncle Han, how difficult it is to dance with shackles on. Do you think it's easy to write poetry? Every word, every line is my blood, red as agate, my sweat shimmering like iridium. Now at least I'm happy. Let her weep in that fetid little hovel that stinks of pickled cabbage! As Li Bai says, 'I raise my head to the sky and laugh, as I walk out the door. How long could someone like me be banished to the wilderness?'"

Ge Ping was shaking her head. "How can you talk like that? Do you have children?"

The young man lifted his chin. "Children? Who would be a child of mine?" He pointed at the three-foot-high stack of poems. "Those are my children! She bore me a daughter too, but that's a child of the flesh, and I want one of the spirit—poetry! I should never have gotten married, I should never have had a so-called child. Look at the history of literature. How many poets came to tragic ends because of marriage? Pushkin, Lu You . . . I want to smash these earthly shackles and be a muse soaring freely through the air!"

Han Yitan and Ge Ping exchanged a glance. They were an honest, dutiful, intellectual couple, and never had they encountered such a fraught situation in their own home.

Taking a risk that he might anger the poet even more, Han Yitan said sternly, "Young man, we can't support you walking out of your job without taking leave first—you're abandoning your post. You have to go back right away. Our house is too small for you to stay here—Xinyuan Bathhouse is nearby, and they take overnight guests. If you don't have enough money, I can pay. And tomorrow, it would be best if you got the first train—"

The young man couldn't believe his ears. Eyes wide, he yelled, "Are you not Han Yitan?"

"What's wrong?" gaped Mr. Han.

"So that's the sort of person you are!" raged the young man. "That newspaper article was a total puff piece! You're actually a phony! A connoisseur of talent? Tirelessly panning for gold? Liar! Hypocrite!" He really did feel that he'd been tricked. Why was this world so full of traps? He slammed his hand down on the table. "What the hell? If you people aren't interested in finding hidden gems, why would you publish such a dog-shit article?"

Ge Ping was terrified. A lunatic in her home, which was meant to be a place of peace and tranquility. How could this be happening?

Han Yitan truly didn't know how to make this young man understand. "C-calm down, just c-c-calm down! You ought to know the work of literary production isn't so simple. You shouldn't have walked out on your job and family and run off to Beijing. Even if your work is good enough, it won't get published right away. Do you know how long publishing lead times are? It's March now, so our current issue will have gone to the printer in January. In the meantime, proofs of the April issue are being checked, the May issue is being typeset, the June issue is more or less edited, and submissions are being read for the July issue. Even if we went full speed ahead, it's not likely your work would make it into the June issue—July would be the soonest. So you see, if we did want to print your work, the very fastest it could happen would be three or four months. Are you really going to wait around in Beijing all that time? If you're talking about a collection or a book-length poem, it'll be more than a year before you have the book in your hands. And that's if we accept your work. If it doesn't reach our standard, then it won't matter how long you wait. You might as well go home."

The young man hadn't expected the world could be this cruel. Sunk in the deepest torment, he nonetheless didn't lose one speck of self-confidence, but declared, "I've chosen this road, and I'm going to walk down it! What's three or four months? What's a year or two? I won't rest until my work is published! I declare war on the world of poetry! I'm going to climb to the top, or die trying!"

Han Yitan stared, mouth open. "How will you live? Where will you stay in Beijing? What will you eat when you run out of money? Anyway, the city doesn't allow rural migrants to hang around indefinitely."

"How will I live?" The young man let out an explosive burst of derisory laughter. "I came looking for the man who tirelessly pans for gold. I thought he'd care about gold, but after all that talk it turns out his brain is filled with the most vulgar, mundane rubbish. How will I live? To a poet, what life is there to speak of, outside of poetry? I'll sleep in the street, scavenging empty cigarette packets for paper and used matchsticks for pens, and keep writing. I'll never ever return to that nauseating job or the little hovel that stinks of pickled cabbage! What was your question? How will I live in Beijing? I know what you mean—earning money. To you people, earning money and eating food is all there is to life. Fine, so I'll tell you: I know how to cut hair. I'll buy a set of barber's tools—I still have a bit of money for that—and go to the farmers' market every day to cut the farmers' hair. I'll earn enough to feed myself and to buy writing paper too. Mr. Han the editor! Don't look at me like that, I didn't come here to borrow money from you. Listen, I'm going to get published and make my name, even if you won't help me. Wait and see!"

They were at an impasse. Han Yitan felt his heart soften. He gazed at the tower of poems and sighed. "Since you've come all this way, I'll look at them.

I don't really have any standard in mind—and anyway, with literature, and especially with poetry, it's difficult to say what's good or bad. Also, I hope you'll understand, but I can't possibly read all these poems. I have to go to work every day, and whatever I don't get done in the office, I bring home to finish in my spare time."

Seeing Han Yitan prepared to read his work, the young man calmed down. "All right, all right," he said. "You're busy, I get it. Just read a selection!"

Han Yitan removed his glasses and picked up a manuscript. Looking at it closely, he was moved by the craftsmanship of the binding and the calligraphic script of the title, which must have taken a lot of effort. Inside, the poems were handwritten so neatly they could have been printed without a single correction. All in all, this truly was "blood red as agate, sweat shimmering like iridium." This was the verse drama, *Waves on the Aegean Sea*, but the opening of the prologue already had him confused:

> *When the bell of Notre-Dame de Paris tolls,*
> *Rousing mighty Caesar from his slumbers,*
> *When the drifting, enrobing, caliginous whirlwind*
> *Stirs the Aegean Sea awake in its cradle . . .*

Frowning, he said to the young man, "Why would you write this? Julius Caesar lived in the first century BC, but Notre-Dame wasn't built until the twelfth century AD. How could he have heard a bell from more than a thousand years in the future, never mind that they're in completely different parts of Europe? Also, how could a 'whirlwind' be 'drifting'? 'Enrobing' and 'caliginous' are far too obscure, you don't need to load your writing with such fancy words . . ."

The young man was unimpressed. "I'm writing poetry, not history. Anyway, this isn't a high school essay, why shouldn't I express my feelings the way I see fit?"

"The poetry you write ought to begin with the existence you're familiar with. You've spent your life in a Chinese county town, why write about ancient Greece and Rome?"

Han Yitan set down the manuscript and picked up another; the young man gestured at it. "Well, that one talks about something familiar—it's when I was sent to work in Inner Mongolia."

Han Yitan glanced down—it was the long narrative poem, *Prometheus of the Grasslands*. First was the contents page: Venice by Moonlight, Apollo in the Mountains, Anna Karenina in a Yurt, Astro Boy on Horseback . . . He didn't dare finish reading the list, let alone look at the poem itself. A huge number of ridiculous poems had passed before his eyes, but this young man's efforts outdid them all. As *Dream of the Red Chamber* has it, "Nonsense on a shaky foundation."

"Uncle Han," said the young man, respectful again, staring at him with hope and pleading in his eyes. "Please tell me where I've fallen short. The sharper your critique, the better."

Han Yitan had no idea what to say. He put the manuscript back and took one from the bottom of the pile: *One Hundred Lyrical Poems*. He turned to the first page, and, merciful Buddha, at least it was free of Western gods and people. The poem even scanned quite well . . . but wait, didn't it seem familiar? The first two lines looked like they were taken from Li Ying, the middle section was all Ai Qing, and the last two lines were Shu Ting's . . .

Just as he was wondering what to do, Ge Ping and Zhan Liying walked into the room. Sensing that something was wrong, Ge Ping had decided to get rid of this half-crazed literary youth—but how? It didn't seem worth getting the police involved. Should she go to the residents' committee? But the situation was hard to explain. In the end, she decided it made the most sense to ask a neighbor for help. The only person who'd ever visited them, apart from to collect for the water or electric bill, was Zhan Liying. And so, while the young man spewed his discontent, she'd slipped out to ask Nanny Zhan if she would help dispatch the intruder. Nanny Zhan heard her out, and bellowed, "What? He won't stay a minute longer! You two are far too kind. How do you know he's even a poet? All kinds of strange things are possible these days! What if he's a con artist? A burglar? An escaped convict? You'd be dead if he attacked you—a couple of bookish types without the strength in your hands to truss a chicken. Come! I'll help you kick him out!"

As soon as she stepped into the room, without even looking at the young man, Zhan Liying bellowed, "Hey! Kid! Where've you come from? These people don't even know you. Why are you here so late? Do you know where you are?

This is Beijing, our capital, and the police keep a tight watch on things. So you'd better go, all right? Or the police will send over one of their volunteer officers, and then you won't be able to leave even if you want to!"

The young man seemed shaken by Nanny Zhan's attack. He had no idea who she was, but her aggressive stance put him in a panic. He stuffed the poems back in his bag and pulled the zipper shut, gasping, "I'm going, I'm going. Now I know the truth about Beijing, the poetry world, and this so-called gold prospector!" He dashed from the house, and then the courtyard.

Han Yitan and Ge Ping stood frozen while Zhan Liying clapped her hands gleefully, chortling.

After this, Han Yitan jumped like a startled bird whenever he heard footsteps approaching their yard. He told the receptionist never to give his address to random visitors. Phone calls from strangers now made him tense up, and he insisted on talking for a while, until he could be sure the caller wasn't the literary youth, before he admitted that yes, he was Han Yitan.

Later, he began getting angry letters from other literary youths, asking why he was so greedy for their manuscripts if he never replied to their submissions. Actually, he'd done his best to respond to everyone at the beginning but was soon overwhelmed by the sheer volume. Even if he did nothing else twenty-four hours a day, not even eat or sleep, he still wouldn't be able to answer the blizzard of letters that arrived each day. He used to buy his own stamps, but that became unfeasible too—it would cost more than his entire monthly household budget. He started placing his personal rejections into the department's outgoing pile, to be mailed at the office's expense—but though no one said a word, he felt so bad about this that he stopped. Finally, he allowed the submissions to pile up unanswered, which brought him an onslaught of hatred and abuse.

The reporter got in touch about writing a follow-up to the "panning for gold" profile—a horrifying prospect. Not wanting to add to his troubles and anxieties, he declined.

It wasn't until autumn that envelopes "for the personal attention of Han Yitan" and letters to "respected Mr. Han" began tapering off.

One Sunday, their daughter and son-in-law came to visit with their grandson. During the meal, one of Ge Ping's dishes went down particularly well. Their daughter picked a large mushroom off the plate and asked, "Where did you get these, Mom? They're really good." Ge Ping replied, "Oh, a young poet stopped by in the spring and insisted on giving us these . . ."

Han Yitan choked. "These are his? I can't accept anything from him!"

Ge Ping retorted, "Who's talking about taking anything from him? When he left that day, we clean forgot to make him take his mushrooms with him. I tossed them into the dish cupboard and didn't think about them, then I came across them a few days ago while I was tidying up. I thought of returning them to him, but what's his address? Do you remember? And if the neighbors saw us getting rid of perfectly good mushrooms, they'd think we were losing our minds. Besides, he presented them to us of his own free will. You read his poems and gave him some suggestions, didn't you?"

Han Yitan shook his head. "You're a teacher, how could you be so unprincipled? Just because I've read someone's poems and said what I think doesn't mean I ought to accept gifts from him. Besides, he wasn't right in the head. You should never have fed us these mushrooms."

Ge Ping resentfully thought about how she'd spent hours on this dish, only to face this barrage of criticism. "If you're so principled, don't eat it!" she snapped.

Their daughter interjected, "That's enough, Dad! Go on, stand by your principles, I know that's what you do. You've done it all your life." She picked up another mushroom and popped it into her son's mouth. "Come on, open up. These are delicious!"

His daughter looked distraught. Han Yitan bowed his head, feeling a sudden weight on his chest. His face turned the dark purple of pig liver. "Stand by your principles, I know that's what you do." Those words were like an awl going straight into his soul.

She was referring to a moment in 1968. Aged seventeen, she had been about to graduate from high school when the Cultural Revolution caught up with her.

Their family of three was flung around by this red tornado. A nervous person, Han Yitan thought only of self-preservation. Ge Ping thanked her lucky stars that she was only teaching first and second grade—the kids in the fifth and sixth grades were busily denouncing their teachers. Their daughter didn't become a Red Guard, but also wasn't counted as a "black brat." She didn't dare go off on her own as a "free spirit," and showed up at school every day to take part in whatever activities were happening, just going with the flow. She was young and susceptible to influence, though. One afternoon, she came home for lunch, and while they were sitting around the table, she repeated some nasty rumors she'd heard about Madame Mao. Scared out of their minds, Han Yitan and Ge Ping immediately yelled at her so harshly that they all lost their appetites. Ge Ping was due to attend a struggle session in the neighborhood that afternoon, leaving Han Yitan and their daughter alone at home. A seed of terror took root in his heart. Their neighbor was the leader of a rebel faction at a factory (this was before Tantai Zhizhu's family moved in). Surely this neighbor had heard his daughter's "evil attack"? In any case, he felt tremendous guilt for his daughter's words—this behavior couldn't be tolerated. There was only one way out—to come clean and hope for mercy. And so he dragged his sobbing daughter to the police station so she could turn herself in.

When he recalled this incident now, it didn't seem possible. If it had happened to someone else, or been in a novel or narrative poem or memoir, he'd have looked at the manuscript and told the writer, "You can't just make up things like this! This scene doesn't make any sense."

But the fact is, it really did happen.

Even harder to believe: he rode his bike to the station, with his daughter perched on the rack. His bicycle! Why a bicycle? Was he hoping to get to the police a little quicker? To condemn his daughter to death sooner? Why didn't his daughter run? Why did she obediently sit on the rack all the way there? The way she was crying and carrying on, why did she come at all?

It was 1968. He'll never forget. This bizarre, nonsensical incident really took place. He and his only daughter, his flesh and blood. He was thirty-nine years old, his daughter just seventeen.

What happened at the station? A hundred different scenarios could have played out at a hundred different stations. "Public security has broken down," everyone said at the time. All procedures and protocols had been flung aside. What would his daughter's fate be when he marched her into the station? Would she be handed over to the revolutionary mob to be paraded through the streets? Would she be beaten so viciously she'd end up taking her own life? Anything was possible! He planned to plead for mercy—surely a good denunciation would be enough? Couldn't they put her through a couple of struggle sessions and call it a day? A verbal struggle, if possible, please, not a struggle of the flesh . . .

What happened next was like a dream: Good people happened to be on duty at the station that day. The two soldiers behind the reception desk listened poker-faced to his sweaty, rambling "confession" about his daughter's "evil assault," while she hunched over, quivering. In the end, they didn't even rebuke them, just glanced at each other and said at almost the same moment, "That's enough, go home—be more careful next time," and "Go, just go, don't come back again."

Against all expectation, that was the end of it. Han Yitan brought his daughter back home on his bicycle. Only then could he look at the wall they shared with their neighbor and not shake with fear. The daughter was sobbing so hard she could barely breathe, belatedly realizing how much danger she'd been in. She'd only come out unscathed through an incredible stroke of good luck, something that made no sense in those times.

Her respect for her father disappeared that day. He begged her forgiveness after the Gang of Four's downfall, and although she agreed to let bygones be bygones, she never smiled or looked at him the way she did her mother. They never chatted casually or supported each other—these things were no longer possible. When he was hospitalized at fifty, his daughter visited but only asked in a businesslike tone, "Are you better? Have you taken your medicine? Did they give you an injection? Is the food okay?" No warmth at all, as if she was being forced to visit a stranger.

Only he could truly understand this great sorrow, brought about by the course of his life.

He was born into a family of impoverished bureaucrats in 1929. His father was still lost in "dreams of the former capital," but in reality was a "peach blossom after the calamity"—a downtrodden civil servant. After his grandfather died, the household fell apart, and his father was out of luck too. Han Yitan had at least graduated high school, and managed to find a job as a clerk. After Liberation, he got a place at North China Revolutionary University, which despite its name actually only offered a short training program. There was a great shortage of cadres in all areas, and Revolutionary U funneled these newly qualified cadres into the various ministries. Han Yitan became an editor. That was thirty years ago, and although a number of chief editors have passed through the Editorial Department, he's been a constant presence through these "dynastic changes."

He became the editor with the longest CV, mainly because he was obedient. Give him an order, and he would carry it out without missing a single step. To start with, this was just his nature. Later, as he watched his colleagues being denounced during one political movement or another for "being thorny" or "carrying out independent activities," obedience became one of his most prized traits. When the higher-ups wanted him to publish poems conforming to the Campaign against the Three Evils and then the Campaign against the Five Evils, he sought out such poems. When they urgently needed some verses celebrating the Purge of Counter-Revolutionaries, he stayed up all night soliciting them and commissioned accompanying illustrations too. When they said he should show them some "airing of views" in line with the prevailing spirit, he selected a few of the more opinionated submissions and forwarded them to the higher-ups to make sure they were acceptable. When they said it was now time to "sound the horn of anti-rightism," he swiftly gathered some "anti-rightist ladder poems." When they asked him to rush out a special folio of folk songs for the Great Leap Forward, he read six thousand and chose thirty. Then came the Three Years of Hardship, and the higher-ups said everyone was having a difficult time, so why not make the poems a bit lighter? Right away, he pulled together poems and sequences designed to refresh the reader's eye: "Waltz on a Summer's Night," "The Swift-Flowing Brook," "How Beautiful You Are, Red Leaves," "Hearing a Flute in the Mountains." Some were even set to music and became popular ditties. Later, they told him it was no longer acceptable to "condone the tide of revisionist artistic thought," and so he rejected countless submissions from the aforementioned poets, urging them to "keep in step with the changing times." He then discovered a new batch of writers and published a series of their "rev-olutionized" writings. This went on until July 1966. A day before the entire Editorial Department was disbanded, he published a piece a worker had written in his spare time, "An Iron Broom Sweeps Clean the Three-Family Village." After a couple of years of "struggle sessions, self-criticism, and reform" and another three years or so in a cadre school, the Editorial Department was reinstated in 1973, and Han Yitan was among the former editors allowed to return right away. Why was that? Apart from knowing that he would be useful to them, the higher-ups also valued his familiarity with the scene: he knew each writer's past, what they'd published before, how readers responded, and how the department had dealt with whatever issues arose. The bosses only had to ask these questions, and he could answer right away—a living database. From then until 1978, you could say the poems he edited were an endless series of right angles: rhapsodizing the "fighting spirit" to "do battle with capitalist roaders within the Party until the end"; lauding the worker-soldiers for their service in the May Fourth Incident; odes to "the Great Proletarian Cultural Revolution, which we are so glad is here"; exhorting a billion Chinese people to overthrow "rightist revisionist behavior"; jubilation at "the great joy of humanity, that the Gang of Four is shattered"; "cherishing the memory of our revolutionary forebears, whose great achievements must never be forgotten"; heeding the call of "May Fourth spirit" and gazing toward a glittering future; "an ecstatic chorus of a hundred souls" for the "opening of ten Daqing oil fields"; declaring that "'always' should not be in the vocabulary of a materialist"; cheering on the "ministers sensitive to the People's needs"; solemnly presenting "Paean to Getting Rich" . . .

Thanks to the vicissitudes of life, editors came and went. Some were cut loose and banished, others retreated out of shame; some departed never to return, others made the rounds and came back again. His colleagues, too, were always in flux, though a few older editors remained like rocks in a river, fixed in place and covered in moss. Han Yitan was one of them.

Everyone acknowledged that he was a consummate professional who knew his work inside out, in addition to doing as he was told, being generally compliant, and serving as a human database. To be fair, he also had a great eye for poetry. Looking at a bunch of poems with the same theme, he had a knack for quickly sorting through them and rigorously weeding out the ones that lacked a literary sensibility, sifting to find the most artistically accomplished ones. He was a skilled editor, and would often merely shorten a line or change a single word to transform the whole piece, like a form of alchemy. Authors admired him, the chief editor was satisfied with his work, and Han Yitan was proud of himself.

He didn't write poetry himself—he was happy to remain an editor. Inwardly, he sneered at those of his colleagues who scribbled away at their verses as if intoxicated, imagining they could use their positions as a springboard to the realm of professional poets. He had no problem with birds or mice—but took issue with bats, who claimed to belong to whichever species was more expedient at the time.

Without his noticing, his hair had started graying. Like the woman in Qin Taoyu's poem who bragged of her skill at embroidery but wouldn't compare her beauty with others', he had cultivated a life of quiet contentment, defined by conformity. He'd had moments of fear, of being adrift, of loss—but they were all temporary. For instance, during the first two months of the Cultural Revolution, in the tumult after the rebel factions rose up in arms and the former bosses were all mowed down, he was uncertain if he ought to throw his lot in with the rebels or stake out a conservative position. When he was suddenly pulled into a work unit, he thanked his lucky stars that he hadn't "joined a school of fish" or grown close to any "capitalist roaders." Then the work unit was hauled on stage for a struggle session, and the rebel faction split in two and began infighting. The situation was scary, but ultimately it was just a squall, and soon things were clear again. With the Central Cultural Revolution as the highest authority, you couldn't go wrong sticking close to the two newspapers and one magazine—the *People's Daily*, *People's Liberation Army Daily*, and *Red Flag* magazine—so he felt he had no choice but to become a dutiful citizen, shaking with fear the whole time. He had a subscription to *Red Flag*, and all his copies were underlined heavily in red from his careful reading.

For some reason, a sense of panic and loss has been rearing up in him these last few years. When he tries to think about it rationally, it must be because the world is changing so fast; his churning brain can't keep up or digest what's going on. He doesn't know whom to obey anymore.

These days, a young, unproven writer can publish a book of selected poems with their name and signature on the title page. This would have been unimaginable prior to the Cultural Revolution. Qin Mu, Yang Mo, Guo Xiaochuan, and Du Pengcheng were all well known then, but which of them could have brought out something like this? What authors ever had their photos published? What's more, these whippersnappers, deficient in years and experience, get invited all over the place, traveling by plane, staying in hotels, giving speeches, wandering over hill and dale, sometimes even going overseas and getting their names known far and wide. Is this just? Does it make any sense?

Top-ten hits on the radio; pop stars like Li Guyi and Su Xiaoming; bell-bottom trousers and windbreakers; stacked heels and long hair on men; Astro Boy; silver-fungus pearl cream; White Orchid washing machines, Snowflake refrigerators; "I'm a Hitachi kid"; "leading the global wave"; "Comrade Hu Feng has provided a written statement"; *A Compendium of Modern Western Writing*; sixteen-inch standing electric fans on timers; hanging lamps with decorative plum-red shades; wall calendars with celebrity portraits; coffee-table books of French impressionist paintings; households with more than ten thousand yuan buying cars; private firms hiring workers; "plum blossom and soaring crane qigong, Master Hai Deng practices the two-finger 'chan'"; "apartments are now on sale in the newest elite residence in Shenzhen, Gaojia Garden—inland relatives are welcome"; Hiya Kiogan pills, active ingredients: ginseng, ox bezoars, musk, bear bile—"famously efficacious, trusted by the public, pay in Hong Kong, receive your order on the mainland . . ." Truly, this is an information explosion. How is Han Yitan supposed to cope with this? What's right? What's wrong? What's good? What's bad? What's going to fade away and what's going to stick around? What can he do without getting into trouble? And what should he stay far away from?

So many new things under the sun, so many worries in Han Yitan's mind. Facing a world like this, he tosses and turns late into the night, wallowing in nostalgia for the old days.

Still, his life is fairly stable, and like so many others, his household has been moving toward electrification the last couple of years. On the afternoon of December 12, 1982, he sits on his couch flipping through today's *Beijing Daily* while his wife does the laundry in the kitchen. The washing machine is a little loud, but it makes them happy to hear it. Ge Ping, feeling relaxed, returns to the living room and sits at her desk to grade her students' assignments.

When Han Yitan sees the missing-person ad, he feels an immediate panic. A young man from the northeast who "left home for Beijing with a big stack of poems." Who is he coming to see? A shiver shoots through him.

"Ge Ping," he says, "we're in trouble."

She ignores him, and continues grading.

Han Yitan reads out the ad, repeating the threatening words in a loud voice.

Now she's agitated. "Oh no! Whatever happens, we can't let him into our house again."

"Yes, yes," says Han Yitan. "If he shows up with more mushrooms, make him take them away! He's not to leave them on our table. Not even on our windowsill!"

After discussing this for a while, they feel sufficiently prepared to guard against the enemy, and gradually calm down again.

Ge Ping grades another three or four papers while Han Yitan glances at an ad for that evening's performance of *Little Cui, the Fox Spirit*, starring Dai Yueqin and Li Deqi, at the Eastern Ironworkers Club by the China Pingju Opera Theater troupe. The washing machine finishes its cycle. All of a sudden, there is a rap at their front door.

With a start, they turn to look. Through the glass, they see the figure of a man. Oh no—he's actually shown up!

Now what?

CHAPTER 23

A young hoodlum approaches the Bell and Drum Towers—
it's not looking good.

To many adults, the Great Proletarian Cultural Revolution feels like it happened just yesterday. Ten years of turmoil put a sudden stop to many developments that had been well underway. When the chaos was over and people tried to pick up the threads of the past as they righted themselves, they had no choice but to treat the last decade as a blank, as if time had frozen in the summer of 1966 and thawed in the fall of '76. For the last few years, newspapers have been referring to writers in their late thirties, or even those pushing fifty, as "young authors." Most people, including the writers themselves, feel they deserve to have ten years deducted from their actual age.

But what about those born just as the Cultural Revolution was kicking off? Aged sixteen in 1982, they've lived through infancy, childhood, and their teenage years, and are now about to enter young adulthood. They've been quietly growing up.

One of them is now walking north along Drum Tower Street.

His name is Yao Xiangdong—"Xiangdong" as in "facing Dong," meaning Mao Zedong. Many people his age have "Dong" in their names: "defending Dong," "establishing Dong," "praising Dong," and so on. (Names referencing more controversial individuals, such as Weibiao—"protecting Lin Biao"—or Xueqing—"learning from Jiang Qing"—were swiftly changed after their namesakes' fall from grace.) In kindergarten, their minders sang lullabies about "defeating turncoats, traitors, and thieves of work." Toward the end of elementary school, their teachers told the story of Grandpa Liu Shaoqi's great achievements. During the time of "open-door schools," they took part in activities to "further the journey of Socialism and block the road of capitalism," and the teachers raised their awareness by screening the Maoist film *Pine Ridge* and calling a session afterward for them to denounce the character Qian Guang's selfish, corrupt behavior. When they were about to graduate from middle school, the national obsession with grades was at its height, and in order to help get them into a good high school, the teachers worked on their writing abilities by screening *Dawn of New Hopes* and getting them to write critiques of the extreme leftists violently trampling the reasonable hopes of country folk. Society told them love and money were shameful, but now love is everywhere, and households with more than ten thousand yuan are lauded, sending a signal that having more money is glorious. At this young age, having barely experienced anything, central nervous systems still not fully developed, they had to deal with these enormous, constant dramatic reversals. What psychiatric problems and mindsets did they develop as a result?

Anyway, Yao Xiangdong is idly walking north along the street, hands in the pockets of his pale-yellow padded windbreaker.

He's just been kicked out of his home. The reason? That pale-yellow windbreaker.

Yao Xiangdong's father is a former army man; in the late 1960s, he switched to being a security guard at a district-level government department. He's always been very strict with Xiangdong. Ever since Xiangdong was four or five, his father's been filling his brain with the notion that he should join the army as soon as he's old enough. Xiangdong's mother is a typist and naturally also hopes her son will grow up quick and become a soldier. When he was a kid, she sewed him a little uniform in army green, complete with red trim on the collar, and of course a tiny soldier's cap adorned with an authentic five-pointed red star—his dad asked an old army buddy to take it off his own cap. Until he was ten or so, Xiangdong's heart brimmed with a sense of superiority, pride, and confidence. "My dad was in the People's Liberation Army, and I'm going to join up when I'm grown! My dad has so many old army buddies. If I live to be grown, he just needs to say a word to them, and I can enlist!"

When Xiangdong was in first grade, he was on his way home from school when he saw a ruffian stealing someone's hat. A high school student was walking down the sidewalk when out of nowhere a guy on a bicycle sped past, reached out, and grabbed his army-green cap. The high-schooler yelled after him, but the guy turned into an alleyway and was gone. This exhilarating scene left Xiangdong feeling the hat thief was very cool and made him treasure army-green objects even more.

When he was in fourth grade, society began changing all around him. Street thugs no longer stole army-green caps, and high school students gradually abandoned the fashion of dressing in army uniforms or caps. At some point, everyone had started wearing blue: blue shirts, blue trousers, and snow-white sports shoes—the very definition of stylish. In the winter, there was a fad for leather jackets—or "pleather," if they couldn't get hold of the real thing—and round woolen hats with ear flaps. Ruffians started stealing these woolen hats. The next winter, wool was out and shearling hats were in, so of course the thieves switched targets yet again. Fashions kept evolving, and now, the winter of 1982, windbreakers are the latest thing. No one aspires to join the army anymore. Anyone whose grades aren't completely hopeless wants to go to college. Those like Xiangdong, who didn't get into a key high school after he failed to get into a key middle school, those whose grades are going from bad to worse, are clearly not going to get into college, but they no longer dream of being soldiers either. They end up sitting at home waiting to get a job, their minds in a fog, with nothing to hold on to.

Xiangdong's parents haven't relaxed their strict discipline. His father despairs of the boy's poor grades and frequently rages at him, or worse, takes off a slipper and whacks Xiangdong. Inevitably, it takes his mom weeping, screaming, and holding him back before he'll stop. This lesson never takes hold, partly because he's teaching it all wrong, and partly because he doesn't understand this swiftly changing society himself, nor can he cope with it. He has a bellyful of torments and anxieties, which makes him say strange things in front of his son, although his son isn't allowed to talk back. When his son asks a question he can't answer, he takes his rage and confusion out on the boy. The theories he's spouting to his son have grown more and more abstract and out of date. That's the main reason Xiangdong is becoming harder to raise. He's learned to be a phony and only shows his parents what they want to see.

Although Xiangdong is not at a so-called key school, his teachers still work fairly hard. On one hand, they put a great deal of energy into supporting the few students who're actually interested in learning, helping them navigate the choppy seas of academe to surpass all expectations and get into college, thus vindicating themselves and bringing glory to the school, which may then be able to get coveted "key" status if it's able to produce enough such success stories. On the other hand, they try to keep "backward" students such as Xiangdong under control, so they don't cause too much disruption during school hours or get arrested after class. Education has never been a panacea, though, and perhaps these educators are a little too harsh in disciplining Xiangdong. He's learned to lie to them too.

Today, just before lunch, Xiangdong's mom noticed her son's windbreaker wasn't the acrylic one she'd bought him, but a padded cotton one—though the color and style were similar. "Where did you get that?" she asked.

"Swapped with a classmate," he said nonchalantly.

"How could you do that?" she lectured. "That's padded cotton, it must have cost half as much again as yours. If you ruin it, how will you pay your friend back? Isn't your acrylic one just as warm? Why do you need to be so fashionable?"

Xiangdong's father happened to walk into the room just then. Overhearing, he glanced at the windbreaker and flew into a rage. Xiangdong had already owned a padded jacket, made out of his father's old army coat. After wearing this over his blue duds for a while, he began clamoring for a new one. "Who's still wearing ragged old jackets like this?" he'd pleaded. "All my classmates have windbreakers!" His father had held his temper. It's certainly true that kids go around in windbreakers these days—it seems their parents have money to burn. Some even buy their children genuine leather coats. The Yaos are probably among the poorest of the parents—they both work for meager wages with no side jobs, and send their parents money each month. Xiangdong's elder sister graduated from teaching college and now works at a kindergarten. She isn't a Party member yet, so she only earns enough to support herself. Given their financial situation, when Xiangdong pestered his parents for a windbreaker, the best his mom could manage was an acrylic one. Rather than being content with that, he's now somehow managed to acquire a classmate's more expensive garment. Will he never be satisfied?

Seeing his useless son slouching around in a borrowed windbreaker, Xiangdong's father hollered, "You shameless boy! Take that off at once!"

His mom hurried over and tried to soothe her husband. "Your blood pressure! No need to get worked up, let's talk this over, nice and calm." Then, to

Xiangdong, "Tell your father you know what you did was wrong. After lunch, go find your friend and swap back. You hear me?"

Feeling like he had his mom's protection, Xiangdong sat fearlessly at the table and said, "What's the big deal? All we did was swap clothes." With that, he picked up his chopsticks.

This enraged his dad beyond measure. Stamping his foot, he declared, "Don't touch that food! This house has no room for someone like you. Get out of here right now!"

Xiangdong stood, shrugged, and walked out the door, ignoring his parents' screams.

He wandered eastward to the Shicha Seas and squeezed into a crowded pavilion—a few local residents often gather here to sing Beijing opera. Naturally, Xiangdong isn't actually interested in opera, he just enjoys making fun of how stupid the musicians and performers look. Next, he went to the Front Sea, currently frozen over, and menacingly "borrowed" a pair of ice skates from another guy his age. After some skating, he suddenly felt ferociously hungry, and that's how he ended up on the wide avenue leading to the Drum Tower.

Here he is, striding north along Di'anmen Main Road, passing by any number of restaurants, his sense of smell keenly trained on the aromas emanating from each shop front.

At the southernmost end of this street is a large national-enterprise snack bar with a wide selection, as well as a smaller private place specializing in fried filled pancakes. If Xiangdong were to search his pockets for coins, he'd probably be able to scrape together enough to fill his belly with items from these two places—but he doesn't notice them. He's on the west side of the street, and as he passes the crossroads, a batch of three-delicacy buns is just coming out of the steamer at Tianjin Goubuli Buns, a newly opened restaurant, and they're releasing a warm cloud of the most enticing fragrances into the air. Unable to help himself, Xiangdong steps up and peers through the glass. Wow, what a lot of people—some still waiting for their food, others standing behind them, breathing down their necks. Tables piled high with bowls and chopsticks that the waitstaff are too busy to clear away. Deliciously scented steam wafting from the deepest reaches of the room like fog. But who has the patience to stand in line to place an order, then wait again for an open seat? Besides, even if he checks all his pockets, he might not have enough for more than a single bun. Sighing, he steps back down and continues on his way.

Past Guangming Medicines and Eternal Youth Textile Services is Luming Garden Wonton Restaurant. There aren't too many people inside, but he keeps moving, whistling a jaunty tune. Wontons don't interest him—he's in the mood for a proper cooked meal. Now, how can he get hold of a "steelworker"—a five-yuan coin that has a steelworker on one side? Or maybe even a "unity"—a ten-yuan coin with people of all nations depicted—that would be amazing. Without noticing where he's going, he passes by White Rice Alley, Rainbow Clothing, Beijing Cultural Artifacts, Houmen Bridge, and then he sees Heyizhai Snack Bar. Just as he's making for the entrance, a shrill voice calls out, "Hey, Klutz!"

Referring to him, naturally. Xiangdong turns, and there's his classmate, known affectionately as Stinky. He's on a shiny girl's bike with twenty-six-inch wheels by the side of the road.

Xiangdong goes over to him.

Stinky is a plump little guy with a round head atop a round body, respectively encased in a shearling hat and a distinctive-looking leather jacket. His mouth opens and his high-pitched, brittle voice comes out. "Hey, Klutz! Why the fuck are you walking around here?"

Klutz, that is, Xiangdong, grabs Stinky's shearling hat, puts it on his own head, and says cheerfully, "What do you care, you son of a bitch? Where are you off to, looking for whores?"

Stinky reaches for his hat, but Klutz ducks. "Give that back!" Stinky says grouchily. "You already tricked Goatboy out of his windbreaker, you dick, isn't that enough? I have stuff to do!"

Sensing an opportunity for extortion, Klutz says, "I haven't freakin' eaten yet. Pay for my lunch, you son of a bitch, and you can have your hat back."

After an exchange both coarse and intimate, both bullying and brotherly, Klutz finally returns Stinky's hat to him, and Stinky lends Klutz one yuan.

In elementary school, Xiangdong started out obediently doing as his parents and teachers said. He never insulted anyone, nor did he use a single swear word. Then he started seeing people denounced for ideological crimes and led through the street in dunce hats. The accused, being paraded like this, naturally had their dignity trampled into the gutter, but the raging mob surrounding them weren't much better off, with their twisted, shrieking mouths, violent behavior, and utter disregard for the community. Xiangdong's young mind asked the question: *When I grow up, will I be tortured, or will I be doing the torturing? Obviously I should be the tormentor!* To make this aspiration come true, when the kids were playing "struggle session" in third grade, he got his classmates to string up Stinky as a "representative of the three evils," then they rolled up their sleeves and pummeled him, exactly how "counterrevolutionaries" were regularly treated. Finally, he scowled and sternly proclaimed, "Active counterrevolutionaries, your hats are in the hands of the People!" After 1976, parents and teachers ought to have devoted their efforts to rebuilding these youngsters' self-esteem, but given the sweeping changes at the time, Xiangdong's father was having trouble keeping his own balance and certainly didn't have the capacity to deal with his son's mental health too. Instead, he jumped on the boy's every little mistake, berating and hitting him, which caused what was left of Xiangdong's fragile self-respect to completely collapse. Faced with the large-scale alterations to the exam system, teachers were forced to focus on grades and pass rates, which meant treating Xiangdong and his classmates' filthy language and mayhem as no more than behavior to be clamped down on. At moments of stress, they were reduced to sneering, "Look at you, little hoodlums!" not realizing this would further erode Xiangdong's self-esteem and push him in the other direction, a sort of defiance: "You're calling me a little hoodlum? Fine, then I'll be a little hoodlum. Happy now?"

It turned out that getting to know other little hoodlums was the easiest thing in the world—they gathered in public bathrooms, ice-skating rinks, swimming pools, in the crowds of stamp speculators at post offices, at soccer stadiums waiting to resell tickets. Xiangdong's downfall came with the offer of a cigarette in a restroom, a violent collision at a skating rink, the loan of some flippers at a swimming pool—and his first illegal act was following his bros to the post office to sell fake stamps, and the soccer stadium to hawk out-of-date tickets. He scammed less than a yuan, which he spent on five ice pops. Gobbling those down one after another gave him diarrhea for the next two days.

In the summer of 1982, he slipped into someone's yard, boosted a two-foot-tall jade-green cactus, and ran straight to Back Sea, where he threw it right into the water. It's not like he needed this—the only reason he destroyed this beautiful object was to earn the cheers of his bros.

Now Xiangdong takes Stinky's yuan and swaggers into Heyizhai Snack Bar. It's full, as usual, but the line for a table isn't too long. His eyes light on a bubbling clay pot at a nearby table, the surface of the broth twinkling with specks of grease, tofu slices protruding from the thick liquid. Just as he's deciding that's what he will order, he realizes the people digging into this clay pot are his homeroom teacher and his family! Yes, there's no mistake—this older woman must be Mr. Wang's wife, and the boy and girl are surely his kids. They present an attractive tableau, tackling the hot broth with porcelain spoons.

His eyes meet Mr. Wang's, who seems even more embarrassed than him. Teachers fear nothing more than being seen by their students doing anything human—eating, drinking, sleeping, going to the toilet. For his part, Xiangdong stopped seeing teachers as sacred beings in second grade, when his homeroom teacher suddenly bent over in class and vomited into a spittoon. So teachers could get tummy aches too. They could be ill, throw up, and make fools of themselves . . .

"Mr. Wang!" says Xiangdong in a mocking tone.

Mr. Wang blushes like a thief caught red-handed. Xiangdong is surprised and amused. Mrs. Wang and the kids gape at him too and don't look pleased. It takes Mr. Wang a few seconds to say, "Oh it's you, Yao Xiangdong. Are . . . are you here for lunch?"

"No," Xiangdong improvises. "We have guests, so my mom sent me to fetch some snacks."

"Oh, I see, very good, go ahead," says Mr. Wang, smiling and extremely cordial.

It's not like Xiangdong needs his permission, but for some reason he suddenly becomes very polite, and bobs his head a few times before heading to the counter.

Still chewing, Mrs. Wang says approvingly, "That student of yours seems nice."

Mr. Wang reaches for more food and says, "Actually, he's one of our troublemakers."

Xiangdong doesn't hear this little exchange, but he senses Mr. Wang turning to look at him. He doesn't need any snacks, but still spends eighty cents on a small combination platter, specifying it's to take out so the server wraps it for him.

251

As he steps out of the restaurant, regret washes over Xiangdong. What he needs is a clay pot of tofu broth, not this dried-out platter of snacks! He trots across the road and, by the southeast corner of Houmen Bridge, finds a restaurant without any signage. He goes in and sees that they sell beef noodle soup. His stomach is rumbling, so without thinking any further, he scrapes together all his change and buys a bowl of noodles, then dumps in the snacks from the platter (a few strips of beef and some fried peanuts) and gobbles it down. The bowl is so overloaded that some of the soup dribbles out, creating little rivulets down the plastic tablecloth. By the time he notices, it's too late—he yelps in anguish at the sight of a large brown stain on his fancy windbreaker.

This windbreaker belongs to the class chair, Yang Qiangqiang. Surprisingly, Xiangdong gets on quite well with Qiangqiang, even though one of them is a member of the Communist Youth Party and the other a mere backward student. Qiangqiang's parents are both actors with the National Experimental Theater Company. His grades were pretty good in middle school, but he managed to mess up his final exam by not fully addressing an essay prompt and didn't get into a key school—that's how he's ended up with the likes of Xiangdong. Mr. Wang sat them next to each other in class, hoping Qiangqiang could help Xiangdong, but Xiangdong doesn't think he's been a huge amount of help—all he's done is suggest Xiangdong read beyond their textbooks, which isn't likely to happen, and insist on lending him Lyubov Kosmodemyanskaya's *The Story of Zoya and Shura*, though Xiangdong didn't even make it as far as the war against the Germans. Next, Qiangqiang tried to make him read *Romance of the Three Kingdoms*, which was even more painful. Xiangdong said, "I'd rather read comic books," to which Qiangqiang said, "I have the complete set of *Romance of the Three Kingdoms* comics, all forty-eight issues." Xiangdong asked to borrow them, but Qiangqiang replied, "I don't lend them out. You'll have to come to my house." So Xiangdong went over, and Qiangqiang brought out a cardboard box, which did indeed contain the full set of *Three Kingdoms* comics. His parents had bought them for his elder brother before the Cultural Revolution, and the family had held on to them. Xiangdong read a couple and was hooked. Qiangqiang was the only boy in their class who didn't use Xiangdong's nickname, and he didn't swear, but neither did he object to Xiangdong and the others liberally salting their words with "bastards" and "fucks." In class, the teachers were always having to restrain Xiangdong with "Don't do this!" or "You're not allowed to do that!"

Then they'd ask Qiangqiang to help, and he would ask Xiangdong, "Why did you have to do this?" or "Wouldn't it be better if you did that?" For instance, as Xiangdong became completely engrossed in the comic books, Qiangqiang said, "Why don't you take a break? Wouldn't it be good to do a few geometry problems now?" Xiangdong wanted to copy Qiangqiang's assignment, and Qiangqiang said, "Sure, I guess it would be good for you to understand at least one solution." And indeed, he explained precisely one answer to Xiangdong. Qiangqiang is so easygoing, it's hard to dislike him. When they were voting for their class chair, Mr. Wang had initially favored one of the girls, but Xiangdong abruptly threw his support behind Qiangqiang. As a result, every single boy voted for Qiangqiang, and since some of the girls liked him too, he won the election.

Xiangdong's parents no doubt imagine he bullied Qiangqiang into surrendering that windbreaker, but that's not the case. Yesterday, Xiangdong came by Qiangqiang's house after school, and they enjoyed a game of army chess. As he was saying goodbye, Xiangdong noticed how much more stylish Qiangqiang's windbreaker was than his own, and spontaneously piped up, "Shall we swap for a day?" Qiangqiang agreed, so he wore it home. What's the big deal?

And now the windbreaker's been stained by the bastard soup. What bad luck! If it were anyone else, Xiangdong wouldn't give a fuck, but Qiangqiang's been really good to him. Who else would have let him sit there and read his way through all forty-eight volumes of the *Three Kingdoms* comic books?

Xiangdong leaves the noodle restaurant in a foul mood. He'd love to pick a fight with the first person he runs into. All you have to do is say, "Who the fuck do you think you're looking at?" and you can thump them to your heart's content. Unfortunately, the first person he runs into is a PLA soldier in a four-pocket jacket. Regiment level or division level? Red star on his cap, red badge on his collar. As a little kid, this is who Xiangdong longed to be. But now you need to get into officer cadet school if you want to be an army officer, and they only let you in if you have the right grades. "Grades, grades, everything else fades." Xiangdong doesn't have the grades. That sucks!

Next to the noodle restaurant is Yimin Consignment Store, which is gaining quite a reputation in Beijing, and may soon be as well known as Zhongchang Consignment on West Huamen Street. Xiangdong barges in. There are various items of furniture—spring mattresses, folding sofa beds, and the latest addition, a batch of chrome-plated clothing racks with sockets on top where you can fit light bulbs, so they serve as standing lamps too. Xiangdong isn't interested in any of this stuff. But they sell clothes, and here we are—windbreakers! Padded cotton ones! There are little zippered pockets on the sleeves—that's neat. What cool stuff would you keep in there? The brand is in gold lettering on a black background, written in English so he has no idea what it says, but maybe Qiangqiang will know. His English isn't bad. Argh! They're forty-five yuan each! That's way too much. But if he could find the money to buy one, that would be great. He'd take it to Qiangqiang and say, "Hey, bro, I got your windbreaker dirty, but I'll make it up to you. Have a—what's that English word? Have a 'look-see.' Here, take this. Well? It's even better, right? How about it? Cool enough for you?"

Xiangdong leaves the consignment store in a funk and keeps walking north. Oh, there's Hat Hutong. Qiangqiang lives there, in quarters provided by the Ministry of Culture—quite a few people from the Experimental Theater have homes here. Should he go see Qiangqiang? Looking like this? What a disgrace! Even as he has the thought, he's already crossing the road. Get as far from Hat Hutong as possible! He stumbles his way to the northwest end of the street, where he sees Makai Restaurant, from which an alluring aroma emanates. He realizes he's still hungry and instinctively walks right in. It's take-out downstairs, and a sit-down restaurant upstairs. He stands by the stairs and reads the menu. He hasn't sampled most of these dishes before, but just reading the names is enough to make him drool.

Boneless Dong'an chicken	Sea cucumber stew
Oil-braised prawns	Braised dog meat
Deep-fried sparrow	Spicy squid
Sweet and sour fish	Stir-fried battered eel

Once again he thinks how good it would be if he had a steelworker or unity in his pocket—but he's now penniless. And so he trudges back out of Makai, swallowing hard.

He walks toward the Bell and Drum Towers. He doesn't know where he's headed. Out of nowhere, the jade-green cactus pops into his mind.

CHAPTER 24

Believe it or not, wedding banquets have their thrilling
moments too.

The third round of hot dishes arrives.

Chicken fried with walnuts, cooked in the imperial style—Lu Xichun was afraid the Xues wouldn't be able to get hold of walnuts, so he brought three taels' worth in a plastic bag—oil still sizzling as it arrives at the table; a whole crispy duck, into whose mouth Xichun has placed a rose carved out of a carrot with celery leaves attached; a sweet and sour fish, not particularly large, but the crosshatching and sauce amply prove it was cooked in the correct manner; and a dish of cabbage with chestnuts—the chestnuts are large and yellow, the cabbage juicy and green, a simple dish compared to the other three, but still enough to make you drool.

With these four dishes on the table, Seventh Aunt gives up finding fault with everything, and utters some sincere praise. "My word! What a celebratory spread. Imagine our Xiuya having such a fine chef on her very first day in her household. Isn't she a lucky thing?"

Uncle Xue is delighted to hear these words. The sweet and sour fish, which looks, smells, and tastes fantastic, makes him even more emotional. When he was little, there would be a fish on the table every New Year, and just like this one, it would have sizzling gravy ladled over it, but the fish itself was made of wood! The family was too poor to afford an actual fish but didn't want to miss out on the good luck it represented, and this was their solution—apparently the custom came from Jiangzhe district. After the meal, the wooden fish was washed and brushed clean and hung up, ready for the following year. Their fake fish was already in the family before Uncle Xue was born, and he "ate" it every year until he entered Longfu Temple as a lama. One of his siblings must have taken it, though presumably it's no longer in use. He has a sudden urge to ask Jiyue's eldest aunt if she remembers it, but can't see her—she's still in the other room, handling the side banquet there. As for her daughter and her husband, they've taken their children and left. Uncle and Auntie Xue tried persuading them to stay, but the cousin-in-law was adamant, refusing even to hang around for a rare taste of sweet and sour fish. His new daughter-in-law sweetly says in his ear, "Dad, try some of this fish!" He takes a chunk of meat from the cheek, pops it solemnly into his mouth, and chews carefully. It really is the most delicate flavor.

Xiuya has a mild headache from the noise, but her heart is full of joy and pride. All her coworkers from the photo studio stopped by earlier to offer their congratulations, insisting they'd just eaten and couldn't force down another thing, though the hosts urged them to—they just drank a toast to the couple, sat or stood for a while to join in the fun, and said their goodbyes. The professors' son, the one getting a bit of a reputation for his eye-opening techniques, was among them. Xiuya thought back to the designs she'd had on him, as well as the way he and his intellectual family politely rejected her, then reflected that he remains single to this day—and somehow or other, she found herself raising a glass of baijiu and saying to him, in front of everyone, "Come on, let's have a toast!" He was flustered and lost his composure for once. "I can't handle baijiu—I'll have wine instead!" Everyone bayed with laughter—how could he abandon grain for grape? He was forced to down the baijiu, eyes shut tight and nose crinkled, at the same time as Xiuya. She felt an enormous sense of satisfaction and almost said out loud the words in her heart, "Maybe it's time to open your own eyes."

The guests make short work of the third course. Luo Baosang has no sooner finished chewing on a large chunk of crispy duck thigh than he's assaulting the sweet and sour fish. Xiuya notices Jiyue isn't eating much, and his chopsticks don't even go near the fish, probably because it isn't very large and he wants to leave it for the others. She grabs a large chunk and puts it on his plate. "Have some—it's not bad at all!" she says. Watching this little scene, Baosang winks and nudges the perspiring Manager Wang and says in the voice of an old-style peep-show operator, "If you look in that direction, sir, you'll see a couple getting up to no good."

The fish's arrival at the table has triggered wave after wave of nausea in Jiyue. The deep-frying has turned its head glossy brown, making its eyes protrude and its mouth gape, bringing to mind his time as an army cook, when he cut open the fish from the pond to find their guts inhabited by parasitic worms from mouth to anus. He wishes everyone would pick this fish's bones clean so he can stop looking at it. Instead, Xiuya grabs a chunk of the very thing he's trying to avoid and plunks it down on his plate. He reels back a little. His stomach is a churning sea, slopping vicious waves right into his gullet. Baosang's raucous voice swells, and Manager Wang's half-drunken coarse laughter washes over him too. He loses control and, with a cry, throws up.

Just like that, the atmosphere of the wedding is ruined, and you can imagine the chaos that comes next. Auntie Xue probably feels worse than anyone else. Xiuya's shock, Seventh Aunt's accusatory glare, and the disgusted reactions from their guests all feel like the most enormous humiliation. In a panic, Auntie Xue gets her nephew Jikui to take Jiyue out to clean up and change his clothes, then turns to everyone else and frenetically explains, "This never happens to Jiyue. It's been years since he threw up. Maybe he's a little drunk? But he's been drunk before, and nothing like this happened. Anyway, just a little accident . . ." She's still talking, but already Seventh Aunt's eyebrows shoot up and she starts interrogating Xiuya. "Did he tell you he has stomach problems? Did you both get physicals before signing the register? He may need a stomach X-ray, just to make sure everything's okay. You really didn't know he had stomach problems?" Uncle and Auntie Xue frantically answer this volley of questions. "Jiyue's stomach is absolutely fine! This really never happens . . ." The room is growing more tense.

Xiuya isn't actually that bothered by the vomiting and doesn't think there's necessarily anything wrong with his stomach. She looks down at her own suit—she thought she felt herself getting spattered, which is the main reason she's upset right now. Luckily, her jacket and trousers look pristine, but oh no! There are disgusting globs on one high-heeled shoe! She wants to get them off right away but has nothing to wipe with. Her face flushes red, and her lips grow pinched. For the first time in this banquet, she looks unhappy and anxious.

Zhaoying is exhausted, but makes an effort to rally and save the situation. Although she despises everything right now, she keeps a smile on her lips and a bright stream of words coming from her mouth, trying to calm everyone down. "It's fine, Jiyue will have some hot tea to sober up. He'll be okay. I'll get this cleaned up in no time at all. Do keep eating, everyone." Moving nimbly, she cleans the table and floor in a few swipes, and hands Xiuya some Kleenex for her shoe.

Jikui helps his cousin back into the room. Jiyue says to everyone, "I'm okay! I'm not drunk, and there's nothing wrong with my stomach, I just hate fish. I don't eat it, can't even stand the sight of it . . ."

"Tell you what, I'll dispose of it for you, and it won't offend your eyes any longer." Baosang pulls the platter over and tucks in heartily. Even Manager Wang finds this disrespectful, and nudges his shoulder. "Hey, maybe don't say anything for a while."

Seventh Aunt isn't about to let this slide. He doesn't eat fish? He hates fish? That won't do! Fish is auspicious! It represents prosperity! Is he just going to be poor? She whips around to Xiuya. "Did he mention this while you were dating? It's a major problem; he shouldn't have kept it from you."

Before Xiuya can reply, the door opens and more well-wishers pour in. Some are connected to the Xue family, others are people they'd never have expected to show up; some came specially, others you can tell are on their way somewhere else—taking their kid to North Lake Park, say, or they have a shopping bag, meaning they're heading to the department store. Some are Xiuya's acquaintances but strangers to everyone else, others are known to the Xues but not Xiuya, or known to just one of the Xues. Too many people to introduce everyone to everyone else. The room is too small for everyone to sit, so some stand for a while, drink whatever they're offered, and try a couple of dishes; others accept a piece of wedding candy, wrapper removed by the bride or groom. The noise, the crowd—there's far too much going on, and it's overwhelming.

Yao Xiangdong arrives amid this bedlam.

He wandered into this hutong and noticed the red double-happiness wedding decorations, the multitude of bicycles by the siheyuan gate, the confetti on the road outside, and the enticing smells (Lu Xichun had lifted the lid off the pot of steamed beef with powdered rice).

The gaggle of well-wishers was arriving just then, chatting and laughing merrily as they surged into the courtyard. Xiangdong made a snap decision to insert himself among them, and now here he is, at the front line of the banquet.

He's a little nervous to start with, worried that someone will grab him by the arm and yell, "Who are you? What are you doing here?" He lurks in a corner, heart thumping like mad. After a few minutes, though, he realizes that many of the others don't know each other either, and no one seems inclined to question him. He gradually calms down.

Baosang is about six-tenths drunk by this point. Feeling a sudden urge for more beer, he reaches behind him for another bottle, but they're all gone. As his hosts greet the sudden influx of guests, he bellows, "Isn't there any more fucking beer?" Manager Wang grabs him and says, "Forget it, have some malt syrup instead." He pours them both a cup of the stuff. Baosang takes a swig and his face contorts. "What the hell is this crap? Taste that! It's not fit for humans!" He spins around and holds his cup up to the person behind him, who happens to be Yao Xiangdong. For a second, Xiangdong thinks he's been found out, and his soul just about leaves his body. After a few sips of malt syrup, he realizes Baosang is tipsy, and quietly congratulates himself for fitting in. He looks over Baosang's shoulder at the dresser—the top two drawers don't look secure. His fingers itch. What might be in there? He remembers one time, he was squatting in a public toilet chatting with a pickpocket, who shared a story about being at a wedding and peeping into the top drawer of their new dresser—it was where they'd stowed all the cash gifts from the day, and it wasn't just steelworkers or unities either. If Xiangdong could help himself to a few of those, that would be more than enough for the windbreaker from the consignment store.

Having successfully forced Xiangdong to sample the malt syrup, Baosang shuffles back around and raps the table, roaring louder than before, "Beer!" The room is so noisy that no one pays him any attention, which makes him feel empty. He stomps out, evading Manager Wang's ineffectual attempts to stop him, and heads to the cooking tent. Seeing Lu Xichun, his heart fills once more because he is here today to be served, and Xichun is clearly here to serve him.

Xichun is sweating hard, and his eyes are bleary with fatigue, but he feels elated. His efforts have garnered praise from all the guests, and he is pleased with himself. He paid particular attention to Seventh Aunt's reaction—if even she can't help but compliment him, he must truly have produced a beautiful meal. After three rounds of hot dishes, the high point has passed, and the fourth round needn't strive for resplendence. He'll give them three hearty dishes with rice to round off the meal: beef with powdered rice, beef stew, and shredded pork with garlic shoots, plus the perfect grace note—apple fritters in pulled toffee. Before this final round, he'll bring out a tureen of carefully prepared "four-happiness soup." The tradition at Beijing wedding banquets is when this soup reaches the table, the hosts will present him with a red paper soup envelope, which will contain an even number of two-yuan bills, at least two and as many as eight or ten, which is the cue for members of the bridal party, such as Seventh Aunt, to withdraw. He's not here for the soup envelope, though. Should he turn it down? But that might upset the hosts—he should probably just accept it. Or maybe he ought to serve the four-happiness soup last? He'd very much like Seventh Aunt to admire his apple fritters. Not only are the toffee strands exceptionally long and glossy, but every piece of apple is fried to perfection, gleaming with a golden sheen. What exclamations of delight might this elicit from Seventh Aunt?

As he ponders, Baosang pops up in front of him. "Are you already drunk, Baosang?" asks Xichun. "There's still four dishes and soup to come!"

Baosang grumbles, "Not a single drop of beer left! What a poor show! Stingy bastards—imagine not having enough beer."

"Didn't you buy the beer?" Xichun reminds him. "They're not being stingy, they just couldn't get hold of any more."

Now Baosang remembers, but he's already worked up a head of steam. Smacking Xichun on the back of the head, he bellows, "You son of a bitch, do your job and serve us!" He grabs the ladle from the tureen and scoops some soup toward his mouth. Xichun snatches the ladle back, spilling half its contents onto the ground. He tips the other half back into the tureen, replaces the ladle, and picks up the tureen by its earlike handles. "You're drunk, Baosang! I've got nothing against you coming here to eat—I bet you don't often get to taste a feast like this. But behave. How's anyone going to respect you if you don't respect yourself? Go back inside—I'll follow with the soup. There's enough here for everyone. When you're back inside, I'll put some in your bowl, and you can enjoy it then!"

Baosang glares at Xichun, but doesn't move. As Xichun is wondering what to do next, Zhaoying appears and says, "Most of the new guests left—we're back to the ones around the table. Go serve the soup, then you can have a break, and I'll catch my breath too."

Xichun exits with the tureen.

Uncle and Auntie Xue have followed the departing guests to the courtyard gate, and the banquet suddenly seems a lot quieter—just the bride and groom, Seventh Aunt, Cousin Jikui, Manager Wang, Mr. Yin, and a few others. Second

Aunt's son and Jiyue's boss, Master Tong, have gone too. Without the crowd, the objects around the room can be clearly seen, rocks revealed by a receding tide. Garish gifts fill every corner, including many cheap decorative objects with no particular function: vases adorned with crudely painted beautiful women, gold-and-silver-daubed ceramic mugs with slightly deformed mouths, linen pillow covers with bizarre prints (actually factory rejects, originally intended as dishcloths). All in pairs, of course, to represent coupledom. Strewn across the dresser, bedside cabinet, bed, and coffee table, they actually look quite festive, magnificent in their own way. This is what greets Xichun as he steps across the threshold, soup tureen in hand.

Back from saying goodbye, Uncle and Auntie Xue hastily return to their seats when they see Xichun with the soup. This is an important moment, signifying that the banquet is winding down. The bride's family will take their leave, and the bride will stay—now formally part of the groom's family.

Xichun waits for the groom's parents to sit before ceremoniously placing the tureen in the center of the table. Clasping his hands together, he says sincerely, "I've done my very best today, and if any of these dishes wasn't authentic or tasty enough, I hope you will forgive me. This is the four-happiness soup. What are the four happinesses? A loving husband and wife, that's one; love between generations, that's two; love between friends and neighbors, three; and finally, the hope that our fatherland will quickly achieve its Four Modernizations, which will be the greatest happiness of all! Please drink it while it's warm—happiness on top of happiness!"

What a great speech! The guests burst out cheering, and Auntie Xue regrets having put just twelve yuan in the soup envelope. They're very lucky to have hired such an excellent red chef. She'd like to pull Uncle Xue aside to see how he feels about adding four more two-yuan notes to the fee. Seventh Aunt never relishes the moment when the soup arrives at the table, but at least this time she has Xichun's words to cheer her up. The bride and groom exchange a look, and sweetness ripples over their hearts. The only person to remain completely indifferent is Baosang, who has tottered back from the cooking tent. Seeing everyone in the room looking at Xichun with grateful admiration, he feels a jolt of envy. Leaning on his inebriation, he narrows his eyes and says gruffly, "Give me soup!"

Ignoring him, Xichun urges Uncle Xue, Auntie Xue, and Seventh Aunt to try the four-happiness soup. The bride fills her in-laws' bowls, while the groom serves her aunt. The three elders sip and proclaim it good. Only then do the others help themselves with their own spoons. Baosang thrusts his bowl at Xichun, green veins standing out on his forehead, and bellows, "Soup!"

Xichun keeps ignoring him. The bride and groom are toasting him for his hard work, and the other guests join in. Jiyue passes him some baijiu, but before Xichun can take it, Baosang's arm shoots out and knocks the glass onto the table, spilling liquor everywhere. Manager Wang tries to calm Baosang down—"E-nough of this nonsense"—but Baosang is already screaming at Xichun, "Who the hell do you think you are, acting all high and mighty? I know your dirty secret! Your dad was a big teapot! You're the son of a big teapot!"

Jiyue and Xiuya have no idea what he's talking about but are alarmed by Xichun's reaction—he looks as if someone punched him hard in the chest. All the blood drains from his face, his lips tremble, and the tendons in his neck stick out.

The older guests understand Baosang right away. In the old society, the staff at cheap brothels were known as "big teapots," the lowest of the low. Not only did they serve customers, they were also expected to wait on the prostitutes—cleaning rooms and beds between sessions, running out for tobacco and snacks, going door to door offering hot drinks from a large cotton-padded teapot, hence the name. The guests might not have believed Baosang, but Xichun's reaction is damning: the young man who cooked this delicious four-happiness soup is the son of a big teapot! Uncle Xue feels only pity for him, Auntie Xue feels both pity and swelling unhappiness, and Seventh Aunt's goodwill evaporates in a second. How could the Xues be so careless? A big teapot's son should never be allowed near a wedding banquet, no matter how well he cooks! The very thought turns her stomach.

Every nerve in Xichun's body twitches with torment. He only found out the truth about his parents after they died. Before Liberation, his father worked as a factotum in a run-down brothel in Tianjin, which his mom was sold into as a prostitute. After Xichun's mother died and he was left an orphan, Luo Shengqi—Luo Baosang's father, an old acquaintance of his parents and his father's former coworker—came to visit him. Xichun made tea, and as Luo Shengqi sipped it, he slowly told him the whole story. His intentions were good—he also brought

Xichun some dried noodles made with strong flour, and left him five yuan before going. As he talked, and Xichun realized what a "big teapot" actually was, he recalled an incident from his childhood: he'd run in dripping with sweat after playing outside. Desperately thirsty, he'd asked for a drink of boiled water, only instead of saying "water," he just pointed and clamored, "Teapot, big teapot!" His father had been drinking, and instead of passing him the teapot, he smacked the boy hard across the face. That was a shock to his little soul. For a long time, he didn't understand what had happened. His father was a coarse, ill-tempered man, but he'd always been affectionate toward his son, and besides, Xichun hadn't done anything wrong, so why did his dad hit him so hard that his face swelled up? Even stranger, his mom was usually very protective—once, when his dad accidentally tripped Xichun, she spent a full hour nagging him to be more careful; yet now she didn't hug him and yell at his dad as he'd expected, but joined in the scolding, complaining that all he did was play outside from morning to night, and everyone hated him. Only after his parents were dead, and Luo Shengqi came to visit, did he understand the tears and humiliation contained in the words "big teapot." No wonder, when his teacher asked his father to visit the school and talk about his "miserable past and untroubled present," his father hadn't just refused, but growled, "Don't make fun of me." How could he ever have talked about his suffering? His miserable past was only fit to be washed down to the bottom of his heart with copious lashings of alcohol, where it would remain buried.

Xichun had thought: *Father! My father, who once carried a big teapot and struggled to make his way through the dregs of society—I love you. And I love you too, my mother, you whom every right-thinking person looks down on. Mother! The wrinkles on your face, the "purple petals" pinched into your forehead and neck, the cuss words you uttered with your hoarse voice, none of those things hid your gentle, kind nature. You and Father only married after Liberation, and it wasn't easy for you to have me, but you painstakingly raised me, drawing a veil over the past. How will I ever be able to repay everything you did for me? My dear parents, this shame was forced upon you by a long-gone society. I don't accept this! If anyone tries to besmirch your names, I won't let them get away with it.*

Indignation roils in Xichun like molten steel. He hates Baosang with every fiber of his being. Fists clenched so tightly they crackle, his fingernails drive into his palms. In a moment, those iron-hard fists will lash out and strike Baosang right under the chin. Seeing Xichun like this, Baosang quickly sobers up and breaks out in a cold sweat. He instinctively grips the edge of the table, apparently prepared to flip the whole thing over to shield himself from the flying fists. Everyone can see the whole thing unfold with utter clarity and sits in petrified silence as their hearts rise in their throats.

Xichun's fists are about to let rip, but in the millionth of a second before they do, he catches sight of the bride and groom in his peripheral vision. Jiyue's head is bowed, and Xiuya is leaning into her husband's arm, their faces full of terror and despair.

Just like that, Xichun turns and walks out the door. When they recall this moment afterward, no one, including Baosang, is able to say why he ran off so abruptly.

It takes a few seconds before anyone is able to react. Uncle Xue says in a trembling voice, "You shouldn't have done that, Baosang." Kneading her chest, Auntie Xue echoes him: "Baosang, what nonsense are you spouting?" Jiyue springs out of his cowering and points an agitated finger at Baosang. "It's bad enough that you came freeloading, did you have to cause a scene? Get the hell out of here!" And Seventh Aunt, in the tone of an empress proclaiming "Take them out and give them a good lashing!" booms, "How on earth could something like this happen? Just look at these awful people you invited!"

Now that Xichun has vanished, Baosang is emboldened in his boorishness. Everyone already hates him, why not burn it to the ground? He's still holding the table. He could easily flip the whole thing over—wouldn't that be fun? He bellows, "Fine, have it your way! I'll get the hell out of here." His arms tense. In a moment, the table will fly through the air. Everyone jumps to their feet and shrieks, but before Baosang can make his move, someone darts forward and jabs him in the chest with two fingers. Right away, Baosang's eyes roll back, and his body softens like a cooked noodle. Manager Wang stops him from falling and props him up against the dresser.

The person who knocked Baosang out with two fingers to his acupoint is none other than Uncle Xue's sworn brother, Mr. Yin. Up until now, he sat at the table without uttering a word, all but ignored by his fellow diners. His sudden movement is yet another shock. Xiuya believes for a moment that Baosang has been killed, and throws herself against Jiyue's chest, heaving with sobs.

Mr. Yin waves both hands. "Don't worry, he'll wake up in a moment. I bet he'll be better-behaved then." He returns unflustered to his seat and says, "Come on, everyone, drink your soup. The final course should be arriving soon."

Seventh Aunt lets out a shaky breath and smooths down her clothes, ready to take her leave, but seeing how scared Xiuya looks, she hesitates. Can she leave the girl in this state?

In the cooking tent, Xichun sits on a little stool with his head in his hands, weeping silently. Zhaoying crouches by his side, trying to find reassuring words to soothe him. How can she know the thoughts seething inside him? He's hard as nails, and almost never cries. Normally he would have worked through his feelings by beating Luo Baosang into a pulp, but at the last minute he remembered his responsibility to all these other people. Why did he come? It wasn't for the soup envelope, or his reputation—he came to create something beautiful, a selfless offering to a family celebrating a wedding, their friends and relatives. It's true, he's of low birth. His father was a big teapot, his mother was a whore. They managed to redeem themselves after Liberation and live proper lives, but their past was not to be casually recollected for a school project. What anguish! This long-gone society not only carved its degradation into his parents' hearts, its tentacles reached the next generation. But he's strong, and the more humiliating his origins, the more he will cling to his self-respect. He won't fall! He won't sink! He'll stay at his mundane job and contribute to society by the sweat of his brow. By volunteering at events like this, he hopes to use his skills to offer the beauty he creates to ordinary members of society—only to encounter such cruel humiliation! In order not to turn this family's wedding banquet into a whirlpool of chaos, he had no choice but to swallow the bitterness and retreat. Now he can let out the sadness and resentment that has built up inside him. Imagine a tough guy like him sobbing with his head in his hands! He isn't crying because of the shameful legacy left by his parents, but sorrow at their early passing and guilt at not having understood them for so many years.

Zhaoying goes back into the house and informs the guests, "Chef Lu went outside so as not to cause a scene. He's composing himself now. He's a good person." Then to Auntie Xue, "Mom, why don't you give him his soup envelope? That might make him feel better."

Auntie Xue tells Jiyue to fetch it from the dresser. Before the banquet, she wrapped Xichun's cash in red paper and tucked it into the same drawer as the gold Rado watch. She says to her husband, "Shall we give him an extra eight yuan? This hasn't been easy for him!"

Before Uncle Xue can answer, Jiyue yelps, "Hey! The cash is gone, and so's the watch!"

Everyone in the room—apart from Luo Baosang, who is still slumped against the dresser—is thrown once again into shock and astonishment.

CHAPTER 25

The head of the Administrative Division laughs
off an accusation.

It's almost two thirty, but the car that's supposed to take Zhang Qilin to the airport still hasn't arrived. Dr. Yu phones the office again and is told that Fu Shandu set off some time ago. Why isn't he here yet? How aggravating!

Dressed in a suit, leather shoes, and coat, Mr. Zhang is pacing around the living room, hands clasped behind his back. His plane departs at four, an hour and a half from now. Even if the car gets here now, it will still take them more than half an hour to get there, and another forty-odd minutes to check in, drop off his bag, go through security, get through customs to the departure gate, and board the plane. Every minute, every second that passes increases the risk he will miss his flight. Mr. Zhang is usually unflappable, but his pacing is showing unmistakable signs of anxiety and annoyance.

What's going on with Fu Shandu today? In every interaction they've had since Mr. Zhang took over the bureau, he's always seemed meticulous and reliable. Could this aberrant behavior have something to do with the letter that arrived today? Mr. Zhang's eyes flick to the wall. A pale rectangle marks the spot where Luo Jishan's painting, for which he "banished weariness and stirred unworthy Jishan's brush," used to hang until he got his daughter, Xiuzao, to take it down. Why did Fu Shandu help Luo Jishan get this apartment? For the sake of a painting that he's apparently been replicating over and over? What's up with Luo Jishan's insatiable greed for apartments? Does he plan to sublet them? Zhang Qilin is confused. He is keenly aware of the complex web of connections between the things of this world. Looking at a single node won't tell you much—you need to study an entire network to make any kind of judgment. The whistleblowing letter reveals a single node.

Zhang Qilin wonders, *What's the truth of the network it's linked to? Is Fu Shandu showing up late on purpose so I won't have time to question him? No matter how late he shows up, I'll interrogate him on the way to the airport. And if I still haven't got to the bottom of this—well, at least I'll feel better for having asked . . .*

Dr. Yu sends Xiuzao to keep a lookout at the siheyuan gate, not that this will make the car come any faster. As Xiuzao passes through the outer courtyard, her eyes drift east to the side yard. The four-panel gate is half-open, as if to reveal some unfathomable mystery within. Feng Wanmei must be there. What are she and Xun Lei doing at this moment? Listening to music? Reading? Xiuzao isn't jealous, but she feels waves of aching despondency wash over her. Is anything in the world more painful than loving someone who doesn't love you back? Better if he loved you awhile and then stopped; at least you'd be left with sweet memories to nibble on. She might have stayed standing there, lost in her swelling emotions, but a teenager sprints past, crashing into her and disappearing out the gate without so much as looking back. Pale-yellow windbreaker, hands in his pockets, appearing somewhat drunk. Coming from the Xues' wedding, needless to say. Why are their guests so rowdy and rude? Streaking past like a shooting star, not even saying sorry or glancing back. Shameless! Before Xiuzao can take another step, there is a commotion behind her. Uncle and Auntie Xue with a pack of their guests. She hastily steps through the gate and stands to one side. Remembering that she has a job to do, she shields her eyes with a hand and stares into the distance, but the hutong is deserted. No cars in sight.

Dr. Yu glances at her watch: two thirty. She says to her husband, "We might as well call a taxi. How could Old Fu be so irresponsible? Delaying your overseas trip—to think he promised to get us an apartment! What's wrong with him?" She picks up the receiver, but just as she's dialing the taxi stand, Fu Shandu comes in, breathing hard.

Before Dr. Yu can complain, he's already prostrating himself. "Sorry, so sorry, all my fault, I shouldn't have told Wang to go by the art museum route—we got held up by an accident, then we hit every red light on Di'anmen." He grabs Mr. Zhang's luggage. "Is this everything? Let's go!"

Zhang Qilin calms down now that Old Fu is here. An hour and a half is enough time to get to the airport and do everything that needs doing. Now that he's relaxed, he feels a sudden urge to pee. "The main thing is that you're here now," he says. "I'll run to the restroom, then we can go."

"The airport restroom will be cleaner," says Old Fu. "Why not wait until you're there?"

Dr. Yu agrees. "You'll get your trousers dirty, not to mention your shoes. Ugh, this bathroom!"

But Zhang Qilin can't hold it in. He thinks for a moment, then whips off his coat, goes into the room to pull a pair of regular trousers over his nice ones, and switches to everyday shoes. Coming back out, he grins. "See? Now I'm protected." He heads off.

Fu Shandu is flabbergasted. Why would a bureau chief go to all this effort to use a communal hutong toilet on his way to the airport? Dr. Yu finds it surprising too, but seizes the moment to say, "You see, Old Fu? See how we have to live? You left us stuck here, and this is how we pee. In a toilet like that! Aren't you ashamed of yourself?"

Fu Shandu says, as if making a vow, "Dr. Yu, I truly have got my hands on two good apartments for you. How about this—after I've dropped off Mr. Zhang, I'll come back here and take you to see them. You think it makes me happy seeing Mr. Zhang going to all that trouble just to pee?"

Xiuzao has been distracted since coming back inside. The four-panel gate looms vividly in her mind, until her dad's toilet-going antics jolt her out of it. As her dad hurries away, the image of him in a sharp Western-style jacket with ratty trousers and shapeless old shoes sticks in her mind. Dad! Her father is adorable, she suddenly thinks. What a good dad, to go uncomplainingly to the cruddy communal toilet. She's seen her dad do a lot of things. This may be insignificant, even somewhat comical, but it's exactly what's needed to cement in her heart a sense of his prestige—the prestige of a Communist Party member and revolutionary cadre.

For his part, Zhang Qilin is acting wholly on a physiological imperative. He returns from the toilet, hastily washes his hands, steps out of the old trousers, changes back to leather shoes, puts his coat back on, grabs the briefcase from the table, and calls out, "Let's go!" They troop out into the courtyard, past the chuihua gate, down the narrow entryway, and out to the street. After the luggage is stowed in the trunk, Mr. Zhang and Dr. Yu get into the back seat, and Fu Shandu says to Xiuzao, "Get in!" She smiles and says, "I'm not coming." From the back seat, her parents pipe up, "She told us she didn't want to come. She's grown now, she has her own things to do." Old Fu slides nimbly into the front passenger seat and bangs the door shut, and the car starts. Xiuzao waves as they drive away, and glances at her watch: 2:38.

She goes back into the courtyard and comes to the four-panel gate. Xun Lei and Wanmei are laughing, with music playing faintly in the background. Xiuzao feels as if someone viciously pinched her heart. As she walks dispiritedly back to the inner courtyard, Zhan Liying emerges from the chuihua gate with a slightly balding, bespectacled middle-aged man. Xiuzao smiles as she walks past. From behind, she hears Nanny Zhan's coarse voice, "That's great! After *The Drunken Concubine*, they ought to do *Phoenix Returning to Its Nest*." Xiuzao pays no attention, only registering that Nanny Zhan is annoyingly noisy. As she passes the Xues' cooking tent, she hears a man crying inside—muffled, bass sobs. Who on earth could this be? No one should be weeping at a wedding! She has no desire to investigate, but reflects on the complexity and variety of life. In this world of constant motion and collision, she ought to be rational and strong and not allow this tide of love hidden in her heart to sweep over the dam and swamp her ambition. Back home, she washes her face and hums a breezy tune as she sits resolutely at her desk, where she opens her English textbook and notebook.

Meanwhile, the car passes the Drum Tower, then heads east toward Dongzhimen. Zhang Qilin and Dr. Yu in the rear, Fu Shandu in the front passenger seat. As Mr. Zhang ponders how to broach the subject of the letter, Dr. Yu lobs a series of questions about the new apartments at Old Fu, from the size of the bathtubs to whether there are trees outside the windows, and if so, what kind of trees? Old Fu twists around, gripping the back of his seat with both hands, and answers her queries with enthusiasm.

They're almost at the end of Dongzhimen and will soon turn onto the highway for Tianzhu Airport—there isn't much time left. Mr. Zhang interrupts their conversation to say, solemnly, "Old Fu, I have serious business to discuss with you."

Clearly unprepared for this, Fu Shandu looks startled as he repeats, "Serious business?"

Mr. Zhang looks at Fu Shandu, twisted around in his seat, the model of an old-school bureaucrat. Administrators everywhere carry themselves the same way, with the same facial expressions, whatever their actual appearance. Old Fu is thin and wiry, and his eyes blaze with spirit. His thin lips press tightly together until he speaks, when they open and shut decisively. A scar on his cheek moves along with them, as if it contains sufficient data to back up every one of his statements, removing the possibility of rebuttal.

Cutting straight to the heart of the matter, Mr. Zhang says, "I got a letter from a member of the public this afternoon, accusing you. I'm implicated too." He recounts its contents.

Dr. Yu knew nothing of this and is shocked. Now she understands why her husband insisted on having that painting removed from their living room wall. This is a work matter, so she shouldn't speak up, but she worries that the situation will turn awkward. Why bring the question up in the car, with time so tight? She studies Fu Shandu anxiously, afraid he'll be angry or, just as bad, embarrassed. How annoying of her husband. Couldn't this have waited until after his trip?

Unexpectedly, Old Fu's reaction is to silently heave with laughter. Completely at ease, even a little amused, he says, "Everything in that letter is a fact. The only thing he left out is that I haven't helped myself to just one but two units. Ha! I'd like to nab a third one too!"

Zhang Qilin is stunned. Seeing his expression, Old Fu continues in a more conciliatory tone, "You've never paid any attention to housing allocation, and you really don't know much about it. No wonder you hear the wind and think it's rain. To those of us actually on the ground, what you read in that letter is just how things work in our world."

It's true—Zhang Qilin has to admit that the world Fu Shandu operates in is no more than an abstract concept to him. He has no part in the bureau's housing committee. Even though the Party committee does discuss which names to include on their list of midcareer intellectuals deserving of special treatment, they only ever talk about the people themselves, not the housing—they set the priorities, but the actual arrangements are made by Fu Shandu and others like him.

"How could you block off these units? They're meant for midcareer intellectuals," he says. "This is about the Party putting policy into practice. How dare you!"

Still smiling merrily, Fu Shandu says, "Then tell me—which midcareer intellectual in our bureau deserves an apartment but doesn't have one?"

271

Zhang Qilin thinks about it, but there doesn't seem to be anyone in this situation. Everyone on their list has been given a unit. True, the letter never actually said Fu Shandu deprived anyone of an apartment, only that he'd "helped himself" to the bureau's housing stock.

Sensing Mr. Zhang's confusion, Old Fu explains further. "The housing under our control comes from two sources: first, our allocation of government-built apartments, and second, the ones we build ourselves. The first category includes all sizes. A three-room apartment could be anything from about three hundred to five hundred square feet, a two-bedroom could be two fifty to three hundred square feet. Some only have south-facing windows, others only north-facing, and of course some have windows facing both directions. Some of the bigger ones are badly finished, some of the smaller ones are exquisite. Some great apartments are in terrible locations, or the other way around. Some people ask to swap a three-room for a two-room or one-room, others want to give up their apartment for a house. We deal with all that, and to be frank, we sometimes use our power to get a little something extra for ourselves, but—and this is the truth—most of the time, these maneuvers are for the good of our work unit. For instance, in this latest round, we were allocated twenty-eight apartments with a total area of 12,185 square feet. So apart from our existing stock, we could supply twenty-eight households. It's not that straightforward, though. Take your household—I can't stick you in a three-room, it'd have to be two two-rooms instead. That's how I end up with a shortfall. It's not just your family either—there are plenty of cases that need special handling. Some people truly don't get on with their daughters-in-law, for instance, and to provide the best possible service, I'd put that family in two one-rooms rather than a two-room, which means getting in touch with other work units to swap with their allocation. Even if I didn't do that, they'd still come to me. The give-and-take is never between two departments, it's usually three- or four-sided. This is an open secret. The end result should leave everyone satisfied. In this last round, I made sure everyone who needed housing got housing, and I still had two surplus units on my hands. How did that happen? I shortchanged some households of their rightful floor space. Not much, just two dozen square feet each, maybe three or four, but it added up to two extra apartments. And the shortchanged householders got other advantages—a larger balcony, a desirable floor, or plenty of light. Who have I harmed by doing this? It's all completely well intentioned!"

Zhang Qilin says suspiciously, "I'm still not sure I understand your good intentions. Luo Jishan has nothing to do with our work unit, so how did he end up with yet another apartment? That goes against the rules, doesn't it?"

Once again, Fu Shandu sounds convincing as he says, "Luo Jishan is just using this apartment temporarily. I haven't given him a residence permit, so no rules are being broken. We're just doing him a little favor, just like he's doing us a little favor. It's a form of collaboration, if you think about it."

Zhang Qilin is confused. "Collaboration? Between a work unit and a private individual?"

Frustrated by Mr. Zhang's narrow-minded ignorance, Fu Shandu can't help making fun of him. "You are such a bureaucrat! It's like Tao Yuanming wrote, 'He who doesn't know the Han dynasty, is surely ignorant of Wei and Jin too.' Didn't I just say we produce our own housing stock on top of what we're allocated? You think construction is as easy as stacking building blocks? The land, the design, the materials, the labor—everything is a headache! Luo Jishan isn't just a regular guy with a few paintbrushes. Look at that dorm building we just put up. The water-heating system wouldn't have landed in our laps like that without Mr. Luo's help!"

This is feeling more and more like *The Arabian Nights*. "You mean he moonlights at a boiler company?"

Fu Shandu chuckles. "What a joker you are, Mr. Zhang! Of course he doesn't know how to do anything but paint! His pictures are in hot demand—every hotel and guesthouse wants one. Even before the building is up, they've already decided what size painting they want and where it should hang—all ordered way in advance. He puts in a good word for us, and the hotel finds during the course of construction they have a boiler or two more than they need, which they're only too happy for us to take off their hands. Now we owe Mr. Luo a favor, so why not let him stay in an apartment that's sitting empty anyway? It's only right." Seeing that Mr. Zhang's eyes are still wide with alarm, Fu Shandu adds, "Don't worry, there's nothing untoward here. We paid the standard price for those boilers and signed a receipt—the paperwork's all in order. Luo Jishan didn't get a cent in kickbacks either."

Zhang Qilin still doesn't trust this. "He got himself a place to live, isn't that a kickback? The letter said he got three apartments in this way. That's completely excessive!"

Fu Shandu disagrees. "I'm very familiar with his situation. Despite his grow-ing reputation, his work unit doesn't take him seriously at all. They say he's too young and hasn't done enough to deserve elite status, and wouldn't give him anything but a small, cramped apartment. He's got parents and kids living with him—not even enough room to set up his drafting table. He really had no choice but to get these three other apartments. You're imagining three big units, aren't you? I've been to all three. The first is on the fifteenth floor of a tower block, a one-room he uses as his studio. He says he can't always be in hotel rooms work-ing on commissions, he needs a studio of his own to make real art. Then there's a half basement where he's put his old mother and his daughter so his main apartment isn't so overcrowded. The third place is the only one I lent him—just a two-room that he's done up as a space for meeting guests and to store books and art supplies. That's all. Honestly, given where he's at now, if he decided to go abroad, he'd do pretty well for himself! He could buy a house, maybe get hold of a villa with a garden, all perfectly doable. But that's not what this fellow is after. How could you call what he's doing excessive?"

Fu Shandu's little speech leaves Zhang Qilin with nothing to say. He thinks to himself that even if everything Old Fu said is true, there are still unanswered questions. What about maintenance? Or the allocation process itself? Suppressing or placing limits on people's reasonable material needs, or the transactions taking place within society, will only create greater contradictions and ultimately be a needless expenditure of manpower. Ten years ago, farmers were banned from selling peanuts, and yet almost every household in the city had some because a robust network of black-market suppliers stepped in to fill the need. Now the ban has been lifted and the peanut supply chain is legalized and out in the open, which saves a lot of time and energy on both sides. Hasn't that made life easier and less stressful? When will urban housing also be freed from these shackles so it can be distributed more quickly and simply?

Seeing Mr. Zhang's expression soften, Fu Shandu says, "Old Zhang, you haven't asked me what I did with the other apartment I helped myself to—but I'll tell you. It went to Pang Qibin, the head of your Technical Report Unit. The committee said he didn't have enough points and needed to wait awhile, but seeing as I had an extra place on my hands, I made the arrangements for him right away. Now he'll get a new place soon after starting this job, and he'll work better with one less thing to worry about. This so-called accusation is actually a letter of praise for me. But I'd love for the disciplinary committee to investigate me at once. The more they dig, the clearer my conscience will be."

Zhang Qilin smiles. "You've given us one side of the story. I imagine the disciplinary committee will certainly want to investigate, and the outcome might not be as simple as verifying a few things." He suddenly recalls the pale rectangle left on his wall and can't resist adding, "Besides, what's so great about Luo Jishan? All he does is paint variations of the same image, over and over."

"Ever since antiquity, both in China and elsewhere, there have been countless examples of painters repeating their subject matter. If you don't believe me, have a look at Qi Baishi's work, it's all shrimp and chrysanthemums."

Their conversation loosens up as they banter, and Dr. Yu relaxes too. She looks out the window and says, "Enough of that, you can pick up the argument when Old Zhang is back in the country. Look, we're almost at Tianzhu."

The car takes the next exit for the airport and a very short while later is speeding up the circular ramp to the terminal.

PART SIX

申时

Shen Shi

Time of the Monkey: 3:00 p.m. to 5:00 p.m.

CHAPTER 26

The old people's club.

After three o'clock, the winter sunlight at the foot of the Drum Tower's eastern wall feels precious; its warmth will last another half hour at most.

Around this time, the old folk basking by the wall feel their spirits begin to sink. They already miss the sun's cozy glow and are reluctant or unwilling to return to their homes, where people younger than them are now in charge. Even those treated with filial respect still feel melancholy at the thought of parting from these companions they get along so well with.

Grandpa Hu hates it when the sun—His Lordship—tilts toward the west, because that means the old people's gathering will soon break up, and he'll have to drag his weary feet homeward, where he'll have to face his son's frosty expression, his daughter-in-law's eyes that bulge like gingko nuts, and incidents at the dinner table, such as when his grandson picked up a piece of meat and said, "This is for you, Grandpa!" but his daughter-in-law intercepted it and popped it into the boy's mouth, saying with a fake smile, "Grandpa's happy just eating vegetables. Grandpa wants you to have it!" He thought of helping himself to a piece of meat but didn't have the courage.

When Grandpa Hu is sitting next to Old Lady Hai, he feels like a kid relishing the last little sliver of hard candy in his mouth, reluctant to finish it. They take turns rehashing stories of life around the Bell and Drum Towers in the old days, as if their nostalgia has the power to freeze time.

The story they keep going back to is, of course, the one about the "bean juice maiden" more than a hundred years ago. They'll never grow tired of it, in part because they both have ancestors connected to the people in this tale.

Grandpa Hu is the grandson of a near neighbor of the bean juice couple, one of the very neighbors who witnessed their daughter getting kidnapped by the evil princeling's men. Hence the authority with which Grandpa Hu speaks of these events, all these years later. According to him, after the princeling was mysteriously blinded, he was so scared of further repercussions that he let the maiden go. After some time, the maiden's parents found her a husband who was indeed low-status, a bricklayer. In the Year of the Metal Rat, 1900, the old couple died, and the young couple, along with their five children, joined the Boxer Rebellion. Every time someone says that the maiden, now a matron, became a Red Lantern after joining the Boxers, Grandpa Hu corrects them. "No, she was a Blue Lantern. My granddad knew the family extremely well. His family helped themselves freely to the bean juice, just as the maiden's family were welcome to take as many of my family's kidney bean corn cakes from the steamer as they liked. My granddad told me female Boxers were only called Red Lanterns if they were unmarried. Married ones were Blue Lanterns, and the widows were Black Lanterns." What happened next? According to Grandpa Hu, after the Boxers were defeated, the bricklayer was captured and nobly martyred—they beheaded him. The matron escaped overseas with her children. Where did they go? He can't say, because his grandfather never told him. To this day, he can go to Silver Ingot Bridge and point out where the bean juice stall and his grandfather's house once stood—strangers now live in both.

Old Lady Hai is related to the villain. The evil princeling had a half sister born to a concubine—this was Old Lady Hai's grandmother, which means the blind princeling was her great uncle. Not that she feels any guilt by association. Her great uncle didn't just mistreat regular folk, he tormented his servants and yelled at and hit his half sister. The part of the story about the princeling getting blinded on a moonless night is cathartic for Old Lady Hai. She always says at this point, "Evil begets evil." She also has blood ties with quite a few descendants of Manchu aristocracy—some supported the Xinhai Revolution, others joined the Chinese People's Political Consultative Conference, and still others, who ought to call her "Aunt," are now members of the Communist Party. In other words, Old Lady Hai can count both scoundrels and good people among her relatives—which is the case for most people in society. Nothing unusual here. People often ask Old Lady Hai what happened to her great uncle in the end, and she always answers crisply, "Not long after the incident, he went mad and died. On his deathbed, he howled, 'Too hot! Too hot!' They asked, 'What's hot? The bed? The fire?' And he said, 'The bean juice! The bean juice!' He felt as if someone was pouring scalding bean juice onto his body." Naturally, everyone listens in rapt silence to this tale.

What about the mysterious vigilante youth? Where did he come from? Where did he go? How did he get past the closed doors and windows into the princeling's bedchamber and blind him without disturbing the household? Like everyone else, Grandpa Hu and Old Lady Hai can only imagine the answers to these questions—they have no authority here. Several versions of the legend all contain this detail: on the evening the princeling was blinded, the handsome young man stopped by Beiyufang Tobacconist, on Drum Tower Street. Where exactly was that? They've squabbled over this question before, and for some reason, the argument resurfaces today.

Old Lady Hai says, "Beiyufang must have been where Cooking Supplies is today. The shop faces Tobacco Pipe Alley, so when they'd bought their tobacco, customers would step out of Beiyufang and see Shuangshengtai Pipe Shop at the mouth of the alleyway. You remember the shop sign shaped like a giant pipe? It must have been four or five feet long, with a red banner hanging from it."

Grandpa Hu says, "Of course I remember! There were little brass hoops hanging from the sign that tinkled in the breeze. But Beiyufang wasn't on South Drum Tower Street, it was on East Street, across from where Minkang Hui Eatery is now. You're the one with a poor memory!"

Old Lady Hai raises her voice. "Me? A poor memory? I remember every single thing that's ever happened to me, branches and leaves and everything. Let me test you: Back in the day, where was Zhonghe Pawnbroker on Tobacco Pipe Alley?"

Grandpa Hu's neck tenses up. "Halfway down the street, opposite the temple, facing north. How could I ever forget? I went there on many occasions in my youth!" He is struck with a sudden memory of a summer's day in the twelfth year of the Republic, 1923. The Palace of Established Happiness in the Forbidden City caught fire, and the red glow could be seen from the Bell and Drum Towers. Afterward, a few dozen workers from the palace vault were sent to pick through the ruins. He was among them, a young man still in his teens. After each shift at the vault, they were required to remove all their clothing and hop over a foot-high bench, clapping and shouting at the same time. Only when the supervisor nodded could they get dressed and go home. This was to prevent them from secreting treasures in their mouths, hands, armpits, or assholes. It was harder to supervise them scavenging the burnt-out palace in the open air, and they'd been joined with some temporary laborers, who weren't as disciplined. In any case, the imperial household had been greatly diminished and was not as powerful as it used to be. Like all the others, Grandpa Hu snuck some bits of melted gold and silver into his trousers as he worked. Afterward, when he was safely back through the Gate of Divine Prowess, he hurried over to Zhonghe Pawnbroker. Later, he learned that he could have made much more money if he'd brought them to the bank instead—but how would he have known? He'd never set foot in a bank. This recollection prompts him to ask Old Lady Hai, "If your memory is so great, I suppose you remember the fire in the Forbidden City—"

Before he can finish, she says stridently, "Sure I do! I got married that spring. It was on the fourteenth day of the fifth lunar month, late at night. The next morning, I brought a group to Lotus Market, and everyone was talking about the fire."

Right away, Grandpa Hu forgets about the fire. Lotus Market! These two words evoke so many bittersweet memories. They sink into more nostalgia, recalling the joys of youth and the harshness of human existence.

Lotus Market was a temporary marketplace that popped up each year southwest of this neighborhood, around the Shicha Seas, between the fifth day of the fifth lunar month and the fifteenth of the seventh month. It started in the early days of the Republic and lasted more than twenty years, until the late 1930s. In those days, the Front Sea was covered in lotus blossoms, with a broad strip of earth to the west, half of which was planted with wheat. Lotus Market was on this piece of land. "To the east, lotuses, and to the west, wheat—with market stalls where the soil and water meet." Most of the stalls were made of wooden boards and fir poles, half on land and half in the lake. Some had a peaked roof, others retractable awnings made of woven reeds, and of course more basic canopies patched together from scraps of cloth. For a time, Grandpa Hu was an apprentice at the famous Delixing stall workshop and was sometimes sent to set up stalls at Lotus Market. In good times, Old Lady Hai gave tours of Lotus Market, and in leaner times she had a stall there telling fortunes.

Grandpa Hu and Old Lady Hai excitedly recall Lotus Market at the height of its fame. The "eight-treasure congee," made from glutinous and superior rice stewed unctuously together, served in a small bowl with fresh lotus seeds, lotus root, and water lily seeds, topped with soft white sugar and candied tangerine peel dyed red and green. These bowls were kept ready in a bucket cooled with natural ice from the cellar, and would be frosty to the touch when you got them out. People called these "ice cups," and nothing could be more refreshing! Then there was "Suzhou roast," thin layered pancakes made from a batter of peanut oil, eggs, and refined flour, with a filling of shredded radish and lean pork—drool-worthy, and two to a tael. There were all sorts of other tasty treats and a dazzling variety of toys for sale: "bristle figures," with bodies of clay and legs of braided pig bristles, which you would put on a tray and spin into a dance; kites in all sorts of shapes, such as swallows, sand martins, dragonflies, centipedes, Monkey Kings, beautiful women, and most thrillingly the "butterfly delivering a meal"—a little butterfly clipped to the string of a larger butterfly kite. As it soared, the little one climbed the string all by itself, then at the very top a tiny firecracker ignited, causing the large butterfly's wings to fold so it plummeted to the ground. Ingenious.

They reminisce about the many lanterns you could buy at the market, such as lotus blossom lanterns, which weren't actually made of lotus flowers, but sorghum stalks and bamboo from broken baskets, woven into a watermelon-sized sphere with scalloped paper petals and six-inch green paper tassels, and with a little candle in the center. Children wandered around at night with these on sticks, chanting, "Lotus blossom lantern, lotus blossom lantern, light it today and dump it tomorrow." Then there were lanterns made from lotus leaves stuck together with a candle inside. The river lantern was a nubbin of wood surrounded by a ring of paper, with a little oil lamp fashioned from clay; you set these alight and let them drift away on the lake. Hardest to forget was the mugwort lantern, a branch of mugwort with many lit wicks tied between the twigs. You held it by the stem and waved it around your courtyard or hutong as dusk fell, and tiny sparks swung through the air, trailing fragrant smoke that induced many an inappropriate fantasy in young people!

"Hey, aren't you two talking about that 'rain-shy' place from the old days?" says a man with a more upright back than theirs. He has a birdcage in one hand and a couple of walnuts in the other.

Rain-shy? That's right! Whenever it rained, all the stalls in Lotus Market would quickly shut down, hence the nickname. Old Lady Hai and Grandpa Hu sink into bottomless sadness. Lotus Market ceased to exist whenever it rained. What became of the people who once worked there? What were their destinies? Truly, it's best not to look back at the past!

The man who interrupted their conversation is Luo Baosang's father, Luo Shengqi. He's about a decade younger and has quite a different impression of Lotus Market. Before he turned twenty, he was waiting to join the entourage of a sedan company—that's where young men from the beggars' guilds often ended up, though naturally they wouldn't be holding umbrellas or fanning passengers, but standing in the background waving banners. There were several varieties of banner: green dragon, white tiger, scarlet bird, and black tortoise. When he was first hired, he was only permitted to walk at the very back of the procession carrying a banner embroidered with a tortoise with a snake's tail. That summer, he went to the sedan line every day hoping to be hired, but every single day he failed. He had no idea why. Could it be that rich people weren't marrying their sons off that summer? Finally, he went to Lotus Market with an older beggar for a "hard beg." A metal hook pierced the flesh by his collar bone and attached to an iron ball and chain that dragged behind him. He walked all the way from the south end of the market to the north, but although people pointed and stared, he didn't get so much as a single copper coin! That's why he hates the Shicha Seas—he can't walk past without spitting into them. It bothers him to hear Grandpa Hu and Old Lady Hai praising Lotus Market. Having dismissed it as "rain-shy," he rubs the walnuts in his hand so they crunch noisily against each other and proclaims, "What was so great about the Shicha Seas? So what if they had lotus blossoms? There were also heaps of trash on the shore. Some residents even emptied their chamber pots there. Remember the stink of shit and piss? No wonder there were so many flies and mosquitoes! You two are older than me—you probably saw the Drum Tower smoke long before I did."

Grandpa Hu and Old Lady Hai nod and speak over each other. "Absolutely—one time, there was a plume of smoke a yard high coming from the top of the Drum Tower. People thought it had caught fire, they were screaming and running around—"

"Yes, that's right! And someone called the fire brigade, right? The firemen went up and looked around, but there was no fire. That wasn't smoke—it was a column of mosquitoes!"

"This neighborhood was filthy back then, wasn't it? People used to say the road was covered in ash on windless days and became an inkwell when it rained. They weren't lying." Luo Shengqi smiles, as if these bad old days bring him pleasure. He points at the shops catty-corner to them. "Forget the rest, look at those two—Tailin Vegetables, Hecheng Raw and Cooked Meat. You think anyone would have dared step inside back in the day?"

"Exactly!" says Old Lady Hai. "After we fought those Japanese, prices kept going up and up! I remember the banknotes that were printed after the Japanese came: Confucius on one side, a dragon on the other. The paper was so rough, they were more like napkins than money!"

Grandpa Hu cuts in, "They were! Those were from the North China Reserve Bank—we called them 'little blankets.' Everyone used to chant, 'Confucius says we're done, this ten yuan's now worth one!' Then the Nationalists issued the fabi, but let's not talk about that. Right after the Japanese surrendered, a hundred fabi could buy you a pair of ducks. Two years later, a hundred only got you a single coal briquette! What kind of way was that to live?"

At this moment, an extralong number 8 bus passes by, which sparks off a new wave of reminiscences from Old Lady Hai. "It was so hard for us to get anywhere back then! It was so many years after the Republic, and our street only had the *dang dang* car—you know, the streetcar. The driver would have one foot on the bell pedal as he drove, so it went *dang dang dang* all the way. So noisy!" Grandpa Hu picks up the thread: "No, I remember, it was more like *dangdangdang dangdangdangdang dang dangdang* . . . right? The fare was actually pretty cheap, but you had to wait around so long, it felt as if your brain was melting out of your ears. That wasn't really its fault, there was only a single track, so at every stop, the train coming this way would have to turn onto a little side track until the train coming that way had gone past. Now and then you'd see a few people jump onto the back to avoid paying the fare—just hanging there! There was a saying at the time—"

"'Rickshaw—can't afford the fare. *Dang dang* car—can't afford the time!' Not like today, all these buses and trams, bigger, more frequent, and more routes! If you want to go to Xidan, Wangfujing, Tiananmen, the zoo, all you have to do is hop on a bus and that's it, so convenient!"

Grandpa Hu turns to Luo Shengqi. "Don't you agree?"

Luo Shengqi falls silent. Grandpa Hu's words have awakened memories of his greatest unhappiness—no, not just unhappiness, his greatest humiliation, confusion, and fear. Thirty-six years ago, an agent for the Nationalists paid him, right here in front of the Drum Tower, to attack the students marching "Against Hunger, Against Civil War." For each student he beat up, he got a measly steamed bun. After the protest was dispersed, a long-haired college student jumped onto the back of a *dang dang* car, grabbing hold of the door with one hand and flinging leaflets with the other. Red-eyed with rage, Luo Shengqi ran madly after the vehicle and reached out to grab the student. Unexpectedly, the student kicked him hard. Shengqi instinctively held his leg, pulling him to the ground. They rolled around on the road wrestling for a few seconds, faces *this* close together, eyeballs bulging from their sockets—neither would ever forget what the other looked like. Then suddenly the student got pulled aside, and several people were kicking Shengqi. It hurt all the way to his core. The rescuers weren't the student's fellow protesters but a few burly workmen passing by. Shengqi crawled to his feet and hurled some curse words after them, spat on the ground, and sauntered off to get his steamed buns.

Shengqi kept this shameful episode hidden after Liberation, and it didn't come to light until the Cultural Revolution. Actually, he had already accepted that what he did was wrong—the Communist distributing leaflets wasn't afraid of bloody sacrifice in his noble struggle against the Nationalists, all so beggars like Luo Shengqi could lead better lives. Soon, though, he would plunge into horror and confusion again. A government organization sent a parade of trucks down the street in a campaign against capitalist roaders, and on the last truck was a "black claw" with a black placard around his neck who looked exactly like the protester he'd tussled with all those years ago! What was going on? Why was this man, whom the Nationalists had given him a steamed bun to beat up, now himself being "flung to the ground and kicked ten thousand times" by the Communist Party?

Another few years later, after the Gang of Four's downfall, Luo Shengqi was on his way to visit Xue Yongquan when, at the chuihua gate, he passed by Yongquan's neighbor Zhang Qilin. Mr. Zhang didn't react, but Shengqi's heart began pounding wildly. This man looked exactly like the student protester flinging leaflets from the back of the *dang dang* car and the "black claw" being paraded through the streets. He asked Yongquan a few casual questions and found out that Mr. Zhang was a bureau-level cadre in the State Council, and might soon rise to deputy bureau chief or bureau chief! For the rest of that day, Luo Shengqi didn't touch a drop of alcohol. He crept out of the Xues' home with his head lowered and scuttled quickly from the siheyuan, vowing never to return. He got home and thought about it some more. Maybe it wasn't him? He recalled that the college student had a soybean-sized mole between his eyebrows, whereas Zhang Qilin's forehead was unblemished.

With Luo Shengqi's silence, the conversation falters. A breeze rises, bringing a slight chill. He leaves, still holding the birdcage in one hand and walnuts in the other. Grandpa Hu and Old Lady Hai glance at the chess players, who don't look like they plan to stop anytime soon. The *Beijing Evening News* is out; some of them have bought copies and are deploying the "advance slowly, consolidate your position, gradually move in for the kill" strategy, as used by Lin Minhong against Wu Zhengwei in the "Chess Match of the Week" on page four. Ex-director general Wu, formerly of the local Bureau of Commerce, works through the word puzzles on page three with another white-haired old man. They quickly guess that "four squares in one word, containing all kinds of crops" is the word for "field," 田, but "a strangely shaped mouth, hidden deep within" has them stumped.

Since other people are hanging around, Old Lady Hai doesn't want to leave either. The last heat of the sun is quickly fading away, and the cold is increasing with every second. She looks out into the street, which is just as bustling as ever, and remembers a song from her youth, "Beijing Bamboo":

> *Evening drum, morning bell, and again,*
> *You try to warn us, but in vain.*
> *A city of people strive for gain*
> *Crossing bridges in a fog of pain.*

Since she remembers this bamboo verse by heart, you'd think perhaps she's imbibed its message of how all worldly activity is futile. Well, not really . . .

Grandpa Hu is also reluctant to leave. The more time he can spend here by the Drum Tower, the better. Old Lady Hai heaves a sigh, and he quickly starts a conversation in case she's about to leave. "That siheyuan of yours—they'll be implementing the policy soon, won't they?"

This question gives Old Lady Hai a great deal of satisfaction, and she nods solemnly. "And how! Those Central bureaucrats know what they're doing! They're nothing but sensible—who could argue with that?"

The truth is, Old Lady Hai isn't actually the owner of the siheyuan in question; that's just the assumption Grandpa Hu made from a couple of things she's said and her authoritative bearing. Several times now, he's spoken as if she were the landlady, and she's never denied it. This has gradually taken hold in her mind, and now she behaves as if the siheyuan really were hers.

Old Lady Hai is descended, on her father's side, from the wealthy and influential Hešeri clan of the Manchu Plain White Banner. When she was ten, the family began disintegrating, and soon collapsed. She married into a family of former Manchu bannermen; both her husband and father-in-law worked for the Mongolian and Tibetan Affairs Commission. They managed to live relatively comfortably for two or three years, but her father-in-law passed away and her husband became unemployed, then lost much of their savings to a shady investment scheme. Their finances were deteriorating by the day, so her husband took what he'd learned from a family heirloom book about the practice of physiognomy and went around the Shicha Seas and Houmen Bridge neighborhoods reading faces, which brought in just about enough to support them. He lost his life in the Japanese invasion, leaving her alone and childless. She found a job as a receptionist at the girls' school affiliated with Fu Jen University, then became an attendant at a private nursery. The nursery managed to keep running after Liberation, until the government took it over in 1952. She worked at a different nursery for a few more years, until she reached retirement age. Her whole life has been marked by deprivation—how on earth could she own property? The siheyuan she lives in was once owned by her cousins, but they sold it to the Housing Department a few years after Liberation. Since she is related to the original landowners and has lived there the longest, the other residents got in the habit of handing her their rent and utilities money to pass on. The Housing Department also gets in touch with her when anything needs dealing with. If any of the residents has a problem and needs to call the department, that goes through her too. After many years of this, people have the vague impression that the whole place belongs to her. Now that the Beijing government is acquiring private properties, it's not just Grandpa Hu, but also the other residents of the siheyuan, who believe Old Lady Hai is due a windfall.

Old Lady Hai enjoys being seen in this light. As she answers Grandpa Hu's question, her heart glows with pride and happiness. Though she's careful not to say anything too definite—she's blundered before and almost got in trouble with the law. That's a minefield she'd like to avoid.

In 1952, shortly before the nursery she worked at was taken into government ownership, she recounted to the children a story she'd read in the newspaper, something about the noble exploits of a volunteer soldier. When she got to the part about his heroic sacrifice, she was so moved that she burst into tears. Several of the older children started sobbing too, and one of the girls knelt in front of her and asked, "Auntie Hai, why are you crying?" She replied, "I was just thinking of the mother's sadness, losing her son like that." The girl went home and told her parents, "Auntie Hai's son was sacrificed, and she's very sad." The parents felt they had to say something, so the next time they dropped off their daughter, they said to the nursery owner, "It's so unfortunate that an upstanding young man like Auntie Hai's son was martyred. We're devastated too, and we'd like to express our condolences in person." The owner, a kindly, older democrat, was initially puzzled—Auntie Hai didn't have any children, did she? But then she thought: perhaps dutiful, uncomplaining Auntie Hai had an illegitimate son in the old society and kept it quiet so she could find a job. But no one in the new society would judge her—in fact, they'd sympathize, especially now she'd offered him up to the war effort against America in support of Korea. She brought the couple to see Auntie Hai. The other parents got wind of this and followed suit. At first, Auntie Hai told them they were mistaken, but the owner assumed this was out of humility and bashfulness and just got more sincere and passionate. Finally, Auntie Hai allowed herself to be pushed into accepting their condolences.

Like a snowball rolling downhill, it just got bigger and bigger. Letters and gifts flooded in from the parents, and even bouquets of flowers. A nearby elementary school asked her to come speak to their students. "Even the tiniest incident from your son's childhood would be worth hearing." Soon, Auntie Hai created a martyred son in her mind. He had her surname (Hai) and was called Jingsheng ("born in Beijing"). He'd loved serving others since he was a child and knew right from wrong at a young age. One snowy day, he was walking past the Shicha Seas when he saw a little girl had fallen through the ice, and without hesitation he dashed over to pull her out. In the beginning, Auntie Hai was visibly tense on stage, wooden and stiff as a tree in winter. After a while, the tree put forth leaves—she learned to loosen up. Often, she was so moved by her own narration that she broke down in tears. As a result, even she was firmly convinced that her son Hai Jingsheng was a real person.

A reporter interviewed her and wrote a story about this heroic mother and son, complete with her photograph. The week after the article was published, more than a thousand letters arrived, many from schoolchildren, proclaiming, "Mother Hai, you may have lost one Hai Jingsheng, but you've gained thousands more! We are all your son! Great respect to our magnificent mother!" The vast pile of letters brought her joy but also terror.

There was a huge discussion in the relevant ministry. Someone held up the paper and asked: "Which division is this hero in? What's his unit number? Why wasn't this ministry informed that a hero had been sacrificed? Did they only notify the parent and forget to report to us?" Someone else remarked: "There must have been some negligence on our part, we probably mislaid his file and the notification. We ought to give this Auntie Hai a Martyr's Family Certificate, and extend an apology." Some suggested questioning Auntie Hai to clear up the whole matter; others felt this would be insulting and might lead to public outrage.

Three months passed. The ministry carried out a careful investigation and concluded there was no such person as Hai Jingsheng. Auntie Hai was a liar. Now what? Turn her over to the police and make an example of her? Give her a stern warning and keep an eye on her? After careful consideration, they decided she was just attention-seeking and hadn't actually hurt anyone. Exposing her might confuse the public, particularly schoolchildren. They decided to resolve the matter quietly.

They brought Auntie Hai in for questioning. For the first hour, she didn't give an inch. She was firmly in the grip of her own delusion and put up a stiff resistance, sobbing one minute, smiling the next as she spoke of her motherly love for Hai Jingsheng, whom she missed very much. Eventually, she returned to reality. When she finally understood that Hai Jingsheng didn't exist, the tears and laughter stopped, and she just stared straight ahead, stunned.

After receiving a harsh scolding, she was transferred to a different nursery in a different district. There, she gradually came back to herself, and the public forgot about her. Hai Jingsheng evaporated from her heart, leaving nothing behind.

She'll never behave so recklessly again, yet she still longs for people to think more of her than her actual life warrants, and—within limits—indulges in imaginary scenarios that make her feel better about herself.

In the many multifamily siheyuans in Beijing's hutongs, there are quite a few people whose minds work the same way as Old Lady Hai's.

After retirement, she found her solitary life very lonely, so she adopted her youngest brother's grandson, Hai Xibin. He came to live with her at the age of four, twenty years ago. She's doted on him ever since he was little. He got a job in the Parks Department after high school, and to this day he hands his wages over to her every single month. You couldn't say he doesn't treat her well, yet he's the only person able to call out Old Lady Hai's lies to her face. It saddens her to think how ruthless Xibin can be at these moments. A few years ago, for instance, her rattan chairs broke. It would have been a waste of money to have them repaired, but she couldn't bear to throw them out, so she asked Xibin to hang them over the entryway. He always did as she asked and went to fetch the ladder. While he was up there, with his grandma watching from the ground, Mrs. Xun from the side yard walked by and said, "Oh my, those chairs look completely unusable, why not just get rid of them?" Old Lady Hai gravely replied, "I can't just throw them away. You know who once sat in them? Chairwoman Kang herself!" Mrs. Xun, who kept up with TV news, was flabbergasted. "What? Chairwoman Kang came to our siheyuan? When? How come we didn't hear about it?" Naturally, she was thinking of Comrade Chairwoman Kang Keqing of the All-China Women's Federation, which was exactly what Old Lady Hai had hoped for. Their actual guest, though, was the chairwoman of the trade union at Xibin's workplace, who also happened to be named Kang. Xibin was too busy with what he was doing to pay much attention, but word got around the siheyuan, mostly because Zhan Liying made it her business to tell everyone she met while fetching water, "Chairwoman Kang Keqing came to our siheyuan to visit Old Lady Hai—she must be someone special, I guess!" Nanny Zhan then sought out Xibin to ask, "Did your grandma take part in the Revolution? I suppose she took a wrong turn somewhere along the line? That's exactly what happened to me—she must be completely rehabilitated? What does Chairwoman Kang plan to do with her?" Xibin flushed bright red with anxiety and annoyance, and said, "That's not true—no such thing ever happened!" Back home, he laid into Old Lady Hai. "What's the point of making up all this nonsense, Grandma? You think you look good by sticking gold to your face? Far better if we just lead honest lives! If you keep telling lies like this, I'll have to go live somewhere else. I can't have you embarrassing me like that." Old Lady Hai hunched her shoulders in fear, and her face turned stark white. She mumbled, "I didn't say anything, they just guessed wrong. You shouldn't talk to me like that, Xibin. You think it was easy for me to bring you up?" She dabbed at her tears with her handkerchief, and Xibin was forced to comfort her. "Just stop bragging about these made-up things, okay? Of course I'd never leave you to fend for yourself. At your age, even if I were just your neighbor, I'd still feel obliged to take care of you."

And now, as Old Lady Hai and Grandpa Hu sit by the Drum Tower, reluctant to go home, Xibin passes by on his bicycle. He screeches to a halt and, one foot on the sidewalk, calls out, "Grandma! Grandpa Hu! The sun's almost gone, why not go home and rest?" Old Lady Hai shouts back, "We're just going now!" And Grandpa Hu echoes, "Just going, just going."

Xibin pedals off. Grandpa Hu watches his retreating form, broad shoulders and narrow waist, and says with admiration, "Lucky you! Xibin's such a polite boy. He's even respectful to me." He thinks of his own son and daughter-in-law. Whenever they walk past the Drum Tower with their child on the way to the park or shopping center, they don't even notice him sitting there, or pretend they don't. If his grandson tries to call out a greeting, they quickly drag him away, clearly terrified that the people around them will realize they, a fancy couple, are related to the shabby old gent on the sidewalk. But that's kids these days—Xibin's unusual! Though even his respectful behavior is nothing compared to previous generations. At this thought, Grandpa Hu says to Old Lady Hai, "Speaking of children showing respect, no one can beat Xun Xingwang in your siheyuan. I saw him when he first moved in, right after Liberation. I was a cook at the food stall by their factory gate. On payday every month, his mom would wait by the stall. When Xingwang came out with his pay packet, he'd lead her right in and order a few meat dishes, along with two snow-white steamed rolls, and just sit there watching her eat, not having any himself—he'd already filled his belly with cornbread and pickles in the factory cafeteria. After his mom finished eating, he'd pay for the meal, take a little cigarette money for himself, and hand the rest of his wages to her. She'd wrap it in her hanky and tuck it into her blouse. They'd sit there a little longer, then he'd say they ought to be getting home. I once asked him, 'How come you bring your mom here for lunch every month?' And he said, 'You probably don't know that my mom had to beg in the streets to raise me. I followed her around and promised myself that I'd pay her back. Seeing her eat so well each month makes me happy!' See? Where would you find a son as devoted and respectful as Xun Xingwang in this day and age?"

Old Lady Hai has to agree. "That sounds like something from a play!" She stands up, folds her stool, and says contentedly, "I wouldn't ask to be treated as well as Xingwang treated his mom. Xibin does more than enough for me!"

Grandpa Hu stands too, picks up his little bench, and looks lingeringly at the setting sun. Trying to delay their departure a few seconds more, he ekes out the conversation. "That's true! Xibin's made something of himself, hasn't he? Got a good job right out of high school, didn't he? And he met a Central leader soon after starting work, right?"

This upsets Old Lady Hai a little. True, Xibin graduated high school in 1975 and got a job in the Parks Department right away. A few months later, he met Madame Mao, which Old Lady Hai has mentioned to Grandpa Hu before. All this is true, but why bring it up now? The one thing she doesn't want to talk about! "See you tomorrow," she says, and heads home.

CHAPTER 27

"Not At All." Madame Mao is a character in this novel too.

Everyone at work calls Hai Xibin "Not At All."

The origin of this nickname lies in his sole encounter with Madame Mao, Jiang Qing.

People his age were in high school during the Cultural Revolution. The rallying cry at the time was "Education must be Revolutionary, spend less time at school." Middle and high school were reduced to two years each, and thanks to the strategy of "not just book-learning, but learning to be workers, peasants, and soldiers, to critique the capitalist class," they only spent maybe half a year actually in the classroom. The school year began and ended in spring. Before New Year 1975, Xibin graduated from the muddle of his high school education. As an only child, he wasn't sent down to the countryside and was soon given a job in the Parks Department as a gardener.

The park where he worked hadn't been open to the public for a while now, but those with the privilege could go in whenever they wanted. As a result, the plants and facilities were exceptionally well cared for. Even the gift shop was always fully stocked, perpetually clean and gleaming.

One afternoon in the middle of May, the park supervisor got a phone call to say a "Central leader" would shortly be arriving for a tour of the park, and they should quickly prepare for this. They didn't say which Central leader, so he thought it best to assume it was Madame Mao—if the place was good enough for Madame Mao, no other Central leader would complain—and mobilized everyone. They scrambled to get ready, and in an instant the park filled with an atmosphere of tension and fear.

Although Xibin was a gardener, the supervisor put him behind the counter in the gift shop—better handsome, clear-skinned Hai Xibin than the actual sales clerk with his acne-ridden face. Madame Mao would probably saunter past the shop and not actually buy anything, so the fact that Xibin had no sales experience was completely overlooked.

Sure enough, it was Jiang Qing who showed up.

For some reason, she was in a good mood that day. This visit wasn't on her itinerary, but she'd had a bit of spare time between engagements, and this park happened to be on the way to her next appointment. On the spur of the moment, she'd asked her staff to arrange this little impromptu outing.

The weather was pleasant that day. Willow trees swayed gently in the breeze, peonies bloomed resplendently, birds chirped merrily, and butterflies fluttered gracefully hither and thither. Jiang Qing strolled along with the park supervisor, smiling and chatting amiably. They walked by the peony beds and under the wisteria trellises. The supervisor caught sight of a maple tree up ahead. Right away, his heart thudded painfully and cold sweat prickled his forehead. One branch was completely withered, and last year's fall leaves were still hanging from it. The gardening team ought to have sawed it off, but here it was in plain sight. Would Jiang Qing find this acceptable?

Jiang Qing's footsteps halted, and she stared. The smile lines on her face faded. The supervisor felt all the blood in his body turn to tar, and a pit of quicksand opened at his feet. A little bird alighted nearby and let loose a crisp little melody.

With her head tilted to one side, Jiang Qing regarded the tree's crown for a full two seconds. Finally, the supervisor heard her say, "This tree is jade green all over, with just one withered branch. That makes it rather special."

He was so moved by his salvation that his throat spasmed, and he was dizzy for quite a while. When he came back to himself, he realized they'd turned back around and were heading back to the entrance. As they passed the gift shop, Jiang Qing abruptly went inside, right up to the counter. She looked at the various snacks laid out there—no one could have explained what was going on, but it was definitely happening—and said cheerfully, "These all look delectable! How much per pound?"

Xibin was not yet seventeen and, unlike the supervisor, had not learned to be fearful. He was only supposed to be standing there as an ornament, and had never sold a snack in his life. He answered, "The prices are written there on the sign."

The supervisor all but fainted dead away, and sure enough, Jiang Qing lost her temper. "Is this how you treat customers?" she snapped at Xibin. "Good thing I can read. What if I were a poor farmer from some little village? Would you just point him at the sign too?"

Xibin flushed bright red, and he lowered his head as if he were being scolded by a teacher. Jiang Qing smiled at his bashfulness. "Don't worry, young man, as long as you learn from your mistake. Could you weigh out some of these snacks for me?"

The supervisor felt himself coming back to life. *Don't create any more disasters, Xibin,* he implored silently.

Xibin picked up the scales and tongs and was about to bend over the snacks when he asked tremulously, "Some . . . How much is some?"

Jiang Qing's eyebrows shot up. Unexpectedly, she clapped her hands and laughed heartily. At this crucial moment, the supervisor sprinted to the counter, shoved Xibin out of the way, and personally weighed out Jiang Qing's snacks. He put two of everything in the pan, each time returning it to the scale, muttering to himself as he fiddled with the counterweights, and when the balance rose, he randomly wrote down a number and made up a price. Jiang Qing had, of course, already moved on, leaving her entourage to pay and get the snacks. When they were done, the supervisor dashed out of the gift shop and caught up with Jiang Qing. He was astounded at his luck when, instead of chastising him for what just happened, she said breezily, "I hear you have tulips in the summer?" Hastily, he leaned closer and replied, "Yes, we do, and you'd be very welcome to come back to see them, Central Leader."

Jiang Qing sighed. "I'd love to come back, if only I had the time."

The supervisor hadn't had time to deal with Xibin. After being pushed aside, Xibin knew he'd messed up, so he left the gift shop and, not knowing where to go, just stood beneath a pine tree, hands clasped before him.

After ambling a little farther, Jiang Qing turned back to her car with the red flag on it. Unfortunately, Xibin reentered her field of vision. The supervisor was furious at this idiocy—why was the boy standing by a path Jiang Qing would have to pass on her way to her car? His teeth itched with rage. He was completely drained: energy, body, and soul. When Jiang Qing stopped walking and beckoned to Xibin, the supervisor knew his life was over, and soon he would be no more than a puddle of mud.

Seeing Jiang Qing wave, Xibin automatically walked over. She really was in extraordinarily good spirits that day—she patted him on the shoulder, kindness written all over her face, and her tone was touchingly patient. "Young man, your customer service really won't do, and you don't seem familiar with your job at all. How will you serve the People like this? You really must improve."

Xibin nodded again and again.

"How old are you?" she asked.

"Seventeen."

"So young!" she exclaimed. "The newly risen sun. Youngsters like you hold all our hopes."

Xibin bowed, uncertain what to say. Resurrected once again, the supervisor longed to thank the Central leader for her words of encouragement, but he could hardly speak on Xibin's behalf.

Jiang Qing wasn't done. "Have you graduated middle school?"

"Yes, and high school too."

She chuckled, and said with a sigh, "Oh my, I'd never have guessed you were already done with high school. Quite remarkable! You're better educated than me, in that case—I never finished high school! That makes you a little intellectual, I suppose. Just seventeen, and already an intellectual!"

And that's when Xibin spoke the legendary words, "Not at all."

This was seven years ago. When Xibin thinks of it now, it feels like a dream. A report on his behavior that day was sent to the higher-ups. A week later, the relevant authority sent out a notice about the "incident" at the park gift shop, which emphasized that apart from young park workers having to improve their "political thinking and education," the park should also "take immediate action to ensure that unsuitable workers are removed from areas frequented by Central leaders and foreign visitors, to prevent future incidents." The next day, Xibin was redeployed from the park to a greenification team in charge of sidewalk trees, along streets that, barring extraordinary circumstances, would never see a Central leader or foreign visitor. He was transferred a few more times after that, but no matter where he ended up, the story about his encounter with Madame Mao always arrived before him. That's why his peers never used his name—he was just Not At All.

Although Xibin was no longer at the park, his supervisor still used the story of his conversation with Jiang Qing as an example of "the Central leader taking the time to patiently educate a young park worker." When word of this reached Old Lady Hai's ears, she beamed with pride and often swanked about it in front of Grandpa Hu and the other members of the "old people's club."

Very soon, the situation turned upside down: Jiang Qing was deposed. In 1976, the tide turned against the Gang of Four, and the events of that day became the story of "Jiang Qing wildly abusing her privilege." A playwright, accompanied by Han Yitan of this siheyuan, came to Xibin's door wanting him to provide material for a play about Jiang Qing's visit. Xibin recounted the whole story from beginning to end, but the playwright seemed disappointed. He said suspiciously, "Jiang Qing and her cronies were hell-bent on persecuting intellectuals at the time. Would she really have spoken so approvingly of intellectuals in front of you?" Xibin didn't know how to lie, fantasize, or conceal—all he could do was tell the complete truth. He had no answer for the playwright's doubts. Of course he was aware that Jiang Qing and her gang came down the hardest on intellectuals—Zhan Liying from their siheyuan was a living example. Yet that day in the park, Jiang Qing said what she said, and he responded, "Not at all."

The playwright went home and wrote a play exposing the Gang of Four. Although the names had been changed, it was clear which character was based on Jiang Qing. From time to time, she let out a maniacal laugh, and all her lines were hissed between her teeth—the audience loathed her. Han Yitan, Ge Ping, Zhan Liying, Old Lady Hai, and Hai Xibin all went to the first performance and thought it wasn't bad at all. They came away admiring the writer's talent. As Xibin cycled home, he thought back through the scenes in the play and felt that a certain something was missing. What could it be? He had no idea, much less the ability to put it into words.

Now that Xibin's fully grown, he's able to think more deeply. The playwright shouldn't have so lightly tossed aside the material he provided. Of course, the events in the park couldn't have appeared directly in the play, but Jiang Qing's evil actions and those of her supporters were encapsulated in this incident. These weren't just character flaws being displayed, but more fundamental, complex traits that might be instructive to study in more detail.

He's mentioned this to Uncle Han, and Han Yitan encouraged him by saying, "You've thought so profoundly about this, why not have a go at writing it yourself? There are plenty of young writers like you these days—you're in your early twenties, aren't you? Since the political weather is clear these days, you should seize the opportunity and establish yourself. These days, famous writers aren't seen as evil—in fact, they're well supported. Look at the youngsters in our siheyuan. Apart from Xue Jiyue, who's probably being held back by his family situation, there's Xun Lei and that girl he's seeing, Miss Feng. They're both aiming to be translators. Zhang Xiuzao is going to be a professor in a few years, and I'm sure she'll end up as a head engineer somewhere. Then take the middle-aged folk, Tantai Zhizhu and Zhan Liying—one's a performing artist, the other's aiming to be at least a high-grade engineer. No one's willing to fall behind. Xibin, enough with the 'Not At All' business—you need to buck up and decide where your ambition lies."

Xibin's only response was a bland smile. The higher-ups had offered to transfer him back to the park, but he'd declined. It's good to make the streets greener, isn't it? Most young people clamor for higher-skilled positions, but Xibin always asks for thankless, tiring tasks such as watering plants with the giant hose. Even Old Lady Hai says he "oozes foolishness," to which he replies calmly, "But, Grandma, it's not like everyone can be famous and successful in a highly skilled position. I know my capabilities, and I think what I'm doing now is very well suited to me."

It's been said that the most prominent characteristic of young people in 1980s China is their hunger and competitiveness. Xibin seems to lie outside of this stereotype. And yet, isn't his indifference to fame and fortune, and his propensity to be content with what he has, also indicative of a certain mindset only to be found in the generation coming of age in the 1980s?

Hai Xibin's hobby is martial arts.

He was scrawny as a kid, and still quite lanky after finishing school. Then in 1979, he developed a sudden passion for martial arts and started training. You might think he was influenced by movies like *Shaolin Temple* or film stars like Jet Li, but that's not it.

Right now in Beijing, there are two groups of martial arts practitioners. One is under the Sports Administration and regularly gets sent to take part in all sorts of competitions. The winners enjoy public glory and are often seen on TV; some even get invited to be in films, displaying the height of their artistry on the silver screen for all to admire. The other group is just regular folk who practice in parks and other green spaces in the early morning. Although even the more talented individuals might not have a presence in the usual publicity channels, in the eyes of Beijing's true martial arts fanatics, they have an even more exalted status than the superstars of the first group. Of course, there is no conflict between these two spheres, and in fact there's no shortage of instances where they overlap.

Xibin got into martial arts because of this second group of practitioners.

His morning commute on his bicycle takes him past Moon Temple Park. One day, passing by earlier than usual, he saw an old man practicing "ground punches" in a grove of trees. He struck such elegant postures that Xibin had to stop to cheer him on, then went closer and watched for a while. They exchanged a few words, enough to form an acquaintance. For several mornings after that, Xibin woke up extra early and rushed to Moon Temple Park. He got to know the old man better and, from being a mere onlooker, began asking for instruction, until he formally acknowledged the old man as his instructor and began practicing in earnest.

The old man is Duan Yanqin, and though he's almost eighty, he looks no more than sixty.

Duan Yanqin, who has quite a reputation in the amateur martial arts community, first made Xibin learn the basics from some younger instructors, and introduced him to more and more people he could study with. Once past this stage, Xibin was able to dip into one form of martial arts after another. In Moon Temple Park, he learned Chen-style Tai Chi from Lei Muni and leg-bouncing from Ma Changqing. In Xuanwu Park, he acknowledged "the Leopard" Fu Bao as yet another teacher and studied several forms of Xingyi Fist with him. In the little park on Lishi Road, he learned how to do Bagua punches, in which you spin on the spot, from Xu Zengfan. On the east lawn of the history museum, he picked up a series of white-ape whole-arm punches from Yang Qishun, whose day job is selling glutinous rice cakes in the grinding factory's cafeteria. Several years later, with more guidance from Grandpa Duan, Xibin reached a reasonable standard in both the "inner arts" of Tai Chi, Xingyi, and Bagua, and the "outer arts" of Cha, Hong, Pao, Hua, and other types of "long fist."

Old Lady Hai nags at him, "Xibin, what's the point of all this? Don't you dare go around getting into fights and stirring up trouble for me."

Xibin has to laugh at that. When has he ever caused his grandmother any trouble?

His boss once praised him at an assembly: "Hai Xibin has mastered all these martial arts and is prepared for hand-to-hand combat with any villains who try to steal our nation's flora. He will protect our country's property, and apprehend these criminals. His thinking should be emulated by all the young workers in our bureau."

Xibin mumbled to himself, "Not at all." Is Beijing really full of nefarious individuals bold enough to creep into the nursery in the dead of night, hoping to help themselves to a sapling? And how often would Xibin run into them while on night shift? Besides, these burglars might look burly, but they're weak inside—it's hardly necessary to reach this level of martial skill to take them on. Even if his spirit were to be emulated by the other young workers, most people probably aren't able to get to his standard of martial arts—and what would be the point, anyway?

"Not At All wants to be in movies! Who's the director of *Deadly Fury*? Why hasn't he cast our Not At All in anything? Is he still making kung fu flicks? We should recommend Not At All to him!" That's the sort of ribbing he was subjected to, from coworkers nudging him and smacking him on the back.

He chuckled along with everyone else. Him? In movies? Could anything be more ridiculous? If he were ever in a film, there'd surely be a long line of people at the cinema box office—all asking for a refund!

"Not At All's doing it for the ladies! Which girl doesn't want a hunky martial arts expert? Our Not At All isn't a hulking brute, you know, he's the delicate sort—a real gentleman warrior!" Big Brother Wang, the technician on their team, teases him like this in front of young women.

Xibin stays silent. This was never his intention, of course, but it has been the result. He often receives love letters from secret admirers. One girl was even so bold as to mail him her note. Old Lady Hai intercepted it, but being far-sighted, she asked Zhan Liying to read it to her. Nanny Zhan opened the letter, but before she'd even started reading out loud, she was already bent in half with laughter.

In answer to Old Lady Hai's inevitable questioning, Xibin always says, "Don't worry, Grandma. I'll be sure to marry a woman who treats you as well as I do."

He's seeing someone at the moment—they're in the first flush of love. On this day, December 12, 1982, he set out on his bicycle first thing in the morning to meet her and is only returning now, a little after four. If he hadn't had to rush back to catch the 4:05 broadcast of *Soccer Highlights*, he might have spent even more time with her. She hasn't yet told her strict parents about him, so they can't go on proper dates, and Xibin isn't ready to introduce her to his grandmother.

Xibin wheels his bicycle into the courtyard and is about to carry it across the chuihua gate when he sees a drunk man sobbing and cursing as he stumbles out of the Xue house. After a few steps, he turns back to scream, "You've got the wrong man! I didn't do it! You're the thieves, you nest of lamas! Old lamas! Young lamas! You just watch out, I'm not fucking done with you yet! I'll find someone to smash your lama temple! Just you wait!"

The ruckus Luo Baosang causes as he's ejected from the banquet brings everyone to the courtyard. The wedding guests spill out of the Xues' two rooms while Zhan Liying and Zhang Xiuzao peep from their windows. Tantai Zhizhu's father-in-law and Mrs. Xun materialize next to Xibin. How did a perfectly good wedding end up in this state?

Xue Jiyue, the groom, is in a state of near hysteria. The others try to restrain him, but he keeps trying to lunge at Baosang. His hair is mussed up, his suit disheveled, and his boutonniere threatens to fall off. He shrieks, "You're not going anywhere, Luo Baosang! Give me back my Rado watch! Or we can both go down to the police station!"

Baosang struts and shuffles as if ready to fight. "I didn't steal your fucking watch! Police station? No way! I'm not going anywhere? Watch me!" He swaggers away.

Xibin has the impulse to stop him but restrains himself. The situation is unclear, and it's hard to say who's right or wrong. As Baosang leaves, Xibin notices Mr. Yin among the crowd. Ah, so he's one of the Xues' guests too.

Jiyue is persuaded to return to the wedding banquet. Zhan Liying has, naturally, already headed in there to find out more about what happened. Mrs. Xun goes over to comfort Uncle Xue—but rather than asking what happened, she launches straight into trying to cheer him up. "There's a drunkard at every banquet. This is nothing at all, don't worry about it. You need to attend to your guests. Come on, I can help with that. Let's go inside." Xiuzao withdraws into her room but is too worked up to return to her studies right away. She's annoyed by the commotion, and once again a little melancholy at how she and these people will never understand each other. Soon, she'll be moving to a completely different environment, far from this vulgar crowd. That's lucky, isn't it? But Xun Lei's past, present, and a good stretch of his future are taking place in this world. How is he able to put up with it? Tantai Zhizhu's father-in-law is tense—this skirmish has reminded him of his own family quarrel. He goes back home and paces around the living room. Why haven't Li Kai and Zhizhu returned yet? Even Bamboo is nowhere to be seen. Should he go looking for them or start getting dinner ready?

Mr. Yin spots Xibin the same moment Xibin notices him. Mr. Yin is Duan Yanqin's most able disciple, and Xibin has trained in Dacheng boxing with him. People say when Mr. Yin was in his fifties, his Dacheng boxing skills were second to none in the whole city, and he had the ability to "hit an old ox on the neighboring hill." Nowadays he lives near Longtan Lake in the south of the city, where he's made quite a name for himself as a bonesetter. After Baosang is gone, Mr. Yin hurriedly says to Xibin, "The man who just left is Luo Baosang. It's not clear whether or not he stole a Rado watch from the Xues. He's drunk and behaving very badly. If you can, follow him at a distance and keep an eye on him. See where he goes and what he does. But don't get too close and startle him, and definitely don't lay a hand on him. Come back here if he returns home. I'll wait for word from you."

Xibin has been a disciple of Mr. Yin's, and this business of the Xues' deserves looking into. Right away, he turns his bicycle around and heads back out. *Soccer Highlights* has, of course, been relegated to the back of his mind.

CHAPTER 28

The bridegroom's brother finally shows up. Loading and
unloading. A kerfuffle at the faucet.

How many drinking places does Beijing have these days?

Back in the day, there were plenty, with a respectable variety on the stretch
between Outer Di'anmen and the Drum Tower. After the Gang of Four fell,
restaurants began increasing in number and variety, and drinking establishments
started returning too. Toward the end of 1982, one popped up in this neighborhood, in Bell Tower Bay Hutong between the Bell and Drum Towers, a
standalone building called First Fragrance Tobacco & Liquor. Inside are four
or five long tables and a dozen or so benches. Apart from various tobacco and
alcohol products, it also offers boiled peanuts, seasoned jellyfish, pig bladder,
chitterlings, tea-smoked sausage, garlic sausage, eggs fried with sausage, lun-
cheon sausage, tea eggs, pig-head meat, and mung bean noodles. Being on an
out-of-the-way hutong, few strangers stumble upon it, and its clientele tend to
be people who live and work nearby. As a result, the customers mostly know
the staff and each other, and the atmosphere is perpetually lively and convivial.

A little after four in the afternoon on December 12, 1982, Hai Xibin tails
Luo Baosang on his bicycle, per Mr. Yin's instructions. When Baosang stumbles
into First Fragrance, Xibin dismounts, locks his bike, and peers through the window. His neighbor Li Kai, Tantai Zhizhu's husband, is in there too; he watches
as Baosang spots Li Kai and bellows something, then staggers over. Li Kai stands
and grabs him before he falls, looking startled and apparently asking questions.

Xibin hesitates—should he go in? Suddenly, someone calls his name.

He turns around, and there is Jiyue's big brother, Xue Jihui, coming toward him on a bicycle.

Jihui hadn't planned to stop—he was just calling out a friendly greeting—but Xibin flags him down and asks, "Why are you only arriving now?"

Clearly exhausted, Jihui answers briefly, "Overtime."

"Overtime? Do you know what day it is? Your family's in crisis! There was a fight at the banquet—they said someone stole their Rado watch." He nods toward First Fragrance. "Jiyue suspects that guy, but there's no evidence. I can't make heads or tails of it. Anyway, you should go, quick! You might be able to help."

Jihui is perplexed. He looks inside First Fragrance, but the only person he recognizes is Li Kai—surely this must be a misunderstanding! Still, Xibin looks and sounds serious. "All right," he says, "I'll go now!" He puts his foot back on the pedal, wishing he could get there immediately.

Xibin watches Jihui's broad back speeding away and feels a strong sense of sympathy. He remembers the previous summer, when he and some other kids from the hutong went to the Shicha Seas to cool off, and the others somehow persuaded him to get into a wrestling match with Jihui. He'd only just started mastering martial arts and was always eager for an opportunity to show off. He challenged Jihui, who rose to his feet and said, "We don't need to fight. I'll stand here, you try to knock me over. If I fall, you win." He planted both feet firmly, put his hands on his waist, and thrust out his sturdy chest. Xibin tried all kinds of tactics, arms and feet lashing out like a white dragon twining around an iron pagoda, but simply couldn't get Jihui to budge. The other kids hooted and hollered, getting pissed off at him. Finally, Xibin said, "You win, Jihui. Name your prize." Jihui smiled. "Tell you what, Not At All, give us a boxing demonstration and we'll call it quits." Xibin launched into the Chen-style Tai Chi moves he'd just mastered, and when he reached his closing pose, it was Jihui who led the applause. Afterward, Jihui said, "Not At All has skill. I don't know a single bit of kung fu—I'm just solidly built." Xibin has always remembered these words. This is what he needs to learn from Jihui: how to be solid. Of course, his scrawny, wiry body will never achieve solidity, but he can earn it through leading his life with seriousness and dignity.

As you can tell from his name—"hui" means "emblem"—Xue Jihui was born at the same time as the national emblem of the People's Republic of China.

On September 20, 1950, Chairman Mao Zedong announced this new coat of arms, and that very evening, Jihui was born in a side hall of Longfu Temple. The midwife was from Union Medical College Hospital—if this had been before Liberation, Xue Yongquan would never have dared to go fetch him from Sun Pit Hutong, which was just to the east of the temple. When the midwife realized it was too late to bring Auntie Xue to the hospital, he hurried to her bedside with his medical bag and successfully delivered Jihui. He refused to accept any money, saying, "If you'd asked me before, I'd have come too. I never collect a fee for services outside the hospital." He was speaking sincerely, as a Christian—but Xue Yongquan still chose to see all this as part of the good fortune that had arrived in Beijing thanks to the Communist Party's Liberation. He and Auntie Xue were married before they turned twenty and had already had three boys and a girl, all delivered by the temple aunties. Two of the boys were born with the umbilical cord wrapped around their necks and stopped breathing because the aunties were unable to untangle them. The third was stillborn. The girl was born healthy, but when she was three months old, the clerk at Xiugeng Hall Bookstore on Longfu Temple Street helped put them in touch with an official who didn't have any daughters. They handed the girl over and never heard from her again.

The new parents were grateful for the Communist Party and the establishment of the People's Republic of China, so they named their sole surviving boy Jihui, "commemorating the emblem." Auntie Xue's health deteriorated after the birth, and she came down with tuberculosis. After Liberation, a large marketplace sprang up on the Longfu Temple grounds, and Xue Yongquan went from being a lama to having a full-time job there. With the family's improved finances, Auntie Xue was able to seek treatment at the Anti-TB Association in Beichizi, and a few years later she was fully recovered. Now in good health, she gave birth to Jiyue. It's been more than thirty years since Jihui's birth, and both boys are now grown men, with wives and careers. Mr. and Mrs. Xue Yongquan ought to be proud of them.

However, no society and no family can remain frozen at a particular moment. As time flows, any society will inevitably become full of contradictions and clashes, and a human being trying to live out his destiny will have both joys and sorrows.

Jihui was sixteen and in his third year of high school when he got swept up in the Cultural Revolution. He was the very first Red Guard in his school and passionately embraced the ideology of "continuing the Revolution under a dictatorship of the proletariat." He expanded his horizons during the "Great Networking," and came to despise the tactic of "strike, smash, snatch." He insisted that they must "fight with words, not weapons," which caused many heated arguments with his fellow Red Guards. He felt sorry for the school principals and Party branch secretaries who'd been branded "recalcitrant capitalist roaders" for minor errors, and grew increasingly confused at the extreme rhetoric emanating from the Central Committee. None of these things, though, left as deep a mark on his psyche or influenced his worldview as much as the shocking sight of "loading and unloading."

What was being "loaded and unloaded"?

Not, as you might imagine, goods from trucks.

Near where the Xues lived was an even more well-maintained hutong, with a perfectly preserved siheyuan. A personage of importance lived here. This individual was now in his seventies, and his faculties were declining. He was also obese and had trouble with his legs. For some time, he'd been declining invitations and no longer attending events. When everything came crashing down in the Cultural Revolution, he somehow managed to survive the turbulence. On occasions such as International Workers' Day or National Day, he still received an invitation to attend the festivities at Tiananmen Tower. A small car would arrive to pick him up, and his neighbors would stand in a large circle watching the attendants and his family bundle him into the car. Jihui was always among this crowd.

The opening of the car door was already too small for the old man, and his confusion and discomfort didn't help. The attendants and family members had to handle him as if he were a heavy and extremely fragile precious item that needed to be maneuvered into place. First, a young man would go into the car and reach out his arms, ready to receive. Three others would help the old man to the car, then bend his body and lower his head, practically hugging him, to get him inside. Once he was through, he could be eased farther into the car. The whole thing took more than ten minutes. As the onlookers watched in silence, the old man let out what sounded like primal cries: "Ah . . . ah ah . . . ah ah ah . . ." (Being squashed like that must have caused him quite a bit of pain.) Meanwhile, the old man's daughter gave orders in a calm, authoritative voice: "Slower! Don't panic! That's right, put some strength into it! Why so nervous?

Ignore him, push harder! And you, pull! Not just his arm, get hold of his torso! What are you moaning about, Dad? Just get in the car, would you?" All in all, it was an unnerving sight.

When the car drove off, some onlookers remained by the hutong entrance, whispering about what they'd just witnessed. They knew the routine by now—a little over half an hour after the curtain came down on the "loading," the "unloading" performance would commence.

When the old man got to the city gate tower, he'd have to be unloaded. Then he went up the tower, and the people with him would make sure the Xinhua News reporters ticked his name off the printed list with their pencil. When his breath had calmed down, without even waiting for the event to be over, they'd load him back into the car and bring him home, where the attendants and family members would, at the direction of the fiftysomething daughter, perform the final unloading. This was much more difficult than the loading, but also faster, and the daughter's voice would be urgent and stiff: "Don't be scared! Pull! You inside, push! Dad, what are you screaming about? You'll be out in a second! All right, quick, support him! Quickly!"

It's hard to say if the old man was actually willing to be loaded and unloaded in this way. His daughter's attitude was clear, though. One time, when the loading was going particularly badly, a guy who was probably his grandson said, "If he can't get in, just let him stay home!" To which the daughter snapped, "Stay home? He's still alive. If his name isn't on the evening news, everyone's going to think he's been brought down. Let me tell you, if he misses even one of these events, never mind in Beijing, even if we went to one of our other homes, we'd be in for such a stink our lives wouldn't be worth living!" So saying, she shoved the old man hard toward the car, and he let out an even more heartrending shriek than ever. You couldn't call her cruel, because her voice shook as she cried "Dad!" and shed tears in front of everyone. This scene made its way into Xue Jihui's eyes and ears, and he felt that life was teaching him a rich, profound, and painful lesson.

A few hours after each loading and unloading, the nearby loudspeakers that some government organization had set up would recite, in loud, plummy tones, the attendees' names. When they got to the old man, Jihui would clench his teeth, and something would vibrate agonizingly within him.

He was never sent down to the countryside. His batch of students happened to be deployed within the city, and he was sent to his present work unit, first as a cargo loader then, after he got his license, driving a BJ130 truck.

Even before the Gang of Four fell, he'd already turned against the Cultural Revolution—not because of any penetrating or precise insights, but simply his own experiences. This "revolution" was nonexistent. The loading and unloading was just one indication.

He established an article of faith for himself: he had to be genuine. Hypocrisy was worse than a genuine mistake. His harshest criticism of anyone was, "Stop pretending!"

And now Jihui is on his bicycle racing to his brother's wedding banquet, exhausted body and soul, about to plunge into a difficult situation.

Will the bride understand why he absolutely had to work overtime today? Or will she see it as an insult? Today may be the only time in her life when she's the star of the show, and her brother-in-law doesn't even bother showing up. Then there's his mother—she wants everything to be auspicious and hates looking bad in front of others. She's always been loving and proud of him, but will any amount of patient explaining get her to excuse his lateness? She'll say, "Even if you had to work overtime, did you really have to be so late?" He could tell her: He was heading back when a delivery man flagged him down, sweat pouring from his forehead—his truck had broken down in the middle of nowhere. He implored Jihui, "You're the nineteenth vehicle to pass by. Please, I'm relying on you!" Jihui persuaded his assistants to get down and have a look. They crawled underneath the truck and, after a huge amount of effort, managed to fix it. What would his mother say? "Couldn't you have told him you had a family event? You think no one else would come along to help? He says he stopped however many vehicles—and you believed him, just like that? He was trying to win your sympathy with his tale of woe, that's all. Bleeding heart!" That's right, he's a bleeding heart. He can't walk past a fellow human being in distress. He'd never selfishly abandon those who need help to plow his own furrow. How could he not do the right thing, just because he was rushing to his brother's wedding? What's he after? Gratitude? Praise? Cash? An award? None of these things—all he wants is a clear conscience. As he sees it, politics, economics, culture, and society are getting more and more fake. Now that China is putting the Four

Modernizations into place, it's even more imperative that he is solid in his dealings with others and himself.

The encounter with Xibin made his burden a little heavier. If the wedding banquet were going well, his lateness wouldn't be as big a deal. What's the problem? What Rado watch? Whose is it? Who stole it? How did Li Kai get mixed up in all this? It pains his heart to think of his father's cowardice, his mother's superstition, and his brother's childishness. They needed him there to take control of the situation! But instead, he's late and has missed the crucial moment.

Faster! Cycle faster! He banishes the weariness from his every muscle and nerve, revs up his energy, qi, and spirit, and sets off to be a dutiful son, brother, and brother-in-law.

When he gets there, his tension ebbs away a little—everything seems normal. The banquet is in full swing, and though the guests aren't exactly booming with laughter, they seem to be having a reasonably lively time. The sound of frying comes from the cooking tent, and the aroma of shredded pork with garlic shoots comes wafting his way. His little daughter, Lotus, wanders out of the nuptial chamber, lips greasy. "Daddy!" she screams in delight. "Granny! Daddy's here!"

Jihui hurries inside, and meets his mom head-on.

Auntie Xue has run through the gamut of emotions today—everything but happiness. After the business with the Rado watch, a number of the guests said goodbye—only Mr. Yin is left of the original group. Although Manager Wang and the others tried to say some comforting words as they departed, she feels her dignity has been dragged through the mud. Seventh Aunt stalked off in high dudgeon, with these parting words to the bride, which she made sure the entire family heard: "I'm not heading home now, I'm going to see your parents. If this mess isn't sorted out by the time you visit tomorrow, Xiuya, you should just stay in your parents' house!" Auntie Xue can't do any of the things she would like to—cry, scream, argue, defend herself. A new batch of well-wishers arrives, and she is so proud and so afraid of washing her dirty linen in public, she immediately pastes a smile on her face and tells Zhaoying to clear the plates so she can put out new place settings. The next round of dishes is less fancy: moo shu pork, a chive omelet, pork and celery, shredded pork with garlic shoots, braised yellow croaker, and spinach noodles. Uncle Xue tells the newcomers the bride got a little tired and is resting in the next room, but she'll be out to light their cigarettes and drink toasts with them in a moment. Jiyue is really drunk, and he's smiling foolishly as he spouts nonsensical replies to their congratulations. Yang Jiguang, an organization-level cadre at the department store, had planned a well-meaning tribute—reciting "The Cowherd and the Weaver Maid" by the Song dynasty poet Qin Guan: "Feelings flow like water, this blessed moment like a dream, how can we bear to part across the bridge of magpies! If love is eternal, what matters each passing day?" Given the circumstances, no one is capable of listening. He tries to expound on the closing couplet, but no one pays any attention to that either. Finally, as a flurry of toasts and clinking glasses erupts around him, he is forced to give up.

Jihui and his mother stand facing each other. He awaits her interrogation, accusations, nagging, and complaints. Instead, she says not a word, just stares at him, her eyes brimming with worry, resentment, pleading, and hope. Jihui feels as if a needle has pierced his heart.

The newcomers don't realize Jihui has only just arrived, and his parents don't want to ask about his lateness in front of everyone. Jiyue is too drunk for rational thought—he just raises his glass and yells, "Brother! Let's have a toast!" Safely past the first hurdle, Jihui swiftly inserts himself into the general merriment. He feels a little awkward because his clothes are noticeably shabbier than everyone else's, but he really didn't have time to go home to get changed into anything fancier.

After doing his social duty at the banqueting table, he leaves the house and goes into the cooking tent, hoping to find out more about the affair with the Rado watch. As he expected, Zhaoying is here helping the chef. Jihui had been prepared for a barrage of blame from his mother, brother, and even his father, but hadn't worried about Zhaoying. Surely she won't rebuke him? Wrong—she's built up a lot of rage, and now unleashes it. Not caring that Xichun is here, she stamps her feet and rails, "So you're finally here? Why bother! Lotus could fall sick and die, and you wouldn't care! I'm about to drop dead of exhaustion—I bet that makes you happy, doesn't it? I'm no more than a servant to your family! A child bride would be better off than me! Why should I go on living? I might as well smash my head against the wall and die!" She bursts into agitated sobs.

Jihui is completely flustered—he has no idea how to comfort her. All of a sudden, he sees how virtuous and hardworking she is, and how much she has had to bottle up before he appeared. His conscience throbs painfully. He thought about so many people but forgot about her! His kindhearted wife, who loves him with her entire body and soul!

He also ignores Xichun, whom he's never met, and puts his hands on Zhaoying's trembling shoulders. "It's all my fault," he says hoarsely. "You can scold me when we get home. I know this hasn't been easy for you—you must have worked so hard today." Zhaoying presses her handkerchief to her nose and chokes even more violently. He lovingly strokes her smooth, round shoulders. "All right, all right, I know. Life isn't easy for anyone. We just have to be understanding of each other. I'll never abandon you like this again. If there's a burden, we'll carry it together."

Xichun turns his head away and concentrates on peeling the hard-boiled quail eggs. Mrs. Xun sent these over with the suggestion that the bride should eat a few to calm her nerves.

Now that Zhaoying has subsided a little, Jihui seizes the moment to ask, "What happened with that Rado watch? I ran into Xibin in the hutong, and he said there was a scene . . ."

Zhaoying gets worked up again and twists her shoulders to get away from him. Sounding resentful and mean, she says, "Who the hell knows what happened! I'm sure they're all keeping it a secret from me—huh! As if I want to know! Who cares about me? I'm just here to take orders. The fine young lady already has stainless steel on her wrist, but that's not fancy enough, so she has to be given a gold-plated Rado watch! If I hadn't been busy in here, I'd have put it on myself! They said it was in the dresser, and when Chef Lu here brought out the four-happiness soup, they said the soup envelope was in there too. Open the drawer, and what do they see? No envelope, and no watch! Then everything kicked off! Baosang was sitting next to the dresser, so they said he probably took it and wanted to search him. You think he let them? He raised a stink! That bastard Baosang attacked Chef Lu with his filthy mouth. The bride's still crying her eyes out. How much do you think my tears are worth? You'd better hurry up and go back in, or your sister-in-law might get upset again!"

Jihui actually had been planning to ask the bride some questions, but he obviously can't do that now, not after everything Zhaoying's said. He takes her hand and kneads it tenderly. "Don't be like that. Just look on the bright side, we'll get this sorted out soon. We're a family, we need to stay united and show each other some understanding."

In Uncle and Auntie Xue's room, the guests have all departed, leaving a mess of plates and cups on the table, which no one is in a hurry to tidy up. Xiuya sits on the edge of the bed, even more angry and troubled than Zhaoying; her eyes glisten with tears, her lips tremble. Each time she bows her head, the confetti caught in her hair falls into her lap. Jiyue's eldest aunt and Zhan Liying sit on either side, ineffectually comforting her—the aunt is clumsy with words, and Nanny Zhan is brash as ever.

Xiuya thinks: *I've been scammed. Was there ever a Rado watch? If you'd really bought me one, why not let me wear it right away? What a coincidence, losing the watch and the soup envelope all at once. Even worse, it seems Jiyue's dad used to be a lama at the temple. Aren't lamas like monks? Monks aren't allowed to get married, are they? Or eat meat? That's just swell, I'm married into a family of lamas. My coworkers aren't going to let me live this down! My life is ruined! Nice of my sister-in-law not to mention this little tidbit when she introduced us. Why did you hide this from me, Jiyue? Also, you puke whenever you see a fish? What the hell is wrong with you? No wonder you said "I'm willing" when you'd only met me a few times. Seventh Aunt was practically driven away—who the hell brings out the soup after serving only twelve of the sixteen dishes? I suppose you arranged it with the chef beforehand. And what a fine chef you hired! The son of a big teapot! Disgusting! Baosang's a disgrace! Maybe there was a watch and he stole it! How did I get this unlucky? This is what your family's like? What's going to happen now? The way he lashed out! And a thief too! That Mr. Yin is so weird. He can knock you out with two fingers! He's sworn brothers with Jiyue's dad. I guess that makes him a lama too! I've married into a lama temple! My god! What's going to happen to me?*

She covers her face with her hands and sobs.

Zhan Liying hugs her and sways her from side to side. "Hey! This is nothing, you hear me? A tiny misunderstanding. A tiny, tiny problem! You're both young—you have no idea how lucky you are! When I was your age, I had it tough! They denounced me as a rightist! You know what that's like? Getting sent down! Reform through labor! Struggle sessions! Interrogations! Your little troubles don't count for anything. Listen to your Nanny Zhan and turn off the waterworks, wash your face, comb your hair, straighten your clothes, spritz on some perfume, put on a happy face, go back to your wedding banquet, and have a good time!"

Although Nanny Zhan's words don't address any of Xiuya's doubts and fears, this wholehearted enthusiasm does calm her down a little.

Bamboo comes running in. "Here you are, Auntie Zhan! You have a telegram—my grandpa signed for you." He hands her a thin envelope.

Nanny Zhan's eyebrows rise. She takes the telegram and, without pausing to thank Bamboo, rips it open. There are only five words:

Brother ill come quick Huijuan

Huijuan is her husband's little sister. This is a nasty shock. Without pausing to explain herself, Nanny Zhan dashes back home, clutching the telegram tightly. Sitting on her bed, she reads it twice more, stares into space for half a minute, then collapses. Her hand reaches for the pillow cover, and she absently chews a corner of it.

"Brother ill come quick." How ill? Could it be . . . When he came to visit at the start of the year, she cooked him a special meal for the Lantern Festival, and he said, "Each time I swallow, I feel like a Beijing stuffed duck." Was something already wrong with his esophagus then? And he's been losing so much weight! This is scary. All day long, she's busied herself with other people's business! Neglecting her own husband! She sees each of the others as a tragic figure—Ji Zhiman is pathetic, Mu Ying is lonely, the Xues got burgled, the bride is resentful, Han Yitan is indecisive, Tantai Zhizhu feels inadequate—but now the greatest tragedy of all has befallen her! Just as the political situation is finally loosening up, her career is back on track, and she's about to be reunited with her husband, they get ambushed by the demon of illness! *This must have been very sudden, or he'd have sent the telegram himself. Oh no! What if he's already . . . People sometimes say "ill," rather than . . .*

She abruptly sits upright, telegram pressed firmly between her palms, her thoughts in a complete jumble. What should she do? She has to do something. Right now! No time to waste.

Okay. A long-distance call to Sichuan. She'll speak to Huijuan or her husband's boss. And she'll call her own workplace to take leave. It can't wait until tomorrow—she'll have to leave right away, on the night train. Or maybe she should see if she can get a plane ticket for tomorrow, or the day after?

She hurries out of the house but only gets a few steps past the chuihua gate before suddenly turning back and charging toward Zhang Qilin's place. She raps hard on the glass pane of their front door, and calls out, "Dr. Yu! Can I use your telephone?" But the door is locked—Xiuzao has just left. Frantic, she tugs at the lock. Then she strides back into the courtyard and through the chuihua gate. A scrawny young man tries to stop her and says, "Nanny Zhan, look at this—someone used the faucet and didn't clear the pipe, and now it's frozen solid. What are we going to do?" She walks right past him and out the siheyuan gate. An icy wind hits her. She realizes she isn't wearing her scarf. She also forgot to lock her front door. No time to turn back. She sprints to the public phone.

Nanny Zhan is already gone by the time Jihui comes in. "I'm sorry for what you've been through," he says earnestly. "We didn't do everything we ought to—especially me, I should have been here much sooner. Xiuya, I hope you'll come to understand that everyone in this family is a decent person. We won't treat you poorly. Let's be united, and we can all live well, all right? So the watch has gone missing—we'll buy another one. Whoever's offended who, they can apologize and make it right. Why think the worst of every situation? The road of life is wide open! Nothing and no one is perfect, Xiuya. Happiness isn't going to just drop into your lap. It's all about whether we see things the right way and show each other understanding. You have to strive for it, fight for it. I'm putting it badly, but I hope you understand what I mean."

Xiuya is, after all, an uncomplicated soul who doesn't ask too much of life, anyone, or anything. Her brother-in-law's sincere words are enough to stop her sobbing.

Zhaoying comes in with a dish of quail eggs, which she hands to Xiuya with some chopsticks. "Eat up," she says. "They're from your neighbor Mrs. Xun—we cooked them specially for you. They'll settle your nerves. I can get you salt if you need it."

Jihui and Xiuya look up at Zhaoying, touched. More than ever, Jihui understands how bighearted his wife is. She'll only show the negativity building up inside her to her husband, the person she loves most in the world. In front of anyone else, she's all dutiful humility. Shouldn't he cherish her more than he already does?

Life in the siheyuan is just one thing after another. The young couple who live next to Zhan Liying in the east wing have returned home from the neighborhood factory where they work. They're both short and skinny and earn the least of anyone in the siheyuan, though they have the greatest demands on their income—five yuan a month to each of their parents and an extra thirty to the woman's mom, who takes care of their three-year-old son. Like many Beijingers in their situation, they have to keep track of every last cent. The only light in their room comes from a six-watt fluorescent bulb, which they switch on only when absolutely necessary. They never eat snacks, have never welcomed guests into their home, and certainly never have anyone over for a meal, not even a humble bowl of black bean noodles.

Their electric meter only moves a single digit each month. When they pass their share of the utilities bill to Xibin each month, if there's been a shortfall that everyone needs to make up, they'll repeatedly curse the "electricity-stealing rat." They don't need to be as frugal with water, which comes from the communal faucet and isn't individually metered, but if another household drives up the bill by using too much water for laundry or failing to clear the pipe in winter so it freezes, this couple gets furious and complains bitterly for a long time afterward.

Today, they worked the early shift at the factory. After that, having received movie tickets from their union, they went to Yuan'en Temple Cinema and saw two short films: *I'd Never Have Thought It* and *A Cry from the Soul*. Now back home, they busy themselves with their chores. The man, whose name is Liang Fumin, takes a bucket out to the communal faucet for water. The woman, Hao Yulan, sits in their little kitchen dealing with the cabbages they bought before the winter, patiently turning them over one by one and stacking them up again. The vat in their little kitchen can hold four buckets of water, but they're afraid it will crack if the water freezes, so they never put more than two buckets in. They have stored a hundred pounds of grade-A vegetables and two hundred of grade-B, which should last them through the winter. In clear weather, they sun the cabbages in the courtyard, and Yulan turns them over every two or three days so the leaves won't wilt and the stems won't go bad. Much of the couple's frugality is concentrated on food—like many Beijingers, their "spirit oozes through the gaps in their teeth." Their clothes are all right, their furniture no worse than anyone else's, and they have a twelve-inch black-and-white TV, though they hardly ever turn this on, unless there's a particularly good program or their son is home. Normally, they cycle back to the factory in the evening to watch the color TV in the rec room. They are relatively generous with their son—his clothes are handsome, of course, and sometimes they treat him to an expensive Guangdong orange or Panama banana, which they have him enjoy while standing in the middle of the courtyard. Two months ago, they splurged on a trip to Fragrant Hills so the child could see the fall foliage. As Yulan later said to Zhan Liying, just the cold drinks alone cost them eighty cents! They arrived home from that excursion glowing with satisfaction, completely contented with their lot in life.

Today, though, there's trouble. Fumin gets to the faucet and finds the pipe frozen shut! The Xues must have opened the valve first thing in the morning and didn't bother clearing the pipe as they came and went all day. The afternoon was quite warm, but after four o'clock the temperature plummeted swiftly. And now, when Fumin turns the faucet, nothing comes out.

Fumin runs back inside and says to Yulan, "The pipe's frozen. I can't be bothered to light a fire, let's just make do with what's in the vat." Yulan says angrily, "There's hardly anything in there—not even enough to cook rice. What are we supposed to do? The Xues are so selfish—all they care about is their convenience. God knows how many tons of water they used today, and we'll still have to split the bill with them. No need to be polite, just go over there and make them heat the pipe!"

That sounds like it will be awkward, so Fumin stays where he is, still fuming. "I don't know what's going on today. Nanny Zhan's usually so friendly, but when I told her about the frozen pipe, she turned even colder than the pipe—ignored me completely." Yulan stops what she's doing with the cabbages and snaps, "I bet all of them already have all the water they need, so they're not going to do anything about it. You're all talk and no action. If you don't dare to go, I will!" She dusts off her apron and stomps out of their little kitchen. Before she's taken a few steps, Auntie Xue emerges into the courtyard, and Yulan charges over. "Hey! Your family has to take responsibility for this! All you care about is what you need—you never cleared the pipe, and now it's frozen solid. Where are we supposed to get water now?"

Auntie Xue has already encountered more than her share of problems today. The third round of guests have got through half their food and drink, and the bride still hasn't shown her face. Now they're noisily demanding that she "descend from heaven" to see them. Auntie Xue has kept a smile pasted on her face, but this is agony. She's on her way to see if the bride had a change of heart and will deign to put in an appearance for her guests. Alas, before she can do this, Yulan confronts her!

Auntie Xue is taken aback. Yulan is scrawny and small-featured, but added to her generally unprepossessing appearance, her rage and rough speech, arms akimbo, make her downright offensive. Auntie Xue had promised herself that no matter what demons assaulted her today, she would fend them off with nice words, but this unexpected attack makes her lose control—especially as every other household has sent a decent gift for Jiyue's big day: an automatic hot-water flask from Bureau Chief Zhang and Dr. Yu, a whistling enamel kettle with a spout from Old Lady Hai and Hai Xibin, some Hong Kong–manufactured cosmetics from Zhan Liying and Mu Ying, a porcelain Goddess of Mercy from Tantai Zhizhu and her family, a tin of Shanghai Gold chicken biscuits from Editor Han and Teacher Ge, and several items from Master Xun's family, the most expensive of which was a desk lamp with a plexiglass base. Liang Fumin and Hao Yulan, by contrast, presented them with a 1983 wall calendar of movie stars that Auntie Xue knows full well they got free from their factory.

All the rage that Auntie Xue has swallowed comes spilling out now. In her most patronizing tone, she lectures the younger woman. "Is this any way to talk? Can't you see we're in the middle of a wedding? Can't you say what you have to say nicely? Why come shrieking at me like a harpy?"

Yulan feels badly treated by Auntie Xue. She has no idea that while she and Fumin were cycling to work at five thirty in the morning, Auntie Xue came by to drop off some wedding candy but found their door locked. Later, she said to Zhaoying, "Fumin and Yulan have a small child, we should make sure they get extra wedding candy. I'll give it to them when they get back this afternoon—don't let me forget!" Facing an enraged Auntie Xue, all Yulan can think is, *So what if your family's having a wedding? You tightwads! We gave you a brand-new calendar and didn't see so much as a candy wrapper in return. You think I want anything from you? We might be poor, but we have principles. I'm not touching your damn candy, now kindly go thaw out the pipe, if you please!*

With these thoughts going through their minds, the neighbors launch into a yelling match.

Old Lady Hai hears the ruckus and comes running. Taking advantage of her seniority, she inserts herself between Auntie Xue and Yulan, and says, "Quiet, both of you! Enough already. Xue, my girl, you seem busy, shouldn't you be getting on with whatever it is you're doing? And you, Yulan, you've got a mouth on you. Whatever you're arguing about, it's not worth getting your face all blotchy like that, is it? You need water? Okay, let's go over to Dr. Yu's place, I'm sure she can spare you a couple of buckets . . . Oh, the door's locked, never mind, send Fumin over to my place, and he can have a bucketful right away. There! Problem solved."

Jihui and Zhaoying come out to see what the racket's about. The sight of her daughter-in-law makes Auntie Xue redirect her anger and bitterness. "Oh fine! Hide yourself away and enjoy life while the neighbors step all over me. You just turned on the faucet and sauntered away, didn't you? Didn't even bother to look back. The pipe's frozen now—I hope you're happy! Roosters will lay eggs and flowers sprout from stones before you grow a conscience!"

Jihui's throat tightens. Zhaoying will say something just as vicious, and they'll go at it hammer and tongs. Old Lady Hai and Yulan are stunned into silence too. All eyes turn to Zhaoying.

Rage fills Zhaoying's brain for a moment, but she sees the quivering wrinkles on her mother-in-law's face and a few loose strands of white hair shaking in the icy wind. The thought flashes through her mind: *Will this be me in twenty or thirty years? It's not easy for anyone! Poor Auntie Xue has been running around since the crack of dawn, and all she's had is trouble!*

Against everyone's expectations, she not only doesn't return the attack, but steps forward and takes Auntie Xue by the arm. "Don't be angry, it's all my fault, I'll go thaw the pipe now. You should take care of yourself, Mom, calm down or you'll make yourself ill."

The shock brings Auntie Xue back to clarity. She sees the gray-black circles around Zhaoying's eyes. Their hands touch, like yin and yang meeting, and grip each other tight. Their eyes grow moist, and Auntie Xue even sheds a few tears. What more is there to be said? In this whole world, there's no one they should have more sympathy for than each other—and no one they can rely on more.

Embarrassed to be caught in the middle of this family scene, Yulan goes back home, where she finds Fumin staring at a little paper bag. "Oh good, you're back," he says. "You got them all wrong. Look! Zhaoying sent Lotus over with these. Her grandma said we should get extra, for our boy." Yulan takes the bag and pours it out onto the table. Wedding candy, and quite a bit of it!

Including six or seven liquor-center chocolates in gold foil. One jolt of remorse after another washes over her.

Jihui fetches firewood and is about to thaw the pipe when Xichun says to him, "I'll take care of it. I know how to do it quicker." Only now does Jihui notice him. Strange, hired chefs aren't generally this helpful. Xichun has a kind, honest face. His eyes are a bit swollen—maybe the smoke got into them? Touched, Jihui says, "Let's both go. You can show me whatever tricks you know."

Xichun lowers himself into the well, and Jihui crouches alongside to help.

In their little kitchen, Fumin and Yulan grow more mortified by the minute. Just then, Xibin appears with a bucket of water. "My grandma sent this for you—help yourselves!"

CHAPTER 29

An old editor shakes with rage at a "literary newcomer."

As it happens, the person knocking at Han Yitan's door isn't the deranged poet mentioned in the *Beijing Daily* missing-persons ad. Ge Ping smiles to see who's there when she opens the door. "Oh, it's you, what a rare honor! What wind blew you here today?"

A man in his early forties stands there in a rather dashing ensemble: checkered baseball cap, long patterned woolen coat, silver-gray pure lambswool scarf, and waffle-soled Nike sneakers.

Han Yitan feels a strange awkwardness but stands to greet his guest.

The visitor, by contrast, seems at home right away. He chuckles. "An ill wind, a force seven gale!" He removes his hat, coat, and scarf and, not seeing a coat rack, places them gingerly on the empty armchair, then sits on the folding stool by the dining table. Ge Ping scoops up the garments, gesturing that he should take the armchair. "Such nice clothes you have—I'll put these on the bed."

Settling into the armchair, the visitor notices that Han Yitan is still standing and waves to indicate he should take a seat too. Editor Han takes the armchair on the other side of the coffee table.

"How's it going?" says Han Yitan. "What have you been busy with?"

The visitor is busy studying the room. "Time to redecorate, Old Han!" he lectures. "You should have a coat rack by the door. Put a couch beneath the window over there. There ought to be a screen between the two rooms, or at least a curtain. Your guests shouldn't be able to see your bed."

Han Yitan says, "We're not that sophisticated, and we don't have your royalties!"

The visitor shakes his head. "Not that much actually comes to me. That TV show we've been pushing—there's three of us attached. How much do you think that brings in, split three ways?"

Ge Ping brings in a cup of tea and sets it down on the table. The visitor cranes his neck to inspect it. "Jasmine? Green tea? Black tea? Oolong?"

"Just regular jasmine," says Ge Ping.

The visitor laughs. "You should provide more variety. When foreigners have a guest, they always ask in English, 'Coffee or tea? Which do you prefer?' And the guest gets to choose."

Ge Ping claps her hands together. "Wow! But we Chinese aren't so fancy."

"If there's more than one guest and they all want different things, say one person wants coffee, one wants tea, and one doesn't want a drink, you should give coffee to the coffee-drinker and tea to the tea-drinker. As for the person who declined, the Chinese rules of hospitality say you ought to bring him tea or coffee anyway, but in the West he'd get upset if you did that."

Ge Ping is startled. "Why would that be?"

The visitor raises his eyebrows. "Because it shows a lack of respect—he already said he didn't want anything. When someone from China goes overseas and gets asked what he wants to drink, he'll say he's not thirsty. Of course, he's just being polite and is waiting to be poured a drink anyway—because that's what happens here. Instead, only the people who asked for a drink get one, and he has to sit there with a dry throat. But the host is just respecting his choice! If a foreigner asks, 'Does it taste good?' and you say, 'No! It's awful!' your host will be delighted because you told him the honest truth. But if you say, 'Yes, very tasty,' and then only take a few mouthfuls, he'll be angry because you lied."

"Have you just come back from abroad? How come you know all this?"

The visitor picks up his cup and takes a sip. "Me? How would I ever go abroad? I heard all this from X—I was at his place just last night, enjoying some Rémy Martin. A famous brand, though it's really not as good as Pagoda brandy!"

Han Yitan can sense where the conversation is going. The visitor isn't showing off his familiarity with Western etiquette, but how deeply embedded he now is within the literary establishment. This X he just mentioned is one of the hottest authors around, just back from a trip abroad. Actually, Han Yitan has known X a long time—before this visitor was even on the scene—but never well enough to be invited for Rémy Martin, whatever that is. That's the literary scene these days, full of gold—and broken glass that glitters just like gold. Even more levels in the hierarchy than seventeen years ago, before the Cultural Revolution.

Ge Ping is more innocent. She sits on the folding chair, facing the visitor, and picks up the conversation. As the visitor has mentioned X, she's naturally keen to hear his opinion of X's latest book, which he's only too eager to offer—although first he quotes the verdicts of various well-known critics, some of whose reviews haven't been published yet. "Last week I was at his place; he'd just finished reading X's latest, and he wanted to know what I thought of . . ." and "He made me promise not to repeat this, though, otherwise people might think he's trying to set the tone!" Ge Ping sits there, rapt.

Han Yitan frowns. His eardrums hurt. He smokes in glum silence.

This visitor has a rather splendid pen name: Dragon Eye. Han Yitan has known him for six or seven years. He first visited this house in 1975, in a woolen hat with earflaps and a plain Mao suit. He said he worked at a factory and had just come from a Party branch meeting, which gave Han Yitan a good impression of him. He'd brought a sheaf of poems, and respectfully said, "I hope Editor Han will tell me how I can improve!" Han Yitan read through the dozen or so poems right away. They were on the theme of "defending revolutionary model operas" and fairly passionate by the standards of the time, vivid with movement and imagery. The only thing he lacked was experience. When he was done reading, Han Yitan went through them one by one, praising their strengths and suggesting areas for improvement. Three days later, the revised poems arrived in the mail, with a letter that read, "As I'm part of an agricultural unit, I'm shortly being deployed to the farming front line and won't be able to express my gratitude and affection in person. Please make any changes to these that you see fit. You are my teacher—now, in the future, and forever. I will be eternally under your guidance as I devote all my strength to cultural enterprise in support of the proletariat Revolution!"

They stayed in touch. Han Yitan recommended these poems to several places, but they were always rejected—yet Dragon Eye uttered no word of complaint. Each time he saw Han Yitan, he said, "Please don't lose confidence in me! I might just be a rough-hewn rock, but with your patient teaching, I will eventually be molded into an inkstone—even if it's only fit for elementary school children to practice their handwriting."

In 1977, a twelve-line poem of his was finally published, after Han Yitan fought hard for its acceptance. Seeing his work in print for the first time was such a thrill, Dragon Eye couldn't put it into words. The sweet smell of newsprint seemed to open the floodgates of his inspiration, and poems poured from him like the ceaseless flow of Huangguoshu Waterfall. By 1979, he'd published twenty-seven short poems. In 1980, he realized that breaking into the literary scene via fiction would take less time and effort, and so he switched genres, and within a year had published his first short story.

Naturally, Han Yitan was no longer the only editor he knew. He was in and out of various editorial departments and attended a number of academic conferences. Unsurprisingly, he was no longer a frequent visitor to Han Yitan's home.

But he'd changed—rather abruptly, to Han Yitan's eye. In late autumn 1980, Dragon Eye showed up at the journal office. Han Yitan happened to bump into him in the front lobby wearing a pale-yellow baseball cap and a new Earth-brand windbreaker from Shanghai. Although it had been a while, Han Yitan was very happy to see him so unexpectedly. He was just about to ask what he was doing here and invite him up to his office, but Dragon Eye nodded blandly at him and, without a word of greeting, said, "Which is your editor in chief's office?"

Han Yitan froze for a second, then pointed it out. Dragon Eye walked around him and made a beeline for it.

This plot development, without any foreshadowing, caught Han Yitan completely by surprise, to his chagrin. Back in his office, he couldn't settle. Would Dragon Eye stop by when he was done chatting with the editor in chief, even for a moment? No—he never showed up.

Even without Han Yitan bad-mouthing him, Dragon Eye has developed a rather seedy reputation in the literary world—mainly in its lower reaches, of course, among the majority of editors and writers. Everyone says he's one part talent and nine parts maneuvering, or two parts writing and eight parts attending the right events, or three parts craft and seven parts bragging. And yet work by him, or at least with his name on it, keeps pouring forth, in genres as diverse as poetry, fiction, essays, criticism, screenplays, and TV scripts. Others say he's a "living room author" who sets foot in someone else's living room almost every evening—obviously not Han Yitan's, with its lack of coat racks and couches, but rather those belonging to people with authority and prestige in the arts: editors and deputy editors, directors and assistant directors, literary superstars and wunderkinds. From these soirees, he emerges with renewed spirits, the latest gossip, the latest trends, new material, new techniques, and all the industry news. No wonder he remains so inspired and produces such a rich array of work, and no wonder so many people actively seek him out for collaborations and coauthorships.

In the spring of 1982, he was transferred from the factory to an arts organization. Though he had a job title, he was effectively treated like a full-time author. At a literary tea party, he walked right by Han Yitan's table in an extremely well-fitted brown suit. Han Yitan turned his face aside, but the editor in chief reached out to shake his hand. Dragon Eye let their palms touch briefly, then without a word of greeting, asked, "Do you know which table Comrade X is sitting at?"

X was the highest-status person present at that event. The editor in chief can't have been happy, but he said, "The first table over there." Dragon Eye didn't even nod in acknowledgment, just barreled straight for "the first table over there."

Yet here he is now, gliding into their presence. Having removed his coat, he is dressed like a young foreigner in a tweed sport jacket and distressed jeans, reclining elegantly in an armchair, perfectly at ease as if he'd been here just the day before, chatting and smiling away.

Ge Ping has listened to Han Yitan complain about Dragon Eye for the last two years, but hasn't personally witnessed his bad behavior and knows her husband is often hard on people. Besides, their visitor is as warm and friendly as he's always been, so she foolishly gets drawn further into conversation with him.

At one point, he casually mentions "that Soviet film, *Lake Sonata*, which shows us moral issues are on the rise all over the world—"

"What's that?" Ge Ping has to ask. "What sonata?"

"You mean to say you haven't seen *Lake Sonata*? What about *White Bim Black Ear*? *Autumn Marathon*? No? They're always screening them at the Film Archive! Why doesn't Old Han take you?"

"Him?" Ge Ping grumbles. "When would he ever take me? It's not easy for him to go himself. The Editorial Department doesn't get many perks."

Dragon Eye says, "Actually, not that many Soviet films are worth watching. But take Michael Cimino's *The Deer Hunter*, or *Marriage Italian Style*, starring Sophia Loren—these are must-sees! That's what I said to the Film Association's leaders when I met them yesterday . . ."

Han Yitan can't stand any more of this. He stubs out his cigarette and interrupts Dragon Eye's lofty discourse. "Why did you come to see me today?"

Dragon Eye's answer is just as direct. "Of course I wouldn't disturb you without a reason. I'm here to get my manuscript back."

"Your manuscript?" Han Yitan is surprised. "I don't have any of your manuscripts here."

Dragon Eye nods. "Correct. I haven't sent you anything in a while. I'm talking about those poems seven years ago, the ones handwritten on letter paper that I saddle stitched myself."

This is even more surprising. "What do you want with those? The ones rhapsodizing revolutionary model operas? Do you still have a use for them?"

"Yes, and it wasn't just the model operas—I also denounced the way right-deviationists were overturning verdicts," says Dragon Eye frankly. "No, of course I don't have any use for them now. But it's worrying to have them out in the world."

Han Yitan's heart thuds. "I don't think that's a big problem, actually. You weren't the only one writing this sort of stuff back then—we printed quite a few in our journal too, some by fairly prominent poets. I edited them myself. People understand they were a product of their time. Why worry about that? Anyway, this was a handwritten manuscript, you never actually published them."

"If they'd been published, I'd say forget it. But since they haven't been, why leave them out there? Go find them for me, would you? I'd like them back."

Han Yitan stares at Dragon Eye, his heart beating fast. It takes a lot of effort to control his revulsion. A little hoarsely, he says, "It's been seven years. I don't know where I could have put your manuscript, or if I still—"

Ge Ping was in the kitchen fetching the kettle for the first part of this exchange, but now she's back in the room adding hot water to their teacups, and she doesn't think Han Yitan should begrudge Dragon Eye a little effort. "A manuscript?" she pipes up. "When in the last decade have we ever thrown out a manuscript? The cabinet under your bookcase is full of manuscripts, isn't it? I daresay Dragon's will be in there."

"What a marvelous housekeeper you are," exclaims Dragon Eye in delight. "What an eye for detail! Old Han, if I could just trouble you to have a look?"

Han Yitan doesn't move. This couldn't be any more awkward. "Why is this so important?"

In a confidential tone, Dragon Eye says, "Why would I lie to you, Old Han? Having got to the stage I'm at, don't I need to secure my future? My talents are limited. Getting a bit of a name for myself and earning a whole load of royalties, well, that's not difficult. But anything I write is not going to be any kind of masterpiece, let alone win prizes or make me famous. At the end of the day, my most likely career path is as some sort of arts official. Sure, I might not have your CV, but I still have three advantages over you: I'm a Party member—a political advantage! I joined the Party during the Cultural Revolution, but my past can withstand scrutiny—I wasn't ever the leader of a rebel faction, and I never took part in any of that 'strike, smash, snatch' stuff. There are plenty of people like me, who joined the Party around that time—they can't discount all of them. Then there's my published work—a career advantage. They say arts officials should be 'artists leading artists.' I'll never be in the second group of artists, but maybe I can be in the first! And I'm only in my early forties—an age advantage! They want to make the administration more revolutionary, knowledgeable, and younger, and I fit all three criteria! So why miss this opportunity?"

Han Yitan has gone pale. He stammers, "You have an even bigger advantage—you get along with the higher-ups."

"That's right," Dragon Eye happily agrees. "I need them, and they need me. I can give them a quick overview of any situation in a timely fashion, report on trends, provide suggestions, and act as a fixer for them. Old Han, you were right under their noses this whole time. The reason you lose out is you're so stubborn, you need to be more flexible and take advantage of—"

Han Yitan smiles grimly. "Seeing as you have so many advantages, why care about a few unpublished poems? Even if you *had* published them, you're influential enough now that you could make every copy disappear into thin air."

"Of course! It wouldn't bother me if they were published. But they weren't, so there's no reason they should exist. I have all these advantages. Why not make myself a little more perfect? I don't want to leave a single stain."

Han Yitan glares at him. "And if I won't hand them over? What if I dig them out and give them to the authorities?"

Dragon Eye smiles serenely. "What good would that do you? It would be just a tiny bit of trouble for me—a little effort and I'd make the whole thing go away. You can't block my way. I'm on my way to the top, and even if I choose not to punish you, will you ever rest easy? Besides, I know you—you're incapable of such a thing. If you were, you'd no longer be Han Yitan."

Only now does Ge Ping understand that her husband is being viciously humiliated and trampled into the ground—but her realization comes far too late.

Han Yitan abruptly jumps to his feet, charges into the inner room, falls to his knees before the bookcase, pulls open the cabinet doors, and pulls out the stacks and stacks of manuscripts inside, scattering them across the floor. He screams, "Take it take it take it take it!"

Scared out of her wits, Ge Ping dashes over in a frenzy. "Yitan! Don't! What are you doing? Don't get so worked up."

Dragon Eye calmly walks up to the pile, bends over, and reaches for his manuscript. Just like that, he stuffs it into his trouser pocket. Then he goes to the bed, grabs his coat, cap, and scarf, and says languidly, "Old Han, madam—please don't be angry with me. I was just joking—how could a lowly creature like me ever dream of becoming an arts official? Even if I became a manager or something like that in my little workplace, I could never do anything to harm Old Han here. I just wanted these worthless poems of mine to read again, as a memento. That's all! Please calm down, you'll make yourself ill. I'm off now, I'll visit another day as penance for this trouble."

With that, he sails away, coat over one arm, scarf and cap in hand.

Poor Han Yitan! A lifetime as an editor, working like an ox in the field. For over thirty years, he's meticulously and dutifully submitted countless applications to join the Party, but after this blow, all the strength suddenly drains from him, body and soul.

It takes Ge Ping a great deal of effort to heft Han Yitan onto the bed, where she leaves him dozing, still fully dressed. Gazing at the jumble of papers Dragon Eye has left behind, stamped with his waffle-soled footprints, she can't stop tears seeping from her eyes.

Another knock at their door! Ge Ping feels just about ready to faint. She goes into the outer room, calling impatiently, "Who is it?" No matter the answer, this door will remain shut.

"Is this the Xun household? I'm looking for Comrade Xun Lei," shouts a voice.

"No, wrong place," she yells back. "The Xuns are in the small yard on the east side! Why are you bothering us?" She will feel guilty about this later. Why did she have to take her anger out on this innocent stranger?

CHAPTER 30

Someone whose life has been smooth sailing finally
meets a headwind.

As Xinger makes the dumpling filling in the kitchen, Xun Xingwang sits in a
rattan chair nearby, smoking and chatting with her.

The filling is egg and fennel. Xinger adds more salt and stirs. "Dad once told
me you and he both like strong flavors," she says. "If other people find something
too salty, it's just right for you."

Master Xun nods gently, the sharp planes of his face obscured by smoke
from his pipe. Xinger has always detested the stink of Zaoer's pipe, but for some
reason Master Xun's doesn't bother her.

"Please tell me a bit more about my dad, Uncle," she entreats. "I can't get
enough."

Master Xun thinks about it, and slowly says, "Your dad was better at swimming than me. Every Sunday after we'd started working at the factory—this is
before you and Lei were born—we'd set off on our bicycles. One time, we saw
someone by the dam at Gaobeidian looking into the water—he'd dropped his
watch. We both dived in—it's fifty feet deep there. After a short while, my eyes
hurt and there was pressure in my ears. All I saw below me were concrete blocks
from upstream, with metal hooks poking out of them. That was scary. I came
back to the surface, but your dad stayed down quite a while longer. When he
finally surfaced, his chest wasn't heaving like mine—he was breathing through
his mouth. Oh, and he was holding the missing watch. That's quite something,
isn't it?"

Xinger pours off the excess liquid from the filling, absorbed by his story. Hearing Master Xun talk about her dad has made her happier than anything since arriving in Beijing.

Master Xun, too, finds a particular form of comfort in these scattered memories. He remembers another one. "We both joined the workshop as carpenters. Your dad wasn't as skilled as me—on the first day, I put together an eight-jointed bench and brought it to the office to show our supervisor. He tried but couldn't keep up and got so anxious there were big beads of sweat on his forehead. That night, the stubborn so-and-so snuck out and kept going. By morning, he'd finished his bench too."

Xinger laughs, her eyes narrowing into crescent moons.

"Both of us had an eye for flashy things. After getting married, we moved from the workshop dorm to lodgings at the same time, carrying poles on our shoulders—at one end, a bundle of clothes, bedding, and whatnot, at the other end, a big glass diorama from the little market on Baiqiao, past Dongbianmen. About five feet square, filled with blown-glass chrysanthemums—only two yuan or so, at the time. Your mom and Xun Lei's mom walked behind us. Your mom had a bundle in her arms, and so did my wife—what do you think they were? Xun Lei himself, of course, and his sister Lian."

Xinger asks, "Where did the glass flowers go?"

"Ah," says Master Xun sadly, "you kids were so rambunctious, you smashed the diorama. I see you've forgotten—but I remember it keenly!"

As Xinger and Master Xun chat in the kitchen, Xun Lei and Feng Wanmei are having a completely different conversation in his room.

Wanmei has a magazine in her hands, open to Mu Ying's essay, which she's just finished reading. "This woman is your neighbor?" she exclaims. "And you've met her?"

"We know each other to say hello to, but we haven't really spoken. She looks so mousy, I'd never have thought she had such extreme views. Do you think you could accept them?"

Wanmei thinks about it. "She writes beautifully, and her arguments are convincing. But these metaphors—'in the home,' 'in the fields,' 'on the mountaintop'—they really don't stand up to scrutiny. Love is what happens between two people, not one person and a landscape. It's different with places and things—if I get tired of the babbling brook, I'll go look at the roaring river or the high mountains. If I'm sick of my teacup, I can smash it. In short, you abandon what you have when you find something better. But how can you treat a person that way? Someone you love, or even have loved, isn't an old shirt you take off and toss away. We're talking about a living, breathing person. A human life. Someone with a soul worth as much as yours. You loved him once, you've enjoyed each other—even if you don't love him anymore, even if you don't want to go on with the relationship you had, you still have to fulfill your moral responsibility and duty."

"So according to you, if either spouse asks for a divorce, that's automatically unethical? Even if love is completely gone, they still have to go on playing the role of husband or wife?"

"Of course that's not what I'm saying." Wanmei bats away his suggestion, groping for the right words. "Say you have a shirt—even if it's not dirty or torn, you'd be within your rights to get rid of it. But a living person you were once in love with, to whom you're legally bound—even if you think he's dirty or torn, you still can't . . . No, wait, it's not the person who's dirty or torn, it's the relationship that has become painfully cracked. In that situation, I reckon you need to curb your own negativity, think more about the other person, and do your best to rediscover the feelings you once had. That's the ethical standard. Or rather, that's the most basic requirement you could have of yourself."

"But what if you can't do that? Wouldn't you just split up eventually? By dragging it out, you cause more pain to both parties, especially the passive one!" It's clear that Xun Lei actually agrees with Wanmei's viewpoint but feels the need to challenge her argument from multiple angles so its triumph over Mu Ying's can be more resounding.

Mrs. Xun walks into her home. After helping to break up the argument at the banquet, she's been back and forth to the Xue household a few times—this last trip was to deliver quail eggs. She says to Master Xun, "I feel for the parents. The bride threw a tantrum and stormed out of the banquet. She still hasn't been back in, and for all I know she'll flounce back home. What's going on? No one is more obsessed with keeping up appearances than those two. If this gets out, Uncle Xue will be fine, but god knows what Auntie Xue will do! She looked ready to faint dead away."

Master Xun removes the pipe from his mouth and says seriously, "What's the bride playing at? If her heart was set on that watch, and she thinks Old Xue and his wife pulled a bait and switch—well, why don't we put up the money? Xun Lei can go buy it. Put that on her wrist, and problem solved."

Mrs. Xun is startled, then looks more closely at her husband's face and understands what he's thinking: *Daughters-in-law are so entitled these days! Are you marrying a man or a watch?* But probably also: *That poor couple. Back when Old Xue was a lama at the Longfu Temple, he chanted scripture at rich people's funerals. He used to get there at the crack of dawn, do three rounds in the morning and two in the afternoon, the sky would be dark by the time he got back. He played the zangs dung—a six-foot horn! You think that was easy? And he hardly got paid anything. Skipping every other meal, tearing down the east wall to mend the west. Just living one day at a time! He struggled through to Liberation, survived the Cultural Revolution, and now that he's finally able to celebrate his son's wedding, this has to happen! Can we just stand by and not do anything?*

Mrs. Xun says, "That's not a bad idea. But where would we get our hands on so much ready cash? Didn't you put your last three months' earnings into the fixed-deposit a few days ago?"

"We'll empty the checking account, and if that's not enough, we'll break into the fixed-deposit."

"We'd need approval from the bank! Don't you think they'll get suspicious? Putting your money into a fixed-deposit, then changing your mind three days later? They might say you need to get a letter from your workplace, to prove—"

"Uncle! Aunt!" Xinger interrupts. "You're only buying a watch, right? How much is it? A few hundred? I can put up the cash first, you can pay me back later!"

"Nonsense!" says Mrs. Xun. "We can't take your money. Anyway, the banks are about to close, we're not going to sort this out today."

Master Xun disagrees. "Let Xinger front the cash—I'll pay her back tomorrow. Go get Old Xue to come over, but make sure no one sees him. I'll have him describe the make and so on, then Lei can go get one just like it. No one needs to know but Old Xue. We'll tell the others we found it."

Mrs. Xun claps her hands. "Right! I'll say I spotted it by the entryway—the thief must have got nervous and tossed it."

She heads off to find Uncle Xue, Xinger goes to get the money from her stash, and Master Xun summons Xun Lei and Wanmei.

With consummate bad timing, this is the moment that the person who mistakenly went to Han Yitan's place earlier, and whom Ge Ping redirected to the Xun house, knocks on their door.

Xun Lei opens the door to a swarthy young guy, perhaps slightly older than him, tall and skinny with a long, bony face.

The stranger says, "Xun Lei? It wasn't easy to find you! Thank god you're home."

Xun Lei lets him in and offers him a seat. "You are . . . ?"

"My name's Zhao—I'm an editor at a publishing house. You sent us your translated manuscript?"

"That's right." Xun Lei looks at him, full of confidence, thinking, *At last—I suppose he's come to let me know they're going to publish it, or maybe they've had an expert check it, and there are some areas they'd like me to revise . . .*

Wanmei has heard them talking and slips into the room. She, too, believes the editor is here with good news. She followed Xun Lei through the whole translation process, and they went to the post office together to mail off the manuscript. They were determined: no going through the back door, no pulling strings, no tricks, no leaving it to chance. They were certain that the publishing house would appreciate and accept this book, based entirely on Xun Lei's shrewd, timely choice of subject matter; his smooth, readable translation; his precise annotations where necessary.

Sadly, it's not to be. What the editor pulls from his bag is the original text, in a dark-green clothbound hardcover edition, and Xun Lei's neatly handwritten translation. In a sympathetic tone, he says, "My editor in chief told me to send this back by mail, but I thought I ought to come in person."

The blood drains from Xun Lei's cheeks. Ever since he aced the exam to get into the ministry, his life has been smooth sailing in every regard. Without his realizing it, these years of cosseting, including the praise and admiration of everyone in this siheyuan, have burnished his self-confidence and self-respect into something as hard and clear as glass—but unfortunately, just as brittle.

He can't stop his voice trembling. "Was the topic unsuitable?"

Wanmei butts in. "Let's be frank, the topic couldn't have been better. In other countries, these nonfiction documentary-style books often wind up on bestseller lists and get fantastic reviews. This book contains lots of useful reference material for people working in quite a few areas in this country. If I were you, I wouldn't hesitate to—"

Editor Zhao can tell at a glance that this young woman is Xun Lei's partner—they function as a unit. He says, "Before starting this project, you didn't get in touch with any publishing houses to find out how they choose their titles, just went ahead and did the translation and mailed it to us. I admire your spirit and your courage a lot, but that's a risky approach. For translated works of this nature, we'll generally have chosen this year's books last year or the year before. After contracts are signed and editors assigned, they're put into our publishing calendar. It's very hard for an unsolicited manuscript to squeeze in there. Even so, the subject matter you've chosen is an absolute bull's-eye. This is the sort of book we'd translate and publish even if it meant squeezing something out of the existing lineup."

"So why aren't you taking it?" Xun Lei feels as if he has a chopstick lodged in his chest. It's been a long while since he's felt this frustrated.

"Are you saying the translation isn't good enough? Go get it verified by an expert!" says Wanmei agitatedly. "If you don't know any experts, I'll help you find one!"

"My boss didn't actually read your translation, so he can't say it's not good. Why did he veto it? I'll be honest, it's because he looked at your information and said, 'He's twenty-two? No way.' That's all it took to kill this. He didn't believe a twenty-two-year-old could translate this book well. Even if you could, it's not your turn. He can't let the name of an inexperienced, untried translator appear on a book like this. That's why. You weren't supposed to know any of this, but we're about the same age, and I felt I owed you an explanation. That's why I came in person. My boss's hierarchical thinking is deep-rooted, and I believe it's wrong. He's holding back talented translators and preventing our country from modernizing. But there's nothing I can do about it. No use trying to argue with him—in his eyes, I'm a lightweight too because I'm not yet thirty and don't have a proper college degree, only a Worker-Peasant-Soldier one."

As Editor Zhao delivers his candid speech, fury builds in Xun Lei's heart. So his youth has become an obstacle to his success! How will he withstand such a bizarre blow? He can think of nothing to say.

Outraged, Wanmei raises her voice. "What's your boss's name? I want to talk to him face-to-face! Otherwise I'll report him to the Publishers' Bureau. How can you discriminate against young people like that? And you're abandoning this book just because the translator happens to be young?"

Editor Zhao smiles grimly. "Oh, he's not abandoning the book. He asked me to lie in the rejection letter—I was supposed to say we already have this book on our list, under contract to another translator. But actually, before I returned your manuscript, my orders were to first ask X if he'd like to translate it. You know Mr. X, of course, he's got ample experience—"

"But he may not be able to translate this book!" Wanmei interrupts. "I know him all too well—he was the deputy head of a department when my dad was deputy Party committee secretary at the college. He's academically sound, of course, and he's a good person, but it's been more than thirty years since he came back from abroad, and he's barely left the country since. What he knows is older English—I mean English from the 1950s and before. He's not going to be as familiar as Xun Lei with the contemporary English in this book or the lifestyles and milieus it depicts."

"That's what he said himself," Editor Zhao confirms. "My boss said I wasn't allowed to tell him someone else had already translated the book, so I only showed him the original. He said he'd already read it and hadn't liked it. Also, he hasn't been well, and the translation would take him at least a year to finish. It would take us another year to get it into print, so the book wouldn't see the light of day until 1985. By that point, its value as a reference text would be much lower. My boss put his faith in this man, but it doesn't seem to be warranted!"

Xun Lei and Wanmei shake their heads and sigh.

Editor Zhao tries to cheer them up. "The good thing is, there are plenty of publishers out there. 'If the east isn't bright, then the west will be.' Why not try your luck somewhere else? There are people like my boss everywhere, but there are also open-minded editors who give newcomers chances and support them. If you're lucky, you'll find someone who'll propel you into the translation scene, and soon you'll be the Fu Lei of our time!"

Just as Xun Lei is about to spew out the emotions that have been building up inside him, he hears his father calling his name from the kitchen.

With a quick apology to Editor Zhao, he hurries over.

In the kitchen are not just his father and Xinger, but also Uncle Xue.

Why does his father look so upset? Before Xun Lei can work out what's going on, his father grumbles, "What took you so long? I called you so many times."

Xinger stands up for him. "Lei has a visitor. They were chatting when you called, no wonder he didn't hear . . ."

His father puffs away at his pipe, apparently unmollified. Still sounding grumpy, he says to Xun Lei, "Think you're so grand? Aren't you even going to say hello to your Uncle Xue?"

Uncle Xue hastily says, "Lei nodded at me when he came in . . ." But Xun Lei is already saying, "Hi, Uncle Xue!" so he smiles and adds, "Even the children in the siheyuan know how polite Xun Lei is, no need to scold him!"

Of course, this is when Wanmei sticks her head in and calls, "Xun Lei! Come quick!"

Master Xun clears his throat sternly. "You're not going anywhere!"

Wanmei winces and withdraws.

Uncle Xue beckons. "Come, Lei, sit next to me. I have something to tell you. It's like this—your mom and dad are really a blessing. They saw that our household is being blown apart by that foreign watch, so they came up with a plan to save us, but you'll need to do me a little favor . . ."

Uncle Xue describes the appearance and model of the gold-plated Rado watch while Wanmei walks Editor Zhao to the gate. When she gets back, she goes into the kitchen and, seeing Master Xun still looking unhappy, tries to explain, "Uncle, that was an editor from a publishing house. We were talking about Xun Lei's career—"

"Career!" says Master Xun frostily. "Like your careers are such a big deal? I was in the army, and all the while I was a soldier, I never once dreamed of being the commander in chief. Why don't you try thinking like that?"

Xun Lei shoots Wanmei a look that stops her saying anything else.

Uncle Xue thanks them again and departs—he needs to hurry back to the wedding banquet, where Mrs. Xun has taken over his hosting duties. Xun Lei says, "I'll go get the watch, Dad," and leaves. Wanmei scurries across the room and says to Xinger, "Shall we start making the dumplings?" All of a sudden, Xinger feels a great pity for Wanmei, and she says warmly, "Come on, I'll roll the skins out, and you wrap them. These dumplings will be delicious with both of us making them! We won't let a single one split open."

Gnawing on his pipe, Master Xun leaves the kitchen and returns to his room. Leaning back in his armchair, he thinks about what's bothering him. A few days ago, Lei and Wanmei were jabbering away about their "careers," and Wanmei mentioned that some famous foreigner in the olden days—oh yes, some French emperor called Napoleon—once said, "Any soldier who doesn't hope to be a marshal isn't a good soldier!" The two youngsters regard that quote with something like reverence. His wife asked to hear more, and the two young people took apart the words to explain it to her. When she understood, she was merely amused. "But if all the soldiers become commanders, who would they command?" Master Xun, though, finds the sentiment revolting. Why did he become a soldier back in the day? If he hadn't joined the army and thrown his lot in with the Communist Party, he would have starved to death! Why did he go to war? If the Nationalists hadn't been defeated, every poor person would have stayed poor forever! He never once thought about having any kind of "career"! Did he dream of being commander in chief? He didn't even think about becoming commander of his own company. When he joined the workshop, younger men often asked him, "Why did you come home after the war? If you'd stayed in the army, you might be a deputy commander by now." There was some truth to this—some of those who joined up at the same time as him had now climbed as high as lieutenant general. Even so, Xun Xingwang had no regrets. He was an ordinary soldier on the battlefield, and an ordinary laborer in the workshop. Now he's an ordinary cobbler on the sidewalk by Houmen Bridge. His blood and sweat flowed righteously, he served his country and his people, his own life is getting better and better, and he's never done anything that's kept him up at night. He respects himself and has earned the respect of those around him. What's wrong with living the way he does? Yet Lei and Wanmei refuse to be content with what they have. All day long, they clamor after this "career," trying to stand out and rise above others. True, they're not just thinking of themselves; the "careers" he hears them talking about would help the nation too. They're not doing anything sneaky or underhanded and don't plan to hurt or cheat anyone. They'll study hard, become specialists, and achieve great things through their work. It's difficult to say who's right or wrong, but those two clearly have a completely different way of thinking than he does. Xinger's heart is closer to his, it seems.

He's wrong about that. In the kitchen, the two women chat as they wrap dumplings. When Wanmei relates the inglorious story of Xun Lei's manuscript getting unjustly rejected, Xinger gets even more worked up than Wanmei was. "How much does it cost to print a book?" she asks earnestly. "If they don't want to publish it, give it to me. I'll get my brother Zaoer to make it happen!"

NOT THE END

申时

Shen Shi

and

酉时

You Shi

On the Cusp between the Time of the Monkey and Rooster:
5:00 p.m.

EPILOGUE

How should we think of time? Is it a circle? An arrow? A
river flowing to the sea? A pair of dice? An accelerating
spaceship? Can it really fold and bend? Time moves on,
while the Bell and Drum Towers are eternal.

On the northern side of Beijing, the Bell and Drum Towers stand tall.

The Drum Tower in front, red walls and gray tiles.

The Bell Tower behind, gray walls and green tiles.

The Drum Tower was built during the Yuan dynasty, when it was known as
the Tower of Orderly Administration. Only in the eighteenth year of the Yongle
emperor's reign (that is, 1420) was it rebuilt in its present location. To the west
of the Drum Tower today, you can still see an "Old Drum Tower Street," so it's
not difficult to work out where the Tower of Orderly Administration once stood.
The Qing dynasty took over all the Ming palaces, official buildings, and temples,
and in the fifth year of the Jiaqing emperor's reign (1800), the Drum Tower went
through a major refurbishment, once again becoming the northernmost point
of the axis running through the city. It's said that back in the day there were
twenty-four drums atop it, each about one and a half feet wide and made from
a single cowskin. In 1900, the forces of the Eight-Nation Alliance invaded, and
the tower was seized. Only one of the twenty-four drums survives to this day,
and its surface bears the marks of the invaders' blades.

In the Yuan dynasty, the Bell Tower was the central pavilion of Wanning
Temple. It was moved in the Ming dynasty and rebuilt in the twelfth year of the
Qianlong emperor's reign (1747), to its present appearance.

Until 1924, the Bell and Drum Towers were responsible for keeping time for the entire city.

How was time measured?

In the beginning, there was a water clock at the top of the Drum Tower, apparently a national treasure from the Song dynasty, consisting of bronze vessels of various sizes that dripped water evenly. There were four of them, named—in descending order—heaven's lake, level water, extremity, and gathering water. Between the vessels were tiny cymbals attached to a mechanism that struck them at regular intervals, eight times each. It was fairly accurate. The vessels had to be regularly refilled, of course, with warm water in the winter to prevent freezing. The water clock room is still there in the Drum Tower, but unfortunately the water clock itself is missing. During the Qing dynasty, they switched to burning incense, though this was actually a step backward in terms of accuracy.

How did the towers report the time?

By day, the Bell Tower struck once, at noon.

By night, the Drum Tower reported the five watches. The first watch was around 8:00 p.m.—known as "setting the watch." After that, every watch was marked by thirteen drumbeats. The second watch was at 10:00 p.m., the third at midnight, the fourth at 2:00 a.m., and the fifth at 4:00 a.m. All the civil and military officials would get out of bed at the third watch, gather at the Meridian Gate by the fourth watch, and at the fifth watch would file into the court, where they knelt in the Hall of Supreme Harmony on what was known as the "expanse," awaiting imperial edicts.

Each drumbeat was echoed by the bell. At the fourth watch, post-midnight, the bell would sound again; this was known as "revealing the drum." Between setting the watch and revealing the drum, the Bell Tower would strike once every half watch (once an hour in today's terms).

Here's how the drum- and bell-striking took place at setting the watch and revealing the drum: A watchman stood atop each tower, holding up a paper lantern (they called this "facing lanterns") as a signal to his counterpart. Having thus coordinated, they'd strike the beat in this rhythm: eighteen fast, eighteen slow, eighteen medium. This was repeated once more, for a total of a hundred and eight strikes, first the drum and then the bell. The whole thing took quite a while.

The Bell and Drum Towers have been silent for fifty-eight years. It's 5:00 p.m. on December 12, 1982, and they continue to stand mightily there, as if they might strike at any moment.

The years go by slowly. Time flows on without a pause. We arrive in this world, and the first thing we are aware of is the space that surrounds us. Its length, breadth, and height, how it's filled with shapes, colors, and sounds. Then we realize there's something alongside this space, something we can't touch or hold or stop—time. Time moves constantly through the space we're in, and that constitutes our life. It contains our joy, sorrow, rage, and pleasure, our lives, deaths, celebrations, and tears.

No one can possibly exist alone—we share our space with many, many others. This is what makes up society. In a single society, people have different ideas about class, political inclination, finances, mindsets, morality, education, personality, goals, physiology, competition, and opportunity, so they end up clashing, colliding with each other, trading blame, separating, sneering at or envying each other. At the same time, they must also rely on each other, come together in love or admiration, respect each other. All these fluid changes across society, looked at as a whole, make up our history. Yet from our individual viewpoints, they seem like destiny.

In the rush of time passing, how many people have felt or will feel this sacred sense of history, this solemn sense of fate?

◆ ◆ ◆

Everyone's experience of time is different.

On his way back from the Xun household, Xue Yongquan has a dizzy spell and grabs the side of the cooking tent, panting for breath. Hai Xibin comes running and catches him before he falls. "Uncle Xue, why don't you come have a rest in my room?"

Xibin lives alone in the eastern "ear room" on the north side of the siheyuan—possibly the only quiet place right now. Uncle Xue allows himself to be led away.

Once he has Uncle Xue settled on his bed, Xibin sneaks off to fetch Mr. Yin.

Although Mr. Yin is a bonesetter, he's able to make more general diagnoses. He takes Uncle Xue's pulse and says, "You'll be okay. Your blood pressure's rising, and you're not fully recovered from your asthma, that's why you're dizzy and your chest is tight. I'll give you a tuina massage, and you'll feel better." He unbuttons Uncle Xue's collar and kneads a pressure point in his throat.

When Xibin reported Luo Baosang's actions to Mr. Yin, his judgment was, "He went into First Fragrance? Then it's very likely we were wrong about him. If the watch really were concealed on his person, you wouldn't be able to drag him in there." Xibin's respect for Mr. Yin increased in that moment. He watches with admiration as Mr. Yin massages Uncle Xue. Boxing isn't enough, he thinks, he ought to ask if Mr. Yin can teach him tuina and bonesetting too.

Uncle Xue shuts his eyes. The touch of his sworn brother's hands on his throat is unleashing a flood of thoughts, some foggy and some clear.

When Xue Yongquan was a lama, he believed time was an enormous circle, cyclical and endless. According to the Buddhist scriptures he learned from his mentor Ao Jinba, the endless cycle of time is divided into sections, each known as a kalpa, and further divided into creation, existence, ruination, and emptiness. During the ruination stage, the three disasters of water, fire, and wind will arrive, and the world will be destroyed. Only by heeding the teachings of Buddha, devoting oneself to cultivating enlightenment, and attaining release can one finally transcend this circle of time. If not, you're doomed to move endlessly through the six realms of reincarnation: heaven, humanity, asuras, hell, hungry ghosts, beasts.

These days, young people visit Buddhist temples for fun. When they see the words "the wheel of dharma keeps turning" carved in the rock outside, they don't know what the words mean and give them no further thought. Back then, Xue Yongquan felt a jolt of terror each time he saw that inscription.

Time is an unimaginably large circle. When one round finishes, another must start, hence another life. In the old days, when condemned criminals were brought to the marketplace to be executed, they would bellow, "Twenty years from now, I'll be a fine fellow again." Fully confident that everyone in the crowd—which included Xue Yongquan—would agree this was how things worked.

He devoutly believes we are rewarded or punished for our deeds. If we are good in this life and accumulate merit, we'll get paid back in the next life. If we do wicked things, our next life will be spent as a hungry ghost or beast.

This circular view of history was shaken by the establishment of the People's Republic of China. He saw with his own eyes the bullies of the temple fair get their retribution in this life. Like thousands of poor Beijingers, he was guaranteed warmth and food. Day by day, his life has grown more prosperous and less sordid, and with the passage of time, a great number of changes have taken place in the city: the expansion of Chang'an Avenue and Tiananmen Square, the "ten big buildings" appearing at the same time, the rapid development of the bus and tram system, wells disappearing and running water becoming commonplace, the replacement of "sir" and "madam" with forms of address such as "comrade." All these developments have made him conceive of time less as a circle and more as a line. Attending night classes at the store, he's received a basic overview of Chinese history. At one end of this line, apes evolved into humans, and at the other end is Communism. His elder son, Jihui, once told him that actually, time has no beginning or end—before humanity descended from apes, you have apes descending from bugs, and before that life itself being created, the planet appearing out of nothingness, and so on. After Communism, there'll still be contradictions and clashes, and human society will keep developing and changing. Eventually, the earth might be destroyed, and perhaps by then humankind will have moved on to other planets. Uncle Xue is dubious about this, but the basic idea that time isn't a closed loop but a line of progression from apes to Communism has taken root in his mind.

As far as the country is concerned, the line of progress leads toward Socialism. "When the land is at peace, all will fulfill their duties. Both the greatest and the meanest have a hand in our prosperity." This is how Xue Yongquan sees his responsibility. He's very dutiful in his work guarding the warehouse and frequently lectures and encourages his sons to be serious in their work for the nation. As for his own household, progress means his sons growing up and marrying, though he also hopes to have fewer problems with his wife, and for his sons to show filial piety. Jihui and his wife have a daughter; he very much hopes Jiyue and his wife will give them a grandson.

Who would have thought Jiyue's wedding would be such a bumpy ride? Some important friends and relatives have come to celebrate with them and ought to be enjoying the final course of the banquet. Instead, the bride is hiding in her in-laws' room, refusing to come out. At any moment, she might even go back to her parents' house to sulk!

In the stress of the moment, Uncle Xue's former view of time reasserts itself. As Mr. Yin kneads his sternum, he hazily wonders: *Am I being punished for my long-ago sin?* He remembers bringing his newborn daughter to the Xiugeng Hall Bookstore clerk, who would in turn take her to the official adopting her. His guiltiest deed. True, this was not long after the Japanese devils retreated and the Nationalists took over. The temple fair appeared to be bustling, but money wasn't worth as much anymore. Even Gold Elephant Zhang, whose Gold Elephant Stall usually did a roaring trade in combs, pleaded hardship when Ao Jinba came by with his yellow cloth bag collecting rent. The money Xue Yongquan got from chanting scripture alongside Ao Jinba wasn't enough to support himself. On the first, second, ninth, and tenth of every month, when there was a fair at the temple, he went to Dongxiao Market at Hademen to earn a little extra income hauling carts. Not long after Auntie Xue gave birth to their daughter, he was pulling his cart past Hademen when he got hit by a jeep driven by an American soldier. This was clearly deliberate—as the cargo rolled from his cart and Xue Yongquan lay sprawled on the road, he heard a burst of laughter from the jeep. He had to pay for the damaged goods and his medical treatment—there was no way he could support his daughter too. And so he gritted his teeth and gave her away. The official—whose real name was kept from them by the middleman—offered them money, but he and Auntie Xue firmly refused. They weren't animals, to sell their own flesh and blood. They were only doing this because they had no other choice. At least this way their daughter would have food and warmth. They asked to see her once a year, but the official's family firmly refused.

He's heard nothing about his daughter in the thirty-odd years since. He tried to track her down after Liberation, but the bookstore clerk had passed away, and he had nothing to go on. For some reason, the turbulence of Jiyue's wedding is making him miss her. She was taken away wearing a pair of tiger-head shoes Auntie Xue had made from an old cassock. Could today's disaster be his retribution?

A burst of merriment from outside—evidently from the banquet. Mrs. Xun's voice rises above the others, full of good cheer. It seems the celebrations are carrying on. In that case, this can't be his punishment. In a while, Xun Lei will return with the new watch, the bride will change her mind, and everything will go back to normal. Why is he allowing his thoughts to run wild?

"How's that? Are you feeling any better? Don't worry—everything will be fine soon enough." Mr. Yin's knuckles press up and down his back. Uncle Xue's padded jacket is lightly covering him, and Xibin has stoked the fire so he doesn't get cold.

He does feel much better, warmed both by the stove and by friendship. His idea of time, bent almost circular, springs back into a straight line. He smiles and nods. His sworn brother, Yin, used to make a living at the temple fair: he tied three wooden poles into a tripod, and from its apex suspended two leather straps that he hung from, shirtless, performing acrobatic tricks. After they got to know each other and realized they could talk about anything under the sun, they became sworn brothers. Each knew the other would take care of his wife and children if anything happened. Mr. Yin is right—everything will be fine soon enough. It's not just Mr. Yin taking care of him now—this kid Hai Xibin is helping too. And the Xuns, neighbors with whom he shares a communal faucet, have shown themselves to be true friends! Perhaps this is a reward for his virtue in a previous life? No, that's pure fantasy. Xun Xingwang was in the Eighth Route Army, then he worked in a large factory. He's gained the true enlightenment of proletariat thinking and understands that comrades must show each other concern, love, and a helpful spirit.

In the end, his thoughts have come full circle. Everything—external time, the changing world, his own life, destiny—has gone back to the way it was.

Success depends on all human effort. What's more, *When everyone gathers firewood, the flames rise higher.* Mr. Yin presses the webbing between Uncle Xue's thumb and index finger, and he feels perfectly well again. Smiling, he says, "I'm fine now. I ought to get back to our guests. Everything will be better soon . . ."

The Bell and Drum Towers were once public timepieces. They marked time with sound.

The towers are on hiatus at the moment and function only as relics. Now, in late 1982, Beijing has public timepieces in two locations: Beijing Railway Station has two clock towers facing each other, and the Telegraph Building on Chang'an Avenue has one. These towers chime the hours and have clocks facing all four directions. Whenever you like, you can glance at them and know the time to within five minutes.

This is too few public clocks for a thriving city bustling with activity. There ought to be a few more outdoor ones. Different heights, styles, models. We particularly need those quartz digital ones—they're cheaper than the analog variety, and tell the time to the second.

The scarcity of timepieces and their imprecision says we don't make good use of time. Many organizations are rife with catchphrases such as "Let's study the matter," "We'll think about it," "Let's keep talking," and "Hang on," "Wait awhile," "Wait and see," "We'll talk some more in the afternoon," "What's the hurry?" and "We'll take care of this tomorrow."

This is a bad habit. Any reform must begin with changing the way we think about time.

That's the sort of reformer Zhang Qilin is.

It's December 12, 1982—but what time?

Zhang Qilin is on a Boeing 747. He extends his wrist to glance at his Shanghai Diamond–brand watch, which says 5:00 p.m. He understands this is Beijing time, as measured from the Greenwich Prime Meridian. The plane is flying westward, while the earth rotates east. He has no idea of the actual time.

It's 2:30 p.m. in New Delhi, and noon in Moscow. He's heading in the direction of Athens, where it's currently 11:00 a.m., Frankfurt, West Germany (10:00 a.m.), and London (9:00 a.m.). And in the other direction, it's now 6:00 p.m. in Tokyo, 11:00 p.m. in Hawaii, 1:00 a.m. in San Francisco, and 4:00 a.m. in New York.

It pains Zhang Qilin that even though the vast majority of cadres in his bureau have college diplomas, only a small percentage have a truly scientific view of time.

What is time?

From a strictly scientific standpoint, time is an objective form of material existence, consisting of a continuous sequence of past, present, and future. It is the ongoing expression of material movement and transformation.

This measurement of material movement and transformation—the "time" we generally talk and think about—since the earliest human society has made use of the sun, moon, and stars, and grew more and more accurate. These days, every country in the world has accepted Greenwich Mean Time, the mean solar time as measured from the meridian line of Greenwich Observatory in London, England, also known as Universal Time. Of course, making everyone understand the difference between true solar time and mean solar time, then standardizing all the time zones in the world, with their standard time and local time, isn't going to be easy. Even so, Zhang Qilin feels the cadres under his command ought to know how accurately time can be measured. The ancients said, "An inch of time is worth an inch of gold," but this hardly seems appropriate now, given our current value system! In everyday life, the smallest unit of time is the second. So how long is a second? Some people think it's a single tick-tock, others the time it takes the second hand to move one notch. More intelligent people define it as such-and-such percentage of a year, month, day, or hour. But actually, the rotation and revolution of the earth is irregular, therefore any measurement derived from them, such as mean solar time or calendar time, isn't going to be completely reliable. A more stable reference point is needed. More recently, scientists have discovered that when atoms experience a change in energy levels, they absorb or emit electromagnetic signals at a constant rate and can therefore be used as a baseline. From there, they constructed a reliable system of time measurement known as Atomic Time, in which one second is how long it takes a cesium atom to oscillate 9,192,631,770 times. This is how the entire world currently defines one second, the basic unit of time. All other methods, from the Bell and Drum Towers to sundials, have become relics of a former era. Mechanical clocks and watches have become more popular among the populace, and more ornamental. Anything that requires precision now calls for a quartz watch, which these days can be accurate up to nine decimal places, losing less than a ten-thousandth of a second per day. Hundred-meter sprint times are recorded to hundredths of a second. If you can run one-hundredth of a second faster than the current champ, you're the new record holder. So much for "an inch of time is worth an inch of gold," when a mere one-hundredth of a second can be more valuable than a single inch of gold!

If a nation's organizations and structures cannot align themselves with society's sense of time, how will they ever be able to show any leadership or work together?

When Zhang Qilin stepped into this role, his first act was to announce a spot-check at 10:00 a.m. that day. When China National Radio signaled ten o'clock, the electronic clock in the lobby showed 10:03; the wall clocks in various departments had 10:01, 9:56, 10:08, and 10:13; the cafeteria clock said 9:49; and the desk clock in the drivers' room showed 10:06. People's personal timepieces were more accurate, though some were still fast or slow. The designer watch worn by Administrative Division's Fu Shandu was a whole ten minutes slow. Upon closer inspection, there was nothing wrong with the watch itself—he'd just failed to set it to the right time after forgetting to wind it.

At eleven, Zhang Qilin called an urgent meeting for the entire bureau, at which he announced the results of his spot-check and gave an impassioned speech. At noon, he said, the public address system would broadcast China National Radio, and when they heard the buzz at the hour, every clock and watch in the building should be synchronized. Loudly, he exhorted, "From noon today, let us bring this new awareness of time to our work. Technology and economics are advancing across the world, second by second, while we fall behind in many areas of science and productivity. We must develop a sense of urgency and a fervent revolutionary spirit. From noon today, phrases such as 'Let's look into it' or 'Wait awhile' or 'Take it slow' and the bureaucratic attitudes they represent must go in the trash! If something needs looking into, look into it right away! Don't drag your feet, just make a decision! If something needs discussing, discuss it quickly, don't beat about the bush or get caught up in unimportant details! If something needs doing, then do it! Don't delay! If something's due in the morning, don't leave it until afternoon. Today's work gets done today, not tomorrow. If you don't need to do it, or shouldn't do it, then don't! Just refuse!"

What was the result of all his hard work? There was no actual opposition—the so-called conservatives like in TV shows, pouty malcontents or jowly, pot-bellied idlers—but an even more implacable enemy, one present in many people and even to a degree in himself: inertia.

He often feels unequal to the task. What's more, as he puts his plans into practice, he's surprised that in the eyes of the world maxims such as "time is money" or "time is life" are considered outdated. The success or failure of many enterprises no longer depends on completing each task as quickly as possible but on having access to the most recent information. In order to devise the best way of dealing with a project code-named GS, the bureau put together a small team with himself at the head, and they made use of every second as they discussed, drafted, revised, and finalized. In a "mere" ten days, they'd put together a practical proposal—you couldn't call them inefficient. But then Pang Qibin from the Technical Report Group sent over some materials, and it turned out that a plan like theirs had already been published in a foreign magazine, even more thoroughly and logically than in their final proposal! They ought to have cultivated the habit of knowing and making use of all the information available! With the right materials, never mind a ten-day meeting—a single day would have been enough—they could have solved the problem in a few hours or even minutes. Soon after this, he decided to elevate the Technical Report Group, then seen in more of a supporting role, to the Technical Report Unit, and to promote Pang Qibin to its head, over everyone else's objections. He also plans to get hold of the latest computer facilities soon so this important part of his bureau can be fully equipped.

He is full of ambition.

And yet he encounters problems every step of the way. Take the accusation that arrived in the mail this afternoon. Fu Shandu explained away the charges flawlessly, but he'll still have to get to the bottom of this. Obviously he can't take the word of two people from outside the organization, but neither can he simply accept Old Fu's version of events. Time is not the crucial element here, but information. Yet he has limited access to information, so it won't do any good "making use of his time" on this trip to analyze the situation or make a judgment. This being the case, he decides to put the issue in cold storage for now. The ministry's disciplinary committee will carry out their own investigation, and for all he knows the problem will be solved by the time he's back in China.

The flight attendant pushes her gleaming trolley past his seat, and he asks for a cup of pure, clear mineral water. A touch of the button and the light above him winks on. He sips his water and starts to read that day's *China Daily*.

◆ ◆ ◆

Space is a container for time, and time is the form in which space exists. No one can leave either space or time. Some people are more aware of space than time, or vice versa.

By three thirty, Dr. Yu and Fu Shandu are on their way to the Tuanjiehu neighborhood. Zhang Qilin went through customs right away, so Dr. Yu was at the airport for only about ten minutes. The plane hasn't taken off yet, and already she's on her way to what might be their new home. She phoned from the airport and asked Xiuzao to come to Tuanjiehu as quickly as possible. They'll decide afterward whether they should pull the trigger right away or wait for Mr. Zhang to get home before making a decision.

Fu Shandu gets the keys from the caretaker and leads Dr. Yu on a tour of the two units.

Rapt with pleasure, Dr. Yu examines every last detail of the apartments.

They're on the third floor, a good height. She's very satisfied.

The two units are next to each other. The right-hand-side one has two rooms with a window joining them, and although they're a little small, there's a sunken living room that they could put a dining table into, or a folding bed if they get a maid. Behind the other door is a reasonably sized entryway, but all the windows face south—nice and warm in winter, but bad for airflow in summer. That could be a problem. Both kitchens are too small, but the gas stoves in both are a good height and well positioned. One has a sitting toilet and one a squatter, which is fine, but neither has much bathroom space—if you put in a washing machine, there'd be no room for a tub. The built-in closets are all right, the balconies a little small. Anyone wanting to move in would have to do at least two things: get a dado painted halfway up the walls and rip out the ugly light fittings with their plastic shades that leave the naked bulbs exposed, replacing them with more elegant hanging lamps. How would they divide up the two apartments? Maybe the whole family should stay in the right-side unit, at least until Xiuzao gets married, and Old Zhang can have the other one as a study and reception room? Or should Xiuzao have her own place from the beginning? As she turns this over in her mind, Dr. Yu suddenly realizes these two apartments aren't the best arrangement, and if one of them could be exchanged for three single units, that might make things easier.

Xiuzao gets there quickly and follows her mother from room to room, but she's distracted. Will they really be moving here soon? She feels like she's losing something significant. True, he doesn't love her and doesn't even know she has feelings for him. Each time she comes back from her college to the siheyuan, there's no guarantee she'll even meet him, and when she does it's inevitably brief and awkward—like this morning. Under the old rattan chairs at the entryway, she with a basket of fried pastries, he with paper wedding decorations and glue. Even so, she's not sure she's ready to sever her connection to the courtyard. In theory, she'd be free to go back for a visit even after moving to Tuanjiehu, but in practice, she knows she wouldn't have the courage, and her former neighbors would find it odd.

"Look, it's almost half past four. Old Fu and Driver Wang are still downstairs—they must be getting impatient," says Dr. Yu. "Do you like it or not? Just tell me what you think."

"As long as you like it, Mom, I don't really care," says Xiuzao vaguely.

"These doors don't make any sense. Look, this would be the perfect place for a fridge, but the door would open right into it." Dr. Yu has resumed her inspection.

Xiuzao isn't sure which door her mother is talking about.

She wanders out onto the balcony and looks at the jagged skyline. For some reason, she remembers the Victor Hugo poem she copied into her diary a few days ago:

> *Can love govern itself? Why should two people be in harmony?*
> *Go ask the flowing water, ask the gusting wind,*
> *The night moth that seeks out the flame,*
> *Sunlight on the overripe grape,*
> *Ask all of singing, calling, longing, murmuring creation!*
> *Ask the deep, cacophonous bird nests of April!*
> *And the unruly heart cries, "How could I know this, how?"*

Every line of this poem is a direct blow to her vibrating heartstrings, and she almost speaks them out loud. It occurs to her that her situation is not, in fact, that of the first line, "two people in harmony." Bitterness fills her soul, and tears come to her eyes.

"Xiuzao! What are you doing on the balcony? Let's go back down, quickly! Old Fu will be frantic," Dr. Yu calls out loudly.

In fact, Fu Shandu is in no hurry for them to come back down—he's at the public phone by the bicycle shed, giving Luo Jishan a call. Why is this phone call so urgent? What are they talking about? No one knows, except for the two of them.

◆　◆　◆

Zhan Liying is making a phone call too.

She had to go all the way to Di'anmen post office and is now in the same cubicle that Tantai Zhizhu was in just a couple of hours ago.

It takes a lot of effort to place the long-distance call to her husband's workplace. It's Sunday, so there's only a skeleton crew on duty, and they don't seem to know anything about his illness. Nanny Zhan spews her anger and dissatisfaction at them. "What's wrong with you? Where has management run off to? Why don't you care if my husband lives or dies? Why aren't you implementing Central's policies for intellectuals? What? You don't know? Why don't you know? How dare you not know! Let me tell you, I know exactly what you're all thinking—my husband is being transferred out, so you've stopped caring about him. I'm going to complain to Central! You wait and see! What? . . . Look it up? Check? What's there to look up or check? I got the telegram! Wait awhile? How long is a while? You need to speak to your boss? Fine, I'll wait! They won't bully Zhan Liying so easily! I'll have it out with them! You tell them, if anything happens to my husband, I'll set the law on them!"

She hangs up huffily and waits for them to call back.

Someone knocks on the glass to hurry her. She opens the door, sticks her head out, and says, "Go make your call somewhere else! This is urgent—I need this phone."

The middle-aged man with graying hair argues back. "This is a public phone—it's for everyone. You can't just take it over. Anyway, you're not using it right now—"

"I'm waiting for a long-distance call," says Zhan Liying self-righteously. "I can't just let you cut in—I might miss my call." She shuts the door with a bang.

Seeing her standing there, arms folded, while the phone remains silent, the man yanks the door open and leans in. "I just need to make a quick call. Your long-distance call will still get through."

Zhan Liying yells, "Stop causing trouble!"

"How can you talk like that?" the man screams through the half-open door. "You're hogging a public phone—you're the one causing trouble!"

Zhan Liying shouts back at him, but he won't give way. The other customers try to calm them down, and even the clerk comes out from behind the counter to get involved.

The long-distance call from Sichuan comes through, but the voice just says, "I couldn't find anyone from management . . ." Zhan Liying screams, "That's outrageous! Isn't my husband's life worth anything to them? Where have they all buggered off to? I'll tell you, they're enjoying their special privileges. They're grubbing for extra cash. They're living it up. Not a care in the world!"

The person at the other end of the line, who has started to loathe her, thinks, *Ugh! If the Cultural Revolution comes back, I hope she gets properly tortured.* The clerk and other customers are also repelled by this yelling and decide there must be something wrong with her.

Zhan Liying, oh, Zhan Liying, you're actually the kindest, most warm-hearted person. All day long, you've done so many unselfish, caring things to help and comfort others. You've shown this not just in spirit, but materially. Yet all your kind deeds are undone by your disastrous personality! The saying goes, "Dripping water cuts through rock, and a string can saw through wood," yet somehow, after all this time, these thorns on your character remain stubbornly there.

Actually, Zhan Liying's husband fell ill at his sister's house. After his sister and her husband brought him to the hospital, the sister dashed out to send Liying the telegram, then phoned his workplace and spoke to his boss, who rushed to the hospital right away. The doctors quickly diagnosed acute inflammation of the gall bladder, requiring immediate treatment. From the hospital office, the husband's boss called Zhan Liying's workplace and left a message with the duty clerk—"Zhan Liying's husband may require surgery. We suggest you give her permission to leave for Sichuan immediately"—to be passed on to management first thing the next morning. He then called the public phone at the hutong but didn't manage to get hold of her—she was already at the post office. For her part, it didn't occur to her that the person she wanted to speak to might be at the hospital.

Of course, one important cause of this impasse is China's inadequate telecommunications network. Even in the capital in late 1982, only a small percentage of households have private lines, and there are far fewer public phones than needed by the populace. We're only talking regular metal cables here—some countries have carried out successful experiments in fiber optics and have even started using these new technologies. This suggests systemic change. But will the Chinese people, Zhan Liying among them, be able to catch up?

◆ ◆ ◆

Tantai Zhizhu steps out of the elevator and sees her new neighbor, Mu Ying, walking toward her.

They nod a greeting at each other.

Mu Ying is in a good mood. After leaving the siheyuan, she stopped by the ministry clinic—the little apartment here is her real home—and washed and groomed herself meticulously. As the common wisdom goes, women dress for those who please them. When she met Ji Zhiman earlier today, she wasn't thinking of pleasing him, but rather showing her own dignity and cultivation. Hence her modest hairstyle, white woolen scarf, and cinched fitted black coat over a rose-colored jacket and soft-gray sweater with a sweetheart neckline, pale-brown collared shirt, and dark-blue woolen trousers with a pair of high heels the same shade as her jacket. Now that she's on her way to see Qi Zhuangsi, she's been through a complete transformation: she has to look young and dashing, as if she's made no effort at all. Her hair is loose, tucked gracefully behind her ears. The scarf and coat are gone. On her head is a pale-blue woolen cap, seemingly thrown on at the last minute. Her dark-blue windbreaker is the latest style, with charmingly asymmetrical white and gray stripes. The zippered pocket on her left sleeve is just large enough for her hardcover address book, in which she has sandwiched the miniature Stage Art of Mei Lanfang stamp sheet. She also has on a chunky grass-green turtleneck, and no jewelry whatsoever, which makes her feel fresh and unadorned. Her faux jeans are molded tightly around her bottom— she designed and sewed them herself. They look like regular worker's trousers, without the usual broad hems or large pockets, and the legs aren't particularly tight, but the whole effect is stunning. Her body seems extraordinarily graceful and fluid. On her feet are a pair of scuffed black leather high-heeled boots. She isn't carrying a purse, just a pair of pale-blue gloves that match her hat.

Since Qi Zhuangsi told her, "Don't bother me again," she has left him alone. When they bump into each other in the office corridor, even if there's no one else around, she smiles blandly and walks away. Even so, she detects an electric current shooting from his leonine eyes into hers. No need for rational thought—intuition says he actually does like her and only said not to bother him because work weighs heavy on his shoulders, and he has too many revolutionary responsibilities. He doesn't find her advances bothersome at all, clearly. It's on her to make the next move. As long as she doesn't go too far, he'd probably be delighted for her to gently intervene in his life. Of course, she'll have to calibrate this carefully, tread lightly, and withdraw in time—she's playing the long game here!

On the subway platform, in the train, walking down the sidewalk to his building, she keeps feeling as if people are shooting her hostile glances. Her head remains held high through it all. No doubt most of them are just thinking how fashionable she is.

She presses the button for the elevator and thinks: *It's true, I admit it, I'm stylish. What's wrong with that? Should I have spent my whole time on earth in that gray little town I was born in? Those socks with splotches of crimson, green, ocher, and sapphire blue, which I once thought were the most beautiful socks in the world—should I have gone on thinking that?*

As far as Mu Ying is concerned, time is an arrow shooting through the air. She used to be at the tail of the arrow, but she's worked very hard to climb along the shaft, and now she's at the tip. As time zips by, the tip is always going to be better than the tail. Just think how many of our everyday expressions have to do with time: "seize the day," "having a moment," "timely," "in our time," "up to the minute." Being "fashionable" means living at the tip of the arrow, where Mu Ying is proud to be.

Mu Ying has taken as her motto a quote from Chekhov's *Uncle Vanya*: "Everything a person has ought to be beautiful: thoughts, soul, face, and clothes." Of course, everyone's idea of beauty is different. The ideas at the tip of time's arrow are going to be completely different from those at the tail. Mu Ying conforms to the perspective of the tip. When it comes to love, she believes that as long as your emotions are sincerely held and you're not forcing anyone to do anything, then no matter who the object of your affections is, it's rational and ethical to love them. As for her appearance, she ignores conventional ideas of how men or women, young or old, should dress. She does as she likes. As long as you and your loved ones are happy with how you look, no need to conform to anyone else's taste.

When she hears the elevator arriving, a ripple of agitation passes through her. She didn't phone Qi Zhuangsi before coming over but firmly believes he'll be there, and that she'll meet him alone. She'll startle him by not mentioning anything else, just stamps. Yes, she's visiting as a fellow stamp collector, nothing else—what fun! She's not going to simply hand over the Mei Lanfang stamps either—she'll negotiate and demand something in exchange. Afterward, she'll claim she has something urgent to attend to and, before he can say anything, fly away gracefully.

The doors open, and a few people walk out—among them her neighbor Tantai Zhizhu. Mu Ying instinctively nods a greeting. She's never seen Zhizhu on stage, but Zhan Liying has told her all kinds of things about her. She can't understand how Zhizhu has spent such a long time living with a common laborer. Maybe it's because those operas she's always performing in are grounded in feudal values, and the poison has sunk deep in her.

As Mu Ying heads up in the elevator, Tantai Zhizhu leaves the building. After nodding at her neighbor, Zhizhu can't help thinking about her. She's learned from Zhan Liying that Mu Ying not only divorced the college classmate she was married to, but abandoned her child. This alone, Zhizhu finds impossible to understand. The way Zhizhu sees it, marriages should definitely be broken up if they were arranged by parents or matchmakers, or brought about by force or deception. A union that you enter freely out of love, though, shouldn't be lightly ended—this isn't a children's game. Lady Precious Stream waiting in her icy cave for eighteen years, White Snake rebuking her husband at the Broken Bridge, Zhao Yanrong feigning madness to escape the palace—these stories will always have the power to move us because they are about loyal, single-minded love. This seems to be a value shared by many people across the world. How else can you explain that the tragedy of Romeo and Juliet remains equally touching today or that audiences are filled with pity and pain for Othello, even at the moment he strangles Desdemona? Apparently Mu Ying dumped her husband because they had "no common language" and she found him "vulgar and shallow." This doesn't explain anything. Anyone could seize on these excuses to cover up the fact that they're chasing after a new man or hoping to trade up for a richer husband. In *The Bean Juice Tale*, couldn't Mo Ji have tossed out these reasons to justify his abandonment of Jin Yunu? When Li Jia "passed on" his wife, Du Shiniang, to Sun Fu, couldn't he have made these same claims? That would make Du Shiniang's sinking of the hundred treasures look less like a noble gesture and more like a temper tantrum.

Tantai Zhizhu and Mu Ying might be around the same age, but the way they see love and morality is completely different.

After their encounter by the elevator, each silently judges the other for a minute or two, then moves on. They both have their own lives to lead, their own hopes and emotions to deal with.

Zhizhu would like to have spent longer chatting with the critic, but a bunch of visitors she didn't know arrived, so she took her leave. The critic walked her to the elevator.

"Don't worry. The opera troupe is definitely going to be reformed, but it's not going to regress to the way things were in the old society," he said kindly as they parted. "I'll make sure the higher-ups hear what you told me today. See you at dinner tomorrow night. Our plan will go ahead."

Zhizhu glowed. How would she ever be able to repay him? With compassion and warmth, he showed himself to be not set in his ways artistically—he encouraged Zhizhu to continue innovating as she came into her own, to create a brand-new, unique style of performing.

The elevator came, and she got in. The critic waved goodbye and said, "Send my love to Li Kai! Tell him I'll be cross if he's not there tomorrow."

Zhizhu was even more touched.

When she arrived at the critic's home an hour before, and told him everything on her mind, he said sincerely, "How about this—tomorrow, instead of dinner at Cuihualou, bring everyone for mutton hot pot at Yanyunzhai near my place. I'll pay. Tell them I saw your troupe's performance of *Mulan Joins the Army* and wanted to hold a gathering to hear everyone's thoughts—I'd actually been planning to do this for real, but I've been so busy I didn't get around to calling you. I imagine the jinghu player and percussionist will be there? Frankly, I think your troupe works together well, and I want to support your continued collaboration so you can reach higher artistic peaks! Naturally, I also have some specific pointers about everything from your vocal technique and percussion rhythms to the way you style your wigs—I'll be sure to mention those too. I'll take the lead thanking Li Kai—without his work behind the scenes, you wouldn't be able to shine on stage. Sound good? Yanyunzhai isn't particularly well known—it's just a little restaurant run by an educated youth—but the quality of the meat and the service are top-notch. I'm sure you'll be pleased with it. The manager happens to be an opera buff too, which is quite unusual—not many people are into opera these days. We're going to have a good time tomorrow night, don't you think?"

Zhizhu protested, "Whoever heard of a critic paying for a meal? It's always the artists opening their wallets—we're bribing you for your praise. Let me pay for dinner."

The critic laughed merrily. "You accidentally said something very amusing—so my praise is just the result of bribery! Well then, seeing as I'll be giving you my feedback tomorrow, which will be the opposite of praise, it's only fitting that I pay. Doesn't it work like that?" Which made Zhizhu laugh too.

Now she walks toward the subway, having recovered her poise and self-confidence. She glances at her watch—five o'clock exactly. All of a sudden, she's desperate to tell Li Kai about her conversation with the critic. *Oh, Li Kai, my darling! In this whole kaleidoscopic world, no matter how you look at it, no one is closer to me than you. Even when I'm deep in despair, you take my limp hand and lead me back to hopefulness. When I finally pulled my career back together, you were the only one who loved me for my entire self, body and soul, as both a wife and a performer. Do you remember that time one of my fans came backstage? He was probably ready to kneel at my feet, but when he realized that my face is puffy under the makeup, and my varicose veins are so bad I have to massage them after every show, he took a couple of quick steps back, and his eyes clearly showed shock and disappointment! So he only loved the Tantai Zhizhu who appeared on stage. Another time, when I was trying to break new ground by appearing in the Shang-style* Losing Her Son and Losing Her Mind, *one of my falls went badly and I got hurt. The audience let out a gasp, though someone called out, "Well done!" When I got backstage, all my colleagues were saying things like, "What's wrong with you?" or "Didn't that go better in rehearsal?" You were the only one who said, "Are you okay?" The first words out of your mouth. That night, you refused to let me ride home on the back of your bicycle and insisted on calling a taxi. When the admin people disallowed your claim for the taxi fare, you gave up the leather shoes you'd planned to buy that month. Oh, Li Kai, your broad chest is the field that I flourish in. The sturdy stream of your love nourishes my soul. I can't lose you, just like you can't lose me! Where are you now, my beloved man? I have to find you right away, to tell you everything. We don't need to worry about that "elder sister" of mine anymore, we have someone fighting in our corner. We'll get through this. Then let's see if we can truly reform the troupe!*

Zhizhu thinks of time as a stream flowing toward the river, and the river to the sea. She's a fish who started in the stream, and is now in the river, well on her way to the ocean. No fish can just go with the flow—there are dangerous rapids, whirlpools, fishing lines, and nets to avoid. The path to the sea is available to everyone, but only those fish who maintain constant vigilance and courage will be able to reach this promised land.

◆ ◆ ◆

Progress means no one depends on the Bell and Drum Towers to tell them the time anymore. Even if there were a public timepiece available at every street corner, everyone would still want their own. Almost every household has a clock, and almost every adult a watch, some more than one. Now that cheap electronic watches have hit the market, children are starting to wear them too.

Xun Lei's father sent him to Wangfujing, but instead he's parking his bicycle outside the department store at Di'anmen. The Rado watch Uncle Xue was talking about will probably be available here, and if not, the watch shop across the road on Xin'anli Hutong will have it. Why not solve the problem closer to home so the bride can be made happy that much sooner?

He walks into the department store and, as he searches for the watch counter, muses about people and timepieces.

Old Lady Hai's room at the rear of the siheyuan has an old-style hanging clock with a dangling pendulum and a red sandalwood case, carved with clamshell and scroll designs. It has a little door inlaid with an oval of white enamel, on which is inscribed a pale-yellow rose. The casing has lost its shine, its joints are coming loose, the enamel is yellowing, and the rose is strangely old-fashioned, putting one in mind of Western European art from a century ago: candelabras, whalebone-stiffened hoop skirts, castles with turrets and drawbridges. This clock has loyally accompanied Old Lady Hai for decades, apart from during the Cultural Revolution's Smash the Four Olds campaign, when it had to be hidden away. It's been broken for some time. Xibin once asked Xun Lei, "Didn't you repair the Xues' clock? Would you have a look at my grandma's and see if you can fix it too? Or just tell me if it's fixable, and I can take it to the clock shop at Di'anmen." Xun Lei went to have a look and was surprised. "But this is an antique!" he said. Xibin asked, "Does it come from abroad?" And Xun Lei said, "No, it was made here in China, during the late Qing dynasty. Don't take it to the shop—they'll try to buy it from you. Not to put in a museum—we have too much history, and anything more recent than the Ming dynasty isn't considered a worthwhile artifact. They'll sell it to some foreigner for a high price to get some foreign currency for the country's coffers. I don't think these foreigners need so many of our antiques, not even the stuff from the early Republican period. Hold on to this!" Old Lady Hai came in as they were talking and lost her temper. "Xibin, who asked you to take that off the wall?" she nagged. "And who said I wanted this repaired? Stop meddling! No one's fixing this clock! Now hang it back up. I don't need it to strike, I already know the time." At her age, Old Lady Hai doesn't need timepieces to measure time, however accurately. Their purpose is to awaken countless memories in her!

Next door to Old Lady Hai, the Zhangs are fanatical about knowing the right time. All three of them have watches, of course, and they own more than one clock: a rectangular brown battery-operated analog clock in the hallway by the door, an alarm clock from a national enterprise that also shows the date and temperature on Mr. Zhang's desk, a Japanese electronic eight-tone musical one on his bookcase, and probably another one in the other bedroom—all of them synchronized with China National Radio.

The timepieces people choose reflect their different needs, personalities, and interests. The tabletop clock in Zhan Liying's home is bright red, more vivid than blood or flames! Tantai Zhizhu's probably came from a consignment store; it has a cuckoo emerging from a wooden nest carved with vine leaves to report the time at regular intervals. One time, Xun Lei stopped by to deliver a letter to Auntie Mu Ying—she happened to be home for once—and saw a Japanese clock on top of her wardrobe: an ancient Greek goddess sprouting wings from her back, holding up a globe with a clock face set in it. A replica European antique, with a cheap printed-circuit mechanism. Even in his own household, his father bought a made-in-Yantai clock a while back with an old-style wooden case, topped with a little golden horse raising its front hoof, two spiky pillars on either side, a sturdy base in the style of a Buddhist pedestal, and a glass case etched with peonies over the pendulum. The first time Feng Wanmei saw it, she laughed and said, "My god, that's a blast from the past!" Xun Lei quickly shushed her. "My dad's had his eye on a clock like that for a while—first he couldn't afford it, then when he could, things like this were no longer on sale. Now it's finally possible. Like when you managed to get tickets to see the Stuttgart Ballet doing *Eugene Onegin*." Embarrassed, Wanmei glanced toward the kitchen and nodded.

Yes, people are choosing their timepieces more and more because of how they look—aesthetic preferences are becoming more important than actually knowing the time. Take Pan Xiuya, the bride. This Rado watch represents her in-laws' affection and respect for her and demonstrates that Jiyue loves and trusts her. At the same time, it will also earn admiration and envy from her coworkers, neighbors, and old school friends. Now that Xun Lei has understood what this watch stands for, he promises himself that he will visit every shop in Beijing if he has to, in order to find a replacement.

Since it's Sunday, the department store is full of customers. As Xun Lei wanders around trying to find the watch counter, someone rushes past, bumps into him, and drops something.

"Oh, I'm sorry!" says Xun Lei.

"No! My—manuscript! No—" The man scoops it up in a panic and is about to make a quick exit, but collides with Xun Lei again. He is about to apologize when he realizes this is just a kid, much younger than him—so he just snorts and walks away.

This is Dragon Eye, though of course Xun Lei has no idea who he is.

After Dragon Eye left Han Yitan's home with the poems that might have come back to bite him, he walked out of the siheyuan, intending to bring them straight home to burn them. When he passed by the pale-green trash can at the end of the hutong, he thought: *Should I just rip them to pieces and throw them in here? No one's going to pick them out and piece them together, surely. If my wife sees me burning papers, she'll ask questions and I'll have to waste time explaining.* He started tearing the poems, but just then an old guy—he didn't know, but it was Grandpa Hu, the scrap paper collector—showed up with his cart and spiked bamboo pole, and called out, "Hey, Comrade, don't tear that up, give it to me!" Startled, he ripped the poems into small pieces anyway and wadded them into the trash can, glaring at the old man, before making a hasty exit. As he'd planned, he then popped into the department store for a photo album. An editor is dropping by his home this evening for a "casual chat," and he plans to fill this album with pictures of himself with famous authors, to nonchalantly pass around as they listen to the newest Mantovani Orchestra record, showing off his connections without his needing to brag.

Dragon Eye was in a good mood, clear as the sky after rain, but his encounter with the old man cast a dark shadow across his sunlit mind. Now the spark of a thought, *I hope that manuscript doesn't* . . . is dancing around his central nervous system. When he bumped into Xun Lei and accidentally said "manuscript" instead of "photo album," that was no coincidence.

As Dragon Eye charges out of the department store, he drives the shadow from his mind. Gazing at the crowded street, he thinks, *This time will never come again, and no opportunity should be missed. Life is a battlefield, and we have to seize every chance we get!*

To him, time is a pair of dice clenched in your fist.

Dragon Eye's rudeness didn't bother Xun Lei, but the stray word "manuscript" has touched off something in his brain. As he cycled here, he ordered himself to forget about the awful rejection from the publisher, but now he can't help recalling it all over again.

Only because of his youth! He's definitely up to the job, but because it's "not his turn," his work won't even get acknowledged! The strangest thing is, the translation is something the country clearly needs to have done urgently, and the "qualified" translator—who hasn't even started the job—doesn't seem particularly keen to do it, yet they won't even look at Xun Lei's completed manuscript! They'd rather leave the pages blank than admit this upstart into their ranks.

Sunk in thought, Xun Lei roams the department store, thinking: *Western clothes, ties, sunglasses, electronic keyboards . . . All these things were once thought of as corrupt and decadent, and all were banned at one time or another. Yet in the end, it was young people who took the lead making them popular, until their presence was established and they became normal. Now even Party members and our nation's leaders wear Western-style suits. Even films lauding the revolutionary war use electronic keyboards on their soundtracks. We're an ancient race, we ought to be able to open our minds and spirits, to accept and digest new things that are useful to us, to step forward and embrace the world's wave of innovations in technology and manufacturing.*

The world may measure time in seconds, minutes, hours, days, months, years, but Xun Lei prefers to think of present and future as an endlessly accelerating rocket. In the past, technological advances were slow, and the speed and volume of information transfer was absolutely pathetic. Now, computers have reached the fifth generation of development and are approaching the capacity of the human brain! Every day, between six and eight thousand scientific papers are written, and the total number of papers doubles every twenty months or so!

How could we slow down? How could we give up at the slightest obstacle? Xun Lei clenches his fists and thinks: *After I've bought the watch, I'll talk this over with Wanmei. Which publisher should we send the manuscript to next? Maybe this time I should bring it in person so I can also tell them how I feel—lay everything out on the table.*

All of a sudden, there is the watch counter in front of him, and right away he sees the model he needs. Perfect! He walks up to it.

◆　◆　◆

When people drink, they enter a magical realm where time—as far as they're concerned—is frozen.

In First Fragrance Tobacco & Liquor, Li Kai has been tipsy for some time. The dull anger that has built up inside him drags him into a dimly lit cave, deep and full of twisty passages. He stumbles along. Tantai Zhizhu's up ahead—he glimpses her back, her swirling skirt, but can't catch up. A blue bat with a long face keeps flapping around in front of him, blocking his view. He's exhausted and getting no closer to Zhizhu. For some reason, she's dressed for the stage—isn't that her costume from the end of *Mulan Joins the Army*, the "powdering her face at the mirror" scene? He once said to her, "You look better in this outfit than in any of your other costumes." She clapped her hands in delight and said, "Really?" But now she won't even look at him.

All of a sudden, Li Kai notices someone waving happily at him. Who is this? Oh right—it's Luo Baosang, the moron who was at the Xues earlier. If you're alone at a bar, all you can do is drown your sorrows, but two people can make merry. He stands and beckons Baosang over.

Baosang still has a bellyful of rage. When he passed the bar, he decided on the spur of the moment to come in and get blind drunk. Now here's Li Kai, who is married to Tantai Zhizhu, who in turn reminds him of *The Bean Juice Tale*, the opera in which Jin Yunu's father, Jin Song, is the head of a beggars' guild. This connection makes him feel strangely close to Zhizhu. As he settles into a chair, this closeness transfers to Li Kai—though he doesn't link Li Kai with the faithless husband, Mo Ji, who gets beaten up. Our brains make lightning-quick associations but are also good at sifting out irrelevant ones.

To Li Kai's surprise, as soon as Baosang has a drink in him, he begins sloppily praising "Big Sister Zhizhu." Every time Big Sister Zhizhu appears in *The Bean Juice Tale*, he says, he's there clapping for her in person. He lauds her singing and gestures, her makeup, costumes, and props. "She really brought Jin Yunu to life!" he enthuses. "Such range! Such humanity! Remember when people wanted to see *Losing Her Son and Losing Her Mind*, and no one in Beijing could play the role? Yong Ronghuan refused to travel from Tianjin, so Big Sister Zhizhu gave in to her audience and went on stage, even though she was ill! That voice, that body—Shang Xiaoyun himself couldn't do better if he were still alive. Sure, she was a tiny bit stiff 'sitting back,' and someone tried to heckle her. What the hell! You get on stage and give it a try! Big Sister Zhizhu isn't a Shang-style performer, she's just doing this to please you, and you dare to complain? Afterward, I hung around outside the theater, and as soon as that bastard came out, I punched him in the face." He rambles on like this for a while, which is fine, but Li Kai is confused by this turn in his monologue: "So I mean, tell me, Jin Yunu is a good person, right? She gives bean juice and leftover rice to poor people, doesn't she? And if a watch went missing, she wouldn't accuse just anyone of stealing it, would she? When Big Sister Zhizhu's kid went missing on stage, she didn't send her maid Shouchun into the audience to search me!"

Thanks to Baosang's big mouth, everyone in First Fragrance now knows who Li Kai is. They begin crowding around to express their admiration and support. An old guy says, "So you're Zhizhu's husband! I heard you meet her after every performance and escort her home. Hats off to you both! I love Zhizhu's work, she's a pro through and through. In *Mulan Joins the Army*, she had the elegance of the Mei style, the subtlety of the Cheng style, the liveliness of the Xun style, and the explosive energy of the Shang style. That's not easy!" Some middle-aged folk join in, speaking over each other: "What's your wife rehearsing now?" "I guess whenever she takes on a new role, you're the first to hear it?" "It's been a while since we saw *Girl with the Red Whip*, any chance Zhizhu could revive it?" Before Li Kai can answer any of these questions, they've started arguing among themselves. But why? Oh, one of them said, "The scenic design in *Mulan Joins the Army* was too heavy handed," and the others apparently disagree. Now they're really tearing into each other. They're all drunk enough to say exactly what's on their minds. Soon, their faces are scarlet, and they look ready for an actual fistfight.

"Stop it!" Baosang hollers. "If you have opinions you want to share, please tell Mr. Zhizhu one by one. He'll make a note and pass your thoughts on to Big Sister Zhizhu. No need to argue."

Everyone turns to Li Kai with their suggestions and ideas.

Li Kai feels as if he's finally reached the end of the dark cave, and the long-faced bat has flown off. Up ahead, Zhizhu is in Mulan's female garb, slowly turning around . . .

"Okay, enough of that!" shouts Baosang at the admirers who don't know when to quit. "Our Mr. Zhizhu has to go home and help Big Sister Zhizhu rehearse her latest role! No one has time to sit around like you guys, getting drunk and flapping your gums."

Li Kai has sobered up. He solemnly gets to his feet and smooths the front of his shirt. "Yes, I should go. Goodbye, everyone."

They bid him farewell with such warmth, you'd have thought he was a hero sallying forth into battle.

As always, Li Kai sticks a cigarette in his mouth as he heads for the door, but no matter how much he gropes in his pockets, he can't find his matches or lighter—he must have forgot them in his hurry. Baosang smacks him on the shoulder and claps his other hand over Li Kai's. "Here you go!"

Li Kai isn't sure what just happened, but smiles at Baosang and walks out.

He stands outside First Fragrance, the Drum Tower ahead of him, the Bell Tower behind him. A blast of cold air makes him spit out the unlit cigarette and shiver. His mind is very clear.

"Dad!" Out of nowhere, Bamboo is running toward him, his little hands red from the cold. With tears in his eyes, he grabs his father's arm.

"What are you doing here?" asks Li Kai sternly.

"You went out and Grandpa got worried. He sent me to look for you."

"What's there to be scared of? I'm right here!" He dabs Bamboo's eyes with his handkerchief.

"Come home, Dad." Bamboo tugs his arm.

"How can I go home?" He smacks the back of Bamboo's head and says, even more firmly, "Come on, we'll go find your mom, then we'll all go home together."

Thrusting his chest out, he leads Bamboo toward the Drum Tower.

His right hand is holding Bamboo's. As they walk, he realizes the fingers of his left are still closed over whatever Luo Baosang handed him. What is it? Cool and hard, kind of watch-shaped . . . Why did Baosang give this to him?

He holds up his hand and opens it to reveal—a nifty imported lighter. Those aren't easy to get hold of—it's probably one of Baosang's treasured possessions. He feels a jolt of gratitude.

Li Kai reaches into his pocket for a cigarette and pops it into his mouth. Flicking the lighter open, he holds the flame up and inhales deeply.

◆　◆　◆

Time treats everyone the same. Realizing sentiments like "all are equal before the truth" or "before the law" is easier said than done and must be fought for, but everyone really is equal in the face of time.

And yet, although time is fair to us, everyone spends it in different ways, which lead to different outcomes, so not everyone feels the same way about it.

Cycling home, Lu Xichun happens to pass by the Di'anmen crossroads at exactly 5:00 p.m. He's spent almost ten hours cooking for the Xue wedding. When he said goodbye, Auntie Xue, Jihui, and Zhaoying walked him to the siheyuan gate, and Auntie Xue insisted on giving him a soup envelope, one she'd hastily grabbed after the original one went missing. He turned her down, saying sincerely, "I just came to help, Auntie. All I wanted was to practice my craft and see you all happily enjoying the taste and aroma of my food. If you and your guests were satisfied, then I'm very happy. If I'd come for the sake of the soup envelope, there are some dishes I wouldn't have bothered with!" Auntie Xue tried to stuff the envelope into his hands, but he stepped back, and Zhaoying said, "Mom, Chef Lu said no, and I think we should respect that. He's cooked for us all day, and for his pains he got attacked for no reason. No matter how much money we give him, we can't make up for that! Instead, why don't we stay in touch and have him come by as our guest another time! If Chef Lu ever needs our help, he just has to ask, and we'll be there right away." Jihui added, "It's rare to meet a good person like Chef Lu. He even showed us how to thaw our pipes! You're welcome to visit anytime, Chef Lu—not just here, but at our home too. We're in Gongjian Hutong, just east of Beihai Park—very easy to find. I'll write our address—you must drop by." Xichun said, "My parents are both dead and I have no family left. If you really don't mind, I'd love to come visit when I have time." Only then did Auntie Xue put away the soup envelope and say, "Of course you must come, dear Chef Lu! We're your family now."

Neither side had expected to become this close after a single day. The stately Drum Tower looked down at them, savoring this taste of humanity.

Before he got on his bike, Xichun said with unfeigned emotion, "Your kinsman Luo Baosang isn't the brightest, and doesn't have much of a purpose in life. All he knows is eating and drinking and going around scrounging from people. I've known him a long time, and we never got along. Still, I don't think he stole the Rado watch. He's never been a thief, and I don't think he'd have picked today to branch out. Please go easy on him. He's pitiful, in a way. Remember, quite a few people came into the room at the same time, and no one knew who they all were. Could the thief have slipped in among them? Let's not falsely accuse Baosang!"

Auntie Xue was touched by this speech. What a man. Still concerned about Baosang being falsely accused, after what he did to him!

They took their leave reluctantly. They're all ordinary people, but their emotions at that moment were anything but ordinary!

So that was Lu Xichun's day. He made a thing of beauty that many people were able to enjoy. It was a beautiful experience for him too. Of course, there were ugly moments too, but anyone whose work is creating beauty must expect some trouble. His heart is full of joy as he cycles home, and his ambitions have had a shot in the arm.

True, he is still only a white chef in a small restaurant, and the boss will continue to look down on him. This won't last forever, though. Even as a white chef, he can seek out other mentors and escape this dead end as quickly as possible. Chef He once told him many traditional Beijing snacks are dying out: thousand-thread buns, chicken-pork-bamboo buns, three-winter buns; thousand-layer cakes, crystal cakes, hawthorn-honey cakes, and other steamed cakes. Why not revive a few of these at the little restaurant? Customers are sure to love them, and it will do wonders for their earnings! There are sure to be obstacles in his way, but as Teacher Ji is fond of saying, "You need to take a historical perspective."

As the last rays of sun fade on this winter afternoon, Lu Xichun—a perfectly ordinary young Beijinger—cheerfully leaves the neighborhood of the Bell and Drum Towers, his conscience clear.

By contrast, another person is currently lurking on the street by the towers, guilty and uneasy.

Yao Xiangdong's hands are in the pockets of his windbreaker, one holding a wad of banknotes, the other wrapped around the Rado watch. When he slipped out of the Xue home, he felt a wild joy. He'd done it! He fled to Drum Tower Street, feeling like a millionaire. Hey there, Makai Restaurant—when you start serving dinner at four thirty, I'll go right in and order your most famous dishes! What have you got? Dong'an chicken, sweet and sour fish, and deep-fried sparrow? That should be interesting! Imagine a dish being sweet *and* sour at the same time! He swaggers into a food store by the entrance to Tobacco Pipe Alley and has the clerk bag up five cream puffs for him. At the register, he rips open the red paper of the soup envelope, hands over a banknote, and gets change. Picking up the cream puffs in their paper bag, he bites into one before even leaving the shop. He gobbles them down as he walks along the street, and they're all gone before he reaches Houmen Bridge. Now thirsty, he crosses the road to Hat Hutong, planning to get a yogurt drink from the store there. But then—panic! A voice calls out, "You dropped something!" He turns to see an older broad-shouldered gent. On the ground is a scrap of red paper that must have fallen from his pocket. He bends to pick it up, and just like that his courage is gone. Too nervous to buy the drink, he slinks out of the shop. Without looking back, he can sense the older man staring at him from behind. He keeps moving all the way to the southern end of Houmen Bridge before stopping to catch his breath.

Could that be a plainclothes detective? The more he thinks about it, the more likely it seems!

He looks anxiously around. The man walks out of the store and turns in to Hat Hutong without even glancing his way. He lets out a sigh of relief, but the little drum that has started beating in his heart refuses to stop.

He sits down on the stone steps of a souvenir shop. Yimin Consignment Store happens to be right across the road. Inside is a windbreaker even more stylish than Yang Qiangqiang's. All he has to do is sell the watch, and he could have it. His eyes take in the door marked "Buying Dept. No Browsing." He's heard you need to produce a household registration and work pass to sell here.

He has a student card, but does he dare identify himself? He sits there staring across the road, and despairs. He feels as if his hands, thrust in his pockets, are holding live coals. As if the Rado watch has just been pulled from a furnace and is still glowing red, shooting blue and white sparks.

Xiangdong stands. The ground is unsteady, as if he's walking on steel plates shooting off a production line. He stumbles southward, then blunders across the road and turns back north. What should he do?

As a little kid, he loved playing the bad guy with his hutong chums, especially Japanese devils or Nazis. He'd hum a Japanese marching tune from a movie, "*Dah—dee dah—dah dee dah dee—*" or bring his legs sharply together, like he'd seen German soldiers do in films, and swing his right arm out. "Heil Hitler!" It was so much fun being the villain and having people chase after you! He'd happily allow his playmates, as Eighth Route soldiers or Red Guards, to gun him down. Eyes shut, face contorted, even if it ruined his clothes, he'd fall to the ground writhing.

This is the most expensive thing he's ever stolen—now he's a real bad guy, yet all he feels is loneliness and terror.

Everyone walking down the street looks relaxed and carefree. Even the old guy bent almost double and the little wailing boy trotting behind his mom seem better off than him. The old man doesn't care who sees him, and the kid can sob full-throatedly, not scared of attracting attention.

"Hey, Klutz!"

Xiangdong leaps in the air at the sudden cry.

He turns around. It's Stinky.

As usual, Stinky stops his bike and balances with one foot on the sidewalk, looking him up and down. "What the fuck are you still doing here?"

Xiangdong mumbles, "Nothing. I was just . . . going to play chess with Qiangqiang . . ."

Stinky's nose crinkles. "You're not fooling anyone. If you're going to Hat Hutong, why are you walking north? You must be up to some fucking mischief."

Xiangdong's heart thumps. Trying to stay calm, he thinks maybe he ought to show Stinky the contents of his pockets. With that mouth of his, when Stinky says he can do something, you'd believe he could tear down the Bell and Drum Towers themselves. So why not ask for his help to fence the watch? He can take a cut.

Stinky grumbles about something or other, but Xiangdong isn't listening. When Stinky pauses for breath, he says, "Enough of your nonsense. Here, I'll buy you dinner at Makai. I need a favor."

Stinky's eyes narrow, and he smirks. "Now you want to play at being generous? Didn't you just borrow money from me earlier? And now you want to treat? Whatever you're doing, I'm not getting involved!" He pushes off on his bicycle, pedaling hard, and in an instant has disappeared.

Turns out that mouth talks a good game, but he's afraid of trouble.

Xiangdong's legs shake. Maybe he should go to the Shicha Seas and toss in the watch, like he did the cactus. Yes, get rid of the watch and cash. The lake isn't completely frozen yet—he can see a patch of clear water below Silver Ingot Bridge. He'll feel safer then, and he can go home. Not that he wants to go home, where his mom will nag and scream, and his dad will slap and kick. If only he could spend the night out here—but it's a cold winter's night, and he has nowhere else to go. Unless he gets a bus to the train station?

On January 1, 1980, the criminal code of the People's Republic of China came into effect—but high school students like Xiangdong don't get much legal education, and his brain is still stuffed with inaccurate ideas: volunteer officers raiding people's homes in the dead of night, slapping handcuffs on people, shaving their heads and dragging them on stage for a struggle session, putting up a poster with their name and a bright-red tick mark next to it. He has no idea that Article 63 of the new criminal code states that a criminal who turns himself in will receive a lighter sentence; for minor offenses, charges may be dismissed altogether. He could simply turn back now, and return the Xues their watch and money. He hasn't spent much of the cash, and they may not even ask him to pay it back. Or if he's scared they won't understand, he could go to a police station and turn himself in. But these thoughts do not cross Xiangdong's mind.

He has caused others suffering, and now he's suffering himself.

The sky darkens. Soon the Drum Tower is no more than a silhouette against the sky.

◆　◆　◆

Xiuzao doesn't come back in the car. As Fu Shandu gives Dr. Yu a lift home, he can't help asking, "Is something wrong with your daughter? Didn't she like the apartment?" Dr. Yu waves dismissively. "Don't worry about it. That's how college students behave these days—they all want to show how independent they are."

That is indeed Xiuzao's mindset. She doesn't need a lift home in a car from her dad's workplace, and not only that, it's clear to her that this new apartment belongs to her parents. She just happens to be staying there awhile. When she's done with college, she'll move to a cheap hostel or something. It's not that she doesn't want the convenience of a car, and she certainly desires the comfort of a light-filled apartment with all mod cons—but she believes her conscience will only be clear if she earns these things herself, by working hard and contributing to the nation.

The bus ride home, just like the one there, is smoother than she expected, transfers included. She gets off the number 8 outside the Drum Tower.

"Zhang Xiuzao!" calls a voice.

She turns and sees Xun Lei! Their second encounter today. Her heart beats wildly.

To Xun Lei, this isn't a particularly momentous occasion. He was cycling home after buying the watch when he saw Xiuzao and called out a greeting.

Xiuzao stops. Xun Lei gets off his bike and smiles. "What time do you have? Let me check this watch against yours."

To Xun Lei, this is a perfectly normal request. He's already checked the Rado against the department store clock and his own watch, but they might not be precise—whereas he knows every single timepiece in Xiuzao's home is accurate to the second.

Xiuzao had planned to keep walking after giving Xun Lei a polite nod, but there's no reason not to help him. She sticks out her wrist and reads off her digital watch: "December 12, 1982, 4:58:34 p.m."

Xun Lei adjusts the new watch as close to this as he can get. Xiuzao wonders: *Why does he have a ladies' watch? Could he have bought it for Feng Wanmei?* But if he's already at the point where he's buying her fancy watches, then soon they'll be getting . . .

Xun Lei doesn't notice her curious stare. When he's done fiddling with the watch, he says, "December 12—Double Twelve! I almost forgot—it's the anniversary of the Xi'an Incident. How many years has it been?"

Xiuzao is startled—the day's almost over, and she too hadn't realized. She thinks a moment. "The Xi'an Incident was 1936—that's forty-six years ago."

The two young people's eyes meet, and something like an electric charge passes between their souls. At the same moment, they sense something formless and powerful transcending their individual lives, feelings, and work: the force of history itself.

"I'll walk you home," says Xun Lei.

Xiuzao silently nods.

All of a sudden, Xun Lei realizes there are many ideas he can share with this fellow young person. As they walk past the Drum Tower, he says, "I think you're like me—you've had an awakening. In the silent, invisible stream of time, you've developed an awareness of history. When we were kids, the adults made us go to history classes and talked to us about history, but for a very long time, the word 'history' just made me think of homework and grades. Fill in the blanks: In what year did the Battle of the Yalu River take place? What were the eight nations of the Eight-Nation Alliance? I got full marks in quite a few quizzes, but to be honest, I didn't truly understand what history was for a very long time. It wasn't until I got back from England and, after traveling thousands of miles, finally returned to this neighborhood. When I saw the abandoned bell behind the Drum Tower, for some reason my heart started beating faster, my eyes got warm, and my throat seized up. Just like that, I had a true sense of history. You understand what I'm saying? It's hard to put this into words. A mixture of thoughts, feelings, facts, ideals, determination, and faith. To put it simply, I understood for the first time with perfect clarity the places I needed to reach and the responsibilities I needed to take on, within the sweep of time. Maybe that's what people mean when they say they have a mission. The holy sensation of human history and individual destiny fusing together."

Xiuzao is deeply moved. After hearing these words, what she feels for Xun Lei soars beyond mere love. In an instant, her jealousy, resentment, reticence, and anxiety vanish. Every fiber of her being vibrates in tune with him. She says enthusiastically, "You're absolutely right! I feel like I'm moving toward maturity, which means the first shoots of the sense of history and destiny are sprouting. I went to Shanxi with some classmates this summer, and at Hukou Waterfall on the Yellow River, I felt something like the sensation you described. Of course, it was probably much vaguer than what you felt, but I still treasured it!"

They turn into their hutong. Xun Lei feels they ought to continue this spontaneous, fascinating conversation and says, "Why don't you come by my place later for dumplings? When we're done eating, we can hang out. Wanmei's there, and also a—let's call her a cousin, visiting from her village in Hebei. She's got all the latest information about life in the countryside—she'll expand our consciousness. We'll have so much to discuss: time, history, destiny, our calling . . . How about it?"

Xiuzao gladly agrees. All at once, that Victor Hugo love poem doesn't seem so great. Instead, it's the words he spoke on his deathbed that resonate: "Life is the struggle of day against night." How different her days and nights, and those of Xun Lei, Wanmei, and this country girl, must be from those of Hugo's era and society. Their understanding of the struggle can't possibly be the same as this foreign writer's. And yet, during their conversation, she could surely use Hugo's last words to start a deep, lively discussion. She's already starting to miss this siheyuan that she'll soon have to leave, and feels a pang of guilt at not having made more effort to get to know the neighbors her age. As they approach the gate, she screws up her courage and says, "If it won't be too many people, could I invite Hai Xibin too? That way it can be a sort of symposium for all the young people in the siheyuan."

"Great idea!" Xun Lei taps the top of his head in celebration. "You see? We've never done that before—we're turning a new page in our siheyuan. Turns out history can be created by us too."

The two young people walk cheerfully through the gate.

In 1905, Einstein came up with his theory of special relativity and fundamentally shifted our understanding of time. He pointed out that whether or not two events happen at the same moment depends on how you look at it. When you measure a moving object in the direction of its motion, it's shorter than if it were still. Similarly, a clock in motion ticks slower than a stationary one.

This was the thirty-first year of the reign of the Qing dynasty's Guangxu emperor. The despot Empress Dowager Cixi had reluctantly accepted Western technological innovations such as railroads, electric lights, photography, and steamships, not to mention abolition of the imperial examination system, yet hardly anyone in the whole of China knew about or understood Einstein's groundbreaking discovery. The Bell and Drum Towers, looming over the north of Beijing, went on sounding the hours from their outmoded perspective of time.

In 1915, Einstein published his theory of general relativity, which says time and space can be bent, shrunk, or stretched, thus smashing the absolutist view of time people had held since antiquity.

By then, the Qing dynasty had fallen, but the last emperor remained in the Forbidden Palace, living as he always had. The previous year, ambitious Yuan Shikai farcically proclaimed himself emperor, and the progressives had to expend a great deal of energy putting a halt to this regressive move. Ignorance and superstition still plagued our ancient race. Through it all the Bell and Drum Towers struck at the appointed time, and people's ideas about time remained stubbornly the same.

In the decades after that, this country went through a tumultuous transformation. China now has its own scholars of relativity. More and more knowledgeable people are beginning to create their own frameworks of time. In the macroscopic world (that is, the world we are able to observe), time may be seen as a straight line, moving steadily forward. In the microscopic world (molecules, atoms, other particles) and the super-macroscopic world (galaxies, the universe), however, time isn't necessarily straight or even, but might curve or bend. Hypothetical particles known as tachyons would move faster than the speed of light, which was previously thought to be impossible—so if you were to observe a tachyon, you could say time is moving backward. There are phenomena known as black holes, the result of a celestial body undergoing complete gravitational collapse. Their mass and density are so great that any matter or light entering their fields will be "swallowed." Therefore they not only negate time, but can cause time to freeze in their vicinity. If we sent a spaceship to investigate a black hole, it might take a million years for news to come back to earth, even though the astronauts will believe they've only been gone a few minutes or seconds and won't have aged at all.

Ah, time! You flow silently forward, and within you, human communities write their histories and individuals live out their destinies. Oh, Beijing! Beijingers! You who live near the Bell and Drum Towers. Human society and human souls are far more complex and profound than the physical world as described by the theory of relativity. There may be general rules, but how do they manifest in every actual person? What will happen to all these people we have met on December 12, 1982? Will our understanding, judgment, and predictions be validated or refuted by time?

Will Xue Jiyue and Pan Xiuya be happy together? Will Xue Yongquan hold on to his inner peace? Will Auntie Xue keep clashing with her daughters-in-law, particularly Xiuya? Will Jihui manage to forget the scenes of loading and unloading, and allow new information to spur him to action? What happens when the Xuns say goodbye to Xinger, and how will they deal with the daughter-in-law they're stuck with, Feng Wanmei? What will Xinger tell Zaoer and their mom about her trip to Beijing, and how will she feel about this visit afterward? When Xun Lei submits his translated manuscript with Wanmei's encouragement, will he encounter any more problems? Will Wanmei's love for Xun Lei remain strong forever? Will Zhang Qilin and Dr. Yu stay in touch with their former neighbors after moving to the new apartment? What poems will Xiuzao add to her notebook after this "symposium" with the other young people of the siheyuan? Will Pang Qibin retain his position as head of the Technical Report Unit? What will come of the investigation into Fu Shandu and Luo Jishan's shenanigans? Will Zhan Liying ever change her personality? How will Qi Zhuangsi respond to Mu Ying's continued pursuit, particularly after he retires? Will Mu Ying's views on love and ethics be embraced or rejected by more people as society advances? When Ji Zhiman finally awakens from his fantasies, how will he react, and what will become of him? Will Tantai Zhizhu ever become a true artist? Can Li Kai escape the dark shadows of his heart? Will Han Yitan find the courage to think for himself? Will Dragon Eye's determination bring him success? Will Hai Xibin remain indifferent to fame and fortune? When will Liang Fumin and Hao Yulan change their low-income, low-expenditure lifestyle and mindset? Will Yao Xiangdong turn his life around in time, or will he keep sinking? Will Luo Baosang ever find someone to settle down with, or will he continue mooching off people everywhere he goes? Who will Lu Xichun eventually bring to the photo studio for a wedding portrait? How much more scrap paper will Grandpa Hu collect? Will Old Lady Hai's bragging go too far once again? How will Lotus and Bamboo see the world around them as adults?

It would seem that everything contains a certain uncertainty.

Still, there's one thing we can be sure of. Barring some unpredictable catastrophe, Beijing's Bell and Drum Towers will remain as eternal witnesses to history and destiny.

The Drum Tower in front, red walls and gray tiles.

The Bell Tower behind, gray walls and green tiles.

The two towers stand tall, eternally awaiting the next moment, the next day, the next month, the next year, the next generation.

ACKNOWLEDGMENTS

Thank you to the publisher, to the translator, to the editors, and to the person reading this book.

TIMELINE

1850 TO 1864
The Taiping Rebellion against the Qing dynasty establishes the Taiping Heavenly Kingdom

1911
The Xinhai Revolution ends the Qing dynasty and establishes the Republic of China

1912
Yuan Shikai becomes the first president of the Republic of China

1915
Yuan Shikai proclaims himself emperor, only to abdicate a few months later; he dies in June 1916

MAY 4, 1919
Student protests lead to the anti-imperialist, modernizing May Fourth Movement

1924
Puyi, the last emperor, is expelled from the palace

DECEMBER 1936
The Xi'an Incident: Chiang Kai-shek is seized by two generals in a bid to make the Nationalists change their policies

1937

Second Sino-Japanese War begins; the Eighth Route Army is created as a united front between the Nationalists and Communists against the Japanese

1945

Second Sino-Japanese War ends; Beijing is liberated from the Japanese and renamed Beiping; the Eighth Route Army and New Fourth Army are merged by the Communists to form the People's Liberation Army

NOVEMBER 1947

Shijiazhuang is liberated by Communist forces

OCTOBER 1, 1949

After the War of Liberation, the People's Republic of China is formed; Beiping reverts to being Beijing; Chiang Kai-shek's Nationalist government and army retreat to Taiwan

1951

Campaign against the Three Evils (corruption, waste, and bureaucracy)

1952

Campaign against the Five Evils (bribery, tax evasion, cheating on government contracts, theft of state property, theft of state economic information)

1953 TO 1957

First Five-Year Plan launched to improve the economy and develop industry

1956

Mao Zedong coins the term "capitalist roader" to describe those who attempt to pull the Revolution in a capitalist direction

1957

Anti-Rightist Campaign launched to purge "rightists" from the Communist Party

1958

The people's commune is established across China; each commune is divided into production brigades and production teams

1958 TO 1962

Second Five-Year Plan launched to continue the process of collective ownership

1959 TO 1962

The Great Leap Forward, a failed attempt spearheaded by Mao Zedong to improve China's agricultural society, leads to famine and millions of deaths (referred to as the Three Years of Hardship)

MAY 1966

Start of the Great Proletarian Cultural Revolution; Madame Mao (Jiang Qing) begins producing her "model operas"; the formation of the Red Guards (a student-led paramilitary movement)

1966 TO 1967

The Great Networking: groups of Red Guards from all over China converge on Beijing

1968

Many "educated youths" from the cities are "sent down" to the countryside to be with the People

1972

Madame Mao forms the Gang of Four, an influential political clique

APRIL 5, 1976

The Tiananmen Incident, a protest in Tiananmen Square, is held in the wake of Zhou Enlai's death

SEPTEMBER 9, 1976

Death of Mao Zedong

OCTOBER 1976

Downfall of the Gang of Four; end of the Cultural Revolution; educated youths return to the cities

1979

The household responsibility system makes individual families responsible for agricultural production

ABOUT THE AUTHOR

Photo © Jiao Jinmu

Liu Xinwu was born on June 4, 1942, in Chengdu, Sichuan Province, China, and has lived in Beijing since 1950. His short story "The Class Teacher" appeared in *People's Literature* magazine in November 1977 and is regarded as the first instance of China's "scar literature" genre. Liu's other stories include "I Love Every Green Leaf," "Black Walls," "White Teeth," and "The Wish." His novellas include *Overpass* and *Little Dunzi*. He is also the author of the novel *The Wedding Party*, winner of the Mao Dun Literature Prize. He has also written many essays and has been an architectural critic. His research into the classical Chinese novels *The Golden Lotus* and *Dream of the Red Chamber* has been very influential. From 1987 to 1989, he was the editor in chief of *People's Literature*.

ABOUT THE TRANSLATOR

Jeremy Tiang has translated novels by Yan Ge, Zhang Yueran, Yeng Pway Ngon, Chan Ho-Kei, Li Er, Lo Yi-Chin, and Geling Yan. He also writes and translates plays. His novel *State of Emergency* won the Singapore Literature Prize in 2018. Tiang is also the author of a short story collection, *It Never Rains on National Day*. He lives in New York City. For more information, visit www.jeremytiang.com.